Distorted Virtue

Ruth Strickling

PublishAmerica
Baltimore

ISBN: 1-4137-9705-9
PUBLISHED BY PUBLISHAMERICA, LLLP
www.publishamerica.com
Baltimore

Printed in the United States of America

Dedication

This book is dedicated to the three most influential women in my life.

Acknowledgments

So many people have played a part in this book. Trying to give suitable thanks makes me realize just how great your contributions have been. The help and support I received at every turn kept me moving and hopeful.

It would be impossible to personally thank each and every person who gave words of encouragement along the way or did some other helpful thing. I feel deeply fortunate to have all of you in my life but I would like to mention some of you who really went all the way with me.

First, Helen Maris, my first and gentle reader, thanks so much for your effort and very loving way. From your help I was finally able to take the lid off. And I thank you especially for years and years of believing in me.

Pam Marsh and Carole Scagnetti, the most trusted of friends who took time you didn't have to help me move it to the next level. Your words of encouragement gave me the fortitude to put it out there.

Eileen Scallen, your valued input on the story itself and your assistance on the publishing business helped me get past those big fears. Your encouragement meant so much to me when I was at my doubting best.

Thanks to my sisters, Janette and Nancy who have supported me in all of my endeavors. I'm blessed to have such wonderful family behind me. An extra thanks to Janette for the editing assistance. To Margaret and Olen who watch from afar and are probably not surprised.

I've left for last, words of gratitude to my loving spouse, Sandra

Waldrop. I thank you first for a wonderful life and loving relationship. I know how hard you work at that. Thank you also for the gallivanting around the world that has given me both fodder for my books and the isolation that I've needed to motivate the creativity. Our life's adventures continue to inspire me. Thank you most for being you.

Lastly, thanks to PublishAmerica for this opportunity and for all your very professional and helpful ways.

"Nearly all men can stand adversity,
But if you want to test a man's character,
Give him power."
Abe Lincoln

Chapter One

She knew that she had just learned more than it was safe to know. She set her jaw and struggled not to let her face divulge her fear. Her gut was in a knot. Should she make some excuse and try to leave immediately or was it safer to linger and convince him that it had gone unnoticed? She needed time to think.

She had stumbled onto information not intended for anyone on the outside. There were needles attacking the back of her neck leaving that prickly sensation that accompanies terror. Her feeling of foreboding threatened her composure, threatened to expose her. The meeting had broken up, she should try to get out now. Maybe she could escape to the ladies room. She could think there.

"Excuse me," she interrupted, "Where's the restroom?" Her dry throat made her voice sound like it had come from someone else's body.

His focus moved from his file to lock onto her face and she was certain that an accusatory air hung suspended in the ice of his pale blue eyes. The fear gripping her surely revealed her terror, her weak knees threatened to force her collapse.

"Down the hall, second door," he growled.

She moved cautiously in the direction of his gesture wondering if she would really be allowed to leave the room. Before she could contemplate further, she was in the hallway and her legs were propelling her toward the safety of the bathroom. They seemed to have a mind of their own. She raced to gain access to the safe room. Her body parts, not under her control were acting in concert to carry her to safety. Was she moving too fast or too stiffly, was her fear obvious? She slipped into the safety of the bathroom and sagged against the door. As her eyes closed she sighed audibly, her heart was pounding. She nearly leapt from her skin as she found herself face to face with his assistant, Karla.

Back in the conference room, Roland thoughtfully arranged his files and packed his briefcase for the flight to London. He reflected on the meeting and knew that it had gone well. Amanda Chambers was enchanting and he had experienced some difficulty in concentrating on the work. An indulgence he did not allow himself. He was both warmed and irritated by this distraction. Her scent lingered in the room even now and reminded him of her brash femininity. She was charming, but direct, strong, yet somehow soft, almost vulnerable. It was easy to get sucked in by the contrast she projected. She was an enigma, always his downfall with the opposite sex. The incident which had just occurred was troubling him. He'd have to give the matter some thought but it could wait for the flight.

It had been a great strategy on the part of the secretary to send Amanda to this summit, he observed. She was bright and well prepared and she had quickly taken the lead on some of the more crucial questions, especially those around providing drugs to AIDS sufferers in third world countries. She was no shrinking violet and he knew that she was going to add a whole new dimension to these roundtable discussions.

He was amused as he reflected on how several of the hard hitting pharmaceutical boys on the panel were caught with their pants down when the issue of actual R & D costs came up. A smile crept across his face as he recalled the stammering and stalling that had gone on. It was obvious to everyone in the room that diversion and deflection were their stock in trade and she knocked them off stride early in the meeting. She made it clear that the large consortium of drug companies would not slip this by the committee as easily as they had hoped. She alone would cause them to do some homework, simply because she had thoroughly done hers. The other committee members quickly seized on the issue and kept the pressure on. Once she exposed the weakness the others moved in for the kill. Because of this, he had not had to expose his own motives. He really wanted her on his side but knew that wasn't possible.

Shaking off those distracting thoughts of her, he resumed packing. He had so much to do in preparation for the London meeting. It had been a good trip for him. This summit had gone well primarily because he prepared meticulously for all such encounters. His assistant was no Amanda Chambers but he had taught her all of the intricate steps that had to be followed to keep the charade going and the work on track. Karla was a dolt but she was loyal as hell and a very willing learner. He couldn't rely on her decisions but she was almost robot-like in her approach to her tasks. Great at execution but never a real thinker.

He felt a surge of relief and a sense of pride at the completion of sessions such as this. The preparation leading up to it sometimes caused him to question how much longer he could function under the strain. Today, however, was a day for relaxation and reflection. He could feel good about the work of his staff and take personal pride in the team that he had put together and trained so well. Karla's screw up after the meeting remained the only fly in the ointment.

Reflecting on the meetings again, he was intrigued by the interplay of the three divergent interests. The committee work was so open and transparent that he wondered how anything ever got done. It was unending debate which never seemed to move forward or reach any conclusions. Just a lot of wrangling that ate up precious time.

On the other hand, the interest groups, such as today's drug consortium, were tugging in the opposite direction, trying hard not to reveal one item of information and so driven by greed that they would go to any lengths to conceal facts which were practically public knowledge. It might actually be funny to watch if the issues weren't so deadly serious.

But what really made the game challenging was the covert work of his group, the masters of manipulation. He knew that nothing would ever be accomplished if his organization wasn't doing it. He was a facilitator. He worked to get the rubber on the road. If things moved along appropriately, as they had today, he could just let it flow. It was only when things bogged down or got off track that they would roll up their sleeves and force the outcome. The left against the right was an idealistic fantasy that took eons to ever achieve a goal. Thank God he had found the organization known as Gazelle and with it a way to make changes. In their time, in their way. He relished the autonomy that his position as director gave him. Yes, to him Gazelle was a godsend.

Back in the ladies room, Amanda was working hard to regain her composure. She was still stunned and could not find the words to appear nonchalant as she stared into the chilling and accusing face of Karla. She could not remember ever being so off guard. She heard herself talking and hoped that it was small talk as she searched her insides for the required composure. She chastised herself for such lack of control and that anger toward her behavior coupled with a deep breath allowed her composure to come shooting back into her body like a thunderbolt. Her sense of self returned as she strode confidently into the first stall.

She knew she couldn't stay in the bathroom forever. She had to return to the conference room to gather her things and say her goodbyes. There would be time to analyze the information once she was away from here. Just hold it together for another ten minutes. *And then what?* she asked herself. *Don't get ahead of yourself,* was the unspoken reply, *One step at a time.*

She heard the door open and close so she left the stall, splashed some cool water on her face, patted it dry, assessed her image in the mirror, and gave herself a private admonishment sufficient to carry her back down the hall to the conference room.

Roland was just picking up his briefcase as she entered. "Good job," he offered. "I hope everything goes as well in Bangkok in June. I think we're finally making some real headway."

"Ya, so do I," she responded. It took all of her effort to look him in the face. She just wanted to grab her belongings and run. She knew that she must face him and appear as normal as possible. With great resolve, she reached out to shake his hand and thank him for all the hard work. Even in her state of disarray she could not help but respond slightly to his warm smile and good looks. His blond hair was thick and closely cropped, his chin was strong and his steel blue eyes were set off by his fair skin. Underneath this handsome exterior, he reeked of danger.

Taken as a package his appearance and demeanor were somehow seductive but the coldness in those eyes and the rigid posture revealed the falseness of that perception. His reputation was well earned and wide spread and she knew as she stood there assessing him that she needed to concentrate on what she knew and not what she felt.

As she folded up her file, his cell phone rang and while he was otherwise engaged she slipped out the door with a casual wave and a spurious smile. As she hurried to exit the building she noticed Karla talking excitedly with another delegate on the other side of the glass. From her demeanor and the way her hands were dancing around Amanda assumed that she had not completely pulled the wool over their eyes.

Downstairs she hailed a cab. In typical DC fashion it took three tries before one finally swerved over to the curb and compassionately swallowed her up. She mechanically gave her address to the driver. Traveling through the streets of the district past the Lincoln Memorial and across Monument Bridge, encased in the relative anonymity of the cab, she sobered at the task that lay in front of her. What should she do with this information? She longed for a trustworthy friend, a confidant. She was not one to go anywhere without a plan. Certainly not off into something as deep as this. She felt so alone.

She was jolted back to reality by the ringing of her cell phone. "Amanda? Nate, here. How'd the meeting go? Thought you'd be back in the office by now."

Her boss was always so enthusiastic. "Oh, Hi, Nate. It just ended, I'm in the cab now. I've got an awful headache so I decided to just go on home. Can we talk in the morning?"

"Sure. I'll catch you around 9." It was a relief to have him off the phone. She liked working for Nate Tidwell but his demeanor could really wear on you. In some ways the consummate bureaucrat, steady and predictable and at other times he seemed to be conniving and controlling, she had to stay one step ahead of him, she had to manage him and it could be a real strain.

It was through Nate that her suspicions were first aroused. It was weeks ago that he had dumped those files on her desk and announced that she was going to the summit. She was excited to be in charge of the AIDS project for the department. Nate told her that Secretary Denton, himself, was taking an uncharacteristic interest in the pharmaceutical project. He said he was assigning her because the secretary was going to be extremely hands on and since it would require regular briefings, he needed her to handle it.

Her tenure in the department was relatively short when compared to her meteoric rise. She was recognized as an over achiever and her level of responsibility increased rapidly compared to those around her. She was pleased to hear that the secretary, himself had put her on this particular assignment. It meant that he knew of her work and had confidence in her abilities. She took her work seriously and on such days she would go home filled with pride.

In fact, Albert Denton had taken particular notice of Amanda and her work. He was the kind of manager who relied heavily on key personnel within his department and she had come to his attention first by impressing Nate Tidwell.

His relationship with Nate was a muddled one and he leaned on him because he could and because it was his habit. Nate had strengths that he didn't and he believed that it was the mark of a wise manager to surround himself with those who could outperform him. This was how the increased responsibility had flowed to Amanda.

Nate Tidwell and Albert Denton had been working together since they were boys. Denton's Drug Store was the landmark in Preston, Texas. Albert's father, the pharmacist, had hired Nate to unload the trucks and to sweep out the retail portion of the store when the boys were just 12 years old.

These tasks had originally been given to Albert but he had shown that he was unable to handle them. He dropped the boxes and broke the contents and every time he swept out the store something was knocked off the shelves and broken. All in all, Albert had shown himself to be physically inept.

Nate had eventually picked up the physical part of Albert's duties leaving him to spend most of his time sitting in the office pouring over order forms and inventory lists. Albert's father relied on Nate and spoke so highly of his abilities and dependability that Albert had come to believe that he could not function without him.

Years later when Albert got promoted to a management position with the State Department of Human Resources it was a natural progression for him to hire Nate. It was from that agency that Albert went to Washington and made a name for himself as a man who could do more on less. In the climate of smaller government he was a shining star and Nate stayed at his side.

It was in this environment that they had both agreed that Amanda should handle the secretary's pet projects of pharmaceuticals and energy.

She silently pledged that she would find enough time to do an outstanding job on both of these summits that had been assigned to her. At least the pharmaceutical summit was local and she had a personal interest in the issue which would give her a head start on understanding the matters to be discussed.

The energy summit, on the other hand was taking a lot of concentration for her. The issues were complex and the answers just didn't seem to be there, no matter how hard she studied nor how much she looked. While the June meeting in Bangkok was still a ways off, she was already feeling those disturbing waves of panic.

It was when she'd begun her review of those files that she was first gripped by that uneasy feeling that wouldn't go away. After her initial review of the files she'd slumped back in her chair, a deep furrow settled on her brow. Two things were troubling. First, the issue of the AIDS cocktail for Africa had been bounced around inside the beltway for months, even years. Why now had it taken on such heightened importance? It had actually been rather quiet, almost dormant for 6 months or so. She found nothing in her research to indicate a reason for this heightened interest or scrutiny. She'd made a note to investigate who was pushing this summit. She could only assume that her remaining questions would be answered in due course or at the summit itself. Second, and even more perplexing was the question, who or what was Gazelle?

This moniker was referred to in two documents which appeared to be related. They were documents which had been marked up and edited by the time she'd stumbled upon them. They were buried in a file that was only remotely associated with the subject.

The first was a memo in which the sender's name was blacked out. It was addressed to Secretary Denton and dated one month earlier. The first paragraph briefly summarized the issue around the AIDS cocktail having to do with the drug companies' cost of research and development versus the wholesale cost of the drugs. The second paragraph spoke of the difficulties associated with trying to get these companies to do the right thing. An apparent, ethical plea to a corporate hierarchy.

This paragraph concluded with the statement, "While the pharmaceutical companies involved insist that forcing them to provide their drugs free or at severely reduced prices will have a serious and chilling effect on future drug development they cannot be excused from their responsibility."

In the margin directly adjacent to this sentence were written the words, "Gazelle must force this issue even if corporate management change is required. I have alerted R to the gravity of this issue, see attached for further details."

Nothing had been attached of course. There were however, two small staple holes in the upper left corner. There were other marks on the document, in the upper right margin. Two sets of initials apparently affirming that the memo had been received and read. While one set of initials appeared to be "HA," the second was nearly illegible. It looked like the last initial was either an "H" or perhaps an "A." Finally, scribbled at the bottom in blue ink was a notation, "I agree; tell R to put on next agenda." She wasn't sure if she recognized that handwriting but she didn't think it was Secretary Denton's.

At first she was simply curious about the document. She was sure that it was purely accidental that it had reached that file and her desk. The contents were really quite innocuous except for the Gazelle thing. Over time, however, its significance had begun to eat away at her and she realized that there was something furtive about its reference. "Gazelle must force this issue even if corporate management change is required." She found that statement most troubling. The more thought she gave it the more questions it raised.

It was not until two days later as she made her way further down into the file that she had discovered a second document which changed everything for her. This one, she believed, was the one that had previously been attached to the memo as it too had those telltale holes where staples had been removed. It was entitled, "Suggested Management Changes," and it listed three heads of large pharmaceutical companies under the ominous heading, "Eliminate." At the bottom the disturbing question was posed, "Does Gazelle have enough fire power for 3 hits without contracting out?"

It had been this discovery that had started her on the road to inquiry and, as it turned out, intrigue. It had burned into her memory until she was unable to forget it, woke up in the middle of the night with it staring down at her like it was imprinted on the ceiling of her bedroom. She could see it whenever she closed her eyes. It was haunting her.

This had been one of those things that you think isn't really happening, working in a federal agency, running across a document with apparent threats and a strange reference to what appears to be a code name. Unbelievable! This just doesn't happen. She even wondered once if one of her co-workers was playing a prank. There were some who were certainly possibilities. You just don't expect to stumble across anything covert in her kind of work. So was there really any significance to all this? People often spoke in euphemisms. Words like elimination, fire power or hits, could mean nothing more than having someone voted out of power, targeted by shareholders or it could mean much more. Even if this didn't refer to taking someone's life it did reflect interference or manipulation of a company's management, purportedly by someone in government. This alone was cause for alarm.

Days later with the issue built up even greater in her mind; she determined that she had to do something. She wished again for someone to reason this out with, someone who could make sense of it, hopefully just explain it away and let her get back to normal. She decided that Nate was that person. It was, after all, his ultimate responsibility. He had inadvertently gotten the document to her and it was up to him, as her supervisor, to help fix things that were keeping her from doing her job. It certainly was doing that. She could think of little else.

Just walking up to Nate and making a direct inquiry didn't seem prudent. She would either be laughed out of the office or put on the watch list for employees who had too much imagination. Either way it wasn't something that was likely to get her promoted.

She decided to bite the bullet and had chosen a Monday several weeks ago to clear it all up. She had found Nate sitting in his corner office concentrating on a file that he had in front of him. The door was standing open and she gave a perfunctory knock to get his attention as she entered. "Is this a good time?" She inquired. He gave a nod and smiled warmly as he gestured her in and to the chair across the desk.

"What's up?" he asked.

She laid out the story of the anomalous documents she had discovered in the pharmaceutical files that he had delivered to her office. She had chosen not to divulge all of her suspicions. She presented the documents in an air of inquisition, not one of accusation.

Nate was pretty cool. He did not, as she had once imagined, laugh her out of the office. She detected a curious knit to his brow; however, as he stared at the paper she had given him. She wondered once if this was the first time he had seen it. His questions were simple and mostly around where exactly, she had found it. The questions he asked gave her the assurance she needed that he had not known that the document was in the files and, further, that he found it intriguing and out of the ordinary as well.

She left the meeting with Nate assured that she was not crazy and certain that he would get to the bottom of it. She assumed that within the week she would know the source and the meaning of it all. She also left the meeting without the document and wondered briefly on her way back to her office if she would regret not having made a copy. She dismissed the idea as absurd and put it out of her mind.

A week had gone by when, with no further response from Nate, she decided to broach the issue with him once again. They were having lunch downstairs in the cafeteria and she and Nate were the last two left at the long table. She quizzed him about his progress with the memo and found that the subject was promptly and politely dismissed. She returned to her office curious about his response, but decided that she had probably caught him at an unfocused moment. She vowed to follow up with a more direct and formal approach. To do so she called his extension and left a voice mail message requesting a meeting with him about the document she had left with him from the pharmaceutical files. This message was never acknowledged nor returned.

She did finally get some official time with Nate, behind closed doors.

"Amanda, I've chased this document up one hall and down the other. I've been up in the rarified air of the 18th floor and down into the archives of the file room. I'm convinced that this is some kind of hoax or prank."

"What in the world kind of joke could this be, Nate, and on whom is it being played? I'm not sure I buy that. What convinced you it wasn't authentic?"

"The most obvious, I guess, is that it's virtually untraceable and," she cut him off.

"Exactly my point, Nate. What other document in all those volumes of files can't be traced or authenticated? Why this one? Does that reference to Gazelle not raise your curiosity?"

"Military projects aside, I've been able to find no such code word in any of the data bases in any of the federal agencies. I'm convinced it's a joke. Listen to me on this, Amanda, move on!" There was a distinct sharpness in his command.

She'd left that meeting with an uneasy feeling and something resembling a bowling ball in the pit of her stomach. She spent that entire weekend locked in her apartment analyzing and reanalyzing, over and over again, all that she knew, all that she suspected, and all that she could think of that she might do. Her avenues seemed limited. Without Nate or someone with whom she could investigate this, she was flat out on her own. Damn how she hated that feeling.

She had always been a team player. Throughout her youth she had been consumed by athletics and always relished the feelings of support and camaraderie that came from the team sports in particular. Playing all alone was just not to her liking. She loved strategy and believed that more heads meant more information and consequently better plans.

What she knew for certain was that the document existed, although she had no copy or proof of it now. She also knew that Nate was either very complacent or acting a little squirrelly, she wasn't sure which. Either way he would be no help. And, she knew that her curiosity remained and that she must explore further. In her mind, she needed a plan that was safe and would lead to a satisfactory resolution.

By that Sunday night, as she sat in her apartment and looked out over the Potomac and the monuments off in the distance, she knew that she would have to proceed on her own and the only direction that would lead to eventual enlightenment was to discover the identity of Gazelle. That was the first step and an absolute must. But how would she proceed?

Since the direct approach with Nate hadn't worked, she considered the indirect? She could lay some bait in some of her meetings and see if anyone would bite.

The upcoming summit would be a good place to begin since those in attendance were definitely tuned in to the pharmaceutical companies. In three days of meetings, two each morning and two each afternoon she would be exposed to a wide variety of players. She thought of it as trolling. Just pop the bait out there and see who follows along or takes it.

It took several more days of heavy consideration to find just the right approach. She decided to make some ostensibly innocent yet slightly ambiguous comment about the animal, gazelle, and see if anyone reacted or responded. It would be up to her to keep a cool head and show no response if anyone did react.

She knew it was unlikely that something would come of this so she wasn't really concerned about not having a follow up plan. First she would see if anyone had a reaction, if they did she'd proceed from there.

She couldn't believe that she was getting caught up in this intrigue. It was so unlike her. She was not a risk taker. Danger was not usually on her agenda. She wondered then if she was getting bored with her job and with the endless travel and meetings, just looking for some game or diversion. Had her imagination become overactive? It did heighten the anticipation of going to the summit, she had to admit.

Finally the day had arrived, today. She'd set out for the meetings early this morning fully prepared and briefed on the subject. In addition she was armed with the knowledge of those suspicious documents and the unsatisfactory response she had received from Nate. She was on her own and determined to try to make sense of what was happening. She vowed to get to the bottom of this Gazelle thing, if not today she'd try again.

It had actually been kind of fun at the earlier breakouts. As the meetings were concluding and she was gathering up her papers she'd turned to one of the delegates and ask if they had seen the gazelle on the news? Most had responded politely but disinterestedly, even looked at her as if she needed to get a life. Some had even graciously engaged her in conversation about the animals or the zoo assuming that she was trying to be friendly and make small talk.

She was beginning to really have a good time with the playfulness of the exercise. It was relieving some of the boredom and making her feel more important than she was. It was like she had her own piece of secret information. An inside joke, so to speak. Not until the committee meeting on AIDS drugs for Africa had she really learned that this was something to be taken seriously. She had made her now standard statement about the gazelle, putting extra emphasis on the word, at the end of the meeting to no one in particular. At once, an alarmed Karla, Roland Priestly's right-hand-girl, had jerked back stiffly and gasped almost audibly. She looked coldly at Amanda and then quickly left the room with what Amanda had observed to be a Gestapo-like gait. Her reaction was so strong that it frightened Amanda at first as she wondered if Roland may have noticed as well.

It was just moments later when Amanda was in the corner retrieving some notes from her briefcase that Karla re-entered the room. Unintentionally, Amanda was hidden in plain sight. Karla couldn't see her from her vantage point and mistakenly assumed that she was alone with Roland. "That woman is on to you and Gazelle," she blurted.

It was then that Amanda had coughed and turned back to the table trying to appear as though nothing had been said. She made some totally unrelated but purely business comment and looked intently at her notes. She had furrowed her brow in a way that, she hoped, everyone would assume that she was so intent on her work that she hadn't absorbed what was said.

Amanda was certain that she had seen the color drain from Karla's face. She knew that Karla and Roland both knew that she had heard. Gratefully, she thought, they did not know that she had also seen those documents. Things were starting to add up quickly for her and the sum total was pointing directly at Roland Priestly and she knew from reputation that he was someone to fear.

Suddenly her harmless little game had turned toxic. It was then that she had asked directions to the restroom and found her way down the hall for that brief respite which had allowed her to regain her composure and chart her escape.

With her thoughts now back in the cab and in the present she was wondering what forces she had just unleashed. Reconsidering for a moment, she thought that surely this must all be her imagination. After all, nothing had really happened. This was just her perception. Her mind was playing tricks on her because she had gotten all caught up in this crazy game of her own invention.

She wondered if she needed a vacation. Maybe she'd go home to the lake and visit her brother. Well, this wasn't the time but she would talk to Nate about getting on the schedule after the spring meetings were over.

Home for Amanda now was a one bedroom apartment on the third floor of a brick apartment building in Arlington. She thoughtfully gathered up her purse and brief case as the taxi swooped around the circular drive and deposited her at the front entrance under the portico. Management had spent their resources on making the front of the building as appealing as possible while neglecting some of the units and common areas inside. The front was tastefully landscaped with an attractive fountain in the center of the drive. Thriving plants along the entryway were highlighted at night with colored lighting. It made the building look richer than the rent reflected.

Inside, a combination security guard/doorman managed to stay awake about half of his shift and alert even less than that. It was another amenity that made the building appear to be more than it was. Alvin Forslund had been overseeing the activity in this lobby for nearly a decade. Upon moving in, Amanda had begun conversing with him regularly since she knew no one in the city. She knew of his family and often inquired about his wife and the progress of his two sons. It was she who kept the little candy dish on his desk filled with those watermelon flavored candies that they both enjoyed. They even exchanged Christmas remembrances. She greeted him now as she passed through the lobby and caught a waiting elevator to the third floor.

Her palms were sweaty, not from exerting herself, but just from plain old nerves. She knew as she fumbled clumsily with the loop of keys that she had not yet recovered from the physical reactions born from her earlier fear. Finally slipping the correct one into the lock she nearly willed the stubborn door to release and allow her to enter the safety of her home. She leaned against the back of the door momentarily as she exhaled and nearly let herself relax. She put her briefcase and purse on the shelf in the entryway as was her habit, glanced over at the pulsating light on the message machine, and headed immediately for the shower.

With the water hitting her body she began to relax but her mind was still racing. She kept trying to set her thoughts aside so that she could wait and make a logical assessment of it all when she was more calm and refreshed. The reality settled over her as she was toweling off that she was not going to feel the calm that she had been craving.

Choosing to let her hair dry naturally, she slipped into her robe and went out to sit on the sofa in the living room. Here she could look out over her tiny balcony and over to the city. It always gave her a wonderful feeling of calm and comfort to do so. She felt like she could watch all the happenings of the city from the relative safety of her cover. She was like a voyeur, safe in her spot watching people bustling around who didn't even know she existed. As a plane came by lazily descending along the river toward Reagan National Airport she imagined all the people who might be on board and what their jobs might be. This quickly brought her back to the project at hand and to her own mission.

She decided that she needed to attack this as she would any of her work assignments. She had to take each task as a project in itself, organization was paramount. The first step in this process was to define the project as completely as she could. She went to the entryway to retrieve her laptop and returning to the sofa, noticed again the insistent flashing of the message machine. It would have to wait; she needed to get her thoughts together. She sat cross legged, placed the computer in her lap, booted it up, opened a new document and began to organize her thoughts.

The first thing on the page was her observation that she had possibly put herself in jeopardy and had gotten nothing in return. She had tipped her hand and made no gain for doing so. Perhaps she had even exposed herself to Gazelle, she wasn't certain of that. She silently vowed that she would not make that mistake again.

Second was her uncertainty of what Karla's and Roland's connection to Gazelle might be. Her challenge at this point was to learn the identity of Gazelle while not exposing herself or any suspicions that she had around the possible existence of him.

Lastly, there was Nate's reaction to her attempt to enlist his assistance. She felt about as blown off as you could be. She wasn't sure if he knew something he wasn't telling her or if he just discounted the whole affair but he certainly had been no help, *Chalk that up to a major waste of time,* she thought.

She began to summarize the puny amount of knowledge that she had in one column and her crazy suspicions in another. When she weighed the two, she again wondered if she was going off the deep end.

Suddenly tired and somewhat discouraged by her uncharacteristic lack of clarity she set the computer aside and went into the kitchen to pour a glass of wine.

Tempted by the aged brie peering up at her from the cheese keeper she realized that she was hungry and decided to combine it with the wine and some hard pumpernickel she had stowed below. She arranged the three on a tray and before going back outside she hit the rewind and play buttons on her answering machine. Just as she'd thought, two more hang-ups. She lowered her wiry frame into the lounge chair on the balcony and folded her feet in under her in a semi lotus position. She needed some time for introspection and contemplation.

As she consumed the meal she felt a wave of emotion wash over her that left her feeling overwhelmed and near exhaustion. She had an unexpected longing for the safety, security and simplicity of her childhood. She unconsciously set the tray aside and went to the phone to dial the number of her brother.

Willmot Chambers, Jr. had left the hustle of the corporate world behind and had moved back to the large, old, wood framed house that had been left to the two of them when their mother passed away. He had spent over a year lovingly restoring and refurbishing the place and had proudly opened it to the public as a B & B just over a year ago. She was never certain how well it was working out for him financially, but he had blossomed and taken on a kind of serenity when he let go of the rat race. To her he never had seemed cut out for the big city and all the pressures that went with the high end advertising business.

The place was located at the end of a dirt road, not far from town, and it sat directly at the lake's edge. Their childhood there had been almost magical in retrospect. In the summer they spent long days and evenings playing in the sand of the beach, they would swim in the crystal waters either off the floating dock or sometimes out to the island, and there was always time to sail around the bay with its bright green flora, hazy blue skies and white sandy shoreline.

Balmy summer nights were spent around a fire in the sand, sometimes with music from Will's guitar and sometimes with just the songs provided by the crickets accompanied by the crackling of the fire. The spring and fall there held their own rewards, but the winters would ride in on a bitter, Yankee Clipper and engulf the entire region in a clasp of cold and lake effect snow. Once the nights stayed cold enough and the lake froze hard enough, they had their own skating rink just off the end of the porch. These same amenities made the place attractive to the tourists today. Growing up there had been idyllic. Everything from that time seemed somehow more carefree. It was never clear to Amanda whether the times were simpler or the place.

"Hi, Will, it's Mandy."

"Mandy, Hi, I was just thinking about you. I made a pot of Grandma's soup today and it made me think of you."

"I was just sitting here eating dinner thinking about old times and decided to give you a buzz. I've actually been thinking of trying to squeeze in a visit, maybe a long weekend."

"That would be great. Just tell me when and the red carpet goes out."

"Will, I'd like to talk to you about something. Now that I hear your voice I realize how much I miss you. I may try to arrange something in the next couple of weeks."

"I'd love to see you. Just let me know as soon as you can."

"I'll call you." She hung up from the call feeling more alone than ever.

Amanda's big brother had always been a source of strength for her. When they were kids he was her enemy and her hero. Regardless of the hat he wore, one thing was for sure, he was there for her, a steadying force in her life. She longed for that now. She was formulating a plan in her mind and a trip home to the lake seemed like just what the doctor ordered.

Chapter Two

Roland reclined the seatback slightly and raised the leg support of the seat in the business class section of the flight to London. His cell phone was off and with his computer tucked away in his briefcase he found himself with a satisfying moment of freedom from the electronic umbilical cord that tethered him to all the functions of Gazelle. As much as he loved his work, as devoted as he was to the cause, as driven as he was by all that there was to do, this was what he liked most about flying. It was the time that he could get inside himself and reflect on what had been accomplished and chart what was yet to come. Today he was plagued by this nasty little business around Amanda Chambers. He was glad that his assistant, Karla, was not on this trip, that he would not have her needling at his side. He needed this time to himself. This was something that required grave consideration. It could be a turning point for Gazelle.

He adjusted his head on the tiny pillow provided and turned to look out the window. It always seemed to him that you could get out and walk across the clouds when you were above them like this.

The next thing he knew, the flight attendant was asking him to put his seatback upright for landing at London's Heathrow Airport. He couldn't believe that the flight had dissolved so quickly into his sleep. So much for all that time to contemplate, it would have to wait until he finished his meeting. It was premature to bring it to the other members now anyway.

After an interminable cab ride to his hotel near Hyde Park, Roland checked into his usual room, 202. While the bellman unpacked his overnight bag, placing the toiletries on the vanity in his previously prescribed way and hanging his shirts according to color, he set up his laptop and logged on to the internet to retrieve his e-mail messages.

Roland tipped well and sent complimentary letters to supervisors wherever he stayed or ate. Because of this he received outstanding service at every turn and, he had to admit, it made the travel much more pleasant. He was generally greeted by name and the services he required were pre-arranged and seldom had to be requested. He was a creature of habit.

It was early afternoon in London and his meeting would not be until 4. He looked forward to these meetings with mixed emotions. It was always good to come together to focus the efforts or the organization but he sometimes resented the attitude of oversight of his work. Today he was meeting with what he called the "S Group." It was comprised of the senator, the secretary, the short guy, the sponge, and the sonofabitch. He knew these nicknames were disrespectful but he had a right to see things as he chose and no one was going to control what went on inside his head. He feared what would happen, however, if there was ever a slip of the tongue. The only one in the group who ever gave him heartburn was, of course, the aptly labeled, sonofabitch.

His real name was Harry Axelrod and he had been one of the original and founding members of Gazelle. Harry now held the position of President and CEO of one of the largest and few, publicly held energy companies headquartered in Venezuela. He played a big part in all of the energy decisions made by this and the previous administrations of the United States and wielded unprecedented power in Venezuela, primarily because of his connections to the labor unions there. His hand was always in the cookie jar but he was too slick for many to realize it.

He had a way of operating that left little in the way of a paper trail. "Less paper, less evidence," he regularly said, usually accompanied by a large, boisterous laugh and a bone shattering whack on the back. He was always chewing on a half smoked cigar which looked like it had been rolling around in saliva for about a week. Roland found him personally crass and disgusting and although he had at one time had slight respect for him professionally, that was not the case today. Roland felt it unfortunate that the founding brothers of Gazelle had not included a provision for removing a party from the decision making process. At any rate, Roland knew that Harry would be his greatest challenge in today's meeting.

At precisely 3:45, Roland made his way to the small conference room on the mezzanine level of the hotel which had been reserved for the gathering of the great minds of Gazelle. Roland was partial to the round table type of discussion and the hotel had accommodated his wishes with the proper setup of the room. Few in attendance would know of the eavesdropping equipment or of its intended use.

By 4:15 all of the greetings and small talk were out of the way and everyone was helping themselves to the bar and buffet snacks. Roland took a seat at the table near the window and asked the last ones at the buffet to find a seat so they could begin. As expected, everyone was present and ready to begin except Harry Axelrod. This was an action that had been repeated every quarter for the last five years. The spring meeting of Gazelle was about to begin.

Gazelle was not the kind of organization to read the minutes from the last meeting or have the treasurer report on the state of their finances. Things were handled much more loosely. When Roland needed funds he simply transferred whatever amount was required from a readily accessible, numbered account in a Swiss bank. No questions had ever been asked. What would be discussed today would be the next steps for Gazelle. The board was very hands on in this regard. The business was the issue and the issue was the business.

This particular meeting was taking place in London instead of their Washington, DC headquarters because both the senator and the secretary were becoming increasingly concerned about security and possible exposure. It would not do either career any good to be exposed as a member of this organization or just to be consorting with the others in this room. Particularly the presumed assassin called Shorty.

"Gentlemen," Roland began, "We have just concluded a successful experience at the summit meeting around the pharmaceutical issue. As was our hope, our judiciously placed people performed well and very little involvement by Gazelle was necessary once the meetings opened. This new procedure we've been using where we lobby the delegates before they actually start their meetings has really begun to pay big dividends. Should the remainder of our initiatives turn out as well we may find ourselves with even greater capacity in the future."

Before any of the principals could comment Axelrod shot through the door with a thunderous greeting, cigar in one hand and a whisky in the other. "'Scuse my interruption, boys. I guess I'm a tad late. You know what they say. Better late than a dollar short or something like that. What'd I miss?"

Roland set his teeth and said through them, "We were just getting started, Harry, why don't you take a seat?"

Roland turned his attention back to the round table and continued, "As you know, we've been quite successful in bringing heightened attention to the issue of AIDS drugs for Africa. This new drug consortium we discovered has been hard at work trying to stay in the background and keep the spotlight on other world problems. They've been trying for months to bury the issue and the last thing they wanted was for the media to pick this up again and start asking tough questions or, even worse, make more accusations about greed at the expense of human life.

"They'd tried diligently to keep the summit low key, little press coverage was expected which was one of the reasons we got involved. In particular, as you'll recall, we wanted to bring a greater awareness and put some pressure on these guys. We had a nice protest group in place and it brought some good press coverage. We've known that this drug consortium has been hell bent on keeping the drug prices artificially high. They've really been gouging since the latest numbers show a resurgence of the disease in both the US and Africa. I believe that we've just brought a floodlight of exposure, and further, we've made those boys start to squirm.

"I've taken the liberty of printing out a few of today's advanced news reports from the internet which show that skepticism is beginning to reign in several prominent publications and the drug consortium is already out there trying to do some damage control. Some of those news articles are included in your briefing packets." Roland gestured toward the files in front of each attendee.

The secretary spoke up, "Whenever we can realize this kind of result and not have to play as active a role, we are literally playing on the house's money."

"What's your take on this success factor, Roland?" asked the senator.

"Primarily, well placed operatives who are thoroughly briefed," Roland responded.

Harry jumped in, "It certainly hasn't hurt that the pre-summit lobbying of some key delegates included veiled threats and references to people getting hurt," he added.

Roland grimaced slightly as he continued, "While we had people in place to initiate larger and more violent demonstrations and several of our people were strategically placed in the committee meetings, themselves, we were fortunate to not have to activate all those forces. On this one, we've had some sympathy factor playing for us that we won't encounter when we take up energy in June and, of course, the prison reform issue, which is set for the fall, will really be an upstream swim."

"Hold on there a minute. Let me be clear on this." It was Axelrod again. "You think we're gonna have a tougher sell on energy than on AIDS? My God, what've we come to?"

"Look," Roland responded. "You know we've never been about affecting public opinion. We decided from the start that it would be our mission to affect outcome only. Of course we do that easiest where public and political opinions are in tune with our desired outcome. The whole idea of this is not to have to wait for public opinion to change or for the politicians to decide that it's finally prudent to take some action. We are the shortcut, remember. Our purpose is to make things happen on our schedule. Because we see the larger picture we have the impetus to make the changes when and where they need to be made. I'm simply preparing us for the fact that both the public and the politicians have more divergent positions around energy and prison reform than they have around getting AIDS drugs out to the masses to cut off an apparent epidemic." Roland felt himself getting prickly. He hated the side of himself that Axelrod always seemed to bring out.

"What' our next step, Roland?" asked the senator calmly.

"Everything is in place for our enforcement. The publicity from the summit has created the appropriate environment and I have all the documentation necessary. It's my plan, with your approval, to put the proposition to the largest of the three pharmaceutical companies. That would be Hexlar, Inc. in Zurich. If I lay out what's in front of them, I have no doubt that we'll gain their full cooperation. Once we have them on board, I'm certain they'll bring their two friends along as well."

"What's your schedule?" asked Shorty.

"With everyone's approval we'll begin today, I'll contact them at once and arrange the meeting in Zurich for the first of next week. I wouldn't be surprised to see an announcement from them in the press sometime in the next month or so."

Everyone nodded in agreement.

The meeting continued on for a couple of hours with meaningful dialogue for the most part. Near the conclusion Axelrod took the floor and started putting pressure on the group around their approach to energy.

"Here's the deal, men. If we don't get a grip on this thing fast it's really gonna take off without us. We've got to get pressure on this administration and do it now before every other Tom, Dick & Harry put their two cents in. I've got several guys who are set to serve on this silly committee to make it look like this thing's being done on the up and up. I'm tellin ya, the train's gonna leave the station with our butts in the caboose if we don't move now."

In fact, Harry Axelrod's issues around energy and the upcoming summit were much larger than what he would put forth here. It would be helpful to his real cause, however, if he could get this group moving in the right direction. He could use all the help he could get.

Roland thought that he observed a brief and knowing look

exchanged between the senator and the secretary. He failed to comprehend the significance of it.

"Harry," the senator replied, "We're with you on this. It's just gonna take a little time to come up with a plan that comprehensive, let alone get all the operatives in place. Hell, I appreciate that you've got some folks lined up but we've never gone outside for assistance like this before. What's wrong with having Roland put it all together like he usually does? What's pushing this?"

"It's the goddamn mess the last administration made, that's what. These politicos are headed right down the same road makin' a right hand turn instead of a left to get there. Their goin' the same place, I tell ya. Caterin' to the Middle Eastern oil just won't cut it anymore. We gotta steer this thing or I, for one, am gonna get run over."

"Harry, this sounds more like worry over your wallet than concern for the energy policies." The secretary had finally joined in the debate.

"Hell yes, it affects my profits and I'll remind you right now who bankrolls this little think tank and most of that army of ants you oversee out in that little ant hill of a bunker."

Roland brought the matter back under control by proposing that he and the staff would send a preliminary draft of their plan to the members within 30 days and they would hold an interim meeting in May to focus strictly on that plan and its final implementation. That would still give them more than a month to iron out the details before the energy summit to be held in Bangkok.

It was early evening in London before the meeting concluded. Roland had agreed to have dinner in the senator's suite as there were some specific things that each wanted to discuss with the other in a more private setting. Roland was looking forward to having the senator's undivided attention.

Ever since the inception of Gazelle, the senator was the one constant that Roland could count on to stay the course with him. They had both been among the founders and their concept of the agency's work had always been closely aligned. He reflected now on those long evenings where the direction and the methods were hammered out forcefully by four, strong minded and well meaning men. It had started as a group of friends with similar work on the hill. They would often meet for dinner and drinks and as the months wore on the nights got longer and the meetings became more heated.

All of them were frustrated about their work and that was with a capital "F." It was becoming harder and harder to accept the fact that nothing appeared to ever get done in the legislature. The more they kicked around their issues the more right it seemed. After more than a year of yelling, cajoling, and outright arguing, Gazelle was born. It had sprung forth from the seeds of discontent and disillusion to become an unseen force in modern American politics.

The premise was simple. What couldn't be accomplished through the sluggish democratic process with its multiple representatives, numerous meetings, unending interest groups and the constant pressure for votes and involvement of the press would be accomplished through shortcuts prepared by Gazelle. Even the name had been unanimous. The gazelle, an animal which is not only fast, but graceful and slick in its movements would lend them the image that they craved. It was a perfect description of how they would operate. There had never been anything sinister in their purpose. Their motives were pure. It was just the damn frustration with not being able to accomplish things in a timely manner that had driven them to take matters into their own hands. Not one among them had thought that the framers of the Constitution had ever, in their wildest imaginations, envisioned the world as it was today.

Things had really come to a head for Roland, personally, after the congressional debates on health reform. Each of the original founders of Gazelle had been present as one after another of the unending, congressional procession came on to the floor and had their say. Each had their own ax to grind. Each had to make their play to the press and to the voters back home. To Roland, the richest country on earth was turning its back on the poor and disenfranchised and was wrangling over minutia which meant nothing in the trenches. Americans who could not afford the best health care from their own pockets or who did not have the highest paying jobs with the best health benefits would, in the best equipped country on the planet, just have to die.

Roland was personally touched by this as he watched many of the coal miners whom he had grown up around in southern Pennsylvania slowly cough themselves to death from black lung disease. There was little to relieve their suffering. The death of the steel industry in the United States and the attendant closing of the mines had coincided ominously with the onset of their disease. It was as if the poverty and the illness had been aligned to visit the miners in rapid succession. No sooner had they begun to adjust to the loss of their livelihood when the diagnosis with its bleak prognosis was pronounced. They often had to choose between medications for themselves and food for their families as they choked their way to an early departure, many so young that they still had children in school.

He had watched his best friend's father suffer this fate slowly and certainly, a man who had taken him on camping trips and who had taught him to fish. He was a man who had been like a father to him and who had unselfishly given of himself even in his illness. It was he who had taken two wide-eyed boys to their first major league ballgame even though the walk up to the bleacher seats had invoked a coughing spasm which almost sent them back home before the first pitch was thrown.

Roland had watched the legislature slowly debate away men's lives as they struggled to determine whether this disease belonged under the purview of the Workers Compensation law or whether it was simple negligence from the mining companies hence giving the walking dead a remedy in tort. He vowed at that man's funeral and swore on all that he held dear that he would never allow political wrangling to ever again get in the way of what was needed. Years later, after the inception of Gazelle, he proclaimed silently that he and Gazelle would make things happen in their own way and in their own time, whatever it took.

It had been a simple stroke of luck when the shadow government was created and with it came a perfect place to hide their actions. It was originally designed for national security it was said, but as is often the case, it became a double edged sword.

Anytime people are given authority to act with little oversight the opportunity for self serving ripens quickly and ripe can turn to rot overnight. As the leadership void was recognized, those with the most power had just naturally stepped into that void. In this instance it was the secretary who began controlling matters in the undisclosed bunker. As one of the founders of Gazelle, he had taken the lead in the setting up and daily operations at that locale. He had been able to hand pick and control which workers would serve either part or all of their time in the secret, backup offices of the United States government.

Over the last couple of years he had even usurped some of the decision making power on key issues from the president's own cabinet. The administration began to realize that the work could, in fact, get done more effectively if it was assigned to the secretary and his covert working group. They had gained the nickname, "Army of Ants," and "The Hill," had taken on a new meaning among key people in the West Wing of the White House. From there it was like rolling down hill to allow more control to be moved over to the shadow side.

The tide was turning and on certain issues the shadow government was becoming the governing voice and the elected administration, the shadow side. It was a tricky balance of power that got traded back and forth. Simply put, the unscrutinized group could make things happen where the administration could not. Always the consummate politicians, the president and his cautious, vote seeking advisors had seen a certain convenience in turning over to the underground section, those things which they did not wish to have debated in the press. It was a great way to dodge the criticism and avoid having the press ask embarrassing questions.

They had gotten it down to a near science. Float the issue balloon out there but don't take a hard stand, wait for the shadow side to accomplish what was needed and before the press could really get a hold of the outcome, spring forward with their position on the issue. Loud and clear, no room for equivocating. Come out strong just as the issue was to be resolved, usually the next day. To no one's chagrin, it was becoming a real vote saver.

The only loser here would be the democratic process and maybe the Constitution. It seemed by the players involved, a small price to pay to get results that were in the best interest of the country and in some cases, the world. Most of the members of Gazelle believed that this was a temporary solution and believed that, in time, changes could be brought about which would make the organization unnecessary. Most saw themselves as soldiers riding the white steed in pursuit of change for the good of all.

It was simply fortuitous that the secretary had the power of the shadow government and the assistance of Gazelle. By whatever quirk of fate or careful planning they had come together in the same place and at the same time. From his position he was really able to get things done. When they formed Gazelle no one had dared to dream that they could be this effective or have this much clout. They knew they would be wise to take all the actions they could while this ideal environment remained. It was the best of all worlds. Although there was a blurring between the sanctioned actions taken from the bunker and those taken by Gazelle the outcome was working and that was what mattered.

Roland was not particularly interested in all of the issues with which Gazelle was working. His pet project was prison reform. Unfortunately, he had to work through these other items and wait until his was at the top of the agenda. In the meantime he had to come up with a comprehensive plan for how Gazelle would influence the outcome of the energy issue. This was a sticky problem when you looked at the scope of the topic. It had become simpler to manipulate the outcome, thanks in large part to the environmentalist groups and their active approach to the subject. They could be infiltrated and controlled or they could be duplicated and imitated. The implementation would be the simpler part on this one.

Since he would not have time to write a comprehensive plan from scratch, he put Karla onto the research and he would cut and paste from plans which were currently under consideration. Once Gazelle found its objective, he could put together the plan for achieving it timely. Swift and sure, that was the way. He had a large number of very able minds at his disposal and getting the documents that they needed to put the plan in place would take only a few days. He was certain that before the end of the week the substantive portion of the energy plan would be decided and only the enforcement stage would be left.

Chapter Three

As Roland knocked on the door of the senator's suite, an ocean away Amanda was awaiting the arrival of her bag on the baggage carousel at the Milwaukee airport and in Room 403 of the London hotel Harry Axelrod was on the telephone with his contact in the bunker.

Double dealing had never been in Axelrod's vocabulary. Dealing was dealing in his mind and there was little discernable difference between dealing straight or double crossing. A man's objective had to be met and it was up to him to say how and when that would happen. You just couldn't sit around and wait for all the mealy mouthed, glad handing to get things done. Harry Axelrod had spent the last seven years wheeling and dealing in energy commodities and that was no place for the faint of heart to play.

He had gladly been a part of Gazelle when it began. It was the only game in town at that time. He had soon tired of the benevolent role that the group was playing and he had moved on to play hard ball on his own. He didn't mind being the patron of the organization, sometimes they could be helpful and he was skimming so much money off his deals that a few million was nothing. He had placed that amount in the Swiss account to begin and Gazelle's operations seldom used the interest alone.

Buzz was exactly the well placed informant that Harry loved on his side. Over worked, under paid and overly leveraged in life he was ripe for the bribe. He doubted that was his real name but Harry had learned years ago that these were the people who could really give you the edge you needed to stay ahead.

The documents that had come to him from Buzz had put Harry in a bad mood and created an anxiety that made him push the Gazelle group to get this energy policy on the table as soon as possible.

The heightened scrutiny and potential tariffs that were being proposed could be his undoing. He had had one close call a couple of years ago and he didn't intend for that to ever happen again. He would rather work this one through Gazelle if possible because they were as close to government sanctioned as you could get and still not be waiting to see what fate would deal you. Patience was just not his style.

Buzz had left a message on Harry's special number which was their way of making contact. In coded speech now, Harry learned that the last information that he had requested had been obtained by Buzz and placed in the pouch for pickup. Harry hoped that it would be good news. They never discussed content and Buzz had no idea who Harry was or why he was willing to pay such large amounts for an occasional copied document. All he needed to know was that he could access such information and there was a market for doing so that kept him solvent. He went on about his work pleased that the money was secure in his safe deposit box. He had taken yesterday's payment to the bank today and spent a little extra time counting and organizing the harvest from his illicit endeavor. To Buzz, money meant safety.

Will was at the airport to pick Amanda up as promised and as she scanned the circling luggage looking for her weekender, she realized how good it felt to be back in his presence. Grabbing the bag as it rounded the end of the conveyor, Amanda adroitly swung it up over her shoulder, picked up her matching carryon and headed out through the double doors where Will was waiting after retrieving the car. The sweet aroma of spring in the upper mid-west invaded her nostrils and reminded her of long walks on a quiet beach from long ago. She guessed this place would never be completely out of her. So often a sight, a sound or a song would take her right back to where it all began.

Will popped the release on the tailgate of the SUV and Amanda knowingly parked her bags in the cargo area. Coming around the side of the vehicle to enter the passenger's door, she caught a glimpse of a woman who for one startled moment, reminded her of Karla. Her heart leapt up into her throat and she stood there in the midst of a double take recognizing that she was suffering from some level of paranoia.

In the car on the way to the lake, Will and Amanda filled the hour and a half with catch up conversation. Will was preparing Amanda for the changes he had made to the yard and grounds since she had last visited. She was warmed by the enthusiasm in his voice as she thought again of how much he seemed to enjoy being back at the lake. Amanda purposely steered the talk away from her and what she felt a need to talk to Will about. Better to wait until they were both rested and not distracted to get into that.

As they were within a few miles of the house, Will blurted out, "Amanda, there is someone I'd like you to meet." He rarely addressed her by her full, given name.

"Wow, like me to meet as in, 'You're fixing me up,' or like me to meet as in, 'You've found someone?'"

"I've found someone, Mandy and at the same time I've found myself."

"I'm happy for you, Will; I could tell there'd been some change in you. You seem so happy."

"Mandy, it's a man," he cautioned.

"So?"

With that, Will was out of the closet.

"Well now, with that out of the way, what did you want to talk about?" He inquired as a broad, warm smile floated across his face.

"I'd like to wait until morning if that's all right. By the way, what's his name, where does he live and when will I meet him?"

"Charles, Chicago and tomorrow night. He's coming up to meet you."

"Cool," was her reply.

When they arrived at the house, Amanda was buoyed by the cheerfulness and familiarity that greeted her. Willl had indeed accomplished a great deal around the grounds. Where there had once been neatly groomed grass with small shrubs around the house there was now an air of formality that emanated from the plantings. A garden-like atmosphere where once had been expanse of lawn. It really set off the house and gave it a kind of grandeur that she had never assigned to it before. She couldn't wait to wake up here tomorrow and go for one of her favorite walks.

Once inside, Will helped her haul her bags up to her room. Though it had been updated and redecorated to go along with the décor in the rest of the house, Will had very thoughtfully retained the essence of the little garret that had been her sanctuary growing up. Will thoughtfully left her to herself and returned back downstairs. As she moved over to the window which found its access to the outside through a gable on the west roof she was once again twelve years old inside. The room enveloped her and her reverie as it had for all those wonderful and painful years. It had been here that she had spent her carefree childhood years and it was here that she had tasted first love and its pain of loss. She thought about all of the problems that she had analyzed and answers she had come to lying in the bed looking up at that same ceiling. She hoped that tomorrow and her discussions with Will would bring the same clarity to this Gazelle issue.

She reflected on her earlier conversation with Will and was warmed by the serenity that he had found. She was pleased for him that love had come to him and entertained a touch of envy for his emotional growth. She wondered again if she would ever find that certain someone to share her life with.

Roland felt at home and totally at ease on the sofa in Senator Chastain Hampton's suite. All those years ago as a legislative aide on Capitol Hill, Roland had worked for the senator and had, in fact, been the one to introduce the senator to the concept of what had become, Gazelle. They had worked together for several years and Roland would be hard pressed to count the number of times that they had sat like this in some hotel room with files spread out in front of them. Using the coffee table as his desk, Roland could still stay organized and function as well as he could at a five thousand dollar desk.

The senator sat at the desk of the hotel room concluding a transatlantic phone call. They had already discussed several issues and were about to wrap up their Gazelle business.

Roland leaned back on the sofa, looked the senator in the eye and stated coldly, "There is one other thing I would like to discuss with you. This has to be totally off the record and only between us. In other words, if anything comes up about it, we never had this conversation. Can we go there?"

"Ordinarily I resist conversations that start that way, but knowing you as I do I suspect this is something I need to know and judging from your demeanor I will not hear what you have to say unless I agree to your terms."

"True."

"All right then, agreed."

Roland began to relate the story of Amanda Chambers and her references to Gazelle. He had learned from some of his people in the breakout and committee meetings at the summit that she had been making references to gazelles in various ways at nearly every meeting she attended. He had heard it with his own ears in that one instance. To further complicate things, Karla had allowed herself to have a physical response to Amanda's reference and Roland had seen Amanda become unnerved. Finally, the clincher had occurred when Karla had erroneously believed that they were alone and had advised Roland that Amanda was on to him and Gazelle. Gazelle may have been compromised, he cautioned.

The senator's brow was deeply furrowed. "We've always known that this day could come," he observed.

"I'm really in a quandary as to how to handle this, Sir. I have no idea where this comes from and how much is known. I wonder if Amanda Chambers is that cagey and clever. If she is, is she in this alone? I know she's bright but I don't see her as calculating. I'm not even sure why I'm coming to you with this now. It's premature, but I felt a need to talk to you, I guess."

"Are you asking me for advice, Roland?"

"Truthfully, I think I need your help in analyzing this and I also felt that I owed you, in particular, an early heads up."

"Maybe we should start at the beginning, if we separate the known from what we simply suspect, perhaps we can deduce what is needed to construct an appropriate resolution."

Roland was always awed by the clarity which the senator could bring to problem solving and analyzing. He was a clear thinker, could cut to the essence of the issue quickly, and above all, was a strong leader. All attributes which contributed to his success in politics. He really was a natural. Despite his mid-western roots he leaned more to the liberal side, socially but was a fiscal conservative, a perfect fit for Roland.

On top of it all he was fair and even handed, he was a true gentleman. Roland lamented that there were not more like him to fill legislatures all over the country. This was precisely the kind of man that the democratic process needed, he thought. Roland wondered for a moment if he was as good a fit in his position as the senator was in his.

Brought back to the present by the task at hand, Roland began, "Well, we know Gazelle is vulnerable to detection because we've never taken great precautions to control knowledge of its existence. Though we haven't publicized the name, many people have been recruited over the years to support our work. There is a broad awareness of the forces at work even if the specifics of the organization have not been generally known. The bunker and the work that goes on there is a whole separate issue. Its existence can never be compromised. As we've so often observed most people just want this whole system to work but don't really want to know how it works."

"Okay, so Point Number One is Gazelle is vulnerable." The senator inserted, "Given that, what is the likelihood that Ms. Chambers either ferreted out the identity of the organization or that it somehow fell into her lap? Tell me more about her and flesh out your thoughts on this issue."

"She's bright, very bright. Whenever I've worked with her I've been struck by how quickly she assimilates and analyzes information. What she is not is personable. She doesn't seem to care who she angers and she can leave a lot of ill will behind her."

"Sounds like a dangerous combination. What motivates her, Roland?"

"I'd say probably causes. Not money, not power, she really seems to be interested in making a difference and I think she is very courageous and caring particularly for the disenfranchised or oppressed."

"Can you give me an example?"

"Well, this African mess comes to mind, it's still fresh in my mind from the summit. Let me chronicle that for you and you can tell me what you glean from it."

"She first started working on the Congressional Committee on African Issues less than a year ago. At the time the committee was just coming to the realization that the issues absolutely had to be broken down and tackled by sub-committees due to their magnitude. Amanda, Ms. Chambers, quickly grabbed one of the delegate seats on the AIDS sub-committee. She also served as an alternate on Poverty and on the Corruption sub-committee.

"My recollection is that she gained these seats in mid-September and by the time the AIDS group met in early October she was all over the drug companies. She was busy lining up support and suggesting research areas that needed to be covered so that the delegates would be armed with all pertinent facts and figures by the time of the summit. She really got them rolling.

"By the time of these most recent meetings, she had them completely knowledgeable and focused and she wasn't even in a position of leadership at the time, totally effective approach. She actually saved us a bundle of work and any possible detection. I would have thought that she had been involved in that area previously but I know from Nate Tidwell that she had not. She did her homework, did it fast and did it well. That's how she seems to work."

"Actually, listening to your description, Roland, I'm reminded of another promising, young aide that I met some years ago," the senator smiled. "I sense that you and Ms. Chambers have a great deal in common. This could get very interesting. Tell me, would you say that her effectiveness comes primarily from her speed of assimilation of knowledge or from her analytical ability?"

"I'd be inclined to think it is from her ability to take in the information rapidly and retain it. In watching her I believe her analytical skills lag that ability, but probably not by much. She takes in a lot of information quickly and then needs some time and focus to analyze what she's learned. Yes," he said thoughtfully, "I think that's an accurate assessment."

"Then, my friend, I believe you have just uncovered Truth Number 2. Repeating what we know then, Gazelle is vulnerable to exposure and Ms. Chambers has probably come across information that she does not yet know what to do with."

Roland nodded affirmatively, he was again inspired by the man's ability to cut through all those words and hear only the germane nuggets of information that led to the most logical conclusion. "And what do you make of her behavior at the summit that I described earlier?" Roland asked.

"Yes," said the Senator thoughtfully as he stroked his chin unconsciously. "That is troubling. What if she knows everything and is trying to identify the players? That would make Karla's reaction and subsequent statement, as you described it, an indictment of you, my friend. It's also possible that she has some small amount of information and is looking for a place to gain more. Either way, Karla has effectively fingered you, to use the vernacular."

Roland squirmed slightly on the sofa and couldn't resist the need to tug his tie to loosen its grip around his neck. His breathing quickened.

The senator spoke again after a thoughtful moment, "Gazelle is vulnerable, Ms. Chambers has some level of knowledge or suspicion and you have been identified as a link to the organization or to further information about it. Roland, this must stop here!"

Chapter Four

The sun had just set in the quiet Virginia countryside and twilight hung suspended in the embrace of the still humid air. Summer was arriving early and as he moved slowly and inconspicuously along the state road Buzz fantasized about taking the family on a first class vacation this year. He had enough money in the safe deposit box to rent a beach house for a month or maybe take everyone to Disneyworld for a week. He would look into it.

He was jolted back to reality by the adrenaline rush which accompanied his stomping on the brakes and swerving onto the shoulder to avoid the big, black car that streaked out of the side road and straddled the center line as it accelerated away from him and disappeared over the small hill in his rear view mirror. He had only a sense of a black car and dark windows. For all he knew it could have been guided by remote control. No one was visible.

His heart was still thumping in his chest as he turned onto the side road and made his way up the winding road and stopped at the heavy, iron, security gate to gain access to the Sommerset Inn Resort and Spa.

One of the security guards scanned his ID card into the computer while another held out a small pad for his right thumb print to also be entered into the data base. A quick look in the cargo area of the van and a walk around the rear satisfied the cadre of guards that he was ready to enter the premises. As a courier for the compound, Buzz repeated this routine at least twice each working day.

The drive to the main building wound through the golf course, then took him past the tennis courts and pool. Just beyond the three-story, colonial style hotel building he entered a small parking lot. He descended a slight slope into the parking area making it barely visible from the veranda of the grand resort and from the numerous cottages which dotted the grounds. He left the aging delivery van here and disappeared into the building through a door in the lower level of the main resort lodge.

Amanda awoke to bright sunshine. Her soft feelings of coziness and security from the night before were washed from her by a cold dose of foreboding as reality bolted her upright in the bed. She needed desperately to talk to Will.

She could hear him stirring around downstairs as she went into the closet sized bathroom tucked into the dormer of her room and started the water in the shower. It would take the hot water a while to reach the third floor bath and she was thankful that it was spring and there were no paying guests in the B & B.

She peeled out of her sleep clothes and adjusted the temperature of the water. The room was beginning to fill with steam as she stepped under the cascade and turned her face up into the refreshing spray. To Amanda this was truly one of life's most delicious moments.

After spending longer in the water than she should have, she toweled off and pulled on a fresh t-shirt, jeans and jogging shoes, her usual and favorite Saturday attire. She spread her bed up quickly, closed the door behind her and bounded down the staircase with the same squeaks and creaks that she had memorized years ago.

As she entered the kitchen she saw nothing of her brother except his butt. He was bent over pulling freshly baked goods from the large, commercial style oven. The aroma grabbed her and made her seven years old again and for a moment her mother was standing in front of her.

As Will spoke she returned to the present, "Good morning, Sleeping Beauty, I was beginning to think there might be a gas leak up there in your little attic that had done you in."

"I know, I know, I haven't slept that soundly in months. It felt good. Thanks for baking, Will, it smells divine, you must have gotten up with the chickens."

"Not really, it's my usual and I enjoy having you here to bake for. Grab us each a cup of that coffee and I'll take the tray. I thought we'd eat out on the terrace if that's okay."

"Sounds great to me if it's warm enough."

She followed him out through the French doors and along the flagstone walkway to the slightly raised terrace. It was positioned perfectly toward the east to take advantage of the early sun and a full view of the lake, a really wonderful morning spot. They pulled wrought iron chairs up to a round café table and dove into the fresh coffee cake and coffee.

Amanda was anxious to get to the topic of the day but also needed to know how the day would play out. "What's our schedule for today?" She asked.

"Nothing rigid," Will responded, "I need to get some things at the store for dinner and Charles will be here about 4 or 5. Other than that the day is ours."

"I'm going to get another cup of coffee and then I really need to talk. You want one?"

"Just pour it all in one of those carafes above the coffee maker and bring it out here," Will suggested, "We'll just drink and talk all morning."

Amanda returned to the terrace, poured Will and herself a steaming mug of the brew, sat down, put her feet up in the adjacent chair and began to tell all that she had come to know about Gazelle. She left out nothing but was careful to distinguish between facts, suspicions and feelings.

Nearly two and one-half hours later Will was fully briefed and frightfully apprehensive. She had watched his expressions go from doubt, through skepticism and amazement to finally land on pure, unadulterated worry. He had asked questions throughout her tale and he had gained a thorough understanding of what had transpired up to now. He slowly raked his fingers through his sun streaked hair. His brow hosted deep furrows as he spoke, "Jesus, Mandy, this is probably the most incredible story I've ever heard. I just can't think what to say, I need to absorb what I just heard."

Will got up and paced around the terrace going nowhere yet moving with purpose. For a few moments he stood motionless, hands jammed down into his pockets, his back to Amanda, looking out across the lake. Finally he turned, walked back to the table and sat down. He reached out and picked up Amanda's hand in his and looking straight into her eyes he announced, "Mandy, you're in danger."

Harry Axelrod had been back from London less than 24 hours. Though he was not accustomed to running his own errands, going to the drop spot was not an errand that he would trust to even the most loyal person on his staff. His right hand man, his buffer, had been left out of the particulars on this one even though he had arranged the contact for him. Harry knew how this would end up and no one else needed to be involved. The fewer people who knew, the better and he and Buzz were already getting to be one person too many.

He knew he was somewhat conspicuous entering the building lobby in his jogging clothes but he had found that most people avert their eyes from the scantily clad and it was the only place he could go alone without raising questions among his staff. The real challenge had been what to do with the documents once retrieved, but he had worked that out with a plastic sleeve which he wore on his chest under his workout shirt.

He entered the men's room off the lobby and allowed himself to relax slightly when he saw that the last stall was vacant. It had been a problem previously to be inconspicuous when he arrived and found that stall occupied. He went in, latched the door behind him and began to loosen the thumb screws on the plumbing access panel. Once removed, he reached his hand in behind the shut-off valve and extracted a packet of rolled up papers. He replaced the panel, slid the documents under his workout shirt and quickly left the stall and men's room. He walked briskly back through the lobby mingling with the throng of workers going to and returning from lunch. As he emerged from the revolving door and stepped onto the sidewalk he started an easy jog and moved over to use the curb area adjacent to the street. A light mist was descending on the District now, but it was just an easy quarter-mile back to his own office. There he could re-enter the building through the health club on the first floor.

Showered, dressed and alone in his office he pulled out the ill-gotten papers and began to read. As he read anger, dread and fear all fought for first place on his emotional scale. The documents in front of him confirmed what he had feared. A restrictive tariff on Venezuelan oil would probably be announced any day. He needed to intervene. He could be wiped out.

He had been required to lean more heavily on the import business in the wake of Enron and was trying to keep a low profile in the commodities trading right now. The possibility that all the players in that arena would be revealed was slight but the risk was still greater than what he would normally find acceptable. Harry Axelrod only bet on sure things and trading in energy, in particular, the way he did it, was only manageable if you or your friends were in control. He needed the deck stacked or he didn't like the odds.

Insider information and stock manipulation were gimmicks for the rookies. Oh sure, he had done his share of both, had cut his teeth on stock hype trading. It was just one of those old time cons moved to Wall Street but he had gotten a real high out of pulling them off. The anonymity of those internet chat rooms on stocks and the day-trading fools who frequented them had been a boon in the early days but he wouldn't want to be playing in that arena now. The SEC and the Justice Department were all over that stuff now.

He smiled to himself, *It was getting harder and harder to win if you were a small time crook,* he mused. The only way for crime to pay is to be a major thief with an organization or network behind you. Law enforcement is effectively pushing crime up the ladder to become bigger and more sophisticated instead of deterring it. He heard himself laugh out loud.

The second piece of information revealed in the documents in front of him and the item that snapped him back to reality was the looming Russian oil deal. It was really backing him into a desperate corner.

Harry picked up the secure phone on his desk and dialed directly to the secretary, just one of the perks of money, power and influence.

"I want to know about this Venezuelan oil tariff."

"Boy, I'll say one thing for your sources, they're fast."

"Don't screw around with me, what's up?"

"Take it easy, we're handling it. Don't get nervous..."

"Damn it! Don't tell me what to do. I tell you what to do. I want a complete report and I want it now. Meet me now," Harry demanded.

The big black sedans were barely noticeable parked amongst the huge containers at the cargo pier. The secretary emerged from the back door of his car and slid in next to Harry in the adjacent vehicle. It was somewhat symbolic that he made the secretary come to him.

"I want to know your plan. Every damn detail," he began.

After 30 minutes the secretary moved back to his own car and both sped away like two, dark, nocturnal creatures suddenly deterred by each other's presence after gobbling up their prey.

Harry was a troubled man. Once again he had looked to his friends inside the government for assistance and once again he got nothing but a wimpy response. *Why the hell was he spending all this money on them when they never produced results,* he wondered. He would handle this himself, it was too important to him personally. He leaned his head back on the plush seat, closed his eyes and began to formulate a plan.

Back in his office, Harry placed a call to a pager and entered the number of his secure line. Out in the Virginia countryside, in the bowels of the Sommerset Inn, Buzz's pager went off.

Moments later Harry picked up his ringing phone, "It's going the other way this time," he said. "I drop, you pick up. Complete instructions will be included, payment as usual when it's done." He hung up.

Seconds later the phone rang again. Harry picked it up and heard, "This'll cost you more. Where do you want to put these documents, what's this about? Who's the target?"

"It'll be doubled," he replied and hung up again. "How dare that prick," he thought. Harry knew that Buzz was losing his usefulness. He was too curious to be trusted. He was a loose cannon and Harry couldn't afford to have him running around shooting off his mouth. He was certain that Buzz would have to tell someone after he saw the documents that Harry was preparing to plant. He was also certain that the plant along with a well-placed tip to the media would sufficiently discredit the source and with it the plans for the entire tariff. This should put a stop to the influence being asserted behind his back.

Buzz's time had come. This plant would be the end of his usefulness. He dialed a second number and Nate Tidwell answered.

Chapter Five

Roland left the senator's room with the weight of the world on his shoulders. He had so much to consider, so much to decide. Were they really ready to take Gazelle to the next level? Was assassination of someone like Amanda Chambers an option? Up until now they'd concentrated on killing a few reputations here and there. They always stood ready to take out some of the bad actors but they were always people who had screwed someone over. They only resorted to elimination when the players were those who had taken or put at risk the lives of innocent people. It seemed that all Amanda had done was stumble onto sensitive information. *Hardly an indictment,* he thought.

Gazelle had always been about policy and implementation. Execution and assassination would be taking on a whole new meaning in this context. Was this to be their destiny? He knew there were those among them who would welcome that evolution.

The tight tentacles of stress had bound themselves around him and were threatening to choke off his capacity for reason. His thinking was clouded and he couldn't seem to release the furrow in his brow. He decided to go downstairs for a rare nightcap.

Upon entering the dark, wood paneled pub with its ornate furnishings he was instantly struck by her beauty. She seemed to almost glow in the dark. The corner of the bar where she sat was lighter than the rest of the room. Hers was not a classic beauty, more exotic he thought. As she talked with her companions her gestures captured his awareness with a compelling sensuality and held him spellbound. She had an earthiness about her that captured him completely. He could feel it in the gut. He could not tear his eyes away from her. He was beginning to feel self-conscious. Was it from staring at her or was it her brief but knowing glances back at him? He felt exposed, vulnerable, nearly naked. He tugged the knot of his tie as if he needed to assure himself that it was still there.

He gained the strength and presence of mind to turn away from her and, having salvaged some composure, he selected a seat at the bar where his back would be toward her. Sliding onto the stool he looked up to greet the bartender only to be confronted by her image in the mirror behind the bar. Her smile was wry.

Roland was barely into his brandy when she joined him at the bar.

"Buy a girl a drink?" she asked coyly.

"What are you having?" Roland signaled the bartender.

"Whatever you've got looks fine to me," she quipped. Roland wondered if she was referring only to the drink.

"Another, please," he addressed the bartender. He couldn't avoid the sight of her trim thighs as the slit in her skirt strained to reveal more of them. Her eyes were deep and dark, her mouth prominent and pouty. He didn't know where to look next, she was flawless. He was lost.

"Look, I'm not usually this forward, but I find your beauty breathtaking. You probably hear that a lot."

"Well, I do, I guess, but a woman in my position can't put too much stock in that, can't be certain of the sincerity of it I mean."

"I apologize if I've offended you. I assure you, my reaction is nothing but sincere. I'm not very suave and I'm probably way too unpracticed socially. Comes from too much work, I guess."

"I think your darling, sort of quaint. It's quite refreshing," she cooed.

Roland felt a shiver. "What did you mean about, 'a woman in my position' earlier?"

Her laugh was as sweet and melodic as he would have imagined. "Does the name Mira Melong mean anything to you?" she asked.

"If my memory serves me correctly, a young jetsetter, daughter of a wealthy Asian businessman and a world renowned model, not to mention a tabloid regular that the paparazzi can't catch on film. How am I doing?"

"How do you do?" she said as she reached out to offer her hand.

He took her hand, "Roland," he responded, "Roland Priestly, regular guy."

They both laughed.

"Well, Roland Priestly, regular guy, what's your game?"

"Just a simple businessman and a general flunky to those who are more successful than I," he responded.

"What brings you to London? I assume you don't live here since you're in a hotel at this time of night."

"Just business meetings, always business with me," he answered. He was captivated.

Roland opened his eyes to the sunshine pouring through the crack in the draperies, a pounding headache and long strands of brown hair draped across his chest. Mira lay next to him with her head in the crook of his arm which he needed desperately to move at this time or perhaps never be able to again. As he tried to blink the headache away he was flooded with images of a night of playful and gratifying sex. It exceeded his wildest fantasy. Not that he ever allowed himself many of those.

Mira had been the aggressor at the bar and had continued in that role throughout the night taking him to heights unimagined. He had no idea his body could still respond that way and he had a new appreciation for both the quantity and quality of what he could achieve. She was obviously a very talented young woman. He was totally spent yet somehow invigorated. He couldn't wait to take on the day.

He tried moving slightly to see if his body still worked. He needed to stretch. Mira whimpered slightly and rolled over on her back to stretch herself awake. He was instantly aroused at the sight of her naked body. Her perfectly shaped, bronze limbs contrasted against the stark white sheets and her ample, rounded breasts begged his attention. He gladly obliged. He really couldn't help himself. Her physical warmth and eager touches filled up corners, crevices and clefts of him that had been ignored, disregarded and almost forgotten. Consummating their mutual arousal in the shower got the day off to an enjoyable start. Mira was magnificent. His headache was gone.

He politely left the shower to her and completed his grooming while she lingered under the cascade of water. He ordered room service while she dressed and they enjoyed an abundant breakfast on the balcony. The spring morning held promise of the day to come.

Mira kissed him gently as they parted at the door. Both promised to call. He was flooded with conflicting feelings. Roland did not condone casual sex yet he had just engaged in such an encounter and felt all the better for it. Mira was an enchanting woman whom, he thought, he would never see again, yet never forget. She had touched him deeply.

He opened his briefcase on the table and began to spread out the business of Gazelle in front of him. His direction seemed clearer. He realized that over time he had lost sight of what was important. Today he vowed to make that right. He picked up his cell phone and began. He had very frank and direct conversations with two of the members before he was finished. The question of Gazelle engaging in executions and assassinations and the reason for the dilemma were thoroughly discussed. His path had become clear.

Amanda and Will worked thoughtfully as they straightened the kitchen from the morning meal. Will was working out an evening menu and extracting from that a shopping list as he went along.

Amanda was anxious to take a walk and Will elected to stay at the house and finish up some chores. As she set off in the freshness of the spring air, droplets of moisture from the morning dew still clung to the greenery and blooms like tiny diamonds. She watched as they winked occasionally at the early sun and boldly flirted with the rays of warmth that would eventually send them into oblivion. Her favorite path or shortcut as she used to call it was less prominent but still present in the dense, low growth along the lake.

A few new homes had been built in the old vacant patch and she hoped she would not find herself suddenly trespassing on some unknown resident's lot. Instead she found that her trail skirted the newcomers and led her out to the old, nearly abandoned road that would take her toward that familiar town. *She still knew her way around,* she gloated to herself. Unlike those earlier times, her pace was slow as her energies and focus were all in her head today.

As she walked along familiar territory she remembered her time here before Washington and how hard she had been trying to get away. Her mother had been using their home as a Tourist House as they had called it then. She took in families for varying lengths of time during the summer. Often they would have the same people with them for two to three months at a time and Amanda worked hard to help Will and her mother operate the business in a way that provided sufficient income to see them through the other three seasons. This had been their necessity after the early death of her father. Her mother worked hard to make ends meet and Amanda and Will both pitched in willingly.

As she moved along her familiar route today she was transported back to that summer and the days leading up to her job with the agency. She paused now and let the memory of that August day embrace her.

She remembered it clearly and with some fondness now. It had never seemed far for her to go. She had walked effortlessly along the narrow, rural roadway, quiet from the lack of weekend bustle and tourist's cars. She relished making the walk into the tiny hamlet in the sultry part of the day. With lunch cooked, guests served and the kitchen cleaned up she was free for a couple of hours before the dinner commotion would begin and the unending cycle of chopping, cooking and serving the guests would repeat itself once more.

The gravel crunched beneath her feet and she felt herself lulled by the stillness of that August afternoon. The lake lapped gently against the shore and the familiar song of the crickets built a tune inside her head. Boats bobbed slightly on ripples left by the few passing power boats and the sailboats contributed a bell-like tinkle as their riggings tapped melodiously against their masts. The road followed obediently, the shape of the shoreline as it curved softly around the bay and swept into town. She had always found this environment seductive and it would have been easy to get complacent about her future and stay there forever but for her there was also something stifling about this environment. It was the culture, she knew that she would never fit in.

She had arrived at the post office in no time ready to explode from anticipation. She paused for a moment hoping that she could wish a letter into the box. This was a scene she had repeated nearly every day for the preceding several weeks but today was special.

Conscious of every move and acting with deliberate care, she cautiously opened the door to the postal box and exposed the letters within. It took both hands to extract the contents so she had taken them over to the shelf area to sort through and separate the unwieldy bundle. She made one stack for bills for her mother, another for letters addressed to the guests and a final for the temporary, summer employees. She recognized the names easily and had even gotten familiar enough with this task that she knew who many of the senders were by the handwriting and return addresses.

Her heart sank as she came to the bottom of the stack and there was nothing addressed to her. Her sigh was audible. The unwritten message was received. Obviously, she had misinterpreted their interest. This was the day by which they would notify the successful candidate. As usual, she had allowed herself to indulge in unrealistic expectations. Disappointment always followed expectations. What made her dare to dream? Again, she silently vowed to steel herself against the caring. Well, she had new resolve. She could find happiness in a life made just for her, by her, and it could be one filled with meaning and excitement. She was determined to keep trying.

This disappointment had come on the heels of her painful decision not to accompany the man she loved in pursuit of his dream but rather to maintain her independence and make her life around a fulfilling career. He had not been willing to make the concessions that would have been required for them to build a life together and neither was she. She would have had to give up everything, her family and her work to accompany him back to his homeland. She had been unwilling to do that and he could not give up what he had worked so hard for, it had broken her heart.

She had set her jaw in defiance, picked up the mail with determination and left the post office that day with strength of purpose drawn on her face and a trace of defeat in her step.

On her slow and quiet walk back, she'd reflected on her life and why it was that she believed that she could make things different. Every direction she turned the people around her all lived basically the same life. Oh sure, each had its own little twists and there were always unexpected turns but one looked just like the next to her. She just didn't feel like she could settle and that's what it would be for her.

As she'd walked along the blacktop roadway she played road soccer with a fist-sized rock. The harder she tried to aim it, the less control she'd seemed to have over its direction. She wondered if she really had any control over anything. They say control is an illusion. Could she plan her future or was it just going to unfold and fallout all over her. She hated feeling like a victim.

Finally, in utter frustration and preceded by a gentle hop, she'd teed off on the rock and sent it sailing across the road and into the lake. The ripples that it sent out caught her attention and she was captivated by their pattern. She had approached the edge of the water and slowly lowered onto her haunches to watch the little waves as they moved at a precisely calibrated speed until they lost energy and melted into the body of water which had spawned them. A smile spilled across her face as she recalled her father cautioning her that if she ever wanted to know what kind of an impression she left behind she only had to put her hand in the water and, upon pulling it out, observe the hole that was left.

Apparently, she thought now, she had left just such an impression on the interview committee. She had been so hopeful and optimistic as she sat at the conference table calmly fielding and responding to the interviewers' questions. She had pinned all her hopes on that opportunity. If only she could get that job she could gain the independence and challenges that she so craved. She could begin to make plans and put together a direction for her life, begin to heal. Oh, how she yearned to make a difference, to do something of importance to others and to the world.

She recalled how she was jerked from her reverie that day by the sharp clanging of a bell off in the distance; it had persistently summoned her back to work. The pots and pans were calling and would take precedence over the examination of her bleak life. Pondering her place in the universe would have to keep for some other time.

Upon entering the backdoor of the cavernous kitchen and dining hall, she had been hailed by Roberta, the assistant cook who was speaking excitedly and waving a piece of paper in the air. As Amanda got her to calm down and slow down, her Salvadoran accent diminished enough that she could make out that the paper being fluttered in her face was a telephone message which had arrived in her absence. Rescuing the paper from Roberta's outstretched hand, she learned that the committee had chosen to contact her by phone. Roberta, in her excitement, had taken down a somewhat confusing message. Either they wanted her to come to Washington to start work on the 'first of September' or they had passed her by and they had work for their 'first such member.' Well that didn't really make sense, did it? They must have said they wanted her to report for work.

Ecstatic at the prospect she had whooped, hollered and picked Roberta up in a big bear hug and whirled her around in circles. Roberta's short, spindly legs had groped for the floor as Amanda had swept her around the dining room in a distorted version of a waltz. Everyone in the kitchen had been thrilled for her. They had been feeling the strain and waiting to hear right along with her.

She had not been able to wait until dinner was over to return the call. She slipped into the kitchen's tiny office used for planning menus and placing food orders and boldly dialed the number provided in the message. All eyes had been on her as she emerged from the relative quiet of the office into the pandemonium of a kitchen with a meal due. Everyone just knew instinctively, that the job was hers and as they set about their tasks, there was a proud and positive mood in the otherwise humid and heavy atmosphere. Just two short weeks and she would be on her way. Her feet had fairly flown across the floor as she chopped, stirred and served. She knew that her life had just taken an important turn. It would be some time before she would realize the magnitude of that turn, however.

Amanda found herself smiling now at the memory of that time and the thought of Roberta being whirled around the kitchen. She allowed herself a gentle laugh even though she had so much weighing on her mind.

Setting aside Gazelle for a moment there was all the nostalgia that a trip back home can bring. She really missed her parents in this environment and her mind was flooded with images of them as a family. With all the innocence of a child, she had thought back then that things would never change. At what age, she wondered, had she become aware of death? When had she realized that she would someday lose those she loved so much? It certainly isn't real until it actually happens and then, she realized, it's too late to contemplate it. All you can do is feel it. Another of life's ironies she mused.

Additionally, all the flurry of that first love and the eventual pain that follows flooded over her today. Her decision had been difficult but daring. It so went against what she had been taught that young women should yearn for. She had passed on marriage to have a life of her own. She had felt that most of her role models had stirred around her in silent condemnation of the path she'd chosen back then.

And what about this change in Will? she asked herself. There certainly is more than one way to lose someone you love. Her parents had left her through death and Alex through commitment, but would Will now leave her through love? She had never known him to be in love. If he ever had been it was when they were separated physically and she had probably been too self-absorbed and unaware to realize. This time he seemed different. She could actually see the change in him. She was glad he was happy but, at the same time, she was wary about his relationship with her. She supposed it was just uncharted territory for them and everyone has that fear of the unknown. She convinced herself that her reservations would pass with time and renewed trust.

In the grander scheme it didn't matter anyway. If she didn't get this mess figured out about Gazelle she was probably going to get herself killed. It was time to face the facts and own up to the jeopardy she had placed herself in.

Will had told her what he knew of Roland Priestly. His name always came up with those of the most unsavory characters. He was known to have a great deal of influence on Capitol Hill and he wielded it unshyly. Nothing concretely illegal had ever been tied to him but you didn't gain that kind of power and influence in Washington by going to church on Sunday and dropping a twenty in the collection plate. He was ominous and he was dangerous because he was connected, but connected to whom? There you had it, the sixty-four thousand dollar question. He must be Gazelle or connected to him. How could she follow that thread and not get herself hurt or killed? More importantly, why should she? What was so compelling about all this?

She thought back to what had started her down this road of mystery and intrigue. *That damn document!* came the resounding answer.

She wondered if she should try to recover it or at least make a copy. She made a mental note to talk to Will about it. She was having trouble concentrating. There was so much rushing around inside her mind and she couldn't seem to bring clarity to it. Either something wasn't right with her or maybe it was just that she was missing pieces of this puzzle.

She had been so struck by Will's directness about the danger this morning that neither of them had taken the next step. They needed to brainstorm long and hard about a strategy but they had both needed to take some time to absorb and adjust to this reality.

Unaware of her surroundings, she suddenly found herself back at the house. Getting around this area was still second nature to her and she had just navigated the time away unaware of the twists and turns that had taken her home.

Will was unpacking the groceries from the rear of the car as Amanda entered the driveway. The gravel made a crunching noise and slid slightly under her feet as she approached him.

"What's for lunch?" she asked him. "Got anything scrumptiously irresistible in those bags?"

"The best thing in here is some beautiful salmon filets I found. Those are for dinner though, so hands off. I thought we'd do a big salad for lunch if that's okay with you."

"Sounds great."

"There's also a little left over soup if you're interested."

"Doesn't sound like we need to go hungry, let's get at it." She picked up the last of the bags from the rear of the vehicle.

They made their way through the back door laden down with grocery bags just in time to hear the answering machine blurt out its invitation to leave a message after the beep. The response came in the form of a woman's voice making inquiry about availability at the B & B and requesting a call back as soon as possible. The 703 area code on the call back number indicated a Virginia location. Amanda thought the voice oddly familiar but dismissed it as paranoia.

"Don't get many visitors from your part of the country," said Will. "Most of my guests come up from the Chicago area, just for the weekend. Guess I'd better get back to her and see if I can drum up some new business."

All at once Amanda felt like she was about to jump out of her skin. She had that sense that she was watching a story unfold from outside her body. This was about her, she was starring in it but she wasn't really here. Kind of watching herself it seemed. Finally she blurted out, "God, Will, I'm about to explode. You said yourself, I'm in danger and then we casually go about making plans for dinner and booking the damn B & B like nothing's amiss. Well, damn it, Will, I'm scared, what should I do?" she literally collapsed onto the kitchen stool, put her head down on her arm and began to sob.

"I'm sorry, Mandy," Will cooed. "I guess I'm half way between denial and distracted trying to figure out what to do. I don't blame you for blowing up."

Amanda sniffed.

Will put his arms around her and swayed her gently in his arms, "Go ahead and cry, get it out," he said.

Chapter Six

From time to time in the history of the United States of America, the government has determined that it is prudent to provide a completely safe and secure location to which members of congress, the executive branch and key, high level government staff could be moved in order to continue the critical operations of the country's business. Historically, depending upon the country's level of fear or paranoia these bunkers have been alternately built and abandoned with a rhythm which harkens the winds of war. This was a time of building. The current administration had re-opened and enhanced several of these secure bunkers and had instituted a mandatory rotation system for certain key personnel to ensure that matters of government and national security could be quickly moved outside Washington. Maintaining a working presence in the bunkers would make it easier to transition critical functions there as needed.

It was Nate's rotation time in the bunker. At his level he was required to spend thirty of every 120 days on location with this shadow government. The "undisclosed location" or UL as the employees had named it, had become an accepted part of civil service over the last couple of years. Those dispatched to the UL were required to leave their homes and offices for the prescribed time and take up residence and life inside the compound. They all left their families the same 800 number where messages could be relayed to them. They could tell no one where they were physically located nor what mode of transportation they used to get there. For all their family and friends knew they could be anywhere in the world hooked to their real lives by just a telephone line, totally monitored. It was as if they were floating in space somewhere, tethered only by an anonymous, telephonic connection. It was harder for some than for others. Nate had no problem whatsoever with the assignment and, in fact, spent more time there than was required. He liked working closely with the secretary and that was where he could be found.

Nate, dressed in casual slacks, a golf shirt and topsiders shouldered his bag, locked his front door and walked the few blocks in bright sunshine to the metro stop. Once in Arlington, he switched to the blue line and rode it out to Alexandria. The staging facility was carefully located within a block of the metro and he arrived well ahead of his required time. The modest sign read, "Colonial Inn," and it hung slightly askew.

The old, narrow, row house had been converted to a restaurant and inn. There were occasionally a few guests in the dining room but the carpets were sufficiently worn and the paint just drab enough to discourage most local trade. The inn never solicited business and most always operated under a "No Vacancy," sign. Quoted rates were artificially high enough that the vacancies could be offered without fear of many takers. Those who did stumble onto the premises were placed in a wing well removed from the center of action.

Nate moved through the lobby hardly taking notice of the ornate, Federalist period furnishings. He passed beyond the small, single elevator and entered an inconspicuous corridor. The hallway was narrow and dimly lit. He went through a door labeled, "Staff Only." Upon stepping through the door the security routine began. His ID badge was scanned, as was his thumb print. His bag was physically searched while he spent this time with the metal detector, X-ray machine and explosive detection device. Finally, he was patted down. There were several other workers in the room submitting to the same routine and the air was inevitably strained and tense.

On the wall opposite the security station were several rows of lockers. Nate was given a key for number 121. He moved resolutely across the room and opened his assigned locker. From it he removed a golf bag which he laid lengthwise on one of the tables provided. He opened the bag by releasing three latches along the length of it. It was hinged along the back and when opened revealed sufficient capacity to transfer his packed items from his travel bag to the inside of the golf bag. This accomplished he locked his empty travel bag into the locker, shouldered the golf bag and moved through the double, swinging doors where he passed a row of dressing rooms. Here other employees who, for the benefit of their families, had to leave home dressed for travel changed into their provided golf attire. Nate continued into the lounge where he would await their prompt, 3 p.m. departure.

By 2:45 the shuttle bus was available for loading. Nate exited the rear of the building with his golf bag on his shoulder and joined the other masquerading employees walking down the loading ramp. He approached the 20 passenger, green and white shuttle bus with the name, "Virginia Golf Tours," emblazoned on the side and rear. The driver waited by the open cargo door as Nate and the others put their bags inside. He boarded the bus and chose a window seat about halfway back. The only thing he had kept out for the journey was the current issue of Time magazine which he knew would keep him occupied during the ride.

Two hours later the shuttle bus pulled up to the iron-gated entry to the Sommerset Inn, Resort and Spa. Two uniformed security guards boarded the bus while two others with their canine companion began their search of the cargo area, including the opening of some of the golf bags.

One of the guards on the bus carried an electronic device which resembled the smallest of laptop computers. The second guard took the ID badge from one passenger at a time and inserted it into a slot on the device for electronic reading. Purportedly this would match with the scan that had been done back at the point of embarkation before the bus was boarded. All the scanning done in Alexandria had been uploaded onto the server at headquarters and subsequently downloaded to the tiny computer the security guard now carried on the bus. She also occasionally asked a passenger to place their thumb on the pad on top of the computer. Lastly a picture was taken of each occupant of the bus where they sat. Nate was not sure if this was preserved for posterity, used if they disappeared or if it was some of this new software that compared facial features and structure to ensure that no imposters were on board.

As the guards left the bus the iron gates opened and the bus proceeded inside. They disembarked in the lot on the west end of the main resort building. As they entered a door in the lower level an elongated golf cart, built for that specific purpose and driven by a bellman, moved their bags to the lobby of the resort and from there to their assigned rooms.

Tomorrow afternoon the bus would leave again with workers whose UL time was complete. It would look to the casual observer that the golfers had arrived in the evening, spent the night, golfed in the morning and returned to D.C. in the afternoon. The assigned times and rotations in the bunker were carefully calculated to maintain this appearance. None but the most perceptive would detect the different identity of the golfers on the bus. This careful charade was invented to keep the locals and casual observers in the area from becoming suspicious of the traffic at the Inn.

Nate heard the heavily reinforced door close behind him and the temperature dropped dramatically. The hallways in the bunker were not climatically controlled as they stayed at a constant temperature year around. During the elevator ride to the lower level the group began to loosen up and casual conversations broke out. Everyone seemed more relaxed once outside the obvious glare of security. Here everyone knew they were constantly monitored but somehow cameras put them more at ease than the uniformed guards and driver. Each of them was headed for their respective office areas for a quick briefing and hand off before gathering in the dining hall for dinner at 6:30. This ride to the lower level on the crowded elevator made him think of miners descending into the earth to begin their shifts. The only things missing were the hard hats with headlights attached and the canary.

The employees themselves had decided that breakfast and lunch should be casual and relaxed but the majority had voted for dinner to be served promptly, properly and all together. Nate had just enough time to visit his room to hang up his clothes and set his toiletries out before freshening up and putting on a tailored shirt and tie to wear to dinner.

Entering the dining room he saw several of his regular dinner companions gathering around their usual table and he made his way through the maze of white draped tables to join them. After greetings and handshakes they took their seats. One of the few percs of UL rotation was that wine was provided with dinner. Nate picked up the open bottle of Chardonnay from the tray in the middle of the table and poured himself a glass.

"Any other takers on white?" he asked the entire table. Two glasses went up in the air and Nate reached across the table to fill those as well. Replacing the bottle, he picked up the red, "Who would like the Merlot?" he asked. Several more takers responded, one of which was Buzz. This time Nate rose and walked around the table to fill the glasses one by one. As he leaned around to fill Buzz's he whispered, "Eight o'clock, starter's shack." He moved adroitly on around the table to complete the wine allotments.

Dinner passed with light conversation and some heavier discussions of world issues and politics of the day. Some of those who were nearing the completion of their rotation liked to asked those who were newly arrived about news on the outside, joking that they had no access to that reality. Actually Nate had come to enjoy these times and the camaraderie that they provided. He always started his rotation on this kind of up note and the closer he got to the end of 30 days the more he didn't care if he ever saw any of these people again.

His attention was diverted from these thoughts to the present conversation. Tricia Wells, one of the economists, was talking about the recently concluded summit. Apparently she had attended and had been struck by the tone of the meeting on AIDS drugs for Africa. She spoke of a young woman who apparently had done her homework and who had put the spotlight on the drug companies and their foot dragging. She was impressed with several other issues that had been discussed there and at the level of competence that she had witnessed in some of the younger people involved in this work.

"What's an economist doing on the African AIDS issue?" Nate asked.

"Actually I was there on the Poverty Committee but I had an opportunity to sit in on several other meetings during the conference."

Conversation and small talk continued around the table and throughout the dinner time. Nate was again lost in his thoughts. He was grateful that he didn't sit with other people from his department and engage solely in shop talk. It was nice to be away from it and get other's perspectives for a change. He wondered what these people would think about his second job.

After dinner, as was his custom when he was here, Nate took an evening walk along the golf course. This night he ended his walk at the starter's shack. He found a bench and sat down to wait. A little before seven with the air chilling rapidly and the evening light receding beyond the western horizon, Buzz joined Nate on the bench. It was an isolated area at this time of night, well out in the open where both men felt they could talk freely.

Nate began, "What are you doing screwing around in this deal?" His voice was little more than a harsh whisper.

"Hey," replied Buzz, "Your man's the one changed the thing around, not me."

"What change? You never had any contract, you're just supposed to get what he asks for."

"That's it. This wasn't a get it was a put. To me that's a whole new deal, to me it's more dangerous, that means more dough. That's all I said."

"You've just made this harder than it had to be. I thought we had a good thing going here and you had to screw with it. I told you before that you asked way too many questions and now you're holding him up for more cash. Have you done the thing?"

"Yeh, it's all in place, just like the instructions said, I guess he's trying to set this guy up, incriminate him in something, huh?"

Nate was livid. "There you go. Stop asking so many questions, are you wired?" Nate moved toward Buzz and tapped his hand on his chest and back in a perfunctory but accusing way. "I wouldn't tell you if I knew, which I don't. Unlike you, I try to keep my nose out of the part that doesn't concern me. You'd have done well to do the same and never, never try to hold the man up for more money. I told you he'd be generous with you, that's how he operates. I said you'd see a nice bonus if this went well. Why couldn't you trust that? Jesus, you really pissed him off Buzz."

"Why should I trust someone who won't answer a question and whom I don't even know?" Buzz inquired.

"You knew me, Buzz, you knew me," Nate sighed lowly. Buzz did not take note of Nate's use of the past tense.

As Buzz left the building the next morning for his ten o'clock run he didn't notice the small puddle of liquid under the front axle of his van nor was he aware of the small, almost imperceptible drip that contributed to it. He made his way down the winding incline to the security entrance and endured the usual scrutiny to body and vehicle.

Once out on the road his spirits lightened slightly. He had been trying to adjust the temperature of the outside air engulfing his feet when it happened. He looked up from the controls he'd been fiddling with and directly into the grill of a huge tractor trailer rig. He swerved to the right and onto the shoulder to avoid the massive grill and bumper of the tractor and found himself having to choose between turning back into the trailer or confronting the onrushing bridge. In a split second he decided to avoid the truck and concentrate on maneuvering around the bridge by braking hard to give the trailer time to move out of his way and then cutting back onto the road behind it.

The panic was visible on his face when he stepped down on the brake peddle and to his further astonishment, found that his brakes would not slow him. By the time the realization was upon him the bridge loomed large. His next image was of a large, solid concrete abutment growing exponentially bigger by the moment through his windshield. That was the last image Buzz had in this life. "Damn," was all he had time to think as a warm but brief picture of his smiling family danced across his mind like a cherished snapshot. He was thankful to have had them.

The salmon was silently marinating, the side dishes were awaiting their turns on the stove and Amanda was helping Will prepare the hors de oeuvres when they heard the car in the driveway. Will charged out the door to meet Charles while Amanda discreetly busied herself in the kitchen in order to give them a moment alone. As they clamored through the back door and entered the family room Will wore a big smile on his face, warmth in his eyes and held a bright and beautiful bouquet of flowers in his hand. "I'll get these in a vase," he said. "They're gorgeous. You're so thoughtful, Charles."

Amanda was certain that her jaw had dropped and she was standing with her mouth hanging open. She couldn't seem to do anything about it. As he moved gracefully across the room, hand extended, he was saying, "You must be Amanda, I'm Charles and delighted to finally meet you."

She knew she wasn't going to faint but an audible swoon was a distinct possibility. Handsome wasn't adequate to describe what she was looking at. She finally stammered out, "Nice to meet you," and got her hand up to shake his.

Charles was well over six feet tall and buff. His dark hair, somewhere between curly and wavy, topped his squarely etched face like dark icing on a cake. His features all seemed to be carefully designed to complement each other and to enhance his light blue eyes and splendid mouth. His complexion was olive and clear. She thought him beautiful and to top it off his voice resonated with a very slight but sexy accent which she would later learn came from his early years in Italy. Charles Farino was a hunk.

She realized then that Will was trying to work around her to get a vase from the cupboard behind which she had taken root. She was trying to come back to reality but was finding it difficult in the glow of Charles' aura. She finally got herself in gear enough to ask what he would like to drink. His back was turned and he was taking his travel bag from his shoulder and placing it by the hallway door. His shirt pulled taught across his muscular shoulders and back. He looked just as good from the back she observed and fought to shake her thoughts off again.

"My first choice's white wine but what are you two having?" he responded.

"We haven't started," she replied, "And I saw a Pinot Grigio chilling, that okay?"

"Yes, sounds great," he turned to Will, "Will that do for you also, Will?"

Will responded affirmatively and continued to fuss with the flower arrangement trying to get it just right. Gratefully, both Charles and Will seemed to be nearly unaware of Amanda's presence let alone her reaction.

Amanda's tensions eased as the evening moved along. She felt so good in Charles' and Will's presence that she forgot all about Gazelle and everything else outside of the family room and the warmth that the three of them shared. Neither she nor Will spoke of her predicament though it seemed like every other topic under the sun was at least touched upon. It was a thoroughly enchanting and loving evening. Amanda felt her soul nurtured. She was renewed.

Will and Charles seemed to glow in the presence of each other and would hold hands or place a hand on each other from time to time as though it were the most natural thing in the world and, she reflected, it was! Two people in love, two people who wanted to be near each other and this would, naturally, include a physical closeness. How could people hate love? Some days it seemed to her that the hate in the world outweighed the love. How could that be? Love is a natural feeling and hate has to be taught. How could so many of the world's religions be teaching and promoting hate? Reject what you don't know and you'll eventually learn to hate it.

To Amanda, love was one of those commodities that flourished when shared. Locking love in your heart and never expressing it to those around you only diminished it, maybe even destroyed it. It needed to be exercised. Love needed to be shared, to be spread, to be showered upon everyone and everything. Only then would it flourish. Telling someone you love them encourages them to tell another and so the chain reaction begins. But saying it can be perfunctory, you have to really feel it in your heart, let it in. Love is to hate, as smiles are to frowns. All are contagious. *You truly do reap what you sow,* she thought. How different could the world be if we loved more? Valued each other more? Could hugs ever replace war? She doubted it, doubted the depth of her fellow man, it felt sad.

She realized that the evening had run its course and as she stood to excuse herself to retire for the night, she hugged Will gratefully and kissed him goodnight. Charles stood and embraced her as well and she felt like she had two wonderful, loving brothers. She was appreciative of what the three of them shared. At the same time the green eyes of envy winked somewhere in the recess of her consciousness as she reflected on what Will had found and with whom he had found it. She asked herself again as she had many times before, *Why are the good ones always gay?*

The next morning it was Amanda's turn to arise first and prepare breakfast for her brothers, as she thought of them now. She started coffee going in the oversized brewer and set about stirring up a pancake batter. Setting that aside she began frying bacon. She was sure the smell would reach them and prompt them to search out the source of their olfactory stimulation. The aroma of frying bacon was better than an alarm clock for getting most people up and moving in the morning. She had just placed the first pieces on the warming tray when the faces magically appeared.

Sunday morning was spent in a quiet easiness and disappeared over the horizon before any of them were ready. Will and Amanda found a moment to talk where they agreed that she needed to return to her apartment and resume her work as usual. She would have to act as normally as possible. Will would come to D.C. mid-week and they would put a plan together before he left.

Shortly after 4 the weekend had sadly wound its way to an inevitable end. The two vehicles crunched their way through the gravel in the driveway and moved toward the intersection where they parted company. Will's SUV heading to the airport to deliver Amanda and Charles embarking on his solitary drive to Chicago. Amanda's heart was heavy as she watched Charles turn south while she and Will continued west. She gave one last tentative wave as the divide between them widened. She and Will drove on in silence.

Before reaching the airport Amanda shared with Will her uneasy feeling about the voice on his answering machine and asked him to get as much information as possible when he returned the call. She was back in her investigative mode and ready to move this mystery along.

It was not unusual for individual members of Gazelle to speak with one another or with Roland between meetings. Harry had done just that this Monday morning. He was disturbed yet thoughtful about what he had learned. The idea that these cream puffs had to deliberate and search their souls was laughable to him. They just weren't sure they could get their lily white hands dirty. What a load of crap. He had been right to move on without them long ago. All this hand wringing was making him sick. They didn't seem to understand that to survive in this tough world you had to get a smudge on you now and then.

Harry was distressed that the existence and possibly the identity of Gazelle was compromised. Linking him to certain members of that group would severely endanger his power grid and that, he reflected, could not be allowed to happen. Not now when he needed to wield all the influence he could muster. Also, there was the possibility that identifying Gazelle and some of the projects they'd been working on could expose some of his more violent past. All of which had been necessary to achieve their goals and none of which the lily livered members would consider taking on.

He was certain that the discrediting of the influence peddler in the bunker was complete and effective. The politicos were already beginning to avoid the man and his agenda like the plague. His face was smeared all over the front page of every major paper and most of the tabloids. The media had picked it up as promptly as he had thought. He took a moment to bask in the pleasure of his accomplishment. He wondered how good he really could be. He considered the possibility that the fix was only temporary, and at best, he had bought himself some time and a little space to maneuver. Someone else would eventually pick up that drum and begin to beat it again. They could never seem to quit using the Venezuelan oil issue as one of their bullying points. Now, however, the issue of Russia loomed larger.

Harry knew that the Russian oilmen were itching to get into the American market. This lovey-dovey relationship between the current administration and the Russians which was splashed all over the newspapers and evening news made Harry want to puke.

Several shipments of Russian oil had recently arrived in Houston and it was just enough to whet the Russian's appetite for more. There were those who projected that the Russians could provide one million barrels of crude per day in the near future. Harry doubted that, but he didn't doubt that they were a very real threat to his imports.

A million barrels per day represented about one-tenth of the U.S. import and was about equal to what Saudi Arabia was currently providing. The plan was to take the arctic seaport of Murmansk and turn it into a deep water port that would accommodate the super tankers. Harry was sure that the Russian oil would be more costly but he was not going to discount the determination of the Russians to make it work. For now, he thought, that portion of the imports, that ten per cent, could come from Russia or Saudi Arabia but if both were supplying at that rate Harry's business would be severely diminished and probably devastated, particularly if the tariff was in place besides.

He felt squeezed from all directions. This was exactly why he had started taking matters into his own hands years ago. If you weren't pro-active they'd make you a victim. He had much to do.

Harry considered his earlier problems and took some satisfaction in his skill and ability to survive such crises. Shortly before the rioting over the banking and monetary crisis in Argentina the oil fields in southern Venezuela had been hit by extremely brutal and violent strikes by opposing labor unions who were struggling and warring over control of the oil workers. One union was so well organized and connected that the leadership was all but anonymous. The other, however, was headed by a young upstart who was speaking to swelling crowds outside one of the largest fields every night as the workers changed shifts.

Harry had absolutely no interest in who won this struggle. He cared neither about the well-being nor the plight of the workers. His only concern was to get the issue resolved before work completely stopped and the flow of oil and the revenue it generated ceased. In his mind this was what was good for the worker as well. He reasoned that they needed pay checks more than they needed union representation.

He knew he would have to deal with union issues later but he would cross that bridge when he came to it. He could always put pressure on the unions by slowing the export of crude and forcing the lay-off of thousands. At these times he simply swung his emphasis over to the trading side of the energy market to sustain himself and let the impact of the reduction starve the unions into submission or, at the least, force them to settle for some bone he would toss them. He reveled in his brilliance for being diversified.

Recognizing the need to end this battle of the labor unions, Harry arranged for the fiery leader of the United Petroleros Federale (UPF), one Cesar Rodino, to meet his unfortunate end one night as he returned to his modest home in the rural village of Escradone. A fight broke out, ostensibly with sympathizers from the rival union and someone pulled a knife. It had been so simple to arrange that Harry found it almost disappointing, not much challenge.

With the issue resolved, work in the oil fields returned to normal and to this day Harry had not had problems nor received demands from the union. He wondered if their leadership had somehow detected his assistance in their rise to power. He looked out the window of his office with the elevated view and noted how small those moving around below him seemed.

Lulled into a sense of satisfaction and how in control he was, he permitted himself a moment of confidence. His choices were simple, really, either the Saudi's could supply that ten per cent or the Russians could. Anything else cut into his pocket. He had to stop one of them. The bottom line was he had power and he wasn't afraid to wield it. He'd get this current mess under control by whatever means were needed. If things progressed as he planned it would all be mute before too much longer. What was important was the immediate future and his ability to remain able to fund the all important project. He silently observed, *Harry Axelrod, you're a survivor.*

Amanda arrived home Sunday evening and entered her apartment with a sense of uneasiness. She knew that her being in danger had heightened her sensitivities and even perhaps her paranoia. She also knew that she was paying more attention to her surroundings, was more acutely aware of her environment. She was looking at things more carefully. She was even certain that her hearing had become more acute. She was surprised, however, to find that what escalated her suspicions now was an unfamiliar smell that she detected as she entered the foyer of her apartment. She had smelled it even before she reached around the door frame to put the light on.

She blinked now and willed her eyes into focus. She stood motionless for a few minutes trying to take in her entire visual field. Remaining motionless also enabled her to listen very carefully without masking any unusual sounds with her own rustling.

She heard nothing out of the ordinary and her first, cursory visual appraisal picked up nothing out of place but she remained wary. She crossed the apartment and put her bag down at the foot of the bed. She took her carry-on into the bathroom to unload her toiletries. As she stepped back into the bedroom she stopped, frozen where she stood and stared. The shade on the bedside lamp closest to the wall and window was tilted. A definite change from their usual position.

She knew how she had left them. Not from some obsessive compulsive disorder about having things precisely so. Rather, a general sense of the order around you. When you live alone in a small space you have an awareness of where things are. There is no putting it off to the presence of someone else moving around in the space. You just know and any change grabs your attention, especially when your nerves are on edge and you're feeling vulnerable.

The window wasn't open, so she could not attribute it to the wind. She went over and straightened it and assured herself that it was adjusted tightly and would require a fair amount of force to tilt it. She was certain that someone had bumped it. She could think of no reason for the apartment manager to have been in there, particularly over the weekend, but she would certainly check out that possibility.

She swept through the rest of her apartment checking that the windows were all locked and that the sliding door to the balcony was locked and braced. When she rechecked the front door she found that in her distraction upon entering she had not set the dead bolt. She did so now and admonished herself to take more care.

Back at the front door the smell captured her attention again. She sniffed several times lightly and decided that it was a familiar scent. A perfume, cologne, men's, women's, she wasn't sure. The aroma that remained was so slight it was hardly distinguishable at all but she was as sure that it was there as she was that she was there. Someone had been in her apartment and she was mad as hell. She felt that her privacy had been invaded, she felt vulnerable, violated even. She started thinking about someone looking through her things, touching things that belonged only to her and her blood was ready to boil.

Since nothing seemed to have been taken she assumed it was a search that had occurred. Believing that no one but Gazelle had any interest in knowing what was in her apartment, he rapidly became the object of her rage. Now, more than ever, she was determined to get at least a copy of that document and maybe more. She would put an end to this. She couldn't wait to return to the office.

Chapter Seven

Roland left the Zurich airport and since he had elected not to engage a car for this trip he exited the terminal through the right hand door and went to the hotel, shuttle bus pick-up area. The attendant there asked him the name of his hotel and confirmed that he had a reservation. After a brief consultation over his two-way radio he informed Roland that his wait would be only a couple of minutes. Roland acknowledged his assistance and used the time to stretch out his legs in recovery of the flight from London.

His bag loaded into the trailer behind the shuttle, Roland climbed aboard with a family from California and two Asians who appeared to be businessmen. He was always aware. The ride to the central part of the city was long but on this bus it seemed interminable. In that moment he couldn't remember why he hadn't booked a private car. He would remedy that for the return trip.

Once he reached his hotel, since he was not a regular visitor to Zurich, he sought out the Bell Captain. While the bags were being unloaded he gave complete and thorough instructions to the man as to how his belongings were to be unpacked and arranged in his room. He also asked that he be on the second floor as he had when he made the reservation. The Bellman nodded his assent and understanding. Roland removed his money clip from his pocket and peeled off a very generous tip for the service. He also made a note of the man's name on his brass nametag. If the service was as requested the man's supervisor would be so advised when Roland's letters went out on the 15th of the month. If the service was inadequate the supervisor would also know that.

He left the hotel and walked the couple of blocks to the Central Railway Station where he could get something to eat. One train was carefully inching up to the parking bumper as he crossed the open air, covered depot. He passed the escalators to the lower level and the ubiquitous McDonald's with families crowding around it. He continued through the station and when he emerged on the other side, he made a left turn. Traffic was light and he walked along the sidewalk next to the train awaiting its turn to back out of the station. One block down he crossed the street and approached the hostess of the small, outdoor café. She took him to a table tucked attractively between two potted shrubs. He selected the chair that provided him with a view of the street and city and accepted the menu. He took a few minutes to just survey his surroundings.

Roland loved Switzerland. It was clean, orderly, predictable and beautiful. He made a mental note to do some shopping after lunch. His meeting with the Hexlar people was not until tomorrow morning. He needed a couple of hours of business time this afternoon but that left plenty of time for him personally.

Returning to the hotel after lunch he finished checking in and picked up his key at the registration desk. The desk clerk handed him a message which had been left for him. He found it curious that someone had chosen this method of communication instead of his cell phone.

He opened the note in the elevator and was astounded to see the note card imprinted with the name Mira Melong.

"When I learned you were in Zurich I couldn't resist contacting you. I'll be in the lobby bar at 8. Don't you just love cloak and dagger stuff? M"

Roland found himself too distracted to get much work done. He had so much on his mind with Gazelle, Amanda and now Mira appearing so unexpectedly. *This is exactly why I've always kept my life free from these entanglements,* he said to himself,

Funny, he thought, that he should see Mira as an entanglement, a bother. He really couldn't afford to have her following him around playing her childish, rich-girl games. He fought to bring his mind back to the matter of Gazelle again.

He was observing the heavy, brocade draperies and sheer curtains covering the windows behind them. It was quite grand, he thought, how the heavily and ornately braided ropes tied the draperies back to let the light into the room unimpeded. *Damn*, he admonished, *can't keep my mind on work.* He decided then that his time would be better spent out in the city. Maybe he could think more clearly if he wasn't trying so hard.

Before leaving the hotel, Roland stopped at the front desk and checked out. He went next to the Bell Captain with whom he had done business earlier and gave the man a more handsome sum to move his belongings to a small hotel in the old part of the city near the university. Roland had chosen it from the telephone book and had contacted them from his room. Not his favorite way to choose a hotel, but these were not ordinary circumstances.

He spent the remainder of the afternoon strolling, shopping and turning things over in his mind. Most of all he wondered about Mira. Was this just a coincidence? Maybe he should see her again and see if he could find out if her games were just that or something more. He had that uneasy feeling again, the one that nagged him when things were not on the up and up. He considered it his danger alarm and it hadn't failed him yet.

Roland concluded his afternoon with tea at a sidewalk table in the old square that had once been a pig market and was across from the Fraumunster Cathedral. He watched the tour busses pull up to the sidewalk and alternately suck up and spit out the groups of tourists who flocked to see the stained glass windows by Chagall.

Finishing his tea and having reached clarity around some of his troublesome issues, he walked past the church and crossed the bridge to the old city. The streets were narrow and crowded and he had a hill to climb to reach his new accommodations but he thought the environment charming and was glad he had been forced to move.

He crossed the small but opulent lobby and approached the

registration desk of the quaint hotel. The desk clerk greeted him respectfully but graciously and informed him in deeply accented English that his belongings were all in his second floor room as requested. He completed the registration procedure, took his key and inquired of the desk clerk whether there were any messages for him.

"Nein, er none, Herr Priestly, but there was a call."

Roland's eyes shot up at the man, "A call?" He inquired.

"Why, yes, maybe an hour ago, but the caller did not wish to leave a message."

"Man or woman?" Roland asked.

"Ah, a woman," the clerk replied.

Roland rode the elevator to the second floor and found his room. After a brief look around and assuring himself that his things were, indeed, arranged to his liking, he set about his business once again.

He took out his cell phone and dialed Karla.

The first order of business with her was the progress of the energy plan. He knew they had to move this along quickly to keep Axelrod from taking things into his own hands. If that happened things could get ugly fast. He didn't want Harry Axelrod driving anything but particularly not the energy process. The line between what Roland knew and what he suspected about Harry had blurred over the years. He knew that Harry was greedy and self-serving and he had a strong and unsettling suspicion that he had stooped to violence and killing to further his own purposes. Unlike, what Roland believed, was the motivation and moral sense of the other members of Gazelle.

Assured that the energy plan was coming together, Roland moved to his second item of business with Karla. "Where are we with the Chambers surveillance?" he asked.

"She went to her brother's for the weekend, we followed her to the airport and she was seen boarding the flight. We swept her apartment and it's clean. She's back home and back to work now. We're still watching from a distance. Is it time yet to move in closer?"

"Leave it as is for now," Roland replied. "One last item, Karla, get me all you can on a young, jet-setter named Mira Melong. Probe deeply and send a report tomorrow by e-mail."

"Right, when do you meet with the Hexlar people?"

"Tomorrow morning. I'll call you some time tomorrow and I'll be watching for that e-mail, Karla." He cut the connection.

At her desk at Gazelle's headquarters Karla contemplated the conversation. She had always followed, or at least tried to follow, her boss's directions to the letter, but, full of suspicion and tainted by jealously and envy, she couldn't wait to tighten the noose around Ms. Amanda Chambers' neck. She was certain that the more manpower they put on this investigation the more they would learn and the sooner they would learn it. She would show Roland the truth about this precocious benefactor of the down-trodden.

Karla called her contact in the investigative agency and instructed him to step up the level of surveillance. "I want to know how many times per minute she breathes," she told him. "I'm tired of waiting. We need to get something on her sooner rather than later, if you get my drift." Karla actually hoped that they would plant something if they didn't find it soon. She was still smarting from her mishap in the conference room and she had come to believe that Amanda had set her up.

"By the way, I also need an expedited, Level 1, electronic report on a Mira Melong." Karla spelled out both names. "How long do you need?" she inquired.

"We'll have a preliminary by 10 tonight, complete report with all info verified by noon probably."

"I'll be expecting it," Karla signed off.

The Zurich sun had descended behind the mountain and left the city washed gray in a calm twilight. Roland stood looking out the window of his room watching the traffic crawling slowly along the narrow streets below like colonies of ants making their way into and out of their hills. Lights were coming on across the valley turning the scene into a twinkling, serene photograph.

He had a plan and did not want to meet with Mira until he received the report he had requested. He crossed the room and sat on the antique loveseat as he placed a call to his former hotel. He left a message for her with the bartender of the lobby bar. He was regrettably tied up this evening but would appreciate seeing her. Perhaps she could be at the same place tomorrow evening. He would wait until 9. That should give him enough time to get the report and be fully briefed.

He took a few minutes to reflect on his behavior and admonished himself for what he considered to be a loss of control. How had he allowed himself that time with her? He was distressed at his actions professionally because such lapses could place his work in jeopardy and he was repulsed at himself personally for the gratuitous nature of his deeds.

While Roland sat on the sofa and continued to chastise the little boy inside, across the city in her posh hotel suite, Mira was just concluding a phone conversation with Harry Axelrod.

Will arrived at Amanda's apartment as planned and the two had quickly set about strategizing how to get Amanda out of this predicament. They had finally narrowed all of the possibilities down to two. The first, Will's choice, was to get Amanda out of danger by physically removing her from the proximity of Washington. Since Amanda could see no end to that option and envisioned herself living out her years in exile, she had talked Will into the second scenario which they were now putting into action. Will had gone along with her only on the promise that if this did not resolve immediately she would go quietly along with his "safe house" proposal. For now she had him working with her and that felt good. She was hopeful.

The timing had worked out perfectly. Nate's off-site rotation had come up taking him out of the office at this most fortuitous time. Even better, he had left her with "acting delegations" which meant that she was supervising the department in his absence. This gave her full access to his office, desk, mail, files and even limited signing authority.

One of her first such acts was to request full, unrestricted access to computer files for her secretary. It had taken nearly two full days but she had just received the disk with his security information on it. She knew that all these acts could be traced to her but the proof would be difficult and time consuming and she was so sure of her ultimate success and incrimination of Nate that time was all that she needed.

She had to find that document or some other information which would lead her to Gazelle. She wondered once if Nate was Gazelle but she had dismissed that after considering his relative stature at work and in life. Nate was a plodder, he was more comfortable taking orders than giving them and he was averse to risk. She was certain that he knew something about it but was not likely to be the brains or the boss.

She and Will had concluded that Gazelle was one to take action, dynamic. The phrase, "Tell R to put on next agenda," which she had seen on the document inferred an ongoing kind of activity with procedures or rituals. It had also meant that Gazelle did not work alone. The fact that a note such as that was being conveyed to others and that they were holding meetings with an agenda implied a group, probably more than two since there were two sets of initials in addition to the author.

They now knew that they were looking for an active group of operatives, either within the government or somehow connected to it since it was addressed to the secretary and even without further identifying information, it was presented in a format which she recognized as being consistent with internal memos for her department and division. She was sure they were looking for people close to her. She wasn't clear at all what the secretary's role was but it was certainly addressed to him, imputing to him knowledge of it at the very least.

Amanda sent her secretary to the central file room with a list of documents to retrieve which she was certain would keep him there for the remainder of the morning. With him out of the way she sat down at his computer, inserted the new security disk and began her own form of hacking. By 11:30 she had no information but several potential leads that she wanted to follow up. She needed to return to her own office and wait for the afternoon access to the computer. As it turned out she had to continue this secretarial subterfuge for several days before her break came.

Will was growing impatient with Amanda's plan. Unknown to her he had been in contact with Alex, the exchange student who had been a part of their family for several years and Amanda's first love. Alex had attended the University of Wisconsin for both his undergraduate and master's degrees. The university had a program for foreign students which matched them with a volunteer, "host" family in the area. It was the family's job to help the student adjust to life in an American community and they, in turn, had an opportunity for a cross-cultural experience. Usually a member of the family helped the student set up and use bank accounts, transportation systems and deal with any other trials that may beset them. The student spent holidays with the family and was generally, "taken in" as a relative would be.

Alex had always felt himself fortunate that he had arrived at the office of the Dean of Students as the Chambers family had come up in rotation for assignment. It was a good match for both and Alex had always felt like one of the family.

Back in Bulgaria now with a doctoral degree, Alex enjoyed his days at the University in Sofia. With a full professorship he had the pleasure of combining lecturing with ample time for research and writing. His apartment in the Doktors' Garden area of the city permitted him to walk to his office.

Alex left his third floor apartment and walked down the stone stairs to the front of the building. Reaching the entrance he was greeted with a light spring rain. He put up his umbrella and moved past the plastic table and chairs idle now but awaiting the arrival of the coffee seekers who would eventually arrive to spend the greater part of the day. He moved along the uneven sidewalk, weaving his way around and through the cars parked there and thought about his most recent conversation with Will.

He was distressed that Amanda may be in danger but he could not really understand what Will was explaining. He knew that neither Will nor Amanda were alarmists so he felt some obligation to accept all this at face value. He had not seen either of them since their mother's illness and he had to admit that the idea of Amanda coming here was exciting. He had tried to describe the environment and the cultural ways of his country when he was in their home. He had always been the foreigner, the visitor and he looked forward to showing off his city and Bulgarian life for a change. He had always wanted the entire family to see his home, but especially Amanda. Their parting had been painful.

Amanda's break at the computer came in the form of a document stored carelessly on Nate's hard drive. It was an outline of his entire filing system and she felt like she had found the treasure map at last. Scanning rapidly down the list she started investigating every e-mail, document and note that looked from the name like it might be related to Gazelle or the African AIDS issue. She found nothing.

She had taken a break for lunch and decided to spend her time on this beautiful spring day on the mall. She took her tuna sandwich and coke and walked the two blocks to Constitution Avenue. There she sought a bench in the warm, spring sunshine and sat down. Fellow workers walked and jogged past her, some alone, many engaged in conversation with companions. She was wondering if she should give up the hunt. Other than the fact that someone had been in her apartment there was nothing but her paranoia and Roland's reputation to make her think that she was in jeopardy. *Well Nate certainly had acted strangely as well,* she thought.

Suddenly she stopped chewing. She sat there frozen as the thought washed through her mind leaving the clarity of crystal clear glass behind it. It had been right in front of her and she hadn't seen it, hidden in plain sight as they say. She jumped up excitedly, tossed her lunch in the trash can and fairly flew back to the office.

In Nate's office she sat down at his desk and booted up his computer. Arriving at the screen which required a password, she entered, "G A Z E L L E," and waited. The computer hummed for a moment before flickering up a listing of files. Did she want documents or e-mails, it politely asked. She leaned against the back of the oversized chair and was sure that her mouth was hanging open and her eyes were probably the size of dinner plates. "Eureka," she whispered.

At that same, exact moment, out in the Virginia countryside, somewhere in the reinforced basement of the Sommerset Inn Spa and Resort, a message popped up on the computer on the secretary's desk.

Security had been breached. The secretary picked up the phone and dialed his contact. They had needed to know how far Amanda would push this. They were getting their answer.

Amanda had no way to know that she had been set up. Before leaving, Nate had cleaned his files and left just enough interesting information to make things convincing if Amanda continued to pursue Gazelle. He had changed his password and left with the trap baited. She had taken the bait like a lunker to a lure on opening day of fishing season.

Amanda now began opening and printing documents as fast as she could. She couldn't wait to show Will her findings, she had Nate for sure and hoped reviewing these papers at home with Will would unravel the rest of the mystery. She was totally unaware that she had tripped the spring on the trap.

The secretary's conversation was brief. The options had already been arranged. If Amanda Chambers violated Nate Tidwell's computer looking for Gazelle the events would be put in motion. If A, then B, it was logical, simple and without debate.

As a precautionary measure and because the secretary knew that surprises were not good, he placed one more call and advised the recipient of the gravity of what was unfolding even though the man rarely concerned himself with day to day matters. Since no good deed goes unpunished the secretary was soundly chastised for contacting him at all. He was ordered, in no uncertain terms, to stay within the established chain of authority. Therefore, his next call was to the senator.

Karla's stepped up surveillance had naturally included some carefully placed bugging devices. She was receiving daily reports from the results of the eavesdropping and had learned of Amanda's and Will's investigation into Gazelle. She was trying to decide how and when to report this information to Roland. Further, when she did, she would have to admit that she had not followed his instructions, had in fact directly violated them to gain this knowledge. Perhaps she needed something more to increase the impact of the news and lessen his potential outrage at her insubordination. She decided to have both Will and Amanda followed and to have one additional and more thorough search done. This time it would include Amanda's apartment, car and office, as well as her office and laptop computers. "Leave no stone unturned," she told the agent.

Back in her own office, Amanda gathered her voluminous array of documents and literally stuffed them into her briefcase. She turned off the computer and desk lamp and forwarded her phone to voicemail. She walked across the office, retrieved her jacket from the hanger on the back of the thick mahogany door and turned off the office lights. She hesitated there for a moment struck by the lights and sights of D.C. It never failed to move her but she seldom slowed down to take notice. From up here the chaos was all visual, a silent city in perpetual motion. She cautioned herself to make more time for the small pleasures in life when this mess was over. As an afterthought, she went back to her desk and removed the security disk she'd obtained for her secretary and put it in the single drawer of the end table next to the guest chairs. She was careful to put the small packet of Kleenex on the very top of the drawer to conceal its other contents. If anyone looked inside they would not notice the disk at the bottom unless they were really digging around.

She closed the door and took the elevator to the parking garage where her aging Volvo waited. Driving home she wanted to call Will on the cell phone and tell him of her discovery but she was trying to be discreet and cell phones, she thought she'd heard, were not secure. Anyone could listen to those conversations. Curbing her enthusiasm she endured the traffic on the remainder of the drive. As she entered the parking area of her building she had to swing wide to avoid the plumbing van which was parked so near the driveway entrance as to be a nuisance. She would never know that two men and a myriad of electronic devices were ensconced inside.

As she had hoped Will was impressed with her find and they worked well into the night reading, sorting and eventually rating the documents by importance. They got out post-it notes and stuck them to the papers they'd determined to be most germane to their cause. They wrote short summaries on the post-its. They made their way through two pots of coffee and a pizza and both were near exhaustion when they pulled the last page from Amanda's case.

Will suggested that Amanda take the morning off and call in sick so that they could assimilate what they had. He had a nagging sense that they had just gone through a very tall stack of smoke and mirrors, an exercise in futility, but he was too tired to explore it now.

Amanda called the voicemail of a co-worker and reported sick. She asked him to sit in on a morning meeting in her place and told him she would try to be in by noon. That behind her she barely had enough left to brush her teeth before collapsing on the bed.

She awoke four hours later to the sounds of Will rustling around in the kitchen. Over coffee Will agreed that she should go to the office in the afternoon and leave him to do an analysis and evaluation of the facts they'd gathered. He didn't tell her that he had been up for two hours re-arranging and assessing the stacks they had made. Doing so had done nothing to alleviate his sense of re-arranging deck chairs on the Titanic. They really had nothing concrete to take to any authorities. He would spend the day looking to be sure. At the most, they may be able to implicate Nate in something shady to the Office of the Inspector General (OIG) but there was nothing of a criminal nature for sure and it surely didn't seem to implicate anyone else.

After Amanda's departure, Will set to work. By 5:30 in the afternoon he had finished his review and, as he had feared, the results were really inconclusive. He had a lot of circumstantial information that raised a lot of questions but he had not found a nail for the coffin.

While Amanda was gone, Will had taken her laptop computer down to the computer service and had an access tracking software installed. It was not sophisticated but it would provide a log of every time the system was logged on or off. Most importantly it would show when repeated attempts were used in the password field.

Amanda worked until almost seven catching up on some neglected work whose deadline was approaching. She was trying to get as much off her back as possible to free up her time and mind. That accomplished she made a bee line for home. By prior arrangement with

Will, she stopped by and picked up another pizza since neither of them was up to cooking.

Too distracted to pay much attention to eating, Amanda was attempting to launch back into the investigation of the documents when Will stopped her short.

"Look at me," he demanded, "I want you to hear me on this! There is nothing here, Amanda, we've struck out."

Amanda opened her mouth to speak.

"Don't try to argue with me, Mandy. I've been through all this a number of times and I didn't reach this conclusion lightly."

Amanda's hopes fell with her as she collapsed backward into the overstuffed chair. Will was crushing her hopes and perhaps with them, her future.

"I was so sure we had what we needed but a part of me knew it wasn't so," she lamented. "God, Will, I'm so lost, what do we do?"

"I've been thinking about that, Mandy, and I think it's time you left. We need to move to Plan B for your protection."

"No, Will, I can't, not yet," she responded.

'Mandy, it's not safe here"

"Let's do this. Let's work through next weekend, at least and I promise if there's any other sign in the meantime that someone's after me, I'll go willingly," she suggested.

Once again Will found himself giving in to the pleas of his little sister. The deal was struck.

Chapter Eight

Roland was having trouble absorbing the information in front of him. He had received the investigative report on Mira electronically. Karla had attached it to an e-mail and forwarded it to him as promised. As he reviewed the information he was both surprised and embarrassed.

She was good he decided. He had no indication that she was anything but a casual meeting back in London. Not until she turned up in Zurich had his antennae gone up. He was now chastising himself for not being more careful and at the same time questioning what was becoming of his standards that he had let himself be seduced by a pro. Was he slipping that much or was he no longer able to cover his weaknesses. He'd always prided himself on the fact that he was the ultimate professional and didn't allow himself the luxury of human frailties and needs. These things had to be kept in check or you would put yourself and your work in jeopardy. Maybe he needed a vacation. What a ridiculous thought. Where had that come from? He'd never taken vacations. His work had always been enough for him.

Looking at the screen again the one thing that hopped off the page and buried itself in his memory was the time that Mira had spent at the Granby Academy. He wondered again whether this was a coincidence. His mind whirled back nearly twenty years to that beautiful autumn day in New England. Before he jumped to any conclusions he would have to have more information.

He immediately responded to Karla's e-mail message and requested that she get more information on Mira's time at the academy. "Leave out no detail, no matter how trivial it may seem," he wrote.

In the meantime he would meet with Mira and determine what he could about her motives.

His morning meeting with the Hexlar people had gone even better than he had hoped. He had been prepared to make veiled threats if necessary to bring the pressure to bear on them. They seemed to still be reeling from their drubbing at the summit and had quickly seen the wisdom of agreeing to take the lead with the other members of the pharmaceutical consortium. They would make a concerted effort to get these drugs into a form that could be brought to the masses in Africa. He knew it wasn't going to be that easy. He'd have to keep the pressure on but at least everyone knew what the game was. They knew he was watching now.

He found it interesting that even these greedy bastards had been appalled by the recent announcement by the Catholic Bishops in Africa that it was not appropriate to use condoms to control the spread of AIDS. Roland wondered sometimes where these people's basic sense of decency was. *You had to wonder,* he thought, *what kind of vision these religious leaders had that enabled them to condemn and sentence so many innocent people to such a horrible death. What god was this that they worshipped? Certainly not one with any compassion,* he thought.

His mind wandered next to the other ill-conceived message which was being sent across that continent. That being the belief that those infected with the AIDS virus could be cured by having sex with a virgin. He had been appalled when he saw the most recent statistics of the increase in rape of young women, even babies, as a result of this misinformation. He just couldn't see where this was going to end. It absolutely had to be treated and attacked as a war but it was becoming more and more difficult to get people's attention. All efforts and attention had been refocused on terrorism and homeland security, whatever that is. *Who actually lives in a secure home?* he wondered.

His pharmaceutical work concluded here he was ready to focus on

Gazelle's next most pressing issues, Amanda Chambers and energy. Now he had to determine where Mira fit into this. What was her game? Was she part of the Amanda issue or was she playing in the energy game. One thing was certain; she was trying to get close to him for a reason. He was sure he'd have an answer to that soon enough. Once he knew what she was about he was certain that he could develop an effective strategy to deal with her. His fact-finding included meeting with her tonight.

He had enough information from the investigator to know that she was a player and not what she had first appeared to be. The knowledge he had could be used to learn more about her intentions.

He decided to grab a cab early and detour out by the lake for a drink before heading off to meet Mira.

As he emerged from his hotel the sun was just setting. The air was so fresh and spring felt so renewing that he didn't want to spend his time inside the hotel room. It would feel good to be about in the city for awhile before entering a dismal bar to do business with the enemy. Interesting that he now had Mira in that category. Roland was not a particularly trusting guy but once he'd been betrayed or lied to he was unforgiving and vindictive in a very cruel way. Mira would be sorry she'd been exposed, no pun intended, he chuckled to himself.

A couple hours later he was nursing his way through a drink while waiting for her in the lounge. He looked up and a breath nearly caught in his throat as he saw her coming down the steps toward him. She was a beauty. He remembered at that moment how easily he had been taken in by her. He suspected it was because he wanted to be.

Regaining his composure he stood to welcome her. After a polite hug and a peck on the cheek, he gestured her to the chair opposite him at the table.

"You're looking beautiful this evening," he said. "What will you have to drink?"

"Why thank you, Roland, you're always such a gentleman. Scotch and water would be fine," she responded throatily as she looked deeply into his eyes and held his gaze a little too long to be proper.

Roland sat back down and watched as she crossed her long, shapely legs in front of him and allowed her short skirt to slide further up and expose even more of her firm thigh. Her foot came to rest against his calf. This was going to take all of his self-control. She knew him now and would be going for his weaknesses at every opportunity. He had every confidence in his ability to withstand her advances. She had no idea who she was playing with. He had handled some of the best in the game and by comparison she was absolutely transparent. His experience had taken him into and around the spy game during the cold war. He had dealt with CIA, FBI and even KGB. She was just a beginner and way out of her league with him.

He thought back to the electronic report and stifled a smile at the amateur league she'd been in up till now. *He would play her like a Stradivarius,* he vowed, *She may be very useful.*

"Well," he began, "What brings you to Zurich?"

"Does a girl need a reason to chase a good looking, eligible man around the globe?" she cooed.

He managed a wry smile. This was going to be a very long evening.

"Let me put it another way, then. How did you know I would be in Zurich?"

"Ah, I have my very good sources."

"Okay, we're not getting anywhere with that, I see. Let me ask, then, what was your interest in seeing me?"

"I could give you another flattering response to that question and continue to play games or I could cut to the chase and lay this all out for you."

"Thank you," he said. "I would really appreciate the direct approach for a change. Let's start with your real name and vital statistics."

"My name is Randi," she began, "The rest of the story is for sale. I can assure you that, should we come to an agreement around the value of what I have to say, you will find it very interesting and pertinent to your work."

"Do you have an opening bid in mind?" Paying to get it all out would save him hours of time and a great deal of energy instead of playing games for hours on end to extract the truth slowly. He knew he could test its veracity.

The next couple of hours flew by quickly as Roland listened to her story. The most pertinent part of which was that Randi was hired by Harry Axelrod to shadow Roland and report to him what Roland was going to do with Amanda Chambers. It seemed to Roland, as the story unfolded, that Harry was most anxious to have Roland, and therefore, Gazelle, get their hands dirty and this was a good time for that to happen. Harry no longer wanted to be the only heavy player in this arena. He was trying his best to back Gazelle into a corner where they would be required to move to the next level, that being extermination, well, murder. He even had trouble calling it by its real name.

While Roland resisted this with everything he had he also knew that their work had become so important that it was possible that a human life here or there would become expendable for the greater good. They had long ago crossed the threshold into violence. From time to time persuasion had to take a more physical form than mere emotional intimidation. He had even resorted to hostage taking in one instance but was glad that it had ended without the loss of life. His moment of reckoning had come. The decision was looming upon him. What was he willing to do?

Before departing for the evening, Roland made arrangements to meet Randi the next afternoon for payment and a few follow-up questions. He thought that this whole arrangement with her had come about too easily and he knew that she was either setting him up or that whatever information or skills she had would always go to the highest bidder. Above all he must remain wary.

He took a cab back to his hotel and pondered the wisdom of his work along the way.

Two days later and that much closer to the weekend deadline, Amanda worked doggedly at the computer terminal. She was possessed with the need to find some kind of incriminating information or proof of the existence and identity of Gazelle. Opening document after document, she scanned each for the kind of illumination she sought.

Back in her apartment Will had made a discovery of his own. He was standing in the living room talking with Jake, a representative of Discreet Detection Services. He had found their listing in the Yellow Pages and had enlisted their services immediately. Will had checked the log on Amanda's computer as he had been doing each morning before she arose. This time it had revealed that at 7:14 last evening, while he and Amanda were at dinner, someone had logged onto her computer and had stayed on for approximately 15 minutes, probably about long enough to read her most recent e-mails, he thought.

Immediately troubled by this discovery he had found and engaged Jake. He was now learning that indeed there were bugging devices in the living room, bedroom and kitchen. Will had a terrible knot in the pit of his stomach. He was standing there looking at hard evidence and feeling the gravity of it descend over him. He was confronted with the reality that had moved out of the dark corners of abstraction to take the form of a harsh enemy. He finally had an image in his head of Gazelle and it was worrisome.

No longer able to put this off to Amanda's overactive imagination or even paranoia, Will could visualize a real and dangerous enemy. This was not a game. It had, in fact, turned deadly. He had to act at once. Adrenaline cascaded through his body and his thinking became clear and focused.

Will paid Jake in cash and thanked him for his assistance. He commented that he would rely on the company's promised discretion and slipped him an extra fifty for his cooperation. Will waited anxiously as Jake packed up his electronic gear into a small and, he had to admit, discreet case. After showing him out, Will went directly to the phone to call Amanda. As part of their plan to extend the investigation to the weekend they had decided that any communication between them that referenced their mother would be an emergency alarm that would abort all further activity and bring them to a meeting at their favorite bookstore outside the Pentagon City Mall.

A light sprinkle was falling as Will made his way to catch the Blue Line to Pentagon City. He didn't notice the unmarked van pulling away from the curb adjacent to Amanda's building nor the large, dark sedan that passed him in the next block and pulled up in front of the same address.

The eavesdroppers had been alerted to the detection devices operating within Amanda's apartment by their own sophisticated scanners. The high pitched whine that came over their headsets said that the premises were being swept for bugs. Upon reporting to the secretary that their security was breached, they were immediately pulled off the case. They took pride in the fact that they were packed up, battened down and rolling away from the premises within less than five minutes of detection. The second level of the operation would move in behind them.

It seemed an eternity to Will before Amanda joined him at the table in the bookstore where he sat with a café latte untouched in front of him. He had so much on his mind and his thinking was suddenly so much more focused and clear that he couldn't run through his plans fast enough. Everything was easier to strategize when you were working with something known. Gazelle was suddenly as solid as concrete in his mind.

Will filled Amanda in on the events of the morning. Her head drooped and her face got longer as he talked. She was getting discouraged and defeated just as he was getting energized and working up a full head of steam. Perhaps this was best as she would agree more willingly to visit Alex in Sofia. Will, on the other hand, could not afford to lose focus. He would need every bit of the energy he was feeling to complete his part of this. This was no longer just about protecting his sister.

Will continued to talk excitedly but quietly about their next steps. He agreed with Amanda that it did little good to send her away and leave things as they were. It was necessary for him to take up the responsibility for the investigation and to try to bring Gazelle down. She, however, had to stay out of his way and, more importantly, out of harm's way. He could not handle both the investigation and her safety.

Alex was on board and ready to look after Amanda personally, this would leave Will free to move forward on Gazelle and make Washington safe for Amanda's eventual return. He feared the size and gravity of the assignment but saw little option for either of them. They were in it now and the only way to end this was to see it through to its natural conclusion. You couldn't leave it halfway through. Amanda would be in danger as long as Gazelle pursued her.

Amanda kept insisting on returning to her apartment to pack and to her office to put things in order before leaving. Will was equally insistent that she not go anywhere near her residence, office, car or anywhere that she would be expected to be. Control of the situation was moving from Amanda to Will and she had lost her enthusiasm to fight.

Amanda felt real ambivalence about going to be with Alex. She thought sometimes that she still loved him but other times wondered if it was just that tenderness of the first time you fall in love that encourages feelings of love to reside always within the memory of that person. Perhaps Alex was just the personification of that affection within her. She didn't really think so. Theirs had been a longer, somewhat more enduring love than what you think of as puppy love.

Alex had come into their family little more than a year after the death of her father. While she didn't think that her love for him was in any way connected to what she had lost in her father, she did think that the maturity which had come with having to cope with the loss of a close loved one allowed her to approach her feelings for Alex in a more adult way. She was not agog over him the way her school friends tended to be with their loves du jour. She had dated enough to know how boring and tedious boys her own age could be. Alex was a junior in college when she was a senior in high school and that extra maturity that he displayed had been very seductive to her.

From the beginning they had taken great enjoyment in each other's company. They got to know each other within the structure of her family as Alex was invited to spend holidays and weekends with them. They had spent long evenings in front of the fire with Will and some of their cousins involved in conversations ranging from heavy, world politics to their tastes in popular music. Alex enjoyed many of the same things that she did and they would take long walks along the beach in the summer and through the woods or park after the snow arrived. They sailed, they ice skated, they went to movies and they fell deeply in love. They had continued their relationship throughout Amanda's college years while Alex worked on his post-graduate degree. They had settled into a very loving, stable and fulfilling life together.

It had not been until that last Christmas that Alex had approached her with the idea of them moving to Sofia after school was out. He had been in contact with the university there and they were excited at the prospect of him coming back home to teach and research.

Alex had come to the United States to go to school because of the state of higher education in his home country. Unfortunately the nearly half century of communist censorship had taken a tremendous toll on the academic community there. Materials and individuals who potentially promoted ideologically subversive ideas were systematically eliminated from the learning environment. This resulted in the purging of the libraries and removal of individuals who were educated in the west or who belonged to professional organizations which would bring them into contact with capitalist collaborators. University libraries were left with materials that were reminiscent of the 1800's and lecturers were chosen for their safe thinking rather than academic acumen. Critical thinking was literally wiped out and publishing was eliminated wherever possible. *This should be a real lesson for all of us to beware when government gets involved in academics,* she thought.

Close on the heels of this situation was the arrival of the omnipresent corruption on the academic scene. It had become commonplace to purchase grades and in some cases, often through intimidation, an entire degree.

Alex was determined to return to his home and begin the long process of bringing the academic standards up to where they needed to be. It meant everything to him for higher education in his country to have the respect that would be needed for it to be included with other institutions of higher learning throughout Europe. His dream was to teach, research and publish so that he could bring honor and respect to the university and ultimately to his country. He hoped that others would join him in his efforts. They had much to make up for. A long ways to go to catch up but he was up for the challenge.

Alex had hoped that Amanda could somehow share his dream and his life. He was just old fashioned enough to think that a wife should support her husband in his career. Maybe it wasn't so much old fashioned as it was wishful thinking. Men had been able to pull it off for generations and he had hoped that he could too. He wanted to have both his career and his relationship. Unfortunately, being an emancipated woman she did too.

He had been devastated when Amanda told him that she would not accompany him back to Bulgaria. He understood that she would have adjustments to make but so had he when he came to her country to live. He couldn't understand why she was not willing to give that back to him. She had surprised him around spring break by saying that she would consider the move if it were temporary. She could live that life for a period of time but they would have to come back to the states in the long run and raise their family here. This he could not do. His was to be a life long commitment to academia and to his homeland.

They parted full of love and deeply damaged. Neither could really understand what had happened. They had seen each other a couple of times over the last few years and they managed to keep things light and friendly. They never discussed their love or relationship again. Alex had not had any serious relationships since Amanda and she hardly even dated. They had both become workaholics.

Will guided Amanda out of the bookstore and over to the metro stop. They boarded the Blue Line inbound and detrained at Arlington Cemetery.

Will watched carefully to see who left the train with them, his senses were alert now and he was constantly scanning the environment. A young couple, probably honeymooners, walked arm in arm up toward the visitor's center. A middle aged man in blue collar attire also stepped onto the platform from one of the other cars. He also set off in the direction of the visitor's center. Will and Amanda crossed to the other side and waited for the next train back toward Alexandria. There were no other passengers on the platform as the train pulled along side them and the doors yawned open. One woman left the car that they entered and Will kept her in his radar as the train eased away from the platform with a lurch.

This time they passed the Pentagon City stop and stayed on the train to Reagan National Airport.

Will was able to get Amanda on a flight which was a non-stop to Munich on Lufthansa. This would require a plane change to continue on to Sofia but it was as good as they would find as direct flights into Eastern Europe were as yet uncommon. He was pleased with the brief layover and felt that she would be safe. Based on their indirect path to the airport, he was certain that they were not being followed. They had several hours before Amanda's plane would be ready for boarding. He checked with her to make sure that she had cash and credit cards as she would have to buy everything she needed. Suddenly he looked at her with an expression of dread.

"Where is your passport, Mandy?" Will asked.

"I keep it in my safe deposit box. At the Arlington Branch of Bank One. We can reach it off the metro," she responded.

"What about the key?" he pressed.

"In my lockbox at home, I'm afraid."

Will thought for a moment. He wasn't sure how to gain entry to the safe deposit box without returning to the apartment and he was certain that the apartment was being watched. He sat quietly for a few moments.

"Are you the only signor on the safety deposit box?" he asked.

"No, actually Mom was on it as well," she answered.

Will was getting nowhere fast. He couldn't pose as his mother and had no other woman that he could ask to try such a charade. The scrutiny by the bank would be impossible without the key. He was afraid that he would have to return to the apartment to get the key and then take Mandy to the bank to retrieve the passport. Either that or report it lost and proceed through that red tape. He finally decided that it would be cleaner, even though more dangerous, to retrieve the original. Amanda laid out a plan which he believed just might work. Besides, it was all they had.

Will and Amanda took a cab back to her apartment but had the driver stop one block away and just around the corner. They paid the fare, got out of the cab and began to walk away from her building. Once the cab had left they stopped and turned back toward their intended destination.

Large trees lined the streets in this area providing them some shelter. They stood on the sidewalk as if engaged in conversation. Will had positioned himself so that he could look past Amanda and study the activity around her building. He was alert to anything that might appear unusual but since his heightened sense of security had come about so recently he realized that he had been moving in, out and around that building for nearly two weeks now without really seeing the environment. Consequently he was disadvantaged where it came to observing what was outside the norm. He concluded that it would be best for him to enter the building alone and that if he wasn't back in fifteen minutes Amanda would proceed to the airport and report her passport lost when she arrived there. It would be a mess to deal with but preferable to endangering her here.

A half a world away, in Zurich, Roland was relaxing in his hotel room. He was awaiting a response to a call he had made to Karla. It was still early in Washington and he knew that she would return his call as soon as she entered her office. He was anxious to hear what she had learned about the Granby Academy in particular. He hadn't been able to get it off his mind.

Roland's memory was flooded again and he found himself standing in the plaza of the academy as real as if it were yesterday. He and his wife, Diana, had driven their twelve year old daughter, Debra, to her first day at boarding school. Debra was entering seventh grade and was showing a great deal of promise academically. Additionally, as an only child, both parents had become concerned that she was not developing socially and had decided together that the Granby Academy was the best place for her for now. They would revisit the situation when she was ready to enter high school. That day had been a difficult day for parent and child. It seemed now to Roland, looking back, that it had been the beginning of the end. That was the point at which his life had begun to turn. His family had begun to fragment.

He could feel himself in that moment. The temperature a perfect 75 degrees, the sun shining brightly but at a more acute angle as autumn rushed toward winter. The trees wore leaves of subdued and complimentary colors and they danced gracefully following the lead of the gentle wind. An occasional gust lifted them and hurried them along as if they were scurrying out of the way so that winter could rush in behind them. The beauty of the day was disturbed only by the purpose of their presence in this serene place. Roland realized now how much he was saying goodbye to then. Within a year Diana would be leaving him for another man and less than a year after that, his darling Debra would die at the hands of a drunk driver. He had said goodbye to family and love that autumn day in New England. He had thrown himself into his work after that and never looked back.

The presence of the Granby Academy in his business now seemed almost like a cruel twisting of that knife. His reverie was shattered by the ringing of the phone.

"Hey, Boss, it's Karla."

"What have you got for me?" he asked.

"It's coming to you by e-mail but the short story is that Mira Melong never attended Granby Academy. There's more in the report about her social activities, the real schools she went to and a lot of conjecture about her whereabouts now. Nothing outstanding or interesting from my perspective but maybe it will shed some light on whatever you're looking for. If not, let me know and we'll keep digging," she offered.

Roland concluded his business with Karla and turned his attention to his computer and the files in front of him.

He made a mental summary for himself. Mira, as she was known to him at the time, had come on to him in London with a purpose. She had tried to gain his trust and get him to let his guard down. She followed him to Zurich where she again made contact and sold him a story in a most transparent way. The jury was still out, in his mind, on whom she was working for. She was now Randi and she was either trying to incriminate Harry Axelrod or she really was working for him. The next issue was if she was working for him was she double crossing him or pretending to do so for Roland's benefit? Lastly, whoever put the phony file together for her had deliberately made reference to one of the most painful and vulnerable times in Roland's life. This may be a cruel stab or a veiled warning. That remained to be seen. Before he could answer that he would have to know more about Randi and what her true job description was.

Roland had two files open in front of him. One was titled Randi and the other, Mira. Only the Randi file made reference to Granby Academy. The real Mira Melong had been nowhere near New England for her prep schooling. If he could find for sure who developed Randi's Mira he could track down their motives around the academy reference. He was looking at the pictures of the two Mira's as teenagers in their respective files and thought to himself that Randi's future was written all over her even then. Of course it was easier to see in hindsight.

Chapter Nine

Harry Axelrod was just arriving at his Washington office, while out at Dulles airport, his pilot was busy preparing the company jet. He was awaiting further instructions about departure time before filing a final flight plan. The pilot's cell phone rang. The instructions were brief but complete, they would leave at noon or as soon thereafter as they could get clearance and would fly directly to the west coast. Harry liked to use the Oakland airport for San Francisco access because it was lower profile and less scrutinized on the private side.

He had arranged the meeting for Tuesday afternoon at the Pan Pacific Hotel. This city was far enough from Washington; large enough to get lost in; and the hotel, conveniently located in the theatre district, was far enough from the hustle and bustle of the tourists and the business center to provide the relative anonymity they sought. Satisfied that all preparations were in place, Harry readied himself for the meeting.

He was still uncertain which road to go down. He thought about the relative vulnerabilities of the two countries and their oil supplies. On the one hand, Saudi Arabia was already pumping and shipping their oil to the United States so to take them out as a supplier was to unseat the king from the throne. Russia, on the other hand, was in no position to start filling orders next week. This could give him an added edge because he could pick up some of the slack created by the lack of Saudi oil in the interim. Before and until Russia was able to get production up to a million barrels a day, Harry would have first crack at filling that void. One thing was certain, if he took out one of them the dependence on Venezuelan oil would preclude any further talk of tariffs of that he was sure.

For a moment his greed made him consider taking both countries out of the picture. He would be invincible if he were supplying that extra ten per cent himself. Tempered slightly by reality he backed off of that delusion and returned to the issue at hand. Which country and their oil supply would be easier for him to take out of the equation? Russia was vulnerable because it wasn't producing at that level and didn't have the port to ship that large of a supply. Saudi Arabia's vulnerability was around the political instability in the Middle East. That was a wild card which always trumped good sense. Once that dog was unleashed, however, there was no telling who all would be bitten.

The Saudi's could be taken out so easily by his political clout, Russia though, had the mafia to assist him. *Which would come with the higher price tag,* he asked himself. He would have to decide soon.

Harry's car was waiting at the curb as he exited his office building. He acknowledged the driver who was waiting by the open door and who reached out to take his bag. After Harry was safely seated inside, he stowed the bag in the trunk and went around to the driver's side to begin the trip to Dulles. Harry was on the phone immediately trying to keep things working smoothly in his empire. Traffic moved slowly through the district at this time of day and he welcomed the surge that he felt as the car finally accelerated its way onto the beltway.

He'd have time for a few more calls before they reached the plane. He liked to get as much of his work done as he could while on the ground because he relished the environment on the Gulfstream and he really wanted to be free to appreciate its opulence and comfort, once on board. For him, flying was about being free. Free from the constraints of the ground in as many ways as possible. For this reason he almost resented the conveniences on board which would allow him to work. He preferred to spend his time aloft in the salon portion of the plane, not in the office. He occasionally had to use those amenities to avert some disaster or other in his business but he considered a trip successful if he never entered the office for the duration of the trip. Today he would start with a massage and really give this oil import issue his undivided attention. He had to make it work big for him in the short term. That was where he would make his gains.

A short time later, on board the smooth flying Gulfstream Harry was relishing the plush environment and enjoying that long anticipated massage. It had been a real coup to find Tina. She had been working at the fitness club where Harry belonged and he had actually hired her for her shiatsu massage skills. It had been fortuitous that she had just enough secretarial experience on her resume that he could justify putting her on the staff. She acted as flight attendant, in-flight secretary and massage therapist all rolled into one employee. He realized that she would be hard to replace and he treated her well.

He was struggling to keep his mind on his work. He had a precipitous decision to make and he was under increasing pressure to make it now. He would be in San Francisco within hours and he had to make his direction clear to those with whom he was meeting. The time for action had come.

Harry was not sure if he had dozed off or if he had been so swept up by his thoughts that he had zoned out temporarily. In any event he was somehow startled back into the present with clarity of purpose. His decision was made, the path was clear.

Will stood looking at Amanda's apartment building and listening to her cell phone conversation. After a protracted debate they had decided together that the best chance they had of getting the key to her safety deposit box without being detected was to enlist the assistance of Alvin, the doorman/guard in her building. Amanda was on the phone with him now arranging a meeting. She had spoken carefully and had said some things covertly which they hoped would make Alvin aware of her identity without broadcasting who she was to any possible eavesdroppers.

The one thing most in her favor was that she was the only one that she knew of who called him Al. "Hello, Al? This is Candy. I spoke with you this morning. You remember, about the weather vane. Do you remember?" she asked. She was hoping that he would recall their brief encounter in the lobby this morning where they spoke about the strength and freshness of the spring wind. The fact that she kept the candy dish on his desk filled with hard candies accounted for the name she used to identify herself. She hoped that he would catch on quickly. She waited cautiously praying that he would recognize her voice.

Alvin hesitated, there was no response.

Amanda, not leaving him much time to say the wrong thing, continued, "I wanted to get back to you about the weather vane, you know the wind, spring wind measurement." She spoke with a heavy emphasis on the words weather and wind. "The answer to your question is three hundred and twelve," she said to him. She was optimistic that he would translate that into her apartment number, 312.

Amanda decided to continue on as though Alvin had caught on. "Will you please pick it up as soon as possible? I was thinking within the next hour. Does that work for you? I think you've met my assistant and he could meet you at your house. Can you be there within an hour?" She inquired.

Finally Alvin began to respond although he wasn't sure to what. He thought this was Amanda and could only assume that she wanted to talk to him away from the premises. He stammered out, "Ah, ya, I can be there. You remember where I live?" he asked.

"Yes, of course, I'll have it there within the hour. I hope your wife will enjoy the gift," she continued the deception. "Good bye and thank you for your support," she signed off.

Alvin stared at the phone and scratched his head in wonderment. At the same time and down the block, Amanda was saying to Will, "I think he got it, he should meet you at his house at once. I hope I wasn't too transparent otherwise."

"You'd better get going," she added, "I'll go over to the coffee shop on 34th and wait for you there. Please be careful and try not to put Al or his family in any danger. I worry about this spilling out on other people," she cautioned. "And Will, be very careful." She knew she was repeating herself but she was scared now and couldn't seem to help it.

Will gave her a quick peck on the cheek and agreed to meet her at the coffee shop. "If I'm not there by three o'clock, take a cab to the airport and report your passport lost. Don't miss that flight," he instructed. "Also, change cabs at least twice between the coffee shop and the airport. Don't go directly and above all, stay alert."

Will turned and walked down the block to the metro stop. She watched until he was out of sight. As she turned to make her way over to 34th she saw Alvin leave the lobby and head toward his car. She felt her fingers cross inside her pockets.

Will emerged from the metro station at Virginia Square and walked the 8 or 9 blocks to Alvin's address in no time. He was relieved to find Alvin standing across the street leaning on the fender of a car. Will stepped off the curb, emerged into the street between parked cars and approached him hopefully.

"Hi, Alvin, I'm really glad to see you here, for several reasons," he began.

Alvin looked at him askance. "I wasn't really sure that I understood Amanda on the phone. That was her, wasn't it? Why was she talking in code? What's goin' on? Why are you here?" Alvin was thoroughly confused by the clandestine nature of all this and was looking to have the mystery explained.

"Can we talk for a minute? I think I can explain it quickly enough."

Following Alvin's gesture, Will slid into the front seat of the car and turned to face Alvin. He began to brief him on Amanda's situation. He told him only that she was in danger, being followed and scrutinized and needed to get her passport to get out of the country. Will didn't want to tell him any more than necessary in order to keep him out danger if possible. He felt badly enough enlisting his assistance but they were desperate.

Alvin asked questions which Will deftly avoided once he was certain that Alvin was going to help.

"Alvin, we can talk about this more, later. For now, time is squeezing us and we need to talk about how to get into Amanda's apartment."

The conversation continued for twenty minutes or so and the plan was laid. Because he was in the building anyway, Alvin was the one who could enter the apartment and retrieve the key. He could move about freely and without suspicion throughout the common areas of the apartments. His only risk was if the apartment itself was under surveillance. Will was certain there had not been time to install any new electronic devices since Jake had been there that morning but he was no expert. The sooner they moved the safer it would be. Definitely, the greatest risk would be if someone was watching the apartment specifically and not just the building.

The two men parted. Alvin drove back to the apartment building with a key to Amanda's apartment, so he wouldn't have to use his pass key, and all of the information he needed to retrieve the safe deposit box key. They had talked about specifics trying to minimize the risk of detection. Alvin had to choose his time to enter the premises carefully and he would not touch anything inside except the doorknob and the drawer where the key was kept. He would not turn on any electrical devices, including lights. Will went to wait.

Alvin arrived outside the building approximately twenty minutes later and circled the block looking for the right place to leave the car. He didn't find the ideal one and pulled up into the circular drive of the building to go back around the other way. He realized that his palms were sweaty against the steering wheel. He hadn't been involved in something this furtive since he was a young boy playing pranks in his neighborhood. It gave him that same feeling.

Back out on the street and luck was with him. A car was just pulling away from the curb almost directly across the street from his building. There was a low hanging branch that would partly conceal the side of the car away from the street. He actually got excited over the suitability of the parking place.

Alvin left the car and crossed the street to his place of employment. He put his jacket on the back of his desk chair and began moving around the lobby in his usual manner. He greeted one of the other tenants who entered the lobby returning from the park with her little dog. He moved to the elevator and pushed the "up" button as he saw her approaching. Alvin continued about his work for the next thirty minutes or so.

At the designated time he gathered together the items that he might need and put them in a canvas bag. He placed the bag in his cart which he used to deliver items to the apartments from time to time. This done he went to the freight elevator and pushed the button to summons the bare, elevator car. As planned, Alvin went first to the basement and made a couple of stops there. He unlocked and entered one of the storage rooms where he picked up a box and added it to the other items on his cart.

Back on the freight elevator he pushed the button for the 8th floor. When the door gaped open, he pressed the hold button which would cause the car to remain at that location until he returned. He removed a small box from his cart and took it to the locked utility room on that floor. While at the front of the building he moved over to the hallway window and while running his hand around the perimeter as if checking the glazing he looked out on the street to see if anything appeared to be amiss.

Satisfied that all was in order, Alvin returned to the bank of elevators and rode with his cart to the 3rd floor. He exited the elevator, this time leaving the door of the elevator open and the hold button engaged. He looked right and left only to assure himself that no one else was in the hallway and proceeded directly to Apartment 312. He fumbled slightly getting the key into the lock and realized that his nerves were on edge.

The door opened, he stepped inside. He hesitated just long enough to assure himself that no one else was inside and proceeded directly to the drawer that Will had described. He located the key quickly and turned to leave the apartment. He looked first through the peep hole in the door to see if anyone was in the hallway. Seeing no one, he opened the door cautiously and partially to look right and left again. Next he closed the apartment door and went directly to the elevator. Arriving back in the lobby, he returned his cart to the storage area and replaced the other items he had taken with him. The key remained safely in his pocket for now.

The afternoon darkened from rain clouds moving over the area and thunder could be heard off in the distance. Soon the rain showers that the weatherman had promised would arrive. Alvin turned on the lamp on his desk and sat down to look through some invoices and other papers. He needed to kill at least fifteen minutes so things didn't look suspicious.

Will waited nervously across the street in the parking structure of another apartment building. He could see no unusual movement on the street but he stayed wary and tried to take in every movement. He watched everyone who was in or around the parked cars in particular. The waiting was killing him and eating up precious time that he and Amanda would need to get to the bank. But if they moved too fast they would tip their hands and Amanda would be followed. This they wanted to avoid above all else. Will watched as Alvin left the building, went briefly to his car and then returned to his desk with a newspaper he had retrieved from the car.

This was Will's cue. He looked around carefully now and seeing nothing out of the ordinary, walked from the parking garage toward the entrance to this apartment building. Will started to enter the building and then, as though he had forgotten something, turned and walked to Alvin's car. He opened the passenger door and leaned inside to retrieve a small paper bag from the seat. The car was almost totally concealed on this side by the low hanging limb, Alvin had placed it perfectly. Will turned from the car and entered the apartment building. He walked directly through the lobby, passed the bank of elevators and exited through the rear door. Less than five minutes later and certain that he was not being followed, he joined Amanda in the coffee shop and handed her the key.

The difficult part was done and all that was left was to retrieve the passport from the bank and get back to the airport undetected. They had just less than three hours before the flight's departure. Will and Amanda began by hailing a cab outside the coffee shop and taking it the Rosslyn Metro Station. Arriving there, Will paid the driver while Amanda walked the two blocks to the bank. Will went into the convenience store and bought some snacks, a toothbrush, toothpaste, hair brush and deodorant. This was a start. He used the ATM in the store to withdraw his daily limit from his account and then browsed through the magazines and newspapers.

In short order, Amanda joined him in the store. She had her passport and had made as large a withdrawal from her account as she felt was safe without raising suspicions. She had engaged in small talk with the teller about her long awaited vacation hoping he would not think her suspicious. With what Will was withdrawing from his account for her and the exceptional exchange rate in Bulgaria she would be in good shape financially unless this dragged on too long. She chose not to even consider that possibility.

They left Rosslyn Station back on the Blue Line riding out of Virginia, under the Potomac, and into the District. They got off the train in Foggy Bottom carefully watching all of the other passengers detrain and leave the station in one homogenous bundle. They boarded the next train through and left that train at Farragut East. They walked for awhile stopping frequently to look in windows and partake of the snacks. They would face each other and talk giving themselves plenty of opportunity to observe those around them. Satisfied again that they were not being followed, they boarded another taxi for the ride to the airport. They did not talk much on the way. It seemed like everything had been said at least once and most of it repeatedly. Will had done his best to impress on Amanda how to watch out for her own safety once she was out of the city. They had prearranged ways to stay in contact and a few emergency code words and meeting places if the need arose. They were both near exhaustion but there was still so much ahead of them. Will decided that he could not look that far down the road. He had to stay focused on one step at a time or he would get overwhelmed.

Arriving at the airport with less than two hours to spare, they both felt some level of relief. At least this part of the operation was nearly over. Will had to leave Amanda at the security check point so she was really on her own from there on. They had arranged for her to call him from Munich during her layover there so he could do nothing in the meantime except worry about her. He vowed that he would not let that distract him from the further work which had to be done and which now was solely on his shoulders. He felt a sudden need to talk with Charles and dialed his number on the cell phone from the rear seat of the cab taking him back to Amanda's apartment. He was lonely.

Roland was moving about his hotel room with all of the verve of a zombie. He had spent a miserable, sleepless night. He was due to meet

Randi for lunch and he needed the morning to organize himself. It was time to get focused.

His first call of the day was to Karla. Roland was up early enough to catch her at home at a reasonable hour in the evening. It was imperative that he identify who had put the Mira bio together. Once he solved that mystery he was sure that he would know the meaning behind it. He had spent a good part of the night reliving that part of his past. It had been almost like losing them all over again. Whoever put that bio together had successfully delivered a punch to his gut. He was really strung out emotionally and couldn't seem to stop the minuscule memories of both his wife and daughter that flitted across his mind, just flashbacks he knew but disturbing nonetheless. He couldn't seem to hold his focus, it was damn distracting. His frustration was beginning to dominate his mood. He hoped that Karla would have the information he would need to be able to trace the source.

Karla picked up the phone, "Hey, Boss." She always knew it was him from the caller ID and he hated her calling him, "Boss," but couldn't seem to get her to stop it. This morning with his mood it put him over the edge.

"Damn it, Karla, I've asked you not to call me that, now I'm telling you," he began.

Half a world away Karla looked at the phone and rolled her eyes, "Aren't we in a mood this morning?" she responded.

Roland ignored her retort and continued, "What have you got for me on the Mira bio?"

"Well, I think what I've found may surprise you. Our investigative agency used three different information services in compiling the report. We tracked them through our data banks and turned up one hit. One of the agencies used is called Omni Intelligence. Omni Intelligence is a wholly owned subsidiary of Gratiot Industries. Gratiot Industries is the general partner of a holding company called Pinnacle Partners. One of the companies which Pinnacle owns is Eco-Energy which I'm sure you recognize as being loosely affiliated with Dynamo and one of your good friends."

"Harry Axelrod," he muttered. Roland stood quietly and looked out

115

the window. There was a great deal to contemplate. This information had long reaching implications and he needed to analyze this carefully. "Have you any information on Randi or how the report involves her?"

"Just this, Randi has been employed by Axelrod at least one other time that we've found. More importantly, though, she has a history of playing both sides of the fence. She doesn't seem to need to remain loyal to her employer. She demands a careful look." Karla answered.

"How easy was it to learn that piece of the information?" Roland inquired.

"That's interesting that you asked. We had to really dig for it. I would say on a scale of 1 to 10, 1 being front page news in the Washington Post and 10 being buried in the tomb of the unknown soldier, this was about an 8. Most people wouldn't find it. You'd have to have extraordinary intelligence connections and take a fair amount of time to learn that little tidbit," Karla responded. "Basically, you'd have to be playing for very high stakes and have a lot of time and money."

Several moments later, with the conversation concluded, Roland considered his options. If Randi was hired by Axelrod had he done so knowing her propensity to switch her loyalties or had he been unaware of this? He still could not tell if she was a set up, a trap. He considered the possibility that the answers were with Randi and how he could get to the truth. He certainly could not trust what she told him. He began to prepare for his encounter with the wily Ms. Randi and her disloyalty.

Part way into his preparations, in the midst of making some notes, something still wasn't fitting right. Roland challenged himself to separate fact from fiction. He needed to get down to the fundamentals as he knew them and not get distracted by everything that was bombarding him. The first fact was that Randi had been hired to contact him. No doubt there. This raised the issue of the purpose of this contact. Was it to shadow him as she had said or to gain some other information from him? Perhaps it was specifically to deliver an emotional blow to him. He pondered those options carefully.

The first alternative, to shadow him, made some sense in light of the Amanda Chambers issue. Roland was plagued by the sense that it was important to Axelrod that Gazelle move into the mean side of this game. He had pushed illegal activities from the beginning and recently had unquestionably been promoting assassination as a practical resolution to the energy impasse. This was a viable answer and one to consider.

The second option, to gain further information from him, was remote at best. After careful contemplation, Roland could think of no good reason for anyone, including Axelrod, to go this route. He could think of nothing important to be learned from him that wasn't already fairly common knowledge. Even Axelrod was fully apprised of the matters with which Roland was currently occupied. They had all been debated openly and fully through Gazelle. It was clear what Roland's position was and Axelrod would not need subterfuge to learn any more details.

Number Three, the emotional distraction, was a real possibility. If this were the purpose, he thought, it was working pretty well. He was on the edge and it was taking a whole load of extra effort on his part to stay on track. Why, he asked himself, and to whom would that be important? The why was probably to distract him, get him off his stride, maybe even make him stumble somehow. Who would want that at this time? Well, unfortunately, he could think of many. Certainly the drug consortium he had just leaned on was a possibility, also the energy group or even Amanda Chambers if she had become convinced that he was on to her. Lastly, there was anyone in Gazelle who was taking a contrary view on any of the issues currently on the table. He began to run down the likelihood of the contenders he had identified.

He dismissed Amanda as a suspect in this intrigue as being too unsophisticated and lacking the professional acumen to have put this type of plan into effect this rapidly. With her out, the list shortened to drugs, energy and Gazelle. Roland realized that two of those three had one person in common. Harry Axelrod was a key player in international energy and he opposed Roland's position on both drugs and energy through Gazelle. He just opposed Roland, period. They saw eye to eye on very little. Axelrod appeared to be the one who had hired Randi and consequently would have had a hand in the creation of the bio. All doubt was set aside.

Bottom line was that Randi was hired, by Axelrod, to either monitor where he was going with the handling of Amanda Chambers as she had said or to knock him off stride, at least temporarily, while Axelrod proceeded with some unknown plan, probably around the energy issue. Given the inclusion of the Granby Academy item in the Mira/Randi bio it seemed more likely that the intent was to disrupt Roland emotionally. There would be no need for such a message if this was just about Amanda. That would be a rare slip for Axelrod, to risk detection just so he could take a jab at Roland personally. Harry Axelrod did not generally allow himself such trivial folly.

The remaining question was whether he had hired her knowing that she would switch loyalties or whether that would be an unexpected outcome. This was tougher to distinguish. He decided that only two people would have the answer to that. Would he be able to get the truth from Randi or would he need to get it from Axelrod, himself? Threshold to that was whether Randi knew the truth of Axelrod's motives. He decided that she may not know and in any event, anything he learned from her would be suspect. He would never know the truth except from the man, himself. Randi had become a waste of time. He decided to stand her up and stiff her for the money he had agreed to pay her for her story.

His final decision was to choose his risk, whether to try to learn the truth from Axelrod or whether to risk relying on the depth and efficiency of his intelligence sources. His information certainly indicated that Axelrod may not be aware of Randi's nasty little habit of switching uniforms in the midst of the war. Karla had assured him that the data on her was rather deeply hidden. The key was to gain more information about her previous employment by Axelrod. Had she pulled the switch on that one? Roland prepared an e-mail to Karla to get her started on the investigation and began to pack.

Will was sitting at the table in Amanda's apartment just finishing his morning coffee when his cell phone rang. It was Amanda. Without acknowledging that she was traveling, she spoke to him as casually as if she were around the corner.

"Hi, I didn't want you to worry about me so thought I'd better give you a call," she began.

"Thanks," he continued the ruse, "I talked to Connie and she told me what you two were up to so I wasn't concerned. I hope you're having a good time. That's the main thing."

"Ya, I am, just like I planned. How are things there?"

"Just like you left them except I'm eating everything out of your refrigerator. Maybe we should go to the grocery store tomorrow," he wanted anyone listening to think she would be back directly. "Tell everyone hi for me. Wish I could have gone with you."

"Will do," she responded. "I'll probably give you a quick call later, before I start back."

"That'd be great. I'll hold down the fort here. Miss you, Mandy. Take care."

They hung up quickly hoping to avoid a trace. Will felt a slight relief knowing that Amanda had arrived in Munich without further incident. He knew she would call him once she was settled in with Alex. He knew that Alex would look after her. He loved her as much as Will did. They were family in the broadest sense of the word.

Will allowed himself to let his mind wander and he thought it interesting that the meaning of the word, "family" seemed to change throughout life. When we are young and dependent we see only the safety and security that abounds with a mother, father and siblings, if we're lucky enough to have that. As we grow and move out into the world we have to be willing to loosen our hold on safety and begin to search out the new. Sometimes the same people are there but the roles have to evolve. Relationships which were born from childhood expand as maturity and growth dictate. Sometimes parent becomes child as child turns into parent and often siblings scatter to the winds. *One thing seems certain; we all seek family in some form,* he concluded.

Strange, he thought, *that there are those who wish to steal that from people who do not match their idea of what a family should look like. If skins are of different colors, don't mix them. If the genders are the same, deny them. If it doesn't fit what someone thinks is traditional, invalidate it. If you really want tradition,* he observed, *we could go back to living in tribes.*

What could possibly be the cost to one person of what another found was family? What is a family if not the people that you love and choose to live with? He wondered. *Shouldn't everyone be entitled to their own vision of that? Now that would be a real 'family value!'*

He thought warmly of Charles and Amanda and the wonderful weekend they'd spent together. He was thrilled that they had hit it off so well. It felt like family to him and that's what it really was. Will came back to his coffee and shook his head as he stood. *When will this hate stop,* he wondered?

Back on track for his day's activities, Will shaved, finished dressing, splashed on some aftershave and ran a comb through his hair. On the way out the door he double checked to make sure he had money, cell phone and the address of his appointment. He checked his watch and assured himself that he had plenty of time to reach his destination.

He spoke briefly with Alvin as he passed through the lobby and out into the morning air. The spring mornings in Washington were brisk and refreshing and he felt an extra bounce in his step as he made his way to the metro. The trees were beginning to call attention to themselves by flaunting their unique versions of green. He was uncertain whether life was just damn good or whether it just felt that way today because of his optimism. He had settled on a plan that he felt would take care of this mess once and for all. With Amanda safely away, Will felt he could take some chances that just hadn't been possible before.

Less than an hour after leaving the apartment Will was sitting in a coffee shop across the table from Karla. He had decided to go directly to what he perceived to be the source of the problem. Looking at her now, he was certain that Roland's assistant would hear him out. If need be he could try playing strong arm stuff but he didn't want to endanger himself as well as Amanda. Not that they weren't already in plenty of danger, he just didn't want it to get any worse.

"Thanks for meeting with me," he began. "I'd like to get right to the point. My sister has been followed, her apartment has been bugged and searched and there have been some other indications that she may not be safe. I'm here because she seems to think that your employer may have something against her. I have two questions for you. First, are you or your boss involved in these things and if so, what will it take to make it go away. As you can imagine, I want my sister safe."

Karla was nonplussed. All sorts of thoughts chased through her head. If she said no, what would she be admitting or implying. If she said yes, where would this go? She was instantly sorry that she had agreed to this meeting. It had seemed right when she got the message through the committee chairman that Mr. Chambers was trying to reach Mr. Priestly. She returned the call because she'd hoped to get more into this Amanda thing. Not only that, she alone had been responsible for the bugging and tight pursuit and if it was about any of that she needed to take care of it herself. She wasn't ready for Roland to know that. She felt like a contestant on a game show. The clock was ticking and she couldn't figure out how to answer this inquisition, this frontal assault. He was so direct, she hadn't expected that.

Will sensed that she was bewildered by his directness and decided to help her out. "Look, I don't mean to put you on the spot personally. Maybe we can come up with some way for you to help me learn what I need to know without jeopardizing your confidentiality with your employer."

That sounded good to Karla, but again she needed time to think it through. Finally she stammered out, "What exactly are you proposing?"

"Well, how about this, what if I ask you some specific questions and you tell me whether you have any first hand knowledge of the matter?"

"Why don't you tell me the kind of question your referring to and I'll tell you whether I want to answer you or not?" Karla was proud of herself for answering quickly and she thought, conservatively.

Will was encouraged by her response and knew that Karla had information. What he didn't know was how shrewd she might be. He continued, "Would I be correct to think that your boss has a reason to have my sister followed? I'm not asking you to say that he is actually doing so. Just does he have a reason to care where she goes and what she does?"

Karla studied her hands for a moment and then replied, "I don't think I should be talking to you. I thought when I got your message that this was about something else." Again she felt proud of her response.

Will was convinced that she knew exactly what was going on. He was also convinced that Karla and her boss were behind the surveillance but he had not gotten what he came for.

Will continued, "What will it take to achieve a truce of some sort? As I said earlier, my interest in coming here is to make my sister safe. I'm sure you can understand that. Is there someone else I should talk to? What do you want from Amanda? Information? A promise? Something you think she has? What will it take?" He pressed.

After hanging up from her conversation with Will, Amanda proceeded to her gate for the flight to Sofia. As she walked through the glass and chrome environment she had a surreal feeling. She found the building to be like a house of mirrors and being fatigued from her trip as well as skittish about her safety only heightened the sense of disorientation. She thought she saw a familiar looking man watching her through the glass. He was moving in the opposite direction from her on a moving walkway but through the glass he seemed to be smiling, no, more like leering, as they passed. She thought she had seen him briefly in the waiting area where she sat when she called Will. Arriving in the gate area for her flight, she decided to use the restroom before they began to board so she crossed the hall and went into the ladies room. Several minutes later as she was exiting, the man with the leer stopped in front of her and with a menacing grin on his face, he mumbled, "Guten Morgan, Ms. Chambers."

Amanda dropped her carryon and leapt backward bumping into a woman who was just leaving the restroom. Her heart was pounding, her knees were weak. She turned to see who she had banged into and when she turned back the man had completely vanished. Her carryon lay at her feet. For one brief moment she wondered if it had really happened. She was tired but that had been real, he had been there and he had spoken to her.

Amanda returned to the gate area and fumbled to find her cell phone.

She was grateful that in her travels she had acquired one that worked internationally. She entered Will's number and waited anxiously until she heard his voice. She had reached him in the middle of his meeting with Karla. Amanda related to Will what had happened to her and though he spoke softly and soothingly to her his anger rose and his gut began to churn. He could feel his teeth clench together in rage.

Karla fidgeted as she waited and was getting more uncomfortable and nervous by the moment. She couldn't think what to say to Will and decided that she needed to leave. She turned from him and stood and as she turned back to face him she saw that he too was now standing. His face was suddenly painted with anger and in two giant steps he was around the table and in her face. Before Karla could excuse herself or speak, he growled at her in a low, cruel half-whisper. "I want to know who and why my sister was accosted in the Munich Airport. I will not rest nor will you until I know that she is safe and this is resolved. I know who you are and where you are and I fear that you have underestimated me and my connections." Will stomped out the door before Karla could close her mouth.

Amanda boarded the Airbus 300 without further incident and took her seat at the window. She had looked into the face of every man in every seat as she made her way along the narrow aisle. Unless he was seated behind her, she was sure that he wasn't on the plane. The encounter had made her angry. Fear had been transformed into determination and she was feeling less like a victim again and more like a strong, determined woman. *Who the hell did these people think they were?* She set her jaw in determination and looked forward to arriving in Sofia and briefing Alex. She would get him working on this as well.

Less than 20 minutes later they were airborne and Amanda watched as the countryside below played hide and seek with her through the scattered clouds. Whenever she got a glimpse of the ground she was awed by how beautiful the snow covered mountains were and each little valley that she peered into seemed to be bursting forth green and lush with the promise of an abundant summer to come. She let her thoughts leave reality and follow fantasy and she found herself imagining what the people were like who lived in these gorges and valleys. Wondered what their lives were like, what their day would look like, she thought of the things she'd been taught in school and wondered if there was any link between that and reality.

Her first impression of Bulgaria was out the window of the Airbus as it stubbornly relinquished elevation to the pull of gravity and swept across the fields of small, outlying, rural villages. The quaint farmhouses of brick and tile became tumble down hovels of rock and crude brick held together by a red, earthen mortar as her lofty view was gradually surrendered to the pull of the earth. Rectangular fields of varying shades of green cuddled up around the structures like blankets of spring velvet spread upon the ground for lounging.

Nudged by the sudden reality of how perception changes with perspective, she had a sense of history interminably tied to the soil and of structures which surpass the ages. The antiquity of the buildings was overshadowed by the force of their number. They seemed to be dotted across the countryside like freckles on suntanned skin. She was conscious of a culture where generations have struggled to make a life on the same piece of earth and where family has spawned hope in the same way that the soil has produced life.

The mountains surrounding the city reminded her of descriptions of Sofia that she'd heard from Alex. That it resembled a small Denver. It was surrounded by snow-capped mountains containing ski resorts and historical vestiges of times long past. It also seemed to trap air pollution in its valley in the way that Denver jealously hugs its abused air and emissions close to its terrain.

After clearing customs she hired a taxi at her peril and set out for the drive to downtown. She and Will had decided that it would be safer not to inform Alex and perhaps half of the free world of her arrival. Instead she would go straight to the hotel and make contact with him from there. The number of vehicles around them increased as they neared the city and in just moments they'd arrived in the traffic gridlock known as the city center. After winding their way through a convoluted system of one-way streets and glorified alleys, past designer dress shops, restaurants, coffee houses and bars they arrived at a busy intersection. Here, in the heart of the city, Amanda was greeted by signs boasting the presence of McDonald's and the Sheraton Hotel. She knew she had arrived. She allowed herself the luxury of exhaling.

Once she was in her room and still wearing all of the trappings of severe jet lag, she placed a call to Alex at the university.

Chapter Ten

Nate jumped, startled by the ringing of his phone. He was back in the office after his rotation in the bunker and he had been day dreaming about his time there. Often, after returning, it would take him several days to get back into the swing of his daily routine. It was a strange experience, somewhere between a vacation and a prison sentence he presumed. He picked up the phone and answered by saying his name as was his habit.

"Nate, this is Will Chambers, Amanda's brother. I'd like to meet with you if you don't mind. Is there a convenient time for you in the next day or two?" He inquired.

Nate was somewhat taken aback but didn't skip a beat. "Sure Will, would you like to have lunch tomorrow?"

"That'd be fine, how about meeting at the DC Deli across from the park? That's just about a block from your office. Noon okay?"

Nate agreed to the meeting and they hung up. "Where might this be going," he wondered. He pondered whether Amanda's sick days called in might forebode something more serious.

He had hardly hung up the phone when his pager went off. He checked the number and moved to his briefcase to remove the secure cell phone and return the call. Harry Axelrod was sitting in the working portion of the Gulfstream now and was not particularly pleased to be there. As the phone sounded, he picked up the receiver which was built into the arm of the office chair he occupied.

"Nate?" He inquired.

"Yes sir," Nate responded.

"Got an assignment for you, boy. Can you make yourself available tomorrow around 3 Washington time?"

"No problem there, shall I just stand by the phone?"

"That's the ticket," Harry replied. "I'll be in touch."

Of course Nate wondered what the nature of the assignment might be but he had learned long ago and very clearly not to ask questions. Powerful men seemed to have little tolerance for questions. It was as though it brought the very essence of their power into question which Nate guessed it did if you thought about it. In any event, he would wait to hear what lay in store for him. In the meantime there would be the lunch with Will Chambers.

Harry relished the ride across the Bay Bridge into the city. You had to hand it to these California dandies they'd built a beautiful city on these hills, even if it was populated with leftist wing nuts and the scruff of the earth. As his car exited the Interstate and progressed along Hayes Street he thought what a waste this place had become. He had no patience for liberals, beggars or queers and that was about all he'd found here. The ride to his hotel took him through the Tenderloin District of the city and no one would argue that this place had a shot at winning the award as one of the armpits of America. Homeless, alcoholics, drug addicts and the marginally mentally ill were all that inhabited this neighborhood which clung to the edge of the elite Nob Hill like a barnacle on a pier or more aptly like a boil on a butt, Harry thought.

The Pan Pacific Hotel was as plush as the few blocks up Post Street were blight. Harry's car rolled into the driveway under the portico and stopped adjacent to the green, Rolls Royce which served as the hotel's guest car. Instantly he was attended by a crisply uniformed, white gloved doorman and two similarly clad bellmen. He liked their attention to detail and immediately felt the respect he craved and was sure he deserved. He was confident that this was the best choice for this meeting.

The rooms were lavishly appointed including marble baths and many of those small touches that distinguish a luxurious hotel from an opulent one. This was somewhere between the two, Harry judged.

It was nearly dinner time in the East but mid-afternoon here on the West coast. Harry decided that he would check out the accommodations for tomorrow's meeting. The Bellman took him to the suite which had been reserved for the gathering and he assured him that everything that they might need would be in place including telephones, faxes, a shredder and refreshments of various kinds. He wanted everything to be right and no reason for any of the participants to have to leave the room once this assembly of influence began. He knew that at this same time, a couple of men and one woman of notable distinction were checking into the hotel under assumed names hoping to keep the spotlight off of this get-together. What he didn't know was that arrangements had also been made for a small, discreetly placed camera to allow one other person to share in the knowledge of what would occur in that meeting.

Harry was as excited as he could remember being in some time. This, he believed, was the beginning of a precipitous and possibly world altering event.

Will heard from Amanda and she was safely in Sofia now with Alex. It appeared that the remainder of her trip had gone without incident. He could tell from her voice that she had regained her resolve and she was in a take control frame of mind. It would be hard, he thought, to keep her appeased and quietly out of the way. Alex had his work cut out for him. Will was angry at himself that he had let his emotions cause him to make an error. He was so enraged about the taunting of Amanda by the goon in Munich that he had let Karla know that Amanda was out of the country. He vowed to keep his emotions in check and to keep his cool as he moved through this maze.

After his brief conversation with Nate, Will placed a call to Charles at his office in the History Department at the University of Chicago. Their conversation consisted only of Will asking Charles to come to Washington. Will simply told him that he needed his help. With Spring

Break coming up the next week, Charles only had to cancel one lecture in order to leave town that night. He had the department secretary book a flight and posted a notice on the classroom door for students to find the next morning. That done, he walked the short distance to his apartment, threw a few clothes in a carryon, put together his toiletry bag and headed for the airport. On his way he placed a call to Will and let him know that he should be at National by 7p.m. He just couldn't seem to get with calling it Reagan National.

Charles' flight was on time and he was elated to see Will's face as he exited the arrival area and stepped out into the evening air. After a quick embrace they got into line for a taxi and started talking more intimately. It was so good to be together. They climbed into a Virginia cab and gave the driver the address of Amanda's apartment. They made small talk and smiled at each other as they rode along the expressway. Both were oblivious to the landmarks they passed. Will wanted to wait until they were out of the taxi to tell Charles why he needed him there.

Arriving at the apartment building Will noticed as they passed through the lobby that Alvin wasn't there. Will didn't know what his hours were. Surely he couldn't be there 24 hours a day. He had seen others on duty in the lobby at various times but never this guy. He passed off his observation as slight paranoia or heightened awareness and joined Charles in the elevator for the ride to the third floor.

After they were settled into the apartment, Will made a light snack for them both and they sat down for the briefing that Will had gone over a million times in his mind. He related everything to Charles, leaving out no detail intentionally. He needed Charles' help and he would be most effective if he had all of the facts. Will was sorry that Charles had not been in on the story from the beginning. He was sure that he was putting his own slant on things.

Hours later with the time approaching midnight, the two men decided to give it up and get some sleep. Will felt that Charles was fully briefed and they had done a little strategizing as well. Charles was totally cooperative and supportive and Will felt that he would give him all of the assistance he needed.

Will slept like a baby in Charles' arms that night.

Over coffee the next morning, Will and Charles talked about options. They agreed that the best approach was to enlist the assistance of Charles' father and his considerable wealth and political clout.

Charles did not have a cozy relationship with his natural father. In fact, to say that theirs was a relationship was probably a stretch. Charles' perception was that he and his mother had been abandoned when he was just a toddler. His father was an ambitious man who grew up the oldest son of an automobile factory worker in central Michigan. His grandfather had opted early on to keep his family in a small community and out of the Detroit area. Charles' father had lived and thrived in a small, semi-rural community in the 50's. He married his high school sweetheart just a couple of years out of school and they immediately had Charles. The post-war boom time and the geographical environment had shaped his thinking and led him to make his life in politics and business. As was often the case, those two went together like coffee and cream, an easy and appetizing mix.

Charles' father, like those who mentored him, had done an outstanding job of making his fortune and using it to gain political clout. Charles and his mother had been dumped like excess baggage as his father found fame and apparently unlimited fortune in a marriage to the daughter of one of the state's greatest power brokers. After the divorce and subsequent marriage his career had experienced an astronomical rise and, as they say, the rest is history.

Not until Charles was twelve had his father had any contact with him. He didn't know to this day what had prompted the reunion but he remained skeptical of the man's motives. Charles' life had been shaped by his stepfather, the only real father he had known. His loyalties remained with the simple educator who had provided moral and financial support for him and his mother throughout his childhood. Charles had taken his stepfather's name, Farino, while still in grammar school. He'd even spent summers in Italy with his adopted family and learned the language and to love the culture while still a youngster. His own career in teaching and his doctoral degree in history had been a tribute to that man.

His biological father, on the other hand, was always trying too hard and seemed to want desperately to do something for Charles to make up for his absence and neglect. Charles had wondered skeptically if the man was afraid that he or his mother would come out of the darkness and smear him publicly. Perhaps he wanted them to feel that the score had been evened. That he had done his part.

In any event, Charles took this opportunity to attempt a meeting with the man he could not bring himself to call, "Dad." He placed a call to the number he'd been given, if he ever needed anything, and there he learned from the woman who answered that the soonest he could see him was late the next evening. He would not be back in town until dinner time tomorrow. He also learned that the man had left instructions to accommodate Charles' request if and when he ever called. Charles requested to meet with him at his office at 8 p.m. and was graciously obliged.

Roland's car was just approaching the circular drive at the departure area of the Zurich Airport when his cell phone rang. He had the driver wait at the curb as he listened intently to the information Karla was relating to him. He had been expecting her to call with information about Randi and Harry but had not been prepared for the story which she told. Five minutes into the conversation he decided to get off the phone and give himself time to react to her news. He was furious, no livid, with Karla for acting in direct violation of his instructions but other news bothered him more at the moment.

He concluded the conversation with Karla and instructed his driver to return to the city. He placed a call to the original hotel he had booked downtown near the Railroad Station. Randi would not think to look for him there, in plain sight. He gave the reservation assistant an alias and asked to be transferred to the Bell Captain. Once he had the man on the phone he identified himself and was, of course, remembered. He enlisted the man's assistance and confidence. He would be met near the rear of the hotel and he and his belongings could be taken directly to his room, on the second floor, without having to encounter other guests. The registration process would be handled in confidence in his room. His utmost privacy would be assured.

Thirty minutes later Roland sat on the sofa in his room and glared. He was angry at Karla and wondering how to handle her direct insubordination. He needed to put that aside for now. That would be the easy part. The more difficult issue was the news that someone other than Gazelle was following Amanda Chambers. It was obvious from their actions that they were trying to intimidate her or perhaps do something even worse. Karla had been clear that she had checked again with their agency to be sure there was no confusion or misunderstanding. The scope of their assigned work did not include any international surveillance. They surely would not undertake it if they were not being paid for it and Karla had assured herself this morning that their understanding was correct. They had not even followed her out of the city when she flew to the mid-west to visit her brother, just verified that she had boarded the plane and reported for where it was bound.

This troublesome news deepened the furrows in Roland's brow. He was afraid that several of the bits of information he had churning around in his mind might be coming together in a not too pleasant mosaic of mystery.

Roland longed for one of his patented sessions with his mentor, the senator. He needed to bring clarity to all that was swimming around in his mind. He was further exasperated by the fact that he had spent another relatively sleepless night of tossing and turning and arose this morning feeling unrested. He was tired, grumpy and unable to think as clearly as he'd like, as clearly as he needed to. In the midst of all this he had not been able to give the time to the energy plan that he had intended. They were, by his assessment, behind schedule. Roland was perplexed by what Amanda was doing in Munich. His mind was jumping all over the place.

He decided it was time to settle in and concentrate. He phoned room service and asked them to send up strong coffee, a cheese plate and fruit. His intent was to seal himself into this room and away from the world until he could bring clarity, yet again, to the facts and feelings that were swirling around inside him.

Will arrived at the deli ahead of schedule and found an appropriate table where he could talk to Nate while observing the street outside. He had ordered his lunch so that he wouldn't have to get up after Nate arrived and he had arranged himself with his back to the rear wall and a clear view of the deli and street beyond. His heightened awareness might be blossoming into a full fledged case of paranoia but he was going to hedge his bets from now on. He was so certain after his meeting with Karla that she knew exactly what was going on and he was resolved not to leave this meeting without some further information.

Amanda had told Will of how Nate had discouraged her from following up on the memo she had run across. She had described it as being warned off. Sort of a, 'don't rock the boat,' kind of advice. She'd only gotten that after she cornered him and forced the issue. This seemed a curious response for a supervisor in a federal agency to take.

Nate arrived on time. Will recognized him from Amanda's many descriptions even though he blended remarkably with a deli full of beaurocrats. Will waved and caught his eye. Nate approached the table with his hand outstretched.

"How are you, Will, I'm Nate Tidwell, pleased to make your acquaintance."

"Nice to meet you, Nate, and thanks for coming," Will replied.

"My pleasure, I hope Amanda is all right. I was worried after your call and with her being off ill. Is she okay?"

"Yes, yes, thanks for your concern, this is a different matter. Why don't you get your lunch and we'll talk," Will suggested.

"Right," Nate made his way to the ordering counter and Will surveyed the street outside one more time in his absence. Everything appeared to be in order.

Nate returned to the table and the two men began to make small talk. Nate had to return to the counter to pick up his order and when he returned, Will began in earnest.

"Nate, I'm quite curious about this Gazelle issue that Amanda has mentioned. I understand from her that she has talked to you about it and I'd very much like to get your take on the whole matter. I guess I should tell you before you begin that I do a little free lance writing, you know, investigative pieces, and I'd like to dig into this thing a little further. What can you tell me about it?"

Nate was so shocked at the subject that he actually choked on his sandwich. "My God, Will, you get right at it, don't you? No wonder investigative pieces are your forte."

"Well, I've learned over time that directness is usually preferable to biowing smoke at people and tap dancing around issues, so what do you know about this?" He pressed.

"Give me a minute to think here," Nate responded. "It was awhile ago that Amanda came to me about it. My recollection is that she'd run across some document in one of the files that made some off hand reference to 'Gazelle' and she was looking for the meaning behind it. As I recall I looked through our agency databases for project code names and the like but didn't turn up anything pertinent. Honestly, Will, I don't think there was anything to this and I doubt very much that you'll find a story. I'd save my time if I were you. Seems to me I did."

Will continued to press and eventually Nate began to squirm. Like Amanda before him, Will became convinced that Nate knew more than he was willing to share. Will was more than a little bothered by the possibility of a link between a clandestine operation of some kind and a government employee. He hoped it wasn't what he feared.

Will left the lunch with no further information, only apprehension, but believed that he remained on good terms with Nate even though he had pressed him to the point of discomfort. He actually kinda liked the guy. He was convinced that Nate and Karla both knew more than he did and that connection continued to plague his thoughts. What could an assistant of the infamous Roland Priestly and ostensibly the man himself have in common with a civil servant of a federal agency? Will shuddered to think. As he made his way back across town and out to Virginia he ran a mental checklist. He just couldn't come up with a scenario that explained away the link yet signaled something positive. He was so deep in thought that he almost missed his metro stop.

Back at the apartment he related to Charles the essence of his meeting and the concerns that he had. They decided to put together an approach for the meeting with Charles' father. It was important to

Charles that they be clear about their direction and specific in their request. He didn't want to sit around and make nice with the man, just get in and get out. He was approaching the encounter with trepidation.

They still had several hours before the dreaded meeting and the two of them set about finalizing their approach. Given the fact that they were unaware of his father's connections, who they were and how much influence or clout they could exercise, they decided that they might as well lay the entire thing out to him and let him decide who or what could aid them the best. There was some risk in this but both knew that they weren't getting anywhere with their other methods and desperate times call for a little risk management. Will was convinced that his sister's life hung in the balance and it was time to call in the big guns. He had no idea the reality of that statement.

Chapter Eleven

Harry rose early by west coast standards but none of the participants were going to be in this time zone long enough to adjust so they had set the meeting for 6 a.m. which was a reasonable 9 a.m. in the east. He dressed in casual attire while he waited for room service to send up the ham and egg breakfast he'd ordered before retiring. He had not slept well, his mind raced in anticipation of the day's events. He was reminded of his childhood in Colombia and those sleepless nights awaiting Christmas morning and the hoped for deluge of toys. He was not stupid and he knew what Christmas was supposed to be.

Santa Claus had never come through for him, however. The jolly old man in the red suit and fake beard was always there on Christmas Day but he brought each child in the orphanage one carefully wrapped present and then stood there with a look on his face like he was waiting for the poor little orphan to show more appreciation. Harry had usually just taken his gift and walked away without even saying thank you. It was sort of his way of giving the finger to the whole system.

The children there had been cruel as well. He didn't fit with the others, his skin, his speech, his whole demeanor said, "Gringo." They had never accepted him, had taunted him instead. He had been at the bottom of a heap which itself was at the bottom of society. He knew he'd never be chosen but the hope wouldn't die in a young boy's mind. *Screw them all,* he thought, *I've become my own Santa Claus.*

Back in the moment, Harry picked up his scattered files and packed his briefcase for the brief trip to the 16th floor. He rode alone in the glass elevator and looking out over the tiny hotel lobby he watched life size people moving about below him turn into miniatures of themselves. The excitement of the day was upon him once more.

He strode from the elevator to the suite like a man who owned a better part of the free world. Hell, before this was over, maybe he would.

All of the others were right on time. After greeting the secretary and the senator who'd arrived on the same elevator, Harry turned his attention to Margaret Blanchard as she stepped regally into the meeting room. Everyone had to admit that she was a classic beauty. Dressed casually this morning in a dark burgundy pant suit highlighted by a colorful and flowing scarf, she lit up the room upon arrival. Her dark hair was down and carefully framed her oval face that was highlighted by gorgeous violet eyes that everyone who saw them dreamt of. The look was completed with large silver earrings that reflected the colors from her scarf. She was even more beautiful because she didn't try to be.

Harry knew that she was close to the senator, that they had come to Washington from the same area of the country and that he remained a mentor and friend to her. Something that was hard for her to find with her position, high up in the CIA. He was not offended when she gave him only a perfunctory greeting and headed for the senator with a warm and caring look upon her face.

After exchanging small talk about each other's trips to the west coast and all the other niceties Harry got the ball rolling.

"You all know why were here this morning so I'm not gonna bore you with a lot of introductory crap. Truth is we have to decide here and now how we're gonna handle this whole energy situation. I call it a situation because, as you know, the pressure is on the administration to come out with their energy policy sooner rather than later and, well frankly, there's just too much dickin' around goin on. This has to be resolved now, this morning, without fail."

The others in the room sat looking at the table like the answers to the Algebra test were written there.

Harry continued, "I think I have a plan here that can work for everyone, you know the old win/win kinda deal. I put together a packet for each of you and maybe if we work our way through that you'll get the idea. By the way, these packets will not leave this room, a shredder is provided."

"Unless one of you has some other suggestion, I'll start to make our way through what I'm proposing."

The participants continued their mute approach.

"Well then, the first document in the file is a broad overview of where I suggest this should go. I won't insult your intelligence by reading it to you but let me hit the high points. When I use the word, "I," in this context, understand that I am speaking on behalf of a number of the world's wealthiest and most politically conscious businessmen. I don't remind you of this as a threat but rather as a fact which you may or may not want to keep in mind as you consider the options." Harry wanted to hit them hard early on so they would understand totally who was driving this show.

"I know I'm about to hit you with a lot at the top but I want to be clear about where the money wants to go. As you know that is the single greatest driving force in world politics today.

"We need to break this down into short term and long range plans. I know that each of you is more than clear on our vision for world energy in the protracted future but short term has some problems that I propose to handle personally.

"First thing is this drilling issue. As you know the president's been all over the board on this and finally came down on the side of more drilling in the Arctic. He managed to get a weak sister appointed to the Interior Department and another for Environmental Oversight so the tree huggers will be less of a problem. That is to say, they'll always be there, of course, but they're not going to push anyone around in this administration. That's a non-issue. I happen to think drilling up there is a mistake but that's self-serving on my part so I'll leave it out of the mix for now. The main thing is that even if they suck the goddamn core of the earth out through that tundra and pump it directly into our cars it won't make a dent in this country's dependence on imported oil. Our annual consumption is growing faster than that dinky reserve can even think of handlin'.

"The next issue is just that, our dependence on imported oil, specifically that from the middle-east. The way we are operating now everyone has control of us except us. The United States of America has a proud history of taking care of matters that need our attention wherever in the world that might be. At the risk of being melodramatic, from the time of the Revolution and the tax on tea, no one has told this country what to do until we got ourselves hooked on foreign oil reserves. We're like some damn junkies who are totally dependent on their pushers.

"For me that's a good thing, as you know I make my money in foreign oil. I believe that we should be turning our faces toward Russia now and allying ourselves with them economically. We have friends in all sorts of business ventures who believe that the Arab nations have gotten saturated with our goods and products. Furthermore we continue to fight an uphill battle importing our culture over their religious objections. Our country and our culture are much more closely aligned with Eastern Europe and Russia than with Arabs. Businesses of all kinds see Russia and China as the greatest untapped markets. I believe we'll get the greatest support for this plan if we go the Russian route.

"Bottom line is this; I propose that we take Saudi Arabian oil off the table within the next 12 months. We can do so easily with a slight escalation of what is occurring in the Middle-East as we speak. The trouble with Palestinian plagued Israel and its inability to control these suicide bombers is never going to go away. Considering an energy plan which relies on some sort of peace accord over there is sheer folly. We have to be realists. If we agree that peace is not a possibility then it seems inevitable that over time the rest of the Arab nations will be forced to enter the melee. The lack of stability from that part of the world cannot be the driving force in American economics any longer. We've just been damn lucky that we've made it this far with only a couple of minor hiccups. The most fearful thing in the world is that this great nation not have the petroleum resources that it needs to fend off an attack of some kind and that it should be brought to its knees simply because we were too short sighted and refused to diversify to maintain our independence.

"Finally, and this is where you in this room come in, there is the small issue of Russia not being up and ready to produce at the rate of a million barrels per day.

"Here is what I suggest. We should finance this work for the Russians through direct subsidies to at least two American owned oil companies. We should also pay for building the pumping stations and pipe line to get the oil across the country and last, we take full responsibility for the construction of a deep water port at Murmansk to accommodate the supertankers needed to move the oil to the U.S. I have put together a group of producers who are more than willing to deplete their reserves to supply the extra oil that the country will need until Russia is on line."

Harry hesitated for a moment to give everyone a chance to catch up or catch their breaths. "I know this sounds like a lot to take on but I think you will all agree that it dovetails perfectly into the long range goals that we have for the world's energy resources. These efforts will not be wasted."

Unlike the secretary, Senator Hampton was unaccustomed to being the recipient of someone else's forceful ways. He didn't like the feeling one bit. He rose and moved over to the side table to pour himself a cup of coffee and as he returned to his seat he began, "Harry, you seem to have put together quite a package here. I wonder if it might be wise to give all of us a moment to peruse some of the other items you've included in the files before we continue."

He absolutely hated that this whole political structure had gotten turned upside down. He was convinced that the principles upon which this country were founded included the ideal that the political process, on behalf of all citizens, was intended to be paramount in our system. Business and more specifically, corporations were intended to be included in a second tier of this structure, they were, after all, a creation of the laws of the nation, not the other way around. He became almost fanatical at the thought that this hierarchy had been inverted so that business, rather than the politicians whom he was naïve enough to think engaged in open debate, ran the government. He simply failed to see the irony in this position as compared to what he did with Gazelle.

He hated Harry Axelrod and all those like him. The senator vowed silently that this arrogant man would pay and pay dearly for the sabotage which he perceived that Harry was attempting in this room.

The senator set his coffee cup down on the table and turned to Harry, "It seems to me that we may have a good deal of information to absorb and process. What you are proposing does not just take a phone call or two to implement. This would require a massive campaign throughout the legislature and probably months of debate. I have to say, I don't think you're being very realistic, Harry. Judging from the people that you've brought here you expect each of us to deliver a certain segment of influence in the matter."

"I don't really give a crap what you think, Senator. Maybe I wasn't clear. This is going to happen. It is our choice that you ride this train with us but understand one thing, if not you, then another. There is nothing so unique about you, or anyone else in this room, that this deal stands or falls depending on whether you're on board. There is a line of politicians waiting to get on this train and we're about to leave the station," Harry prodded.

The secretary finally spoke up, "Harry, I don't think the senator was taking exception to the concept so much as the implementation."

"If you don't mind, I'll speak for myself. I consider myself an orator and am quite able to put my own thoughts into words, thank you," the senator cut in.

As the meeting dragged on tempers got short and the air in the suite became heavy with tension and draped over them like an acrid humidity. By 11 o'clock and by mutual consent, business was concluded, papers were being shredded and cool but polite good-byes were passed around among them. Interestingly, everyone was in agreement around the long range plans, it was only this interim phase that had the group at odds.

After the meeting each of them went their own way. Harry was cheerful, the secretary was sullen, the senator was seething and the unflappable Margaret Blanchard, as usual, appeared indifferent. Each returned to their rooms taking their respective moods with them. Each had a different task before them and each of them knew that the powers that be would be expecting more consensus to have come from this gathering. Back in the bunker in rural Virginia the lone remote observer leaned over and switched off the monitor. He'd seen quite enough. He dialed into the meeting which was about to begin on the other side of the glass in the fortified conference room of the bunker.

It was close to seven when Senator Hampton arrived back in the DC area. Going into the district at this hour traffic was relatively light. The commuters who were outbound, however, were forced to creep slowly past the Pentagon and be reminded, once again, of the destruction that had been inflicted on this proud nation. Traffic looked like a kind of funeral dirge. It was almost as if they moved slowly by to show reverence toward the dead and wounded. He wondered how many times you had to pass this damage before you didn't see it anymore, didn't feel it.

After clearing security, his car pulled into the underground parking area of the Hart Senate Office Building and he took the elevator to the second floor. He would have a few moments in his office to take care of some urgent tasks before his meeting at 8. A few of his aides were still at work but his secretary, Marge, had departed for the evening. As was her habit, however, she left his messages in a neat stack next to his phone and a gentle reminder of his schedule was evident as it looked up at him from the seat of his chair.

He looked at the schedule again, wondering if by seeing it written it would make it more real. There it was at 8 p.m. a meeting with Charles Farino.

Senator Chastain Hampton felt a wrenching in his gut every time he thought of his only son, his only child. He had not been a father to the youngster and by the time he had awakened to what he had squandered, the boy had become a young man. A young man, he might add, with thoughts and ideas of his own and a reticence to have any relationship with him. The senator was glad that Charles had been fortunate enough to at least have a solid relationship with his stepfather but his heart literally ached at what he had lost. Did he dare to hope that Charles might be ready to bridge some of that distance?

He was determined to do whatever he could to bring him closer. He knew that he couldn't really hope for a second chance. The boy's childhood was gone and could never be regained but he hoped that something emotional could be salvaged from their physical bond. He wished that he were in a better mood. He didn't really have time to deal with this right now. Harry Axelrod had taken care of that, but it was important to him to be there when Charles called so be there he would.

Alone in his office now he began to make the calls that he hadn't wanted to make from the plane.

The first was to the secretary who, after leaving the meeting in San Francisco, had returned immediately to the Virginia countryside and the relative security of his bunker. The senator knew that he had the undying loyalty of the secretary but it was important to restore their rapport after what Harry had put them through. He had to make sure that the secretary understood completely what his assignment was and that the events of the day had not changed that in any way.

He also needed to reassure the secretary that his silence throughout most of the meeting was neither agreement nor cowardice but rather his choice not to engage the maniacal man in head to head combat where nothing would be gained. He simply preferred not to use that forum for a confrontation, but rather to continue the plan that they had set in motion. Lastly, he owed the secretary an apology for his curtness.

The senator's second call was to Roland Priestly. Roland was still sealed in his hotel room and was pacing around it like a caged lion when he got the senator's call. He had to sit down in order to take in what the man was saying. Roland was never surprised at the tactics that Harry Axelrod used but what he was hearing now was the height of arrogance. Roland listened carefully and made numerous mental notes as the diatribe continued. The senator's appointment arrived and he concluded the call abruptly.

Roland was left to reflect on this new information about Axelrod with the rest of the data that he was trying to make sense of. One thing was ultimately clear at the outset; Harry Axelrod was out of control.

Roland was all the more convinced that Harry was behind the whole Randi issue. It would make sense if he was this far into a patented, self-serving energy plan that it was wise to knock Roland off stride, which he lamented again had happened. Harry needed to get ahead of Roland and Gazelle on the proposal because, as Harry so often and eloquently put it, the first horse to the trough always got the most to drink. His plan had been effective in that he had gotten a very comprehensive plan together before Roland was hardly seated at the drawing board. He had been so involved in Amanda, Pharmaceuticals, Randi, and personal baggage that he had dropped the ball. He felt badly that he had let the senator and other members of Gazelle down but the pain of the past that he had never dealt with was debilitating. Well, he wasn't one to sit around licking his wounds. He had to get up, kick some ass, and take some names. Somehow knowing what the game was made it easier to do what he needed to do.

Roland took a mental inventory of what he now knew. That Harry was operating outside of Gazelle's interests, that he was trying to screw the senator, that he wanted to drag Roland and Gazelle into murder and assassination, that he was going after Amanda Chambers on his own, and finally, that he was greedy as hell. Roland's job was to use this against him and that was precisely what he was best at. He knew just what he needed to do and he had regained his focus.

Roland began by placing a call to Randi's cell phone number.

The secretary had assembled his best team around him. His orders were clear and he was about to put them into effect. These were his most trusted people or soldiers as he preferred to call them. He had held tactical meetings like this before but none with the potential consequences of this project. Secured deep in the bunker, the heavily reinforced briefing room contained limited electronics and some rudimentary video conferencing equipment. The team sat around one end of a conference table and watched the video and slides that were being projected onto the screen at the opposite end of the room. The secretary was standing and pacing around as he laid out for the assassins exactly what was expected of each of them.

After the team was fully briefed the three of them left the secretary alone and proceeded into action. Two of the soldiers departed for Bulgaria and one for Washington.

The unseen observer switched off his listening device and flipped off the switch that permitted him visual access to that room and others.

The secretary would have several days to wait before he would get confirmation that his orders had been carried out. To him, his soldiers were fungible. He had put his best on this project but if they were unsuccessful or met with some tragic end, there would be more to follow. He felt like his power was interminable. He left the conference room and fairly strutted back to his office. He stopped to fix a drink from the bar he kept in his locked credenza. He hiked up his pants and sort of shrugged his shoulders as though an extra rush of testosterone had just pulsed through him. He was already drunk on power.

He may not be calling the shots but that was only because those who were had a view of the larger picture and it was fine with the secretary that they had that responsibility. What he liked most and what he did best was the implementation. To him that meant wielding power and as long as he had the wide ranging latitude that he had now he couldn't be happier.

Will and Charles entered the senator's office looking like two little boys who were sent to see the school principal. Will observed a look come over the senator's face which was somewhere between pride and pain. It was clear to him that Charles' father had real feelings for him. He wasn't sure if it was love or not but surely the man cared for him deeply. The senator came around his desk and shook hands with Charles while embracing his shoulder with his left hand. It was an attempt to make the greeting more than just a cool handshake. Charles, in turn, introduced Will with the explanation that he was his life partner.

Will had never been comfortable with that term, but they didn't have much to choose from in today's world. It sounded so professional.

Others that he knew called their spouses, lovers. He hated that because it sounded casual and temporary, not at all what they had built. During their time together they had made a full and total commitment to each other. That term also played into the perception of the far right and other conservatives that their relationship was passing and temporary. Also, that it was sexual in nature and not supported by underlying love as their own, heterosexual and therefore, loftier, relationships were. In fact, they planned to spend the rest of their lives together and support one another throughout time. Will had decided to only operate the B & B on weekends in the summer and fall so that he and Charles could live together in Chicago. Will anticipated looking after Charles in their waning years, in the home, as he liked to tease him.

There were plenty of people who were obsessed by the physical part of love, Will often thought that it was they who were perverted; their minds apparently conjured up all sorts of sordid images to be put off by. Why couldn't they recognize that love was not restricted by the physical. Two souls could love one another. Not being allowed to marry, spousal terms were legally inaccurate. It was inherently unfair that the culture even refused to acknowledge their relationship in its language. The hue and cry which came from such thinking, he reflected, was that homosexuals wanted special rights. He griped to himself that he'd been paying taxes and supporting their life style his whole adult life but asking that he be given back the same rights that they enjoyed was asking for something 'special.' He wasn't asking anyone to change their religion. He just wanted the same civil contract with his government that everyone else had. Charles often cautioned him to let it go but he burned with an anger so far down inside that he doubted it would ever be released in this lifetime.

Will knew that the senator had been one of the moderates in the senate who had supported gay rights, as they had come to be known, and a woman's right to choose. He had been one of the supporters of the Employment Non-discrimination Act (ENDA) and had actively opposed the Defense of Marriage Act (DOMA) which had already been signed into law over his and others' objections. The close defeat of ENDA and the passage of DOMA had been a blow to same gender relationships since it took away legal recognition of such relationships by the federal government and left in place an employer's right to fire or refuse to promote an employee based on their sexual orientation among a multitude of other unfair policies.

Will would never understand what sex had to do with any of it nor how that was any different than discriminating on the basis of gender, religion or skin color.

He didn't deny that the moral or ethical foundations of our country had their roots in Christianity but somehow the Bible had been allowed to gain greater influence in government recently. Separation of church and state had been an overarching concept of the founding of this country so that all could worship by choice. Now the same language which once protected religion from government was needed to protect the government from Christian zealots who were trying to rob other religions of the same protection. Will would bet his bottom dollar that those same individuals didn't want to live under Shariah if Muslim immigrants happened to become the majority population.

Will had also admired the senator for an enlightened speech which he had given on the senate floor around the abortion issue. While the senator did not believe in abortion personally, it was all the more remarkable that he had understood this to be a two-tiered question. The first was the choice issue and the second was the abortion itself. Women should be given that freedom, he had said, no one was requiring an abortion only leaving the decision to the individual. It was up to the woman and man personally to determine based upon their particular religion or beliefs and was not the business of the state.

Banning that choice by law was another example of placing Christian beliefs into the law for other religions to have to live by. This did not afford everyone their freedom of worship. The legal freedom to choose placed the issue back in the individual church where it more rightly belonged. Those who thought it was murder didn't need to have one; it was as simple as that. Interestingly, most of those who believed that a right to make that choice constituted state sanctioned murder had no problem with the government putting people to death through capital punishment. The senator had been passionate in his delivery.

Reflecting again on these political issues Will thought he would never understand a culture which condoned murder and denounced love if it wasn't between the right two people.

Back in the moment, the senator was inviting his two guests to have a seat as he gestured at the area in the end of his office with a small sofa, easy chair and coffee table. The senator took the chair leaving Will and Charles to sit on the sofa. Will noticed that when they sat, they sank down while the senator seemed to rise above them on his throne. He wondered if this was planned.

Will was having trouble concentrating as the senator and Charles exchanged small talk. He was proud to hear Charles take control of the conversation.

"I'd like to get to the reason we've come to see you if we might," he began.

"Yes, of course," the senator replied.

Charles, with some assistance from Will, laid out the entire story.

The senator was visibly shaken by what he heard. Both Will and Charles, misunderstanding his emotions, were struck by the man's apparent compassion.

Chapter Twelve

Amanda awoke to the sound of birds chirping in the tree outside her room. There was something else, an odor, as she came around she realized that she smelled smoke. Not the cigarette smoke that normally wafted up and in her window from the sidewalk café below but serious, heavy smoke. Something was on fire. She shot out of the bed and began yelling for Alex who met her in the hallway. They both used their shirttails to cover their mouths and noses as they made their way down the front hallway. Alex always left the key to the door hanging in the lock so he was able to open the door quickly. When he did, they were hit with a blast of heat and an overpowering, breath-choking smoke. They began to descend the four floors through heavier fumes. Amanda was having trouble not coughing and when she did, the smoke choked her even more. She thought her eyes were going to burn out of her head they stung so badly. She cracked her shin on something on the landing, a trash can perhaps, she stumbled and it took all of her effort to keep from falling but she knew if she did she'd likely be trampled or lose contact with Alex. It was dark and she could not see where they were going.

There were others on the stairs but she couldn't see them. She just kept moving and the seemingly unending stairs kept taking her down. She clung to Alex's hand and pushed on determinedly in pain and panic. As they burst from the door and emerged onto the street below they joined a large crowd of occupants from the building. Everyone was standing in the narrow street staring up at the top of the building where flames licked out of the fifth floor.

Residents were talking excitedly and Amanda had no clue what they were saying. Alex left her standing among the group and went over to speak with neighbors. When he came back he put his arm around Amanda and thoughtfully explained that the group was concerned about everyone getting out safely. They were taking an unofficial inventory of who was home, hoping that everyone was present and accounted for. Nearly everyone was dressed only in their nightclothes. Some hugged children and some hugged pets. Still others stood in unbelieving shock gaping at the building and shivering from the night and nerves.

Alex had been relieved to see that Mrs. Standovic, a widow who lived alone on the third floor, was seated in one of the plastic chairs from the coffee shop across the street. Everyone looked shocked and sad. Some were crying.

A fire truck had made its way into the street but with the number of cars parked on the sidewalks could not get close to the building. Several of the firefighters were asking those in the crowd to move their cars. Of course, no one had keys. Some of the men started opening doors of the unlocked ones and doing whatever they could to move them away from the front of the building. She saw some of the heftier young men actually lift a couple of the small cars and set them aside.

Eventually the firemen entered the building with hoses in their arms and began the ascent up the stairway that Amanda and Alex had just come down. Although it was only minutes before the men started putting water on the source of the flames it seemed to her that it had been a lifetime and the fire certainly moved much faster than the men. Alex still had his arm around Amanda and he gently moved her down the street to the corner where there was much less excitement and confusion. As they looked back at the building they saw only the inferno.

Roland had invited Randi to meet him at the small, intimate bar that was just across the street from the Railroad Station and on the edge of one of the world's premier shopping districts. As expected, she was twenty minutes late. Roland was cautiously nursing his scotch when he saw her. He would probably never stop reacting to her beauty. He waved to her from across the room and stood as she approached the table he had carefully selected in the corner and away from the window.

As she approached he watched every step she took in the tightly fitted skirt with its side slit up to mid thigh. It was the kind of thing that drove a man crazy and it was perfect for her sensuous ways. She moved her head to one side to toss her hair out of her face as she joined him.

"Good afternoon, Roland, I was so pleased to get your call after I missed you the other evening. Perhaps we had some mix up," she began. "Whatever, doesn't really matter as long as we finally meet again."

"I apologize for the confusion, Randi and thank you for joining me tonight. May I say you look lovely as usual? That is a very striking outfit and you do justice to every inch of it," he continued. "What can I get for you to drink?"

Roland motioned to the waiter who responded immediately. He too was having trouble taking his eyes off of Randi. The young man nearly tripped over himself taking and delivering her order. Randi played him like a harp and looked up at him as she cooed her appreciation for the service. Roland thought the lad might fall into the potted plant as he left their table and made his way awkwardly back toward the bar.

Randi continued to come on to Roland but he was back in his work mode and totally in control of the situation. He still wondered what had come over him that he had allowed himself that slip in his composure. Well it didn't matter now. He knew what he must do and Randi was a part of his plan.

Roland continued to field her little innuendos, double entendres and outright offers and eventually got her to calm down and focus. It seemed like the only way she knew how to interact but once you got her past that she was a bright young woman who could concentrate on what was put before her.

Roland began his proposal, "Randi, I need to make contact with someone who is deathly afraid of me. It's a young woman, a little older than you perhaps who is being protected by a young man. Both of them fear me and if I were to go anywhere near them they would run like rabbits. I considered using my assistant for this but the woman also knows her and would have the same reaction to her that she would to me. I'm interested in paying you further for your services if you will agree to make contact on my behalf. There should be no danger initially but I must warn you that if they learn that you are working for me they may get defensive, even to the point of using violence. Have I piqued your interest?"

Randi looked at him over the top of her tinted, Coach eyeglasses and allowed a mischievous smile to play across her face. "Why Roland, I think you know that I'd do about anything for you. How much are you suggesting?"

Roland couldn't stifle the laugh, "You're so predictable, I like that."

They continued the conversation until they had reached a mutually agreeable sum and the required facts had been given to Randi to facilitate her making contact with Amanda and Alex. Finding them had been the easy part. With the connections that the senator and the secretary had a couple of phone calls could provide the location of almost any US citizen traveling outside the country on a passport or visa. It was becoming increasingly difficult to get lost on this planet.

The more difficult part of Randi's assignment would be sufficiently gaining the trust of the two and convincing them that what she was proposing was a viable alternative to their predicament. Roland's name would have to stay out of it so the sell job would be all the tougher since Randi would have to present herself as working for an anonymous source. It was either that or tell them that she was working with Will or someone else that they would trust. Roland had considered this but was concerned that Amanda was in touch with Will often enough to know that would not work.

This young man, Charles Farino, was a possibility but he was working closely with Will so the same held true for him. Roland could think of no one else whose name they might use to get Amanda's confidence at this point. She was like a rabbit on the run and the least little thing would make her take off again. Gaining her trust was the key to everything and Roland knew that this plan could only work if Randi could pull that off. Everything was riding on her shoulders, beautiful as they were.

Roland left Randi at her hotel with their strategy complete. Randi would leave for Sofia in the morning. He was certain that she had the requisite skills to pull this off but only if her heart was in it. He was not certain if she had been around Harry enough to know the difference between when someone was being fingered for a hit and when they were being located for more legitimate purposes. If he had been sure which way he would get more buy in from Randi he would have told her any lie to get her committed to the cause.

Harry arose feeling even cockier than usual. He was proud of how things had gone in San Francisco. He took extra pleasure in the fact that the old man hadn't had a thing to say. He basically just took the shit Harry threw at him and sat there like a coward and let it drip off him. A malicious grin spread across his face forcing him to shave around it.

His conversation with Nate Tidwell echoed through his memory as he continued to watch his facial contortions in the mirror. He had ordered Nate to get more information on what the secretary was doing around the energy plan. It had been a stroke of genius to get Nate on the payroll when he did. He had become an integral and trusted member of the secretary's team. The secretary used him for cover within the agency whenever he was engaged in the "off books" work as it had come to be known. He also included him in some of the less tidy work around the edges. He knew that they both had enough dirt on them to keep them in Club Fed long into the next century. That was what made them vulnerable. That and money.

The secretary conveniently directed some of the projects of Gazelle from his fortress of a bunker or he could do the legitimate work of the government without oversight, thanks to the current climate of paranoia. Harry thought that the country hadn't seen this level of fear of foreigners since the McCarthy witch hunt hearings in the 50's.

The secretary was also, as it turned out, able to take freelance work for the benefit of his own personal coffers. Harry liked the way the guy worked. Under other circumstances he could have been a real player, the ruthless type. As it was, he was one to be managed carefully. One thing that Harry had learned about people like himself who dealt from the bottom or middle of the deck, was that they were squirrelly as hell. The man's loyalties today would likely be different from those of tomorrow. He followed one of two things, either cash or power. The guy was in love with both.

Harry knew from previous experience that the secretary would do the bidding of the senator unless someone more influential beckoned. He would hitch his wagon to the rising star and wouldn't let go under any circumstances, of that he was certain. Harry had recruited Nate to keep an eye on the secretary's actions. He had to keep the advantage in this energy market. He would use every edge possible to stay one step ahead. Nate had already reported that the secretary was deploying several of his men to take care of the Amanda Chambers trouble once and for all.

It seemed the senator himself had lost patience with the way Gazelle was dicking around and not getting anything done. It was a loose end which needed to be cleaned up sooner rather than later. The senator, knowing of Roland's reticence to engage in assassination, felt that he was moving too slowly and had decided to go around him. Harry assumed it was his way of taking the pressure off his fair-haired boy.

Well, in any event, the wheels were finally in motion and Harry thought that maybe he should call off his dogs. If Roland was moving on the matter, however slowly, and the senator had put the secretary on it, with Harry's man that made at least three. Hell they'd blow the woman and her family right off the planet. He didn't want them stumbling over each other but on the other hand; experience had taught him that if he wanted to make sure it got done, he'd have to do it. He decided to leave his orders as they were.

Amanda pulled back the curtains on her window at the Radisson Hotel. She had taken a room there after the fire and Alex had gone to stay with a colleague who lived just a few blocks from his previous apartment. The estimate was that the residents would not be back in the building for at least 6 months and most thought it would be closer to a year since the wrangling about costs and the cause of the fire were slow to get underway. That would all have to be resolved before the construction would even begin. In the meantime Alex was looking for another place to live.

Amanda wondered why, if she was not staying with Alex, she was there at all. To her it didn't seem she was any safer in a hotel in Sofia than she would be anywhere else in the world, including Washington. There at least, she reasoned, she could be assisting in the resolution of all this. She felt like she was at loose ends and getting nowhere. She hoped that Will would call today. Maybe he would have something to report that would encourage her.

She was really glad that he had decided to bring Charles in to help him. Besides another mind, he was another set of eyes and ears and additionally, he was great support for Will. She felt badly that she had dragged them into this but she was also more convinced than ever that she had been right to pursue her instincts. Something surely was amiss in or around her agency and she saw it as her civic duty to either cure it or expose it.

The thought burst into her head in a flash. She wondered why she hadn't thought of it before. She couldn't wait to talk to Will. She checked the clock and tried to calculate what time it was in Washington. Deciding that it didn't matter she dialed Will.

He answered promptly and was pleased to hear from her. She had already informed him about the fire and the resultant move. He was concerned that she was staying by herself but felt secure in the fact that no one knew of her whereabouts. He had cautioned her to stay in the hotel and off the streets as much as possible but knew that it was not reasonable to expect her to stay in hiding completely. It was always about managing the risk.

Amanda shared her idea with Will, "If we can get just one competent journalist to go along with it I think they will be rewarded with a sensational exposé before this is over. We need someone with a strong reputation who would be willing to go out on a limb with us. We don't have much concrete to give them up front but if we had such a person looking into it we could finally gain some strength against these bullies." She hadn't given Will a chance to get a word in.

"Mandy, Charles and I have come up with a plan that I'd like to let work before we do that. I'm not saying it's a bad idea, in fact I like it but I think it's a last resort. We had a very successful meeting with Senator Hampton last night and both Charles and I came away feeling that he can and will help us. He can't get back to us before tomorrow or the next day, he said he'd call, but it's very encouraging. The man has connections that we can only dream about."

"Oh, Will, that is good news. I wish you'd talk my idea about the press over with Charles though. I'll try to be patient and hope his father can help. Will, I'm really getting a little stir crazy here, cabin fever. I'm so glad I didn't think I could live here with Alex. It would have been a mistake." Amanda was surprised to hear those words coming out of her mouth. She hadn't realized that the recognition of that had come to her. She loved Sofia and found it a tremendous experience but she knew that living the rest of her life here was not something she wanted.

"Mandy, enough, I think we should hang up now." Will was alarmed that she had made reference to where she was. They still weren't certain if the fire had been an accident or an attempt on her life. Perhaps it didn't matter if they were careful on the phone if they'd already discovered where she was.

"I'll call you as soon as we hear from Charles' father. Please take care and keep your eyes open. Stay as close to Alex as you can. I love you," he concluded.

Amanda put down the phone and began to draw a bath. She had decided to stay in through the morning and read. She was due to meet Alex for lunch over at the university. It was only a five minute walk down Tsar Osvoboditel Boulevard, sometimes known as the yellow brick road, and through the underpass to the University on the other side. He was hoping to have information about a new apartment by then and perhaps they could get her moved out of the hotel and into the relative safety of a neighborhood.

Amanda settled in with her book and bath to pass the morning.

The secretary's soldiers sat smoking at a table in the Irish Pub off the lobby of the Radisson Hotel. They looked like most of the men around them, dark hair, stubble on their faces, dark slacks and shoes and the requisite black, leather jacket. They spoke openly about their plans. The taller one cursed the other one repeatedly for his failed attempt with the fire.

"Who ever heard'a startin' a fuckin' fire on the top floor of a building, Mr. Stupid? You were supposed to go into the storage room over the garage. You remember hearin' that before? What kind'a idiot doesn't know that anyway? Eh?"

"I told you it was locked from the inside, I ran out'a time. You rather I got caught jimmying the door or prying it off its hinges?" The shorter man tried to launch a defense. "What daya care anyway? We just torched a building that isn't gonna matter in this town one way or the other. You act like you had part ownership in the place." He tried to put the pressure on the other man.

"Hell, there's no against being stupid. Only thing that pisses me off is that you take me down with you. The boss never listens to excuses so why should I? I gotta mind to take you out along with the mark. Doubt you'd recognize her if she sat down here with us. Have you even looked at the file?" He continued. "Never mind, you do understand how this is supposed ta go down, don't you? We'll check out the spot this afternoon but the hit is tomorrow for sure. You clear?"

"Yah, yah, I got it already. Meet ya back here at 1:30."

Their meeting concluded and they left in opposite directions to blend in with the crowds bustling along the narrow streets.

Randi had been fortunate with her flight reservations at the last minute and she had secured a seat on a Swissair flight out of Zurich that morning. She had about a three hour flight to Sofia. She would be there before noon and would be able to make contact today she was sure. This was going to be quick money she was sure.

She was unfamiliar with the city and had secured a reservation for herself at the Sheraton Hotel in the downtown business district. Before she could make it up the stairs of the hotel a gypsy accosted her with a child in her arms and a doleful look on her face. Randi shook her off and continued into the lobby. After checking in she learned that the University was a distance from her hotel so she secured the services of a car and driver.

She decided to meet with Alex first as she thought that she could reason with him best. Not only was he one layer removed from the fear and jittery nerves facet but he was a man, her strong point. She reasoned that if she could gain his confidence he would be the one to convince Amanda to listen to reason. She knew that gaining their trust would be the only way to move them to where Roland wanted them. She was uncertain whether she was leading these two little lambs to slaughter or safely out of harm's way. Well, she didn't really care, the price was right; she would be well rewarded either way.

Her next step was to secure an appointment with Alex for this afternoon. After some difficulty with phone numbers she reached him at his office at the University. She told him that she was a colleague from Italy who had read one of his published articles and that she needed desperately to meet with him to clarify an issue before she continued her research. She was only in town for a short time and would be very grateful if he could make a few moments for her today. Randi's pleading ways had reached Alex and he agreed to see her at 3 after his afternoon lecture. He gave her directions on where to find him at the school.

Randi hung up and began unpacking and preparing mentally for the afternoon's task. This just might be even easier than she'd thought. He was so nice she'd been able to manipulate her way into his schedule with a mournful appeal.

While Amanda was lunching with Alex, the secretary's soldiers were once again scoping out the underground in front of the University. The taller one had convinced himself that their homework was complete by assuring himself that his partner was briefed and ready. They had studied the photos of their target and gone over the plan repeatedly. They had chosen this area because all of the foot traffic in the area was funneled through here and while they were submerged in those tunnels they were like ducks on a pond. The shops and casino in the underground created a visual diversion and he noticed that hardly a single person looked up. Additionally, he observed that the casino was pumping its music into the tunnel area to attract attention muffling most of the sounds from the street above. The location was nearly perfect for their task.

The traffic on the busy streets intersecting overhead provided just the right amount of cover for them. They would raise no suspicion by leaving the car on the sidewalk with the surplus of others parked there. There was an overgrown planter next to the railing which had swollen into a 7 foot shrub. Its unruly branches would hide the weapons. The construction in progress behind them created enough noise and visual confusion to keep most passersby at bay. They would make the hit from the sidewalk above and escape among hundreds of other vehicles that looked just like theirs, except for the mud on the license plate of course.

Everything needed to be carefully choreographed and the taller one was almost compulsive in his planning of the details. Even the time of the hit was critical as they needed to make their escape complete at the airport, approximately twenty minutes away. Everything depended upon the mark sticking to schedule. They had made reservations on three different flights out of the country so they had some flexibility. Depending on when they finished their work they could take the next flight out and its destination would dictate the remainder of their itinerary. They would be going either to Zurich, Munich or Vienna. It didn't matter to them as long as their exit from Bulgaria went smoothly. Everything was in place at each of those destinations to make their escape complete. As the two men stood on the street smoking and watching the flow of pedestrians below them they went over their precise plans again.

About twenty minutes into their meeting the taller one suddenly stopped talking and jabbed his partner in the ribs with his elbow as he gestured toward the ramp on the side of the underpass closest to the University. As the shorter one turned to see he watched as Alex and Amanda made their way down the ramp and across the wide tunnel toward the stairs that led to the Radisson Hotel on the opposite side.

Alex had his hands jammed into his pockets and his shoulders hunched against the cool spring air. He wore only a dress shirt and sweater vest to fend off the chill. Amanda had her arm through his and in contrast to him wore her red, slicker raincoat which she had purchased after arriving in Sofia. It had a convenient hood and since she couldn't seem to keep up with an umbrella it had kept her from getting drenched by the frequent spring showers. She wore it almost everywhere she went. She kept meaning to do some more shopping but hadn't gotten around to it. The two of them were deep in conversation and walked along briskly with their heads down to stay alert to the uneven walkway.

"Just like clockwork," the shorter one remarked. "These two are so predictable we could set our watches by them." The taller of the two had scoped it all out the day before. He could see exactly how it would play out in his mind.

"Yes, my friend, we shall. Tomorrow we meet at the parking lot at noon, ready the car and time our drive over here so that we park the car here on the sidewalk by 12:20. We can start our visit and smoke fest here on the bridge by 12:25. That should give us just 10 minutes to wait for the moment of our friend's fate."

After walking Amanda back to her hotel Alex returned to the campus for his afternoon lecture.

Back at the Sheraton, Randi was busy choosing just the right outfit to wear. She finally decided on black, high-heeled boots, black gabardine pants topped with a beige, bulky knit sweater and a plaid scarf thrown casually over her shoulders. Her face was framed by large, gold hoop earrings. With everything as calculated as she could make it, Randi headed out for her appointment with moments to spare.

As she rode along the streets of Sofia she was struck by the blend of the architecture around her. This city was proud of its position at the crossroads of world trade over the centuries and what had been left behind in the buildings surely spoke to the fact that every major culture had visited here at some time. The Russian Church and Cathedral, the Moorish influence, the Greek columns, and the crumbling, Fourth Century Roman edifice which she could see out of the window of her hotel room spoke of the visitors from the past. Their occupation by the Turks or Ottoman Empire while not invisible was somewhat less obvious architecturally but it had surely left its mark on the culture otherwise. Finally, there were the drab leftovers of the Soviet era.

Upon arriving at the University Randi went directly to Alex's office. She found him in a small, dimly lit room on the second floor of the main building. The afternoon light making its way in through the aged window glass played host to tiny particles of dust that seemed to be suspended in mid-air. Rows of books clung tenaciously to shelves next to him and magazines in various states of disarray threatened to avalanche down on him from behind. The small wooden desk behind which he sat looked ready to give in to the decades of gravitational pull to which it had been subjected. Several books lay open on top of it and the small reading lamp shone down upon them like sunshine on well oiled tourists on the beach. Randi had to throttle an urge to sneeze just looking at the scene. Alex rose politely and seemed to stumble slightly as his reaction to her appearance spread involuntarily across his face. She assured herself that her work was half done.

Randi held out her hand to him as she greeted him and introduced herself. "I'm afraid that I have obtained this appointment under false pretenses," she began. She found that as usual once a man saw her he could forgive her deception.

Randi pressed her advantage and began to work her charm.

The senator paced uncontrollably about his office. He found himself in one of the greatest quandaries of his life. He was reminded of similar feelings some twenty years ago when he had made the choice to leave Charles and his mother and make his way into the heady world of politics. They had become a burden to him then and to find the success he sought he had to rid himself of that weight. The decision had not been easy but as a young, ambitious social and political climber there seemed at the time to be only one road open to him. He had gotten what he wished for but once there he turned around to see that the things that he loved most had been completely cut from his life. It was then that he had made his awkward attempts with Charles.

Looking back on that time he realized that he had always been the impatient sort. He couldn't wait for things to develop over time. When he decided on a career in politics he did what was necessary to make it happen as quickly as possible. He reflected on his behavior and thought that it was no surprise that he found himself today wrestling with the uncomfortable outcome of making things happen on his time frame. *Maybe*, he thought, *you don't always know what's best.* He knew that wasn't true. He wondered how many other great men over the course of history had wrestled with a similar dilemma.

Confronted again with the choice between his ambition and his son he could only think, *Deja vu.* This was not the kind of decision that he could rely on his advisors for. This was a choice based solely on emotion. He had to consider his feelings and weigh those against all he had worked for, all he had achieved. Or did he? Why couldn't he scratch this one task and find some way to resolve the issue of Amanda Chambers without Charles knowing that he was behind it? Perhaps he could find a way to neutralize her that would appease the hungry wolves including the quiet man in the background who was driving the entire process. In his head he knew that the decision was bigger than that. He wanted his son as much as he wanted his success. He realized that neither alone would ever satisfy him completely.

He called for his assistant to bring him the file hoping that something in his notes might spark a resolution.

Over the years he had gained a reputation for heavy hitting and hard driving. He had never minded this perception because in many ways it made his work easier. Some of the more faint of heart just stepped aside and let him steam roll by. Those who called his bluff raised his anger. He saw himself called to a destiny of greatness and nothing or no one had loomed larger than that mission.

Underneath it all he was a deeply troubled man. He didn't particularly like what he had become. It had started slowly with the creation of Gazelle. It had felt so good to finally be able to move some of the work along. After years of fighting an uphill battle in the legislature he had found an outlet for his frustration and a way to bring some very valuable programs to fruition. The funding had not been a problem with Gazelle's backers and many throughout the country had benefited from his vision. It had been an easy step from Gazelle to get into bed with Harry Axclrod, the financiers and finally with his true superior. It had only taken one expensive, well drafted program that he couldn't get through the Congress to send him into their lair. It had turned out to be a one way door.

While the scope and impact of the programs had gotten larger and more global in their reach the cost of doing business with the big money of the world had come at a higher and higher price for him. While he was not exactly a man who revered power he understood that to lead at the magnitude that he intended and to direct policy on a global scale required a supremacy to which others bent. *It was not what he sought but what he was born to,* he thought. He was troubled by the control which money continued to exert within nations and upon the world stage. It was a not so small loose end that would need to be dealt with. In the meantime he needed those backers who shared his vision of a greater world. The people deserved all his efforts, nothing less.

Chapter Thirteen

Randi's meeting with Alex went longer than either had expected. While he was open to the idea of a resolution to Amanda's peril he was of course, extremely cautious. It didn't help that she had to work on behalf of an anonymous person. She sensed that Alex trusted her and believed what she had to say but he knew instinctively that it would take more to convince Amanda than it had to win him over. He was just more open and reasonable by nature.

Randi was patient and continued to talk with him in the hope that the longer she was with him the more he would trust her. She moved the conversation off into less volatile areas and tried to put him at ease. By the time they decided to part she was feeling fairly confident. Alex agreed to sleep on her proposal and to set up lunch for the three of them the next day. He felt strongly about her ideas and agreed that he would put them to Amanda before the meeting to try and soften her to the notion but he made no promises.

Randi left the meeting feeling optimistic. At least she hadn't been thrown out and she would have an opportunity to meet with them again. Riding back to her hotel she leaned back on the seat, closed her eyes and reflected on tomorrow's work. Women were always more trying. She laughed at what a sexist she was. She wondered why most people thought that men were so much more analytical and less emotional. She found it to be just the opposite. It just depended on what emotion you were referring to.

She was exhausted and needed a drink and a good night's sleep to confront tomorrow. She found a Mexican restaurant on the plaza outside the Sheraton and ordered a taco salad and a Corona. She decided, all things considered, she liked her life.

Amanda rose to another day of sunlight streaming through her window. She decided that springtime in the Balkans was very pleasant. The temperatures varied, the sun gained warmth with each day and the intermittent showers bathed the environment in fresh smells. She had breakfast in the hotel dining room and returned to her room to take on the day's tasks. She had promised herself some shopping this morning and Alex had asked her to join him and someone he wanted her to meet for lunch. She set out to make her preparations.

She decided to walk the distance to the shopping mall downtown near the Sheraton. It was quite a distance but the morning was pleasant and she hated the Sofia taxis. Her shopping spree proved fruitful and before she realized it the time had slipped away. She was so proud of the light, spring jacket that she'd found that she decided to stop by and show it and her other acquisitions to Alex before she returned to her hotel.

She found him ensconced with his books in his second floor office. She was bubbling with the enthusiasm that he loved so much as she shared with him her precious purchases. He was particularly fond of the spring outfit that she'd selected and he told her how seductive she looked. An awkward moment passed between them. Amanda felt her face flush as a charge of sexual energy coursed through her. She quickly gathered up her purchases, made her exit and hurriedly made her way to the hotel to get dressed for their luncheon meeting.

She was so flustered by what had exchanged between them and so distracted that she paid little attention to where she was going. Just yards from the entrance to the hotel as she hurried along the crowded sidewalk making her way around parked cars, other pedestrians and the prolific construction zones she stepped into a sink hole in the sidewalk and twisted her ankle. As she sprawled on the cobblestone her packages sailed through the air and landed several feet in front of her.

To her amazement a bellman in front of the hotel observed her graceless dive and came over to retrieve her and her packages. Her ankle began to swell immediately.

Settled in her room with her foot up in the air on pillows and a huge ice pack resting on her ankle she called Alex to tell him that she couldn't make the lunch. The concern in his voice was touching as well as comforting and he promised to come over and check on her. It was then that he noticed that in her rush to leave she had left her precious raincoat behind.

Alex had no way to reach Randi so he couldn't cancel the meeting with her. He decided to wait until she arrived and then explain what happened. Somewhat out of character, Randi arrived on time. Alex told her what had happened to Amanda and suggested that they go ahead and eat as planned. He could ask her a few more questions that were troubling him and he could pick up Amanda's favorite shopska salad and take it to her at her room. As they prepared to leave his office a cloudburst descended. The oversized rain drops hammered the old windows and the room went even darker from the lack of sun. Randi lamented that she had not brought an umbrella so Alex offered her Amanda's overused, red raincoat with the practical hood.

On the way to lunch Randi was happy to have the hood that Alex had told her Amanda so prized. It had kept her dry for the several blocks they walked to the small restaurant on Shipka.

Alex and Randi spent a leisurely lunch talking further about Randi's proposal. Alex had thought of little else since Randi arrived and he was anxious to get Amanda out of danger if at all possible. He wasn't sure why but he trusted Randi. Toward the end of their lunch Alex ordered a take out for Amanda. The two of them rose and Alex intended to walk Randi back to his office where her car waited. Instead she suggested that she accompany him to the hotel where she could be introduced to Amanda. Randi was anxious to gain the woman's confidence and playing nurse for the afternoon might go a long way toward that end.

Alex agreed and they set out for the hotel. The rain had let up but a light mist persisted cloaking the campus in stealth like fog and encouraging Randi to keep the hood up on the raincoat as she and Alex entered the underground and headed toward the hotel. They were talking enthusiastically about the potential plan for extracting Amanda from Sofia when the shots rang out.

The single soldier sat in a vehicle outside Amanda's apartment in Arlington where Will and Charles were having a lazy Sunday morning. He had been studying the layout of the apartment, the building and the neighborhood over the last two days and had decided on his plan. He was a man who thought that explosives were the ultimate weapon. They did the job, took most of the evidence with them and created their own diversion for a secure escape. He felt totally in control when he used them as he could even choose the form of detonation; time delay or remote device. Much of his information about the apartment and the building had come from a colleague who had been working as a substitute guard/doorman in relief of the regular man who had suffered an unfortunate accident. His ability to move around the building and have access to the apartments by passkey had been invaluable.

He needed one small piece of information to make his plan complete. He was almost ready to go. Perhaps as early as this afternoon, he reflected. He liked to get it done as soon as was practical. Waiting too long often raised more and more alternatives and the whole process could get tangled up in trying to make it too perfect. Paralysis by analysis he called it. He had seen it happen too many times to real pros. You wanted just enough information to be thorough without getting yourself tied up in a knot of knowledge.

Tim, his colleague inside would be diagramming the utility hall and vacant apartment on the second floor at this moment. Once he had that it was just a matter of preparing the little bundle in the trunk of the car and making the insertion. *It would be a good day's work*, he thought.

As he watched the building he saw Tim approach the front lobby window, remove his hat and scratch his head. He put the hat back on and walked over to the lobby entrance leading to the parking garage below. That was his signal.

He turned the key in the aged, non-descript Toyota and waited for it to respond. He had considered leaving it there on the street and taking public transportation to get around until the hit, but the little old crate responded easily so off he went. The last thing he wanted was for this job to fail due to a faulty tool. He should have gotten a better car, he chastised himself. That was a stupid place to scrimp; causing himself unnecessary worry and stress. That was the problem with the people he worked for, they wouldn't just pay the bill and trust the man they'd hired. He was given a set sum for expenses so the cheaper he could do the job, the more profit he could realize. God, that was so government. *He needed to broaden his client base,* he observed to himself. He drove into the parking garage where Tim waited and put the window down to receive the paper.

"You got that area blocked off to parking like I said?" he asked curtly.

The man nodded once affirmatively.

He responded with a return nod and drove off. With everything in place but the time and the exact placement of the explosives, he headed over to the mall to have lunch and spend some quality time with the diagram he'd acquired.

This would be a good time to check in with his employer and finalize the time so he picked up his cell phone to punch in the number. Glancing down at the phone after turning it on, he found the display was dead. He'd forgotten to charge the damn thing. He hated these gizmos. He wondered if the old Toyota's cigarette lighter worked and then, realized, he hadn't brought the adapter. His phone was useless. He decided to call from a pay phone at the mall.

He blended in with the rest of the diverse crowd as he enjoyed a lunch from the Chinese buffet in the food court and watched the families strolling along and enjoying a Sunday afternoon at the mall. Their behavior was so American. They weren't really shopping and they weren't really socializing, just kind of moving along through the commercial environment each displaying their particular brand of strollers and clothing and each silently passing judgment on the others the same way they would by comparing cars out on the interstate.

He was not particularly surprised at the state of the American family. The politicians and other pontificators could find all kinds of things to blame this on but the truth was that they just didn't interact with each other any more. They were too caught up in competition, including on their kids' soccer fields. He saw no irony in the fact that he, a hired killer, was passing judgment on the way American families lived their lives.

With less than two hours to go before the hit he found a pay phone and called in. His report was brief and gave only an estimate of the time, never any details. He neglected to report that his cell phone was inoperative. No further instructions were given so he decided to return to the Toyota and finalize his preparations. He needed to go over the final diagram and be exact in his calculations of the placement before heading out to implement his plan.

The senator sat alone with a glass of scotch in his hand and looked out over the city whose power he coveted so deeply. From his window he had a full on view of the White House and the Washington Monument beyond. It was one of those days where the sun slides in and out between threatening clouds and the skies intermittently spew sunshine and showers. He felt like his mood changed almost directly in response to that rhythm.

He was distressed at himself that he had not been able to make a clear cut decision around this dilemma but he knew that at a minimum he could buy some time. He placed a call to the secretary.

"Where are we on this Chambers deal?" he inquired.

"I just had a report in on the Washington detail and that's all set for this afternoon," the secretary responded. "I'm afraid the news is not so good from the foreign front," he continued.

"What the hell does that mean? Wait, did you say this afternoon? We've got to call off Washington. Do you hear me?" He began to sound frantic. "Call it off immediately."

The secretary responded, "Of course, I'll call it off." He went on, "We got the report from the team abroad and all seems to have gone well including a successful extraction." He continued. "The disturbing thing is from our assets in place over there. The news is reporting some confusing information about the victim."

"That doesn't make any sense to me at all. What do you mean confusion about the victim? Is she dead or what?" The senator felt his shoulders sag and his gut knot up. His face was aflame with anger and agitation.

"Yes, yes, she's dead. It's just that the locals are reporting a different identity. I'm not sure what's going on. I know this is confusing. Can I just get back to you when I know more?" he pleaded, "I'm waiting for a call any minute."

"Yeah, fine, but most important and hear me clearly on this. The Washington job must be called off. Please repeat that to me," the senator demanded.

The secretary said, "I'll call off the Washington job at once." He was anxious to please after the possible foul up on the Bulgarian end.

"One more thing," the senator continued. "Call me to confirm that this has been done."

"Yes sir," came the brief response.

They hung up and the secretary dialed the cell phone number of his soldier in Washington.

While he waited, the senator continued to search his mind for a resolution to this problem. He may be able to buy a little time with the wave of his hand but calling off this entire chain of events was not going to be so easy. Eventually, those with much more to lose than he would step in and take over. He was not at the top of this food chain, as much as he hated to admit it. If it were totally his call to make he'd have no problem knowing what to do. Such was not the case, however. He pondered possible alternatives and it seemed that everything that he came up with had some unworkable aspect to it. He finally hit upon an idea which he thought had some merit.

He decided to call Roland in from the field and seek his counsel on the matter. Often when the two of them got their heads together on some issue the effect of the total brain power was greater than the sum of the two minds. He knew that his emotional involvement was clouding his thinking and bringing Roland's more calculating approach just might help. If not, it was always good to be able to talk to a trusted friend during troubled times. He was surprised to hear himself admit that. It seemed like a weakness, a vulnerability which he had not heretofore acknowledged. He needed friends, he needed family, he needed both Roland and Charles in his life. He had to admit, he needed love.

While he waited for a return call of confirmation from the secretary on one line, he placed a call to Roland on another.

As usual, when the senator called, Roland asked no questions but agreed immediately to return to Washington to meet with him. The senator hung up from that call and began to wonder why he had not heard back from the secretary. He resumed his pose at the window and with it his atmosphere of agony around his future with his son.

Amanda found herself once more observing the earth out of the window of an airplane. After the traumatic killing of Randi who everyone realized was supposed to be her, Will and Alex had quickly moved to get her out of Bulgaria and back on the run. She knew that both men were badly shaken by the murder. Poor Alex had seen that woman shot right off his arm. Amanda shirked from the images that conjured up in her mind.

She looked out the window to try to make the mental pictures go away. She watched the coast of France slip past the edge of her tiny window leaving only a few islands to stand between her and the expanse of the Atlantic. She settled down into the seat to try to get some sleep. *At least*, she thought, *I'll be back in America, even if not at home.* Realizing just how deadly this game was she had been somewhat more pliant in agreeing to the trip to Los Angeles.

Amanda cleared customs at Hartfield International Airport in Atlanta and seamlessly transferred to her flight to California. Only a few more hours and she could settle in to the comfortable bungalow belonging to her aunt in Long Beach. She couldn't imagine that anyone would think to look for her there. She'd thought the same thing about Bulgaria however. Her ankle was still tender and it was beginning to swell again after sitting for so long on the airplane. She reached down to rub it and the reality that a fluke injury such as this had saved her life flowed over her consciousness leaving a flood of murky emotion. She felt like someone had just stripped off her armor and any other device that she had to protect her. She felt naked, exposed and totally vulnerable to her surroundings. For a moment she was that little girl again. Riding in on the tail of that sentiment was the charging steed of anger. She was disgusted every time she thought about how these people were trying to steal her life. She was determined that they would not succeed. She would see them and their wicked ways revealed.

The secretary was getting frenzied in his attempts to reach his Washington soldier. At the same time, reports about the hit in Bulgaria were coming in and the dread that the job had been badly botched descended over him like the curtain of night. This was turning out to be the day from hell. He would try one more time to reach the soldier and if he was still unsuccessful he would have to call the senator back with news which he didn't want to deliver.

He didn't know why he wanted it called off and he didn't care. His job was simply to give the order. The job he loved. Whether putting the hit together or calling it off he got the same charge of excitement. Someone's life was in his hands. He was affecting whether they lived or died. Just a word, a nod and it was done. Finding himself unable to exercise that power now, was creating a performance anxiety which could leave a power monger feeling impotent. He didn't like it one bit. He found himself absolutely infuriated at the soldier whom he could not reach.

Finally, in a state of near panic, he called the senator.

"Sir, I don't know what's going on, don't know what to say, I can't get a hold of the man in Washington and we are within an hour."

"Jesus, what do you mean you can't get a hold of him? You have to." He screamed into the phone. "The man has to be stopped immediately. Stopped at all costs!"

"He's not answering his phone." The secretary continued.

The senator interrupted, "Do you have any idea how stupid that sounds? I can't deal with this right now, stop him or else!"

The secretary was at a loss, he couldn't believe this was happening, why didn't they have a backup form of communication in place? Well this wasn't the time. He needed to do something fast. Finally he blurted out the only thing that he could think, "I could have him arrested." he proposed.

"Christ, you're a piece of work in an emergency," the senator yelled. "I've got to make another call. Get on it, do something to make this stop," he warned.

The senator threw down the phone without cutting off the call and picked up another. He dialed the number that Charles had given him. He needed to get him out of that apartment, out of danger, at the moment if nothing else. He held the cell phone to his ear and listened to the empty ringing on the other end as he made his way down the hall and anxiously pushed the elevator call button to get to the garage below. Gratefully, on a slow day in the building the elevator arrived at once.

Hearing no answer on the phone, he disconnected the call and hit the redial. He was becoming more frantic by the moment. Suddenly his son's life was in his hands. That somber understanding crept slowly across him leaving in its wake the grim reality that within minutes his son could be dead. Dead at his hands. He was on the brink of hysteria but couldn't allow himself to go there. He needed to remain rational.

His thinking was clearer now and once in the car he told the driver to head for Arlington as fast as possible. At the same time he used the car phone to contact the secretary again. He needed an address he realized. He knew only that Charles and Will were staying at an apartment in Arlington and vitally, he had Charles' cell phone number.

After reaching the secretary, he gave the address to his driver and admonished him to move faster. This had become a bona fide emergency. A light rain had been falling and cars lined up one behind the other snarling themselves into a clog of traffic with a stranglehold on the entire District. Singularly they resembled snails making their way slowly toward undefined destinations; together they were a centipede with no head and no apparent bearing. His usual irritation at the inconvenience of too many people in the same place at the same time had, today become a lightning rod for all his frustration. He wanted to jump out of the car and start throttling people one by one. The rhythmic slapping of the windshield wipers like the ticking of a clock heightened his sense of time and the ringing sound coming through the cell phone continued in his ear. He found he was now getting angry with Charles for not picking up.

He never got an answer on Charles' phone. His ostentatious limousine looked out of place among the emergency vehicles as it rounded the corner onto Amanda's street just moments after the last of the charred bodies and burn victims had been removed from the building and the ambulances wailed their way through the rain slicked streets like keening mourners.

Under other circumstances Harry might have laughed at what he had just heard. His man had stood casually by and watched as the senator's well-ordered machine took out Roland's carefully placed operative. What a comedy of errors except it wasn't particularly funny. Of course, while all this was going on Amanda Chambers had headed out to parts unknown. At a minimum it would take a couple of days to find out where that was.

Harry wondered sometimes why he had to stay affiliated with such a bunch of bungling losers but he knew that the answer to that was the perception of legitimacy. To attain the heights that they intended they needed a front man such as the senator.

He thought again at how the man had cowered in front of him at the meeting in San Francisco. Gratefully that was not the way he presented himself on the national or global front. He was not intimidated by any politician and among world political thinkers he simply had no equal. He was definitely the right man for the job but he never could stand up to money. It was his Achilles Heel.

Harry had been pleased with what he had learned through Nate of the actions that were being taken from the bunker on the energy plan. Of course there was the official energy plan for the benefit of the administration and then there was the plan which was being implemented directly from the bunker itself. The politicians and the press wrangled and argued this way and that. Everyone but the White House dog was on the Sunday talk shows with this dribble and that sound byte. They sounded like they'd all been implanted with the same computer chip.

He was thankful that Gazelle was there to get the work done or at least to get it started; it would take something more than Gazelle to really get it finished. He shuddered to think if they'd had to wait for all this haranguing to be over before even beginning a move. The U.S. would be so far back in the bus that they'd never even see through the windshield let alone get to the driver's seat. He was continually amused that the American people could delude themselves that this system worked. He knew what really worked and that was why he would control it.

He was pulling together the biggest cash cows from all corners of the globe and once their little group sat atop the syndicate things on this planet would finally begin to change. In the meantime he had to concentrate on getting the Russian oil producers up and running. The bunker was taking steps to ensure that Saudi Arabia would soon be out of the picture. He'd heard reports already this morning that one of their princes had announced that they had reversed their position of allowing U.S. military strikes from their soil. *Hang on,* he thought, *we're in for a hell of a ride.*

He moved to his desk, removed his suit coat, rolled up his shirt sleeves and prepared to delve into the day's chores. He was still a ways from attaining his dream team. There were key members of the world community that needed to be brought into the fold, who needed to be more forward thinking. With money came a level of responsibility and that was what Harry relied on as he put his proposition to those whom he sought. He began to work his way down his list of potential patrons.

Will shook off any further attention by the attending nurse in the emergency room. His upper back and the backs of his legs were the most painful but the medication was already taking affect and trying to make him succumb to an unwanted sleep. He kept trying to find out where Charles was, how he was. He wasn't sure if they weren't hearing him or if they were just refusing to respond. The veil of fog was fighting to envelope him like down. He tried to throw it off and was becoming belligerent at the indifference to his pleas for information. The last thing he remembered that night was the sharp intrusion of the hypodermic needle in his buttocks.

He awoke in the early morning to the intermittent hum, beeping and clatter of a hospital ward. He began his inquiries immediately. After a final and thorough going over by the doctor on duty he was released from the controls and confines of the hospital just after 9 in the morning. He went directly to the information desk in the lobby and inquired whether Charles Farino was a patient there. Thank God he was. At least he wasn't dead.

Will had not known what had happened until one of the nurses in the emergency ward had finally talked with him as she changed his dressings and treated his wounds. He knew that there had been a tremendous explosion. He had taken the trash down to the receptacle that was in the rear of the building and down the driveway a few feet from the garage. It had happened just as he was holding the lid up on the dumpster. A powerful blast that seemed to crush him into the front of the trash bin and seconds later he was hammered from the rear apparently by chunks of cement, blocks and other fast moving debris. He wasn't sure if he'd lost consciousness but if he had it hadn't been for long. The next thing he remembered was the shrieking of sirens and a fireman stooped down asking him where he was hurt. From there it had seemed a quick ride to the hospital. He hadn't been able to find out anything about Charles who had remained upstairs in the apartment.

He felt great relief that he'd found him in the hospital. He asked the kind faced woman at the desk for his room number.

"Are you family?" came the dreaded reply.

Will and Charles had known enough friends who had been through this. In particular men who were dying of AIDS whose families were called from all corners of the country to make decisions about their care. Family who in many cases had nothing to do with the person because they had rejected them the minute they'd learned that they were gay.

He desperately wanted to see and comfort his spouse, his domestic partner, his life partner, his lover, whatever the hell these people wanted to call it. He wanted to be with and care for the person whom he loved above all else in this world and who, he knew wanted him there. He wanted to hear from the doctor how badly he was hurt, what was the diagnosis? The prognosis? What could he do to make him better? To make him more comfortable?

Will thought for a moment that he might start screaming. Instead he was going to have to stand here and have an inane conversation with a well meaning volunteer. Will was determined to try not to begin with a chip on his shoulder.

He began with a calm and he thought, thorough explanation of why it would be appropriate for him to be allowed to see the patient.

Getting nowhere he moved away and went to the administrative office where he asked to see a member of the hospital staff. He waited patiently for the emergence of a middle aged woman wrapped tightly in a business suit with sensible shoes and her hair yanked viciously into a bun on the back of her head. Her reading glasses were perched precariously on the end of her nose and a retainer chain dangled down from the bows so she wouldn't lose them as she undoubtedly had done with any flexibility that she might have once had.

He began his story and his plea anew. Failing to gain permission for a visit or for knowledge of the room number he asked to be advised of his condition. He could be told only that the doctors had listed him as critical. Nothing more could be divulged to the public, only the family, she rubbed in.

Will worked to remain calm through his mind numbing ordeal. He knew that his best chance of gaining access to Charles was to stay polite but firm. History and friends' stories had taught him that. He took time out to spend time in the men's room vomiting as he lamented ever getting Charles involved in this. He wondered if he would ever be able to forgive himself. *Enough self-indulgence* he cautioned, *move on with the mission.*

By mid-morning Will finally found himself hopefully awaiting a meeting with the attending doctor. He fidgeted and worried and tried not to let his mind go all the places it was trying. He was nearly frantic at the thought of what Charles' injuries might be. He wanted desperately for his imagination to be an exaggeration. The pain medication was beginning to wear off and Will was unable to sit. He paced restlessly around the small waiting room in the critical care unit.

After what seemed an eternity a young doctor came into the room with his hand outstretched. He was dressed in those ugly green scrubs. At least he had a matching mask dangling around his neck like a bad choice in accessories.

"Mr. Chambers, I'm Dr. Gardner, I'm attending Mr. Farino. I understand you've had a bad couple of days." He smiled warmly and maybe sympathetically at Will who began to feel more optimistic.

"Off the subject, how are your injuries today? May I?" He reached around and pulled Will's polo shirt up to observe his back. "Ah, yes," he observed. "Sorry, I took the liberty of also looking at your chart before I met with you. How's the bump on your head feeling? Any headaches?" he continued.

"Doctor, if we might get to Charles, what can you tell me? How is he?"

The doctor interrupted, "Yes, I'm sorry, I get too clinical. Look, I did my surgical residency at Mt. Zion in San Francisco and I'm sympathetic to what you've been through this morning. This hospital, given its location still has some rather archaic attitudes by our standards. Thank goodness the medical profession is getting the idea that families don't all look alike. I'll have no problem taking you to see Mr. Farino."

He began to escort Will out the door and down the hall. He talked as they walked, "Mr. Farino has some very serious wounds and at this time his vital signs are unstable leading us to list him as critical. There are some medical decisions that will have to be made, probably today. His father seems ready to do what has to be done. Are you on good terms with him?" the doctor inquired.

"His father?" Will asked.

"Why, yes, Senator Hampton, he's been with him throughout the night. I believe he just left a couple of hours ago, the demands of his work, I guess."

"My God," Will exclaimed, "Charles hardly knows the man. They don't have a relationship. He left when Charles was a baby."

Will was unaware as he bemoaned the unfairness, the real irony of the situation. The man who had nearly killed Charles was taken in as a loved one trusted to make life saving decisions for him while the one whom Charles loved was excluded as an outsider.

"Nevertheless," replied Dr. Gardner, "he will be the one empowered to make decisions, I'm afraid it's the law. Unless of course you've drawn up Health Care Powers of Attorney?" he asked.

Of course they had kept meaning to get that done. They had even gotten as far as getting the name of an attorney. It was just one of several things on their legal list. They needed to have a Living Trust so they wouldn't get socked with extra taxes upon the death of one of them. They needed to convey property to each other but had learned through the sad stories of friends that there were tax implications to that as well. There was so much that had to be handled and paid for separately, more of the stuff that was seen as "special rights." He didn't need to go there right now.

"No, not yet."

"Didn't think so," said the doctor. "Doesn't usually get done till after something like this." They stopped walking and the doctor turned toward Will, "We need to finish talking about prognosis before we go into his room. He's in a coma right now and we're happy to keep him that way for now. I won't go into a lot of medical jargon. The main thing you need to know is that he will have to have surgery on one of his legs, probably this afternoon. There is a remote possibility that amputation could be required. Also, we have a neurologist coming in to evaluate his head injury further. We may have some decisions to make after hearing his recommendations as well. Bottom line, Will, can I call you Will?" he asked.

Will nodded.

"As I was saying, it comes down to the following priorities, stabilizing his vital signs, surgery on the leg, neurological evaluation and at the same time trying to avoid any infection from the burns. The good news is that his injuries are primarily localized. The bad news is they are in his legs where circulation may not be quite as good. I'm afraid he took quite a wallop on the head. There's also a percussive hearing problem we're pretty sure that's likely to clear up in spite of our medical actions," he smiled warmly at Will.

"It could have been much worse, Will. He's got some fight ahead of him but I really think he'll be all right. He's going to need you and a great deal of time and patience."

"I'll be here for him," Will responded somewhat tearfully.

"As will I," said Dr. Gardner quietly. The two men shook hands and Will followed the doctor into Charles' room.

Amanda left LAX on a Super Shuttle bound for Long Beach. After two trips around the airport the driver had sufficient passengers to make the trip worth while so he turned south on Sepulveda Boulevard, went through the tunnel under the runway and literally elbowed his way into the southbound flow of the 405 Freeway. He made his way over to the carpool lane with a practiced expertise and once there, he put the pedal to the metal.

She watched the south bay curve slide by in a blur. She saw the Goodyear Blimp straining against its anchor ropes which clung tenaciously to the big balloon to keep it near the ground. The van slowed slightly at the intersection with the Harbor Freeway and they resumed their wild ride to the southeast flying past the oil fields of Carson and Wilmington. They slowed again at the interchange with the Long Beach Freeway and then sailed uninterrupted to the Lakewood exit where the Long Beach Airport shared facilities with the large Boeing factory.

Fortunately her's was the first of the Long Beach stops and she was more than a little grateful as they pulled up in front of the gray stucco with white trim which she recognized from her childhood visits. *The wildest ride at Disneyland*, she thought, *would never compete with a ride on an L.A. freeway with a local*.

She was greeted warmly by family whom she'd not seen since her mother's funeral. Her mother's oldest sister had always been special to Amanda and they seemed to find a comfortable rapport every time she visited. It had never taken more than a few hours for the two of them to be at ease with each other and Amanda looked forward to that feeling now.

It had been a terrible two weeks. The latest news about the attack on Will and Charles only served to convince her more completely that this thing had moved out of their league and it was time to enlist help from other sources. Her idea about the press still seemed like a good one but she didn't really have anything concrete to give them. Even if she'd kept that document it would be suspicious at the most. The idea that the woman had been shot wearing her coat and then the bombing at her apartment building sounded like something out of a pocket novel. Even if she convinced them that these were both attempts on her life it would never lead to the real perpetrators. Somehow she needed to expose them. They got away with working behind their carefully crafted veil of secrecy that insulated them from their egregious acts. It would be difficult to make the connection but she just had to make it happen. Especially now she needed to play a greater role.

She hoped that she would be here at her aunt's house only over night and then she would proceed on to her safe house. From there she would be able to continue her work on Gazelle. She knew that Will would be involved with taking care of Charles and except for a little help around the edges he would be unavailable to assist in the search for the truth.

She felt that wave of nausea sweep over her at the thought of Charles and Will being injured because she had involved them in this. On the other hand, it was not she who committed these horrible acts. It was becoming more important and more and more personal that she expose them. She was absolutely furious at the games that were being played with the lives that she loved, maybe with the lives of all Americans, she didn't know for sure but she was determined to find out. *They didn't know who they were messing with,* she thought. She'd find a way to bring them down. She had to. If nothing else, she was tenacious.

By the next morning Amanda was feeling somewhat recovered from her long flights but the reality of the near miss on her life and the lives of Will and Charles hung over her like the blade of a guillotine. There was this horrible anticipation of impending harm. Harm to her and to those she loved most. With that her thoughts turned to Alex. What must he be experiencing after what happened to him. The physical proximity of the death and the fact that he'd been talking to this person as her final breath was drawn so unexpectedly. She wished she could talk to him but it was impossible at this time.

Thoughts of Alex led her to the moment in his office before she'd hurried out. She thought about what it was that made her forget her coat. That surge of feeling for Alex. Was it just memories of times gone by or did she still have feelings for him? She shook off the thought. She didn't have time for that. Not now or ever. He didn't fit into her life and she certainly didn't fit in his. It was time to push on and put those feelings behind her. Whatever they were didn't matter because they weren't going anywhere.

Will was dreading the meeting with Charles' father. He was on his way to the hospital now and Will wasn't sure how the two of them would get along. They'd only just met and now found themselves tied together around the challenges to Charles' life and the quality of it. Will was certain that he knew Charles better than anyone in the world and would know best what Charles would want.

Further, their futures were irrefutably tied together and what affected Charles' life affected Will's. As a consequence, he felt that decisions around his well being were his to make, not the senator's. The law, however, saw it differently. He was worried about how the man would act, whether he would respect Will and his opinion about Charles' health issues. All of this bound Will and the senator together whether they wanted to be or not.

He guessed he'd have to call him Senator. It was so cold and unfriendly but Charles called him that so Will felt inclined to do the same. The sun had just slipped behind the late afternoon clouds as it made its way toward the horizon to bring closure to the day. The senator entered the room where Will sat quietly holding Charles' hand and talking to him in a low and soothing voice. He had just gotten back into his room from the recovery area following his afternoon of surgery.

"Sorry, didn't mean to intrude." He whispered as he caught the door to close it quietly behind him.

"Not at all, Senator, I was just trying to keep him focused on the present. Keep him from slipping too far away. Dr. Gardner suggested." Will kind of stammered.

"Will, let's step outside for a moment. I think we should talk, you know, away from," he gestured toward his sleeping son.

The two men walked along the corridor with no destination and no sense of direction. The senator began, "Will, I want you to know two things up front. I love my son and respect what you and he have together. That said the rest, I think, will take care of itself. We both want the same thing for him."

"It would appear so, Senator."

They stood in the hallway and talked at length about the information that the doctors had given them. They both agreed that the news from surgery had been good. They'd been able to do the necessary repairs to his feet and legs without amputation. The next few days would be critical as to whether they might still have to go back and remove the lower left leg. The news from the neurosurgeon was more complicated. They agreed after some discussion that they needed to have one of the medical professionals explain the results to them both in laymen's terms. The senator agreed to arrange the meeting.

Their business was conducted in an amiable and efficient manner and Will thought that he sensed a change in the man from the time they had met in his office just days before. There was something, an underlying sadness or perhaps some preoccupation. He wasn't sure if it was his concern for Charles or just that he was a busy man with a lot on his mind. Will dismissed it and returned to Charles' room with the senator. He was relieved that they were going to work together in an atmosphere of mutual respect and concern for Charles. He liked the man, he decided.

Will was relieved that he had talked with Amanda and she had arrived safely at their aunt's house in California. He needed to feel that she was out of harm's way because he'd switched his energies to Charles. He knew Amanda wouldn't sit still so he had reassured her again that Charles' father was helping. When the time was right he would broach the subject with him again. For now, Will just needed a little time to concentrate on Charles' most immediate and critical issues. He wished that he would wake up and talk to him.

"Will, I'm sorry to disturb you but I must be leaving," the senator had affectionately put his hand on Will's shoulder. As Will turned from the bed to acknowledge his departure he was again struck by the trouble that the man wore on his face and in his demeanor. Will wondered for a moment if he wasn't being told everything.

After Senator Hampton's departure, Will sat quietly holding Charles' limp hand in the darkened room and thought about the quiet evenings they'd spent just being in each other's company. Sometimes there was small talk, sometimes heated discussions of heady issues and sometimes just quiet togetherness. Will cherished those times when there was no need for talk. Just an easy presence. He longed for that. He prayed they'd have it again. He loved him so deeply. They were so much a part of each other. They could finish each other's sentences, sense one another's moods and seemed to have an uncanny awareness of what the other needed. Yes, they could even press each other's hot buttons. Will needed Charles to comfort and cheer him right now. The far reaching tentacles of despair were clutching at him. He felt alone without his soulmate.

Senator Hampton held the phone to his ear as he rode through the recently rain washed streets of the district. He spoke precisely and deliberately to the secretary about the horrendous harm that had been done because he did not have control of the situation. He demanded that the man get off his rear and get an effective system in place. He needed safeguards, backups and above all he needed to maintain a great deal more control over the operatives than he apparently had now. This inefficiency could not be tolerated in the future. He was in complete agreement that you had to hire professionals and it made no sense to tell an expert how to do their job but total control could not be relinquished. Too much was at stake. "There is a great difference between delegation and abdication," he admonished.

He was anticipating his meeting with Roland and hoped that would bring some clarity to his thinking. His stomach was in a knot and his body ached from the tension which sat like granite in his muscles. The near death of his son seared through his mind like a torch. Horrible images, scorched into his memory moved on and off the stage of his consciousness like the final act of a heavy tragedy. He felt like he was out of touch with it yet it encapsulated his life. He tried to regain perspective.

The sons of others had been sacrificed for such causes and surely there were more to come. This, however, was like some strange and twisted whim of unseen gods. It was the right hand not knowing about the left. It had seemed surreal as it had sadistically unfolded. He tried to shake it off and concentrate on the future. On top of all this he still had the consideration of that bizarre meeting with Harry in San Francisco to deal with. What could the man have been thinking? He was going to have to reel him in and regain control of this entire project. They weren't out of this yet and there was still a very long way to go.

He was back in his office, sipping a scotch and wading through the stack of reports and messages that Marge had left on his desk when Roland arrived. The men hugged affectionately and made the appropriate inquiries about each other's health and the like. The senator poured Roland a drink and they went over to sit in the comfortable furniture at the more casual end of the office. They each sat where they could devour the view of one of the world's most amazing cities and began to catch up on recent developments. Roland began by reporting on his experience with Randi and his suppositions about Harry. The senator began by pretending to listen while assessing his own position.

He heard Roland's voice penetrating his haze of preoccupation. Apparently he had posed a question which had not been responded to. "I'm sorry, Roland, what did you ask? I'm afraid I let my mind wander."

Roland asked again, "What was it you wanted to see me about?"

"Ah, yes, this is my meeting, isn't it?"

The senator looked like he had aged ten years in the short time since

Roland had seen him in London. He wondered what was weighing on him so profoundly.

"Can we talk some more about your suspicions around Harry Axelrod? I've just sat through the strangest meeting with the man and frankly I'm puzzled by his behavior. There was something troubling in your words, tell me again what you just said."

"About Harry, I just said that I feel like he is trying to push Gazelle and perhaps me in particular into engaging in assassination. I think he'd like our hands to be as dirty as his but since that's not possible he'd like to push us over a line. One from which we cannot return. I wonder if he's setting us up for blackmail or a double cross."

The senator continued his withdrawn demeanor but Roland could tell that he was pondering this issue. Perhaps folding it in with what he already knew from his dealings with Harry. In any event, Roland knew from experience that the wheels of analysis and most likely reason were turning inside his head and Roland would eventually learn what he was thinking. He also knew from their history that the senator would be straight with him and would tell him what he knew.

The quiet in the office was becoming tense as the senator continued to stare at an undesignated spot somewhere off in the universe and Roland sat quietly waiting for their exchange to continue. After an interminable time the senator rose, returned to the bar to freshen his drink and moved leisurely over to the window where he gazed out over the sights of Washington. The silence continued.

Roland knew this man better than almost anyone else in his life and he had never seen him so distant, so preoccupied. Whatever was eating at him, whatever he was contemplating had far reaching implications. Of that Roland was certain. He decided to make use of his time by making some notes to himself for errands he needed to run while he was in the states.

As suddenly as he had left, the senator returned. He came back to the chair he had previously vacated and began to talk to Roland as if he had just arrived. "Are you pleased with how things went in Zurich?" he asked.

"Very pleased, Sir, I believe all is in order in the pharmaceutical area for now and I'm ready to focus on this energy issue. Frankly, with the distractions we've had I feel a little behind. Now that I'm back here I can get it back on track with a few days of uninterrupted work."

Roland felt that his mentor was back in the present and ready to focus on whatever had brought him here.

"Let's talk about energy, Roland. Brief me on where you are with it."

As Roland laid out his very conservative approach to making the United States less dependent on foreign oil the senator's mind was moving down dual paths. He always had to analyze information for Gazelle while at the same time considering the implications for his more important agenda. Then before he spoke he had to determine the effect they had on each other. He would be relieved when he would only have to serve the interests of one organization.

He heard Roland saying, "Thus we could facilitate the growth of these newer emerging economies and their tenuous work forces. The economies that we have targeted for growth would be much more attractive to foreign investment with their newly found energy sources."

The senator interrupted, "We may need to rethink that list, Roland. The world is changing every day and my recollection is that we put it together almost a year ago. Some of those countries have had political upheaval and changes in power since that time."

"Yes, of course we will revise it before implementation as I'm sure there are even more changes to come." Roland was amazed that the senator was so distracted as to comment on a step so totally out of context. They were barely into the formation of this plan and he was commenting on implementation issues. What, he wondered again, had this man so totally unfocused and unnerved.

Roland waited patiently hoping that this brave man would soon choose to share with him the source of his heavy burden.

Harry concluded his day by checking two more names from his list. It had been a very good day indeed. With a sheik and a sultan on board his sphere of resources was looking extremely impressive. He still had to return the call to the prince; he'd left that for last on purpose. He needed some time to develop the approach he would take with him.

Alone in his office he leaned back in his plush desk chair and took a long drag on his cigar. Coupled with the scotch in his right hand this had become one of the luxuries of the good life that he looked forward to at the end of his day. He realized that if the make up of his consortium didn't change he was ready to move forward with the plan. He didn't need any more than he had now. Success was within their grasp. He savored that idea with his feet proudly propped up on his desk. Life just didn't get any better than this. The years of hard work were about to pay off in big, big dividends.

He opened the top drawer on the right hand side of his desk and removed a remote control. He pointed it at the opposite wall and pushed the activation button. A hum could be heard as a huge map gradually revealed itself and covered the large area adjacent to the conference table. The map was adorned with various colors and Harry began to take an informal inventory of the contents displayed.

He pushed another button or two and he got an enlarged view of the Middle East. Saudi Arabia had been given the dreaded red color while a more courageous shade of yellow swept the curve along the north east edge of the Mediterranean and encompassed most of the "Stans." Pakistan, Afghanistan, Uzbekistan, Kahzitstan and so on it went around and through Turkey. He pushed another button and the display moved north into Russia which was painted a luscious shade of green for more reasons than one. As he moved around the planet South America was a patchwork of various colors. Africa and China remained an unremarkable shade of gray, as did most of Indonesia and Australia where some red and yellow had been spattered around leaving it to look like a whimsical artist's canvas.

They had carved up the world to their own liking and were close to implementing a plan that would alter the life of its residents forever.

The Consortium of Planned Energy (COPE) would be the ones to determine the balance of world power. They had determined who would produce oil and who would produce alternate forms of energy.

Everything had been allotted and allocated even down to wind and hydro-electric power generation. Who would be the recipients of this energy and how much each would get was the subject of another electronic version of the world map.

The most important map to Harry was the one that represented the income that would be derived from each of the consuming nations and whether they represented a positive or negative income. On that map there was a quotient assigned to each country representing the profit or loss factor that could be expected under the current government. This map drove home the point that some changes would have to be made. As they stood now they would not meet their potential and that was unacceptable to those who had so carefully crafted this plan.

"Yes," he mused aloud, "Some changes must be made." As he stared at the map he calculated what it was going to take to get a high profit quotient in as many countries as possible.

The words, "Regime Change," had taken on a nasty meaning in the world. It was no longer an easy sell in the legislature, in the United Nations or in the minds of the public. Fortunately, the current administration was totally on board with it but that would do him little good. While the matter could be debated to death, hashed and rehashed, it was up to him to simply make certain that things moved forward. He had little concern over ruffling a few feathers on the world political stage. If changes in administrations in some locales were what was needed it was exactly what would be done. They had learned from the Saudis and OPEC that the club of control stayed in the hand of whoever controlled the desperately needed energy sources. Never again would they allow such a substance to control world superpowers and, by extension, the world itself.

His pragmatic side had also taught him that to be kept in creature comforts required some places to have a negative flow, particularly in those countries with extremely inexpensive work forces. It was just the natural law of things that some places had natural resources and some places didn't. He knew that there were countries that would always be an economic drain in that respect but he didn't mind paying for goods and services and by God somebody had to do the work. The trick was to crank those positive quotients as high as they could while keeping the negative numbers as low as possible. He gave no consideration to the possibility that those countries with little in natural resources had been raped of them by his predecessors in greed and often by their own corrupt governments. Compassion was a foreign concept to the ambitious Harry Axelrod and his associates.

Leaning back in his chair he took another sip of the scotch and another long drag on his expensive cigar as he let his mind float off to the future and all the promise that it held. He may not be on his way to being the official ruler of the world but he was in bed with the man who was. He knew that whoever controlled the energy set the agenda and by damn that would be them. He was on top of the world. Success was within reach. All that remained was to bring the consortium together to finalize the "Energy Stabilization Plan" and to initiate the controlled flow of the energy under it. He loved the irony of it; he had always wanted to have ESP.

They were ready, at last, to move into Stage Two which included the world summit meeting on energy resources which was scheduled to be held in Bangkok in June. The timing was perfect.

He picked up his secure phone and punched number one in the speed dial. He couldn't wait to inform the real power behind this project that his mission was met. The man at the other end could hear the excitement in his voice and thought how right he'd been in sizing Harry Axelrod up for this project. He was still that little boy who wanted very much to succeed and be recognized.

Chapter Fourteen

Morning came unnoticed in the confines of the bunker. Constant temperatures and the lack of natural light made the hours meld into one another like the timeless waves of a restless sea. Day and night could not be distinguished and therefore did not exist. There was a rhythm to the energy of the workers and obvious changes in personnel, but other than that, time seemed to move at its own pace and crept by with the stealth of a stalking cat.

The secretary sat at his desk and pushed buttons on his new and complicated phone with all the frenzy of a panicked man trying to report a fire. He was distraught at the way things had been handled or more appropriately had not been handled during the botched assassinations. He was determined to make amends. He was bringing some of his key people together for a major restructuring that would assure that this kind of disaster would not be repeated. He was the one with egg on his face and it was not a feeling he relished.

He continued to fiddle with the buttons on this electronic contraption and express his exasperation at his lack of sophistication with this digital technology. He knew he was far enough down the food chain to be easily replaced if he was not effective and he was not going to see that happen. He was as determined about that as he'd ever been about anything. This was one trip that he was not only going to make sure he got to take; he was going to take it in first class. He was unwavering in his commitment to be a part of this new order.

The powers that be had made it clear that he had unfettered control of setting up the security system which would ensure that their programs were carried out without interference and would also protect them should the need arise. He was faced with a large responsibility and he was grateful that the organization was supportive in every way, including financially.

His plan was to structure a hierarchy over which he would rule that would have at least two tiers of management. He knew that he needed to distance himself from the assassins, but the most difficult task was going to be finding the right people to use as his lieutenants. They had to have street savvy with a touch of arrogance to make them leaders. Above all he had to find the most loyal among his group. He didn't want to forget that he needed someone directly under him who had the ability to organize and oversee the hands on work. He chuckled to himself at the visual of that. He was about as good at this as he was at using this modern technology and he had just proved his lack of expertise to the senator on his last assignment.

His real job was as a secretary in this administration, after all, and he was fortunate that his under-secretary didn't need him at all. This new line of work was taking some time for him to get established. He had a lot to learn about the technical end but the administration and organization would always prove to be his strength.

They really did need to put some fail safe procedures in place that would give him tighter control. That was it, they needed procedures and they needed communications equipment, state of the art stuff, star wars or better. He knew that the funds would be available for whatever he needed. They had made that clear. His mind began to race through all the possibilities. He would also need one of those techie nerds, he thought. One that would sit right next to him and make all this yet to be acquired equipment hum. He had a blank check but with that had come one last chance. He couldn't risk another screw up. He would create the best organization with the best equipment and it would all be at his command. My God, he could get high just thinking about it.

He was excited that the organization had gotten strong enough and well enough entrenched in the bunker to have the courage to install their own equipment instead of limping along with that GSA crap. It also reflected a trust in him and particularly in his ability to assert leadership over the bunker while keeping their activities covert. Lastly, it was a strong vote of confidence in his group's ability to continue to meet their objectives undetected from this site. Sure, he had screwed up the Bulgaria deal but considering their lack of sophistication with both equipment and personnel, it wasn't all his fault.

He had been smart to accept the responsibility for that and that had gone a long way toward cementing confidence in him as the man to head up security under the new wave of activity. Anyway, it would all be changing now. It was the dawning of a new era of influence and effectiveness from his little, obscure locale. He smiled, almost leered, to think about it.

He finally managed to reach his assistant on the other side of the wall. It had probably only taken him ten minutes or so with this new fangled, time saving equipment. He obviously needed some more lessons. In the meantime he was reassuring himself that everything was in order for the meeting of his trusted minions, now just an hour away.

Confident that all was prepared, he allowed himself to sit back and relax while dreaming of the dawning of the new order and what it would mean for him.

He was still lost in his reverie when the notification came in over the new telephone that the shuttle bus carrying the participants for his meeting had cleared Security One, the gate at the road leading onto the grounds. He summoned his assistant, more easily this time, and instructed him on the last few things that needed to be moved from his office into the conference room. As his assistant gathered the items, the secretary gathered his thoughts. Everything was ready to go.

The obscure observer switched monitoring stations once more to access the conference room and the imminent meeting.

Amanda left her aunt's house in the clean, middle class neighborhood and boarded a city bus for the trip to the west side of Long Beach. It was ten o'clock at night and she was shivering from nerves even though it was probably 70 degrees outside.

She had gotten the name of this "connection" from a friend in her aunt's neighborhood that she had met years before while still in high school. She used to visit there for a month or so in the summers. She had known way back then that he dealt drugs to support his little habit and since he was still in the same house with his parents and still had the same habit she had gone to him for help in contacting the underworld, as she thought of it. He had arranged everything.

She rode the bus to the corner of Pacific Coast Highway and crossed the street against the light not wanting to stand there by herself at this hour of the night. She was grateful that it didn't take too long to hail a cab. When she gave the driver the name of the bar on PCH, he glanced over his shoulder and, she thought, raised an eyebrow as he sped away from the curb heading west. Just moments later he made a wide U-turn in the middle of the poorly lit, four-lane street and pulled up to the curb in front of the rundown, cinder block building with peeling paint and a flashing neon sign which she neglected to read. She was too busy looking at the environment and trying to assess her safety and escape routes. The cab driver reluctantly agreed to wait for no more than five minutes providing she threw in an extra fifty.

This side of Long Beach was not the place where tourists and families hung out. She was here to pick up her fake ID and papers and, she hoped, continue her life under an assumed name. For a moment she wondered if she would have any more life to live. She thought she actually heard her knees knocking together as she entered the door and parted the rancid, tattered curtains which hung just inside.

As her eyes adjusted to the dimness and her offended olfactory nerves began to recover, she was slightly relieved to find that she and the bartender with whom she was to do business were the only occupants. At least that was all that she could see.

She was going to great lengths to establish a new identity. It was costing a pretty penny to obtain a fake California driver's license, a social security card and a few other appropriate pieces of paper to make her new persona convincing. She thought for a moment what Will's reaction would be if he knew where she was and what she was doing right now. She cleared her head and approached the creep behind the bar with the unwashed hair and lecherous expression.

She gave the name of the man who had helped her with the contact and as she'd been instructed said she was here for a pick up. The bartender moved reluctantly to the far end of the bar and bent to retrieve a package from underneath. In that moment her heart seemed not to be beating. She thought perhaps this was a bust or worse, a shakedown, and wondered if he would pull out a gun. The plethora of scenarios rushing through her brain caused an overload and she was certain that she was unable to speak or move.

Relief gradually washed over her as he plunked the package on the bar in front of her. She in turn pulled the agreed upon cash from her pocket, picked up the package and turned to leave all in one unbroken motion.

She heard him make an unsavory remark as she parted the filthy curtains and slid carefully between them. She was outside before she took in a breath. Safely back in the cab, she instructed the driver to take her to Long Beach State. She knew she could catch a late bus there which would allow her to transfer at the diagonal for the trip to the all night Ralph's market just a few blocks from her current abode.

A few hours later in that still time between night and morning, she left her aunt's house, slipping out quietly and undetected. She didn't want anyone there to know that she had left or when in case someone came asking. The only other person who was awake and moving about was the unseen occupant of the car weaving back and forth on the dark and deserted streets catapulting copies of The Los Angeles Times from its windows.

She carried absolutely nothing with her into this new life except the clothes she wore, the cash and new identity papers in the pocket of her jeans and what was stored indelibly in her memory. She had been required to wait until four when the city busses began their full runs again. The first slivers of morning light were registering their presence as she walked down to the boulevard and waited adjacent to the park for the commuter to take her toward the Boeing plant. There she got the city college shuttle that went from the Carson campus to the PCH site.

She was able to blend in easily with the students. From there it was a short cab ride to the Greyhound Bus Station and the coach that went to Phoenix.

The bus made several stops along its route including Ontario, Riverside and Palm Springs. She wouldn't stay on the same bus all the way to the desert however, so she expected the five hour trip to take the better part of the day. She was certain that no one would be the wiser when she didn't remain on the bus after its stop in the sunny golf haven of Palm Springs. She purchased her ticket for Phoenix, however.

Several days had passed since she'd arrived in the desert. Her name was Sandy Porter now, her blonde hair was cut and dyed a dark brown, her utilities and telephone were all hooked up and signed on in her new name and she seldom went outside the condo without sunglasses and a visor. A convenient part of the desert style.

Amanda was disturbed from her afternoon nap by the ringing of the phone. She answered the telephone now fully free of the worry that someone unwelcome was listening. She had provided her new number and revised her code talk with Will so that he could contact her safely without giving away any information about her location. He was calling from a pay phone and they would not stay connected more than three minutes. She had a sweep hand on her new Timex for just that purpose. She was learning to think like a woman on the run but more importantly, she was looking after her own safety now and felt all the better for it. She was back in control.

After her conversation with Will she was feeling a little low. Charles was progressing but he had a tough time ahead of him and she couldn't help but feel a little guilt. Thank God he had Will and vice versa. Once again Amanda was jolted from her thoughts by the ringing of the phone. This time it was better news.

Amanda had been hanging out at the computer center of the state university located just down the road from her rented condo. She was hopeful of befriending a techie nerd who she could put to good use on her project. It was under these circumstances that she had found Bradley Duncan. Brad was on the phone now with some information that she had asked if he could retrieve from the internet. It was her intention to put him through several tests in order to determine his level of expertise and so far he had not disappointed.

Amanda had asked around the lab for names of those known to be a cut above the rest in computer manipulation without actually using the word, hacker. In reality it was a hacker that she was after and she was becoming more confident that that was what she'd found in Brad. It didn't hurt that he seemed to be attracted to her. That just made it a little easier to get him to do what she wanted. He hardly gave a thought to what she asked of him. It was obvious that he was not thinking with his brain. It also made him very anxious to show off his skills and expertise. She was hopeful about where this could lead. So was Brad.

It was integral to Amanda's plan that she have someone who could access the information that was being passed around among those whom she perceived were associated with Gazelle. She knew that they would have to crack into the secretary's communications at a minimum and she was gaining confidence that she had found the guy who could and would do that.

Back in Washington Roland continued to pace around his tastefully appointed room. He was still having difficulty absorbing what he had learned from the senator. He wasn't sure if he was more surprised to learn that his mentor, whom he thought he knew so well, had a son or to learn that he had put a hit out on Amanda Chambers. He was thinking that it was the latter. The fact that he'd done that surprised Roland, not only because he didn't see the man as being that involved in the dirty side of the business but also because it showed a lack of confidence in Roland's ability to get the job done. He wondered if he was losing credibility with the senator and consequently with Gazelle. He needed to give some serious consideration to the implications of this.

Roland trusted Senator Hampton, heart and soul. Uneasiness continued to eat at him. He had doubts that he had never had before. His mind was jumping around like frogs in springtime. He was chagrined that he had reached a place where trust in that one person he'd never questioned was waning. Was he becoming paranoid or was there something more going on? He considered his recent communications with Harry Axelrod. He had this sinking feeling that there was some connection between the way Harry was dealing with him and something that the senator had said. Or maybe just the way he said it. Something wasn't right. Of that much he was certain.

Roland was getting that old familiar feeling. The one that he didn't particularly like but had never let him down. He had come to rely on it. It was that danger alarm again, the same one that had saved him in his dealings with Randi. He knew without a doubt that he had to honor his suspicions. He hated being in a business where you could never be sure of whom your friends were. He had never had to have that guard up where the senator was concerned. Their relationship had been a safe haven of reason and compassion for Roland. Had he lost even that now? His instincts were kicking in and he was becoming wary.

He would follow up on a few matters tomorrow to determine where things stood. He had known from the beginning that some day things would go awry and when they did it would not be an amicable parting. He would make his inquiries and then he would make his move.

It may be time to activate the emergency plan that he had put in place years before. He picked up his cell phone and punched in the pre-programmed number.

"Is it you?" was all he heard on the other end.

"Yes, it's time for alert status."

"Your code please."

"Double zero, ten, twenty-two," he responded. "If you don't hear from me by midnight tomorrow, activate. Please repeat."

"You have until midnight tomorrow, Godspeed." They hung up.

As he'd always assumed would be the case, he was grateful today that he had started to plan for this eventuality many years ago. He had sufficient assets put away under the control of his Swiss banker to ensure that he would not be without means when the time to disappear arrived. Additionally, he had made arrangements for a new identity and his living arrangements had been procured and protected as well. His life would take a turn but it would continue on.

Roland began making notes of the order in which he would pursue his investigation. It seemed strange to think about probing into the business of his partners. Particularly the trusted ones but that was the nature of this business and he would only survive as long as he could remain detached and indifferent toward the personalities involved. He hardened himself to the tasks that lay ahead.

The secretary's report to the senator had gone well. He was excited about the new organization that he and his consultants had devised and he was anxious to put it in place. He had alerted the senator to the estimated cost of this arm of the new order and had gotten the go ahead to put the entire operation into effect. It was incomprehensible to him that the ever present budget constraints which he was accustomed to from the government had not been an issue. He couldn't wait to get started with the shopping.

Much of the equipment that would be required couldn't just be ordered from a catalog. Most of it would have to be obtained through the black market or abroad to keep from raising suspicions and creating a trail to the bunker. The logistics of it all would be challenging but it was just the kind of thing he loved to do. It had been brilliant of him to include a second bunker location and later expansion to the western states, eventually stretching to three in Europe, six in Asia, three in South America and one each in Africa and Australia. He had gotten Nate started immediately on procuring the new equipment for the current location and scoping out possible sites for expansion.

He was pleased that everyone had agreed that Nate Tidwell would be second in command to him. He trusted Nate and he liked the fact that he was a bit of a techie, unlike himself. He still hadn't caught up with the idea that we'd made it through the year 2000 glitch. He had been certain that all these technological advancements were going to come crashing down around us. That January First had dawned just like all the rest and he was somewhat embarrassed that he was still eating some of the provisions that he'd laid in at that time.

In any event, he was sure that Nate was going to bring just the right blend of technical understanding, leadership and that street instinct that would be necessary to ride herd on the numerous personalities. In addition to those attributes Nate had experience dealing with both the senator and Harry Axelrod, two prime players and he had shown repeatedly that he was cool under fire.

He was particularly anxious to please the senator now, not just because the last two assignments had been bungled and he wanted to improve his image, although that couldn't be downplayed; but more importantly all this talk of a reorganization of the government had his head spinning with excitement. Whether they called it Homeland Security or whatever, the thought of having a position which oversaw the FBI, CIA and who could imagine what all else was a heady concept and one that he dreamt about continually. It had to be the ultimate position for anyone who dreamed of wielding power as he did. He was sure that he had aligned himself with those who were on the track to success and he wanted to ride that train all the way to the end. He could see himself in that position. He was certain that if he performed well over the next couple of months the powers that be would treat him right. The job was his, hands down. He couldn't even think of a close contender, but then politics always surprised him.

Operation Cloud Nine was rapidly becoming a reality and it would soon leave Gazelle to die of natural causes. He thought about the symbolism of it. Gazelle was a creature of the earth, trying to tame the jungle, living out its usefulness then passing away like any mortal being. Cloud Nine on the other hand was of the universe and capable of changing its shape and presence at will or in reaction to the environment. Quite a concept and very apt, considering where they were heading. He knew that there were some who would not survive this transformation but it was looking like he would.

A sense of satisfaction settled over him. If Operation Cloud Nine was successful he would be atop their security system and would be able to implement all that muscle on the grandest scale imaginable. If, on the other hand, their plan for controlling world energy somehow didn't materialize, he stood to grab that position over Homeland Security and wield similar influence over the greatest enforcement and intelligence agencies of the world's greatest power. Either way, he assured himself, he was sitting at the crossroads of two very powerful paths. He had a foot in each camp and he'd be happy for it to go either way.

Bradley Duncan felt the sweat run down the side of his face as he sat in front of his homemade clone computer with the 21" flat screen monitor. It had taken most of his savings to acquire that monitor but he loved it more than his vintage Datsun 240Z parked in the lot outside his apartment complex. He looked down on it as he moved over to close the slider and turn on the air conditioning. Summer was coming early to the desert.

He was excited about what he had been able to achieve while playing around with the websites of two of the federal agencies. Whoever had built the firewalls into the web system had neglected to plug a hole large enough for his browser to slip through. He had been working on this program with Kyle, a friend at the university, and this was the first time he had actually had success moving through one of the walls. He had accomplished it not just once but twice. He was anxious to share his news with Kyle in the lab this afternoon.

Even better, Sandy Porter, whom he had a serious case of the hots for had agreed to meet him for coffee at the Starbuck's near campus. He knew that what he'd found would impress her and equally important being seen with her at the coffee shop would bump up his stock with some of the jocks and suave know-it-alls on campus. Sandy was a looker and the fact that he would love to touch as well as look was pretty obvious. *Well, all in good time,* he thought.

He looked forward to the afternoon for all these reasons. It was going to be a good day.

He returned to the cluttered and wobbly, fake oak desk which held all of his computer hardware and resumed his trek into cyberspace.

Roland was up early and on his way with much on his 'to do' list. He was on his cell phone in the back of the DC taxi speaking to his account representative at one of the older and more prestigious Swiss banks. He was assured that everything would be in order according to his instructions. They were very anxious to please.

His first stop this morning was at Harry Axelrod's office. He was not expected. The taxi pulled up in front of the ostentatious building and the uniformed doorman held the extra wide door open as Roland strode through. He went directly to the bank of elevators in the rear which went express to the upper floors. He took the ride into the rarified air alone.

As he stepped through the elevator door and into the posh and ornate reception area he was greeted by the Miss Broomstick type. She fit all of the stereotypes of all of the beaky nosed, busy bodies that ever lived. He was in no mood for her this morning. He swept past her with all the force and pleasantries of a hurricane blowing down everything in front of it and leaving nothing but destruction in its path. He could still hear her stuttering and muttering that Mr. Axelrod was not available as he opened the hand carved walnut, double door and entered into the sonofabitch's office unannounced and uninvited. He was itching for a fight and knew that he had come to the right place.

Harry quickly terminated his phone call and stood to greet Roland. "How nice to see you, Roland, I wasn't expecting you. Didn't realize you were on my calendar for this morning. Probably just an oversight. Won't you sit down? Can I get you something?

"Cut the crap. I'm not here to drink coffee or to listen to your ramblings. We're going to have a serious talk and I'll be doing most of the listening. I will take your suggestion to sit down, however. This may take a while."

Roland moved easily and calmly over to the guest chairs opposite Harry's desk and settled himself in. He tugged on the hem of his suit coat to straighten out any wrinkles, crossed his legs and looked directly at Harry Axelrod who had returned to his desk chair feeling somewhat safer with the large mass of wood between him and the angry intruder.

"Tell me about this energy plan," Roland directed.

Harry was taken aback not only by the presence of this anal little prick in his office but also by his unadulterated gall. Coming here unannounced, making demands on him, who the hell did he think he was? What balls! He was nothing more than a hired hand and he waltzed in here challenging Harry and requiring that he make time for him and his questions. Well he'd give it to him with both barrels. Harry was feeling untouchable right now. He had very influential friends in strategic places. No one like this lowlife was going to best him. He could feel his face and neck flush with anger but he fought to keep it under wraps and not let Roland see it. Harry was seething and he probably was letting that affect his reasoning.

"Hell, Roland, I thought we all knew about energy. Haven't you been payin' attenshun in our little meetin's?" Harry really laid on the down home talk since he knew how much it irritated Roland. He continued, "Energy's what rules the world, Boy. That there's the only plan a man needs. Maybe I missed somethin' in one a your little lectures," he gestured with his cigar as he mocked Roland.

"Damnit, Harry, I really don't want to play games. Why don't you just be honest for once in your life? Stand up like a man and put this all on the table."

Harry thought he would explode. He was so enraged at Roland's apparent disdain of him. He'd put this arrogant ass in his place once and for all. "I'd be happy to share the truth with you Roland," his voice lowered, his words became more deliberate and his drawl and folksy speech was gone, "But I really doubt that you are up to it. I don't think you can handle the truth."

It was as if all the bad blood between these two men was seeping out onto the antique, Persian Carpet which covered the floor of the office. Roland was slightly shaken by the change in Harry's demeanor and Harry was brimming with resentment from all the years that he had watched this golden boy get pampered and catered to by the old man. Senator Hampton had been the one line of defense surrounding Roland and it had been hands off for far too long.

Now that Harry felt he had the senator under control and the new plan was well under way he was feeling rife with power and wasn't about to treat Roland with kid gloves as he'd had to do in the past.

"Give it to me straight, if you're even capable of understanding it," he goaded.

Harry laughed in Roland's face, "Oh, I understand it all right, do you? Take a look behind you, Roland." Harry reached into the drawer and for a brief moment, Roland wondered if the man was crazy enough to pull a weapon on him. Instead he extracted the remote control unit.

He pressed the activation button and as the humming began, Roland let the fear flow from his body as curiosity swept over him and he swiveled around in his chair.

"Have you ever heard of Operation Cloud Nine? No, of course you haven't. How about the Consortium of Planned Energy? Oh, that's right; you've been iced out of that one too." It made Harry feel powerful to put this man in his place and to watch that look spread over his face like the dawning of his day of execution had arrived. It was all Harry could do not to laugh. He wondered if the arrogant little man might wet himself right then and there.

Harry knew as soon as he'd done it that he'd told Roland more than he should have but he'd been so enraged that reason didn't seem to have a place in his thinking. He had reacted from his pent up anger and it had felt great to watch him squirm. It was like Harry had gotten to be the one to tell him his life was over. He smiled with pleasure, almost laughed out loud, just remembering. Then there was that last little dig, "Oh by the way, your all important senator has sold you out and is working for me and mine." What a dream come true. Harry was reminded again how good it felt to be one of the few chosen to be in charge of the universe. He sat back in his chair to relish the moment but a stiff breeze of dread and concern blew through his office instead. He may have screwed the deal in his enthusiasm to best this pompous ass.

Roland left Harry's office with all of the aplomb with which he had entered it an hour earlier. He had definitely learned more than he had expected to and now he wasn't so sure that he wanted to know it. Well, of course he wanted, even needed to know the truth but it was not as he had thought and his life had changed irrevocably in that hour. It smarted all the more because it had happened in that sonofabitch Axelrod's office. His challenge now was what he would do with what he learned.

As Roland rode through the district in his classic DC taxi with the Middle Eastern driver, he was trying to absorb what he had just learned and was pondering his next move. Back in the plush high rise, Harry was immediately on the phone with the senator.

"That damn Roland Priestly just crashed into my office ranting and raving and making all sorts of accusations and threats against me," he told the senator. "I knew he was about half crazy and this just proves it. How the hell did he find out about Operation Cloud Nine?" he asked. "You got a leak over there?" Harry thought he'd throw the light of suspicion onto the senator's people. He didn't want to tell the senator that he'd got to gloating and found it rewarding to beat Roland over the head with the reality of what was taking place. He felt reasonably certain that things had broken down sufficiently between Roland and the senator now that he wasn't at risk to be caught in his lie. Not this one at least.

The senator responded coolly, "No, Harry, I don't have a leak. I don't know how Roland learned of the operation but it was not from here. He is a bright boy, however, and he was going to have to know about it at some time. We both knew this day would come and I, for one, have been prepared for the ultimate outcome."

"My God, you finally sayin' it's time to waste him?"

"I'm saying he has outlived his usefulness and has become a liability. I'll contact the secretary and see if he's ready to handle this." The senator spoke calmly but inside it was making his gut churn to think of losing Roland. They had a long and illustrious history and he would miss the man with all his heart. This business was not about his heart, however. He had to think straight and do what was best for the future of the world. He had already allowed himself to become conflicted between head and heart where his son was concerned and he had to convince himself that he had not just gone soft. He had to be firm and detached about this one. It was for the best.

The senator hung up from his conversation with Harry and dialed the secretary at the undisclosed location.

The secretary picked up after several rings.

"What took you so long?"

"Sorry, it's these new phones and all their electronic this and that. I can't do the simplest things. I could shout easier. Anyway, enough of that, It'll get better, what do you need?" he asked.

"Is your new organization functioning yet?"

"Not really, we've got a few more gadgets coming in and then a couple days at least to train everyone. This will be state of the art. No more seat of the pants flying and no more near misses. Well, that's not what you called about, is it?" The secretary could not contain his enthusiasm for where his little corner of the organization was going. It was his dream job.

"How long to be operational?" the senator inquired.

"We need at least another week."

"I can give you that but no more. We have a high level operative to deal with but it absolutely has to be done right the first time. Are you sure you'll be ready to handle it?" the senator asked.

"Let's schedule it for a week from today but I suggest we get the lieutenants together and have a strategy session before then. If it's that big and the first one we can't be too careful," he advised. "We'll need a good plan with thorough preparation and a fail safe system of course."

"Sounds fine. Set it up and contact me for scheduling." The senator hung up.

He touched speed dial Number One on the secure cell phone. On the second ring it was answered and the senator calmly advised his superior in Operation Cloud Nine of his decision about Roland.

Roland's mind was everywhere and nowhere. He was having difficulty staying focused. Just as he was concentrating on where to go next, a feeling of nausea coupled with that old sense of betrayal would descend upon him and take him from his rational thoughts to irrational feelings. At least to him feelings were always irrational. They got in the way of clear thinking and without fail whenever he let them cloud his thinking he got into trouble. There was a weakness, a vulnerability attached to emotions and it was not a place that he was comfortable. What the hell was he doing there now? He had such important issues to analyze. *Get off it!* was the admonishment inside his head.

He was not ready to return to the tasks of the day. He definitely had to change courses. He wasn't ready to go back to his room so he had the driver drop him at one of his favorite coffee shops near Dupont Circle.

Roland left the cab at the curb and paused to take in the ambiance of the neighborhood. He loved the quaint combination of antique and modern, the diversity of the inhabitants and the buzz that could be felt as the energy of the day was just beginning to rush through the city's surroundings. It was like coming home.

He entered the coffee shop and was greeted with a light buzz of conversations and ethnic music with a strong, thumping beat playing out over the establishment. Trey, the day manager, was behind the counter. When he saw Roland a smile of recognition washed over his dark face showing off his ivory white teeth and lively eyes. He waved and came around from behind the counter to shake hands and welcome him back. He chose a seat over in the corner that he knew Roland liked and pulled the chair out gesturing for him to sit. "Would you like your usual, Mr. Roland?" he asked in a thick accent.

"Yes, please," It felt good to be back in his familiar haunts and to be with the people he'd chosen for friends. Friends as he knew them were not friends like other people had. It was enough for him to be known by name and made to feel welcome. He didn't need or want people to wade around in his life. He was most comfortable keeping people at a distance. Superficial to other people was comforting to him.

He picked up a previously read newspaper from the adjacent table and pretended to be interested in reading it in order to gain the privacy that he needed. He never could understand people who literally devoured a paper when they read it. It would be rumpled and wrinkled and folded every which way. He always kept it straight and in order so that when he was finished it wasn't clear if someone had read it or not. The only clue was that it was puffed up with air. Today he was having all kinds of difficulty keeping his mind on his business. He knew it was because he didn't like what he'd learned.

Roland finally got himself under control, got focused on his predicament and began to spend serious time contemplating what the events of the morning meant to his future.

It was easier to think in this undemanding atmosphere and he knew that his decisions over the next few hours would shape the rest of his life. He even wondered if his life had any length left to it. It's amazing how, when left alone a person can come to a place of inner calm in the face of a storm. There is an almost meditative nature to that spot. Roland had never been one to meditate or practice any kind of mind discipline but he knew when he reached that comfortable place within himself that answers would come to him and reason would flow through his thoughts in an almost spiritual way. He had wondered before if that was the kind of experience that persons of religion spoke of when they described levels of enlightenment or meditative connectiveness.

No matter, he was about to reach that place now when he needed it most. He continued to hold the newspaper up in front of his face and ponder his world.

Bradley Duncan and Sandy Porter, nee Amanda Chambers, continued to make great strides in the crashing of firewalls on the internet. The had spent a great deal of time together in Brad's ratty little apartment and in front of his much loved monitor and they would laugh and high five each other every time another bridge was crossed. They teased about putting another notch on the barrel of the browser that Brad and his friend, Kyle had developed. It was becoming quite the cyber weapon.

At times it frightened Amanda to think what could be done by some of the most inane minds. People with very little understanding outside the mathematical protocol of computers could tamper with things that they had absolutely no inkling about. They were like the mountain climbers who climbed the mountain because it was there. These people hacked into sensitive material because they could. Just for the thrill of it. Unlike the climbers who simply left footprints and trash in the environment, hackers on the other hand could wreak havoc on the world sometimes on purpose and sometimes unknowingly.

The time had come to ask Brad for help with her specific project. She had put on a rather seductive top and the desert springtime had provided good reason to wear her shorts and sandals showing off her long and well shaped legs. She sat on the threadbare, pizza stained sofa in his living room and set out the challenge. "Do you think you could get into e-mail from a government department?" She asked.

"Don't know why not," he responded. "This thing's getting pretty sophisticated. Every time we take her for a spin, Kyle and I tweak it and make it a little more powerful. I'm beginning to think we're really onto it big time. We were just thinking about trying to tackle some encryption codes. Now that's big time." Brad gloated. "It's a cyber bazooka," he bragged. "Can blast through about anything, I bet." He and Kyle were beginning to believe their own hype. Just yesterday they had spent a skull session dreaming of the possibility of breaching one of the key recovery systems such as those used by the military. These were centers where the code breaking software was deposited while the encrypted message was in cyberspace only to be accessed by the recipient to decipher the message at the other end.

"How about trying this?" Amanda handed Brad e-mail addresses and information that she knew about the secretary's internet access and IP. While all of that was government domain, she also included some of the information she had gained about Roland Priestly's private internet access provider. She handled it in the way of a challenge without actually daring Brad to follow through. He was too blinded by her to feel manipulated anyway. Most importantly, Amanda wanted him to do it now. She wanted to be present when he got into those sites so she could chose which things he opened, read or downloaded. This was critical for her. She continued her coy little game as she moved him along the super highway toward her desired destination and the data she sought.

Chapter Fifteen

Senator Hampton, Charles Farino and Will Chambers all sat in a tight little circle in the solarium of the rehab hospital. Charles had been moved there just days before and the daunting task that lay before him was just becoming a reality for all three men.

Each of them sat silently staring at undefined spots on the scrubbed tile floor. The room was antiseptic and Spartan except for a few carelessly placed, artificial plants and trees. Elevator music hummed monotonously in the background. All three men were lost in their thoughts.

Will had previously shared with Charles that he needed to be away for a few days because of Amanda and Charles had readily agreed that Will should go now while his own struggles were difficult and personal. Hopefully by the time Will returned Charles would have broken through some of the emotional trauma that was facing him. Even though they were gay, neither of them revealed much of their feminine side and any man knew that his emotional challenges were his and his alone to fight through. Feelings were personal. Charles was there now.

As for the senator, he also knew that Charles' war was personal at this point. Of course he wanted to provide all of the support that he could but he knew that this was his battle to face. He was not aware that Will would be gone for the next few days. He looked across at his son in the wheel chair and his eyes bled forth, all of the love that he was feeling. He found it hard to maintain his unruffled demeanor. He was flush with guilt, how would he ever forgive himself. Well, it wasn't really his fault, people had screwed up. Every soldier had to face losses in the war. Bravery was what it was about. Suck it up and move on. The end justified the means. At least his son was alive. He would hold onto that as he pushed forward toward the ultimate objective. It was for the good of all. For the good of the world.

The new world order, Operation Could Nine had already taken many lives; his son's injury was, like those lost lives, an unfortunate case of collateral damage. *Keep your eyes on the goal,* he reminded himself, *regime change comes at a cost.*

Will had not found the courage to broach the issue of Amanda with the senator again after Charles' initial request that night in his office. That seemed so long ago now. There was just too much on their plates and much like Charles with his rehab challenges, Amanda was Will's issue to deal with. He thought about how these next few days could best be used in the further pursuit of Gazelle. Since Charles' injury it had become very personal to Will. The two people he loved most in the world were nearly killed over this senseless game, whatever the hell it was. He was determined to find out and put an end to it once and for all. He would begin by meeting Amanda face to face.

Will was the first to break the silence. "I'm sorry to have to run but I've got several errands to take care of. Before I leave, Charles, I put some clean clothes in the dresser in your room so you'd have them for your workouts. I knew they were getting more strenuous so I stocked you up for the better part of the week."

Charles nodded an affirmation that said both thank you and I'll miss you. Both men knew that it had to be this way. Will moved across the circle and gave Charles a pat and a peck on the top of the head. He squeezed his hand and sauntered out of the room without looking back. Everything that he was feeling was revealed in his posture.

The only errand that Will had to run was to the airport. He had his flight bag stowed in Charles' room. As was his habit, when he swung by to pick it up, he gave a flirtatious nod to the nurse at the station outside Charles' room and told her to take good care of him until he got back.

"Don't you worry, Will, we're on it. You won't even recognize him when you get back. Have a good trip now," she replied.

Will wished that this hospital was closer to the metro but it had pretty good connecting transportation due to the large number of staff and visitors. He could either grab a cab or take the shuttle bus over to the metro stop. He opted for a cab and decided to take it directly to the airport. No spy games tonight, he thought.

He hadn't gone two blocks when his cavalier attitude was overridden by reason and he told the cabbie to take him to Union Station instead. He spent an hour or so walking around looking in the shop windows and having a cup of coffee. He was fairly sure that someone was keeping him company. He couldn't make out the man's features, he never revealed that much of himself, but even though his clothes were not that distinct, Will realized that they kept appearing at the same places. Maybe he was following him and maybe not. Better to be safe he told himself and he went to the payphone near the Amtrak ticketing counter.

He found that he could change his flight from Dulles to Baltimore, leaving just two hours later. Because of a shorter layover he'd arrive at almost the same time. He made the change with the airline and began laying out a confusing route which would eventually take him to the Baltimore Airport. While he was at it he changed his arrival city from Los Angeles to John Wayne Airport in Orange County. He didn't know if they had access to his flight information but it wouldn't hurt to make them dance around a little if they were all set up at LAX. *The diversion begins,* he thought.

Will arrived in Costa Mesa just after seven in the morning. He emerged from the terminal on the upper level since he hadn't checked any bags. He was able to get a taxi easily at this hour but he took enough time before he got in to carefully observe everyone that was nearby in the ticketing area and on the curb. While he didn't expect to recognize anyone, he wanted to put in his memory as many people as possible who were around him for comparison later on. Satisfied that he had studied everyone, suspicious and not, he got in the cab and asked to go to the Amtrak station at the Irvine Spectrum. The cabbie appeared a little annoyed that he'd gotten such a short trip after his hours in line at the airport and he nearly threw Will against the back of the seat as he burned away from the curb. It was a quiet ride to the train. Most of the horrendous LA traffic was going the opposite direction so the trip took only fifteen minutes or so.

Will gave the man a rather generous tip but it didn't seem to appease him as he heard him grumbling in his beard as he closed the door and shouldered his bag. Will loved the feel of the crisp, early air with its promise of a pleasant day to come. He had to admit this place had it over just about everywhere when it came to weather. This part of the Irvine development had come late in the growth of Orange County and as a result, industrial and office buildings were tucked neatly in among the remnants of still productive orange groves. He could stand here even now and smell the orange blossoms as their sweetness clung to the morning mist particles stirring delicately over the environment. He just stood there and took it in for a moment. Thoughts of Charles flitted across his mind and he wished that he could be there with him. Under different circumstances of course.

Will went inside the station and purchased a ticket all the way to San Diego. He had only about 40 minutes to wait for the next southbound train. They ran fairly frequently at this hour because of the commuters between the two business centers.

Will dozed lightly on the rocking train as it snaked its way down the coast. He tried to get up and move around periodically in order to assess once again the passengers riding with him. After what Amanda and Charles had been through there was no way that he wanted to jeopardize Amanda's security. He was determined to take extra precautions.

He stopped at the snack bar and got a cup of coffee. He took it back to his seat and watched out the window as the train pulled into the station at Oceanside. He couldn't remember when he'd seen so many military haircuts as were mingling about on the platform near the station. He waited until the train was just beginning to move forward with its requisite lurch when he grabbed his bag and went as fast as possible to the exit at the rear of his car. The attendant had already picked up the step and was about to close the half door when Will brushed past him and leapt to the ground. The startled trainman could only utter, "Hey, this ain't your stop."

Will just waved over his shoulder as the man accelerated on down the platform with the train and all of its other passengers. Will stood there and watched long enough to assure himself that no one else got off. He went through the station and got in the third cab in line. The cabbies ahead were shouting and one was running toward them as he told the man to take him to the nearest car rental agency. The man was glad to get away from the curb but Will suspected that he was not looking forward to his return to the cadre of taxis and the abuse he would take from his competition. This was a small community after all.

Will rented the car in the name of one of the companies that he had used before opening the B & B. The card was still good and wouldn't expire until the end of the year even though he hadn't used it in a couple of years. He doubted that the name would be linked to him, at least not initially. He drove off to the east and decided he could use the map from the rental agency as enough of a guide to get where he was going. He continued east until he came to the Escondido area. After going north a ways on the Interstate he would have a choice to go through Hemet, across the mountains and drop down into the desert or go through the pass east of Riverside and make his way out to Palm Springs with all the vacationers coming directly out of LA. Either way it was a beautiful day for a drive. He reached down and found some classical music on the radio and settled in for a few hours of peaceful solitude.

Cruising along the highway and confident that he hadn't been followed from the train, Will had a sense of relaxation that he hadn't felt in weeks. At the turnoff to Riverside he decided to play it extra safe and drove on into the once thriving city of citrus packing plants. He found one of the local offices of the car rental company listed in the brochure in the glove compartment and convinced the attendant there that the brakes on the car were defective. It had taken a few minutes to convince the young woman behind the counter that every time he stepped down hard they pulled the car dangerously toward the ditch. He had purposely chosen this small, out of the way office hoping that there would not be a mechanic on duty. Since there wasn't, the young woman agreed to switch cars with him.

In less than thirty minutes he was back up on the Interstate moving toward Palm Springs with a change of car and one more little diversion that anyone trying to tail or find him would have to figure out. He was pulling out all the stops, leaving nothing to chance to protect Amanda's new identity and location.

Sandy Porter left her condo at just after eleven o'clock and took the Sun Bus through downtown Palm Springs. She made a change at the Old Town Terminal and boarded the coach which would take her to the Tramway at the foot of Tahquitz Peak and Mt. San Jacinto. Her heart was thumping inside her chest and her eyes were suspicious, looking everywhere behind her shades and looking nowhere. At about the same time Will took the Highway 111 exit from Interstate 10 and made his way to the parking lot at the foot of the tram.

Each made their way through the maze of steps and paths to the ticket booth and bought passage up the mountain. Luckily, they were on different trams Amanda making the trip first.

When Will left the car at the top his knees were still wobbly from the ride. He had never been particularly comfortable with heights and someone had gone to a great deal of trouble to make sure you could see exactly how high up you were in this glass car hanging precariously on a cable. Oh yes, and the damn thing had to revolve as it went as well. Anyway, he was glad to be off of it and didn't want to think about the return trip.

He took out the instructions that he had received and read them over again to be sure that he knew where the meeting place was.

Will almost didn't recognize his own sister. She had become Sandy Porter in many ways. Had it not been for her familiar slouch as she sat at the table rifling through sheets of paper he might have gone right past her. His heart took a little leap as he approached her in front of the huge windows looking out on the endless desert from 5,000 plus feet. The restaurant was sort of seedy considering its rich setting but he assumed that was from high traffic. He hoped it was that and not the lack of finances as that made him wonder about the maintenance on the cables and all of its mechanisms. *Better not to go there,* he thought.

A huge smile etched its way across his face as Amanda spotted him and rose to greet him. They literally ran into each other's arms and each held the other tight and long. So much had happened since they'd seen each other. Amanda's near miss at being shot and the horrible injury to Charles along with Will's fortuitous near miss at the apartment bombing. Everything felt suddenly so tenuous and Will felt a longing for their carefree, childish days. It was like they'd both aged in the days they'd been apart. He quickly brought himself to his senses and back to the moment.

They sat at the table and chattered like magpies taking occasional breaks to say how much they loved and missed each other. It felt good to both of them to be in the company of the other. For a few hours the horrible and terrifying real world could be held at bay.

Once they stopped the small talk and brought themselves back to reality Amanda shared with Will the direction she was taking and the progress she'd made. She had with her what looked to Will like reams of papers. All printed communications to and from the secretary's computer at his undisclosed location. Amanda had managed to get through most of it and she had a couple of promising leads but there were still a hundred or so more that they needed to wade through. They divided the stack and started their search. It was easy to dispose of a great deal of the mail as administrative and truly government business but there was also an almost equal amount of Gazelle business being done. That was what they saved; the rest could go into the trash. Neither of them gave any consideration to the dozen or so messages that were always tagged as undeliverable. Therefore, neither of them wondered why the secretary would keep writing to an unrecognized address. Consequently, it didn't matter that this had been instituted to provide the recipient plausible deniability.

After another hour or so they had come to the end of the first go through and it was time to go back and read the Gazelle communiqués more carefully. They could only hope that they would find something meaningful. What they found alarmed them both.

First, there were references to something called Operation Cloud Nine and the context in which it was used lead them to believe that it was both sinister and large. They would need more information before they could conclude exactly what the extent and purpose of it was or who, in particular, was behind it. What was clear was that it was not the "government" business of the secretary, it was somehow connected to world energy issues and it was involved in clandestine affairs which may have included assassination. They both wondered if this was who murdered the woman in Amanda's raincoat and had attempted to kill Will and Charles with the bombing.

Secondly, they learned that Roland Priestly was not a part of this organization and the reference they found made it sound like he had become expendable to Gazelle, whoever that was. There was still no clue to the identity of Gazelle, but they felt they were getting close.

Will couldn't believe that Amanda had been able to make this breakthrough. He praised her for what she'd accomplished and he felt a rush of adrenaline at the fact that they were getting closer. He still worried about her safety but he had come to realize in the recent weeks that none of them were safe nor would they ever be until this horrible person was exposed.

The altitude and atmosphere in which they were working was suddenly drenched in a fog of tension. It was palpable between them. They both seemed to get there at the same moment. They looked at each other solemnly and each knew that the other was poised on the edge of panic. On the one hand it was exhilarating and hopeful to be approaching a solution. On the other, they knew that they had stumbled onto something so large that the magnitude of it threatened to crush them.

At least now they had proof that the secretary was linked to unlawful activity, perhaps even murder but they didn't know the whole story yet. Should they turn over what they had and trust law enforcement, probably FBI in this instance, to ferret out the entire truth or would they be safer getting the whole story together before entrusting their futures to others? That was a deep and difficult question to ponder and one with far reaching implications. They needed to consider their next step very carefully. In truth neither of them could put much faith in an organization that housed itself in something called the J. Edgar Hoover Building. That was not a name that fostered trust and wholesomeness.

They sat in mutual contemplation for what seemed like an hour. Finally, Amanda spoke first. "I think I should go back and have Brad hack into this site once more. Maybe if I pay closer attention, now that I know what I'm looking for, we can get the piece of mail that will clinch it. It's even possible that there's something more recent. Things seem to be happening fast for them based on the last day or so of communications."

"I agree Mandy, can you get Brad to do it? Is he safe for you? God, I have to stop thinking like your brother. I have to tell you, I think Roland Priestly is in danger based on that one message," he sorted through the morass of papers and pulled out the pertinent one. "Here, this one," he began to read, "PTB says Priestly and Gazelle have become burdensome. Make a plan within the week. I don't know, Mandy, but I don't see how else you could read that."

"I think you're right," she agreed. "What do you think we should do with it?"

"My inclination is for you to go back to Brad and get whatever you can. Stay here as Sandy Porter and I'll see if I can set up a meeting with Mr. Roland Preistly. I'll take this one e-mail message with me and see if there's any way that we can enlist his aid. Maybe we're on the same side of this and haven't known it. He may not be the enemy. He may have gotten switched to our side without even knowing it."

"On the other hand, he might be the one who's trying to kill us," she added. "Honestly, I do think you're right though. It's exciting to think that we may have a strong ally. He's got a lot more influence and resources than we do. You've got to be really careful though, Will. You'll be taking a huge risk meeting with him," she cautioned.

They parted just as the sunset behind the mountain threw a golden glow over the expanse of desert which crept past the horizon and beyond their view. The lights of the desert communities began to twinkle creating an aura of dreamlike peace and serenity. Between the view, the dropping sensation in the cable car and the sinking sensation at the daunting tasks which lie ahead, Will found the entire experience surreal and wished they would reach the parking lot and terra firma sooner rather than later.

He had said his goodbyes to Amanda at the restaurant and it was now time to make his way to the next phase of his discovery. He welcomed the feel of the now familiar rental car as he left the parking lot and crept along the street with the other traffic heading for the Interstate, back to the city and his potential rendezvous with Roland Priestly.

Senator Hampton sat in the large, leather chair in the den of his upscale, brick, colonial home in the Chevy Chase section of Maryland. Even though it was mid-morning on a weekday he found himself lolling in the overstuffed chair with the day's edition of the Post in his lap. He had been unable to bring himself to go to the office today. He had spoken with Marge and told her that he would be working from home this morning. He asked her to cancel his appointments and forward calls that were of the utmost importance only. He found himself in a terrible funk. She knew from his voice and from his break with routine that something was bothering him terrifically. This was all out of character for the determined and focused man that she worked for.

Besides the innumerable issues that every senator has to contend with he had several problems that were crushing him with the burden of their weight. Foremost, he needed to meet with Harry Axelrod and bring that matter under control, then there was the little matter of getting the secretary up and running with the new "security" measures for Operation Cloud Nine; but the two things that really had him laid out this morning were Roland and his son.

He was asking himself how he had come to this. He thought again about how some men are just placed in a position of responsibility unlike any one else's. While he may have made the decision to enter politics himself, at times like these he wondered if he'd really had a choice at all. It was like being drafted. He thought back then that he could see so clearly what needed to be done to move this strong and promising country toward its ultimate destiny. It had all seemed so obvious.

It wasn't until he got to Washington and got bogged down in the favor trading and back room debates and deals that he realized that his clear vision was being fogged by the process. He knew that was what had been the appeal of Gazelle. Getting results was what it was all about for the men of that group.

Then had come Operation Cloud Nine, it had been a natural enough evolution. He'd been making such great strides on the national level. With Gazelle's help they had really been perking along with one program after another. He had kept unofficial tallies and was amazed at how they managed to be out in front on almost every issue. The consensus on any one bill or program would eventually come down on the side of just and prudent actions but the time that was wasted getting there continued to appall him. He was convinced that with very few exceptions, Gazelle was doing the right thing, just doing it ahead of what the process would normally allow. He never felt that there was anything wrong with that. Maybe they cut some corners, maybe they even suffered collateral damage but it was simply the case of a few suffering for the good of all. It was always damned tough to get through that part though. It always had set him thinking.

This morning he was testing in his mind, once again, the validity of the cause. It had seemed a natural bump in the process to move from national issues and programs to the world scope. Again, he was frustrated by the fact that he seemed to be able to see what was right long before others could come to it. He just couldn't stand waiting around for them to come to a conclusion which he had already reached. It just made good sense to go ahead and get moving toward the solution.

In his mind that was what Cloud Nine was, a trend leading solution to the world's problems. This disparity couldn't continue. The world couldn't continue to survive the lack of a middle class. It had proven itself over and over in country after country. In every economy of the world, wherever the middle class disappeared anarchy would follow. People who toil in endless poverty had to have hope and when there was no bridge, no road up out of despair, no middle class to strive for, they became desperate. Every one knows that desperate people do desperate things. It was too dangerous to risk world anarchy. Once again it was up to him and the powers that be.

The recent outbreaks only served to strengthen his resolve that he was right in his thinking. Everything from small skirmishes to outright war was breaking out around the globe. So much of it had to do with inequality in the eyes of the participants. Even our own foreign policies and dependence on foreign oil were major contributors to the instability. World leaders were hell bent on grabbing or keeping any natural resource within their reach. Land grabbing had been going on as long as man had been on the planet, that's what had spawned most wars, but the population size was dictating that some resolution be reached soon.

Afghanistan was a perfect example, you could no longer initiate a simple Marshall Plan after a war with such a country. You could hand them all the money on the planet and they would be unable to resolve their problems. The know-how just wasn't there. The only thing those people know how to do is fight. War is their legacy. It would be necessary to import skilled people to teach them how to fish. He thought briefly of a college friend who had gone there with the Peace Corps back in the sixties and wondered what changes they had effected, wondered if they'd changed their lives back then. Today, nation building had become the byword. He reassured himself, yet again, that what they had devised would go a long way toward resolving this inequity.

Convinced again that he was doing the right thing he began to think about Roland and Charles. He had pretty much resolved in his mind that Charles was some of the collateral damage that happened as a natural side effect to these changes. Roland, though, he was unable to reconcile. He assumed it was because Charles' life had been spared and Roland's would not that he was having such grave doubts about the path that they were taking. In many ways Roland was more like a son than Charles. He had been there in his day to day life, sharing his work, learning at his knee where Charles had been taught by another. He loved Charles. He loved Roland. The pain was killing him. He thought his heart would surely break.

Chapter Sixteen

Roland left the coffee shop in Dupont Circle with a clear resolve. He knew that the day of reckoning had arrived. He was not a naïve man and he had known that this day lay lurking on the horizon. He just hadn't expected it to come this soon or in this way. He had always thought that the dissolution of Gazelle would be by mutual consent as had been its birth.

As unpleasant as it was, the demise of Gazelle was something he could accept but the news about his friend and mentor was about as devastating as he could comprehend. It had taken him back to that horrible time again, the gut wrenching breakup of his marriage to Diana followed by the raw, cavernous depth of pain and despair that he had experienced with the death of his beautiful daughter. He'd had no idea what being a parent would mean to him. He and Diana had found themselves expecting when they least intended it but both had been happy to take on their new role and they prepared fastidiously for her arrival. It wasn't until after he saw her, watched her grow, learn and develop that he found himself so enchanted and head over heels in love with that delightful being that was his offspring. He'd felt a pride and fulfillment that defied description every time he'd laid eyes on her. "Debra," he whispered aloud for only his ears.

Roland decided to visit his club where he could combine a workout with a massage and some quiet time. He felt like his muscles were strung so tightly across his bones that something was bound to rupture.

It would feel good to work off some of the stress and it would give him a chance to think. He could always rely on endorphins to clear his head and assist his decision making. He waved down a cab and gave the driver the address of his club.

Roland had finished a mile swim and was exerting himself on the Cybex leg press machine when the attendant approached him. By consensus the members had made the exercise room off limits for cell phones but the club provided a service where you could leave your phone with a kind of hat check service and they would notify you of a call. If you chose to take it you did so out in the lobby area and away from others. His call was from Karla.

He picked up the towel he had draped across the machine and went into the lobby dripping sweat along the way. He found that part of working out disgusting but unavoidable. Fitness centers and locker rooms always smelled like public transportation in a third world country on a hot day. Something about body odor said unclean to him. It was bad enough to inhale one's own odor but the acrid air in the workout room reeked of heavily exerted bodies, nervous energy and a lingering mix of expensive colognes. None of which were designed to be put together.

"Mr. P, Karla here," she began. "Just thought you'd want to know that the brother of Amanda Chambers, name is Will, called on your front line and is anxious to speak with you, quote, about a personal matter."

"Well," he paused thoughtfully, "Thank you for calling me. When did he call?"

"Just, like nanoseconds."

He thanked her for her promptness, moved over to the counter area provided and appropriated paper and pen to record the number. He had no place to put the paper in his workout clothes so he decided to end his exercise session and get to work. He handed the cell phone back to the attendant and asked her if she had some cleaning spray that she could use to wipe it off. He couldn't stand the thought of a sweat covered phone against his ear, even if it was his own.

He made his way into the locker room and began to prepare for his rubdown. He knew his time on the massage table would now be spent wondering what Will Chambers wanted to talk to him about instead of dealing with the difficult position in which he found himself. It was not yet noon and he had until midnight to negate his instructions. There was still much to do.

As he'd predicted his time with the masseuse was spent in contemplation of his upcoming call to Will. He decided to cut the session short and get on with it. He was too distracted for the rubdown to do him any good as far as relaxation and he didn't feel he'd worked out hard enough to get sore. Roland returned to the locker room and began his fastidious grooming routine. Forty-five minutes later he was in the salon of the club at a table near the corner, enjoying a properly chilled mineral water.

He dialed the number that Karla had given him for Will.

Will picked up his cell phone on the first ring. He had it conveniently resting on the console of the rental car as he made his way along the San Diego Freeway toward LAX. "This is Will," he answered.

"Will Chambers?" the male voice inquired.

"Yes, how may I help you?"

"You called my office this morning and asked to have me call you, I believe," Roland responded.

"Ah, yes, I think we need to meet in person. I've recently learned some rather critical news. I think it has to do with your future, the quality of it. Do you wish to meet with me?" Will asked.

"It sounds like I may. Can you be any clearer about the nature of your information?"

"Don't think that is wise as I'm on a cell, are you secure on your end?" Will asked.

"Probably not, are you here in Washington?"

"Tell you what, are you okay with the number I called earlier?"

"Yes, of course," Roland answered.

"I'll call you back on that number from a more secure land line. What time?"

"Please call immediately after we hang up. I'll need just a moment to alert my people to patch you through to me on a secure link."

"Done," said Will and they terminated their conversation there.

Will exited the freeway immediately and found himself among a covey of strip malls. If there was one thing the LA area knew how to do it was to create and refurbish strip malls. There was a kind of progression that they all went through. Most had been put up in the 60's and 70's with their plain square buildings and earth tone colors. A trend had begun around the 90's and 00's where they were gradually being refurbished into a deluxe craftsman style with pitched roofs and gables and a glut of beige and titty-pink colors making them look more distinctively southern California. At least that was the case in someone's mind.

He picked one with a gas station cut out of the corner of the parking lot and swung his vehicle in near the side of the building. He found a spot where a pay phone used to be and cursed the devils who had dismantled it. He was lucky on his second try, just one signal further from the freeway, another mall, another station and this time a working phone.

Will stood under the plastic hood which hung like an industrial halo over the narrow counter. He faced the black, wall mounted telephone with graffiti enhanced side windows and used one finger to shut out the street noise to his right ear while through the left he listened carefully to the ringing on the other end. A woman's voice came on the line and inquired of him with whom he wished to speak. He asked for Roland, said he was expecting his call to be forwarded on a secure link and began his wait. The next voice he heard was from Ma Bell asking for some more coins. He had put all he had on the steel shelf and he began inserting them and listening to the melodious 'ka-ching' they created. The same gratuitous voice told him he had another three minutes.

When Roland came on the line Will laid it all out. He told him of the challenges that they faced with what Amanda had learned and that they had not stopped digging for information to bring Gazelle down. He let him know that they knew that it was Gazelle who had made attempts on their lives. He was brutally honest and had decided after leaving

Amanda that this was either going to be their chance for a conclusion or a set up for their demise. It was a huge risk to take but Will knew something about risk management and he knew that the payoff could be great. He had also assessed exactly what the risk was and knew that they were fairly accurate in reading the secretary's communications. Roland was definitely on the "to be exterminated" list whether he knew it or not. Will hoped he already knew because knowing what he did of Roland's reputation he did not want to deliver the news. He feared the "kill the messenger" syndrome.

Neither Roland nor Will wanted to talk about many of the details on the phone so they concluded their conversation with an agreement that they would meet and further their exchange.

Roland convinced Will that under the circumstances they would be safer meeting on the west coast than in Washington. He was more certain of his ability to escape detection in a transcontinental trip. Their arrangements made, they hung up before Will heard from Ma Bell again.

Amanda found herself seated once more on Brad's poor excuse for a couch. Every time she went there she thought it more putrid than the time before and every time, she thought this is the last time I'll have to come here. Today she prayed that it would come true.

She was beginning to get disturbed because all she was hearing from Brad were curse words and other expressions of frustration. His annoyance was escalating after every few key strokes. She got up and went over to her usual post along side him and in front of the monitor. "What's happening?" she inquired.

"Jeez, I wish I knew. Every time I get right to the edge of an opening in the firewall I get slammed. It's like someone's sitting there with a rocket launcher just waiting for me to appear and then kaboom, down I go in flames. Can't figure it out. If I hadn't just been in there it'd be different."

"What's changed?" Amanda asked.

Brad took his hands off the keyboard and turned around toward her with his eyes wide. "That's it!" he exclaimed.

226

"What's it?"

"They've changed programs. Why didn't I think of that? Way to go, Sandy, you're better at this stuff than you thought."

Amanda sat there with her jaw dropped. She hadn't thought of anything, well whatever, "What's changed, Brad? What will we need to do?"

"I think we're done to be honest. They've either installed new software with a much more sophisticated wall or they've just restructured what they had. Have to tell you, I opt for the first. This looks state of the art to me. I keep getting a lot of messages that indicate pure digital. Wasn't getting any of that before. I say it's a new system and it's high tech, high dollars. I don't think we're going to get in there again, Sandy. At least not any time soon."

"But we've got to," she nearly gasped with desperation. She tried to downplay her reaction, "I mean, are you sure, Brad that you can't try again?"

"Oh, I'll keep trying 'cuz I hate these things to beat me but my guess is it could be months before we crack this baby, if at all. It'll be fun trying. I can't wait to get with Kyle and tweak this little puppy again. Hey, Sandy, what's this all about anyway? Why the panicked look?"

She hadn't realized the look of utter despair that had crept onto her face along with the sinking feeling that she was having. This just couldn't be happening. Just as they were close, moving along anyway. Her feeling of utter hopelessness was displayed in her expression and in her posture.

She looked so defeated sitting there in that decrepit chair in that foul cubicle that Brad called home. She was absolutely irresistible. He was so touched by her sudden vulnerability that he couldn't stop himself. He made his move.

At first as Brad put his arms around her and lifted her off of the chair Amanda felt comforted and secure. Though her body was there her mind was miles away trying to fathom the reality of what had just happened. She slowly became aware of a kiss, so boyishly shy yet physically serious. She was shocked back to the moment like some mythical character seated upon a bolt of lightening. Her response was not to the kiss as a physical intimacy but rather to the horror she felt that it was happening, that she hadn't kept things under control as she'd planned. She was both appalled and sympathetic. Kissing this young man was the last thing she wanted to do but she was also aware of his sensitivity and did not want to hurt him. He was nothing but kind and even as bad off as she was at the moment, she couldn't do anything to harm his fragile self image.

She pulled away from him slowly saying, "No Brad, as sweet as you are, I just can't get involved right now."

He seemed disappointed but at least not hurt. That was all she could hope for under the circumstances. She felt despicable that she had enlisted his help, had used him for her own purpose and now he had unrealistic expectations of where that was going. Even in this dark time of fear she had not lost her compassion for others. She was, for a moment at least, grateful for that.

Amanda gathered her tote bag and left Brad's apartment for what she assumed was the last time. She was totally disappointed that she had not been able to get the more recent communications from the secretary's computer but she knew that she couldn't use Brad for that purpose any longer. Perhaps there was another way, she thought as she began to make her way back toward her rented condo. It was a beautiful, desert afternoon. Not yet the time of year when they turned into scorchers but the sun had a reassuring warmth to it that made her think about the most fundamental needs of life. From her recollection, not far behind warmth on that hierarchal list was safety. She'd better get it in gear if she was going to meet that one.

She wondered if Will was having better luck with getting a meeting with Roland Priestly. She noticed as she walked along that her fingers were crossed. She scoffed at herself, *that's not going to help this sort of trouble, Amanda.*

Harry and the senator had agreed to meet at The All Suites Hotel in the Virginia suburbs. Not wanting to attract attention, they had booked the room under a corporate name and each agreed to arrive by cab rather than using their respective limos.

Bouncing along on the poorly maintained road, the senator knew now why he traveled in his Lincoln Town Car. It was incredibly difficult to work in the backseat of one of these cramped little cars with no suspension. It was impossible to write and his notes would fly off his lap every time the vehicle discovered another of the plentiful potholes that dotted the streets throughout the District and these surrounding suburbs. "How much further?" he finally grumped at the driver.

"Just up a couple more blocks, Sir," the cabbie answered.

He folded up his notes and relished the thought of getting out of these worn and odoriferous confines. The taxi pulled into the drive and came to a stop under the portico in front of the registration area. The senator put on a fedora with the brim turned down slightly over his eyes and entered the lobby. He approached the desk clerk and inquired about the corporate room reservation. He was given a key to the suite in exchange for payment which he chose to make in cash.

He advised the young man behind the counter that he was expecting another member of his company and asked that he be shown to his suite. Lastly, he stopped by the coffee shop in the lobby and ordered and paid for two carafes of coffee and a variety of pastries to be delivered to the room. That accomplished he rode the elevator up to the assigned room and let himself in.

The suite consisted of two rooms; one a bedroom and the other, a spacious area with a large work table in the center and a sofa and easy chair balancing the kitchenette on the opposite wall. He judged it to be nearly ideal for today's purposes and set his briefcase on the table.

He had just begun to remove the papers he needed from his attaché when there was a knock on the door and Harry, using the key he'd obtained from the desk, let himself into the room. He had the look of pent up thunder on his face. He strode across the room to the table and literally flung his Italian leather briefcase onto the table with the petulance of a spoiled child in the midst of a temper tantrum.

The senator smiled to himself and nearly let a grin break across his face. "Good morning, Harry, should I assume that you are not glad to be here?"

"Hell no, I'm not. Let's get this done; I've got a tight schedule."

Let the negotiations begin, the senator thought. In negotiating he was without peer. After years of association he knew how to handle Harry Axelrod and today of all days he had made a careful plan. The stakes were high and he was loaded for bear. His future, the future of Operation Cloud Nine and therefore the future of the world depended upon his ability to pull off his finely honed strategy. He knew that he had to get Harry to buy into the structure of this new world order that put him, Senator Chastain Hampton, directly under the leader. The all important pecking order had to be established here and now.

He knew that everything would play off of and be dependent on his opening volley. He began, "Given your reticence and lack of cooperative attitude, let me be direct and to the point, this organization and the wealth which you stand to control will not go forth in its current condition," he knew he had to hit Harry where he lived. He knew that Harry's reason for pushing this vision was greed and nothing more, but the senator had built his entire political career, his entire life around accommodating the moneyed, power brokers of America and he knew very well how to play their game.

"Let me describe to you a scenario and then we can each take an opportunity to express our pleasure or displeasure with the various facets of it. That way we can both have input into the final agreement which I'm certain can be reached. Understand at the beginning that this is not my plan. This is simply an unbiased assessment of where things are currently and where, undoubtedly both you and I are trying to get. I can absolutely assure you that it is where our superior anticipates that things will go."

Harry gave a half nod like he was permitting the senator to continue but not really assenting to anything he was saying.

The senator knew this reaction and, once again, stifled a smile as he knew that he was about to take the doggy for a walk. His well scripted plan was off to an excellent start. He just had to lead this narrow minded man to where he wanted him. Down the path to peace and harmony they went.

The senator took the next fifteen minutes or so to lay out the current state of Operation Cloud Nine. After that he began to paint a vision of untold riches to be controlled through the consortium of the world's wealthy that Harry was working with and finally through the careful use and allotment of energy resources. All this had been discussed at length over the period of time when they had created the vision of the new order. He knew that Harry had to buy into and envision himself in this new environment before he could take him along to the final outcome, the agreement that they so needed. Lastly, he encouraged Harry to picture himself atop the manipulation of the world's energy resources controlling every ebb and flow of the resources that were the precious life blood of the world economy and the management of which the future of the entire planet depended.

Once he could see the glaze of glory reflected in Harry's eyes he knew that he had him hooked. He could almost watch Harry counting his untold millions and more importantly, as he knew the man, he could see him dream of wielding the power that his personality so craved. It was time to move into the structure of the organization and get him to assent to the division of power that was needed.

"Lastly, Harry, and this is important to the life of this order, is the structure and form that it absolutely has to take in order to be palatable to the people of this planet. Many of the cultures with whom we will be dealing have never been free to make decisions or take independent steps of action. We have to get into an area here where psychology, sociology and a whole ton of organizational behaviorism will meet. Remember that more of the world is at war right now than is living in peace. Some are living under the firm hand of dictators and still others are actively engaged in combat.

As a consequence we have to proceed in a delicate manner that is as firm as a parent's controls. I know that this is not your strong suit. You were not parented and you do not foster these ideals in your employees. There are, however, those of us who have spent a lifetime practicing these skills, particularly those of us in politics. We deal everyday with making decisions and rules which are good for our constituents. We spend days and nights thinking and worrying about what is good for others, things that they may not even be thinking about themselves. This is an area where I excel. That is precisely what makes this amalgamation of minds so strong. You bring things that I don't have and vice versa." He paused to give Harry time to absorb and catch up.

Harry was still lost in the vision of a huge boardroom filled with the most beautiful appointments and furnishings. He's seated in a huge, plush leather chair at the head of a handsomely rich table. Around it are seated the wealthy and the powerful of the world. All of their eyes are on him. All of them are waiting for him to speak. He was mellow in his fantasy and he only half listened as the senator droned on. *God, how those politicians can talk,* he thought.

He realized then that he had been asked a question, "What, sorry?"

"I was just asking you if you could agree that each of us brings our unique strengths to this project and consequently, each of us has a unique roll to fill?" the senator repeated. This was an example in negotiating techniques of getting the other party to begin to agree with you on something simple as you move them along to bigger and bigger concessions.

Harry nodded in agreement. How could he not agree with something so fundamentally accurate?

The senator continued on this way until Harry had agreed and was absolutely on board with the separation of powers between the two men that the senator had envisioned all along. He concluded by having Harry agree that he, Senator Hampton, would be the one to communicate with the powers that be. He would act as the deputy, the manager and Harry would continue to coordinate the consortium of money. Finally, he advised that he would have the agreement reduced to writing when he returned to his office and would messenger it over to Harry. This way they would have a reference for responsibility for tasks as the structure of the new organization was taking shape and their mutual vision of world order was about to come to fruition.

After two hours, Harry left the hotel happy as a clam and with visions of grandeur still dancing about in his head.

The senator did the same.

Roland decided on his way to the airport to obtain an extension on the activation of his emergency plan. He picked up his cell phone and dialed the number.

"Is it you?" was the response.

"This is double zero, ten, twenty-two. I need a 48 hour extension. If you've not heard from me by midnight on the 14th, activate. Please repeat."

"You have until midnight on the 14th, a 48 hour extension from your original request, Godspeed." They hung up.

Roland had decided to use a private jet for his trip to the west coast. It left him with a great deal more flexibility in departure times and he could make whatever stops along the way he deemed prudent. Additionally it could be much harder to track him down after the fact as he'd learned that the loyalty of the crew could be purchased. He'd been fortunate that the group he'd used numerous times in the past and who knew of his habits was available and waiting.

As his car swept up alongside the Learjet waiting on the tarmac at National Airport he was nearly deafened by the high pitched whine emitted by the engines and the polluted smell of the air threatened instant lung disease. The shrieking sound stood out against the background of jumbo jets and helicopters mulling about busily above and around him. He covered one ear with his free hand and laid his other over against his shrugged up shoulder to try to block out the painful screech as he clutched his briefcase, nodded to the pilot in the open doorway and rushed up the stairs to escape the repulsive wind and sound. Once inside the attendant pulled the stairs up and secured the door gratefully blocking out that excruciating noise.

"Don't think you've ever had the engines started when I boarded before, Steven," he said to the pilot as he shook the man's hand in greeting.

"Good to have you aboard, sorry, Sir, I know that noise can be unpleasant but I had a sense of urgency from your message and I wanted to make sure we were set to go. I've taken the liberty of filing the flight plan to LAX to get us started and we can amend that in flight as you know. If you'll buckle in we'll contact the tower and be airborne ASAP."

Roland took off his coat and gave it to the cabin attendant before sitting in the front facing, leather seat with a good sized table in front of it and fastening his seat belt. Once he was settled in the attendant took her place buckling into the jump seat outside the cockpit door and the plane began to taxi away from the general aviation hangers. Roland leaned his head back, closed his eyes and began to formulate his plan for arrival.

Before reaching the coast they had put down at three airports and filed numerous flight plans with innumerable amendments. Although it could be done, they would not be easy to track. At the last stop in Boise, Roland had treated all three crew members to a beautifully presented and aptly appointed dinner catered from a topnotch restaurant which specialized in Asian infusion. The food was delightful and they all agreed as they headed back for the plane and their ultimate destination that they had eaten way too much. Roland hoped they weren't going to be sleepy but he knew that the fail safe measures which were in place would keep them safe from such harm. Having a co-pilot who ate completely different dishes from the pilot was a help and he knew the plane was equipped with all sorts of alarms if any erratic movement occurred. Lastly, he knew these guys were pros and they'd had his life in their hands many times before. That wasn't his worry; he had plenty of real ones of his own to concentrate on.

Chapter Seventeen

As Roland was winging his way to the west coast, Will was rattling down it, coincidentally on the SoCal Flyer. This was California's version of a double decked commuter train which made pretty good time between LA and San Diego.

He found himself packed in among business people who were hard at work either reading documents or pecking on laptops and a gaggle of Girl Scout Brownies who were apparently on their first train ride and judging from their excited, non-stop talk, they were headed to the San Diego Zoo. He decided that his best bet for arriving with any fraction of his sanity still in place was to look out the window at the unique countryside that was flying past his personal, little peep hole to the world.

He saw the large, gray, concrete stacks of the San Onofre Nuclear Energy Plant wink at him as they made a brief appearance in the opening through which he could view the passing world. Behind it came a kind of brushy undergrowth which stretched from the tracks toward the sea and then stopped abruptly where the blue breakers of the Pacific lapped upon the white sands of the land abutting it. It was hard to remember everything that was wrong with life in this kind of an environment but he forced himself to concentrate on the meeting that lay ahead, just down the tracks.

Roland heard the tires screech as the jet touched down at a private air strip just east of San Diego. The runway and grounds were now maintained by a private group of airplane owners who kept it busy with their personal aircraft preferring its convenience to that of the main, commercial airport that was closer to the coast and downtown. This airstrip had been built during World War II due to its proximity to the Pacific theatre of fighting and had been maintained through the Korean Conflict in the 50's. It had been closed with the first round of bases in the early 60's and the group of owners/operators had been formed at that time and still continued today. The strip was in good shape but the buildings needed some upgrading and it was anyone's guess if it would survive in this economy.

Roland had reserved a car and was anticipating it meeting him near the parking lot. He entered the small terminal and passed through its lobby with plastic plants, torn naughahide seating and peeling paint. It really looked like something out of the 70's, a kind of Howard Johnson's décor. He emerged from the terminal and spotted a dark sedan parked at the curb with the driver leaning against the front fender. He was holding a sign in his hand with the name Carl Handler carefully printed on it. Roland walked up to the driver, smiled and said, "I'm Mr. Handler."

The driver introduced himself with a half bow and opened the rear door for Roland to enter.

Moments later they were on the freeway cutting and darting among the unending stream of cars whose drivers seemed to have urgent business at the formless termination of this roadway. Of all the places Roland went around the world, *each,* he thought *had its own drivers' personality. From Bangkok to London there was a predictable manner exhibited by the drivers and an unspoken way of communicating to those around them. None of those,* he observed, *was more unusual or more consistent throughout the state than Californians on their freeways.* He sort of shut his eyes and chose not to watch.

It was only moments before they exited the freeway. Roland pressed the button which opened the roof and found himself riding along a winding, eucalyptus lined, road where the air felt fresh and damp and the aroma of the peeling trees filled his senses like the cold remedies of his childhood. The driver maneuvered the car into the parking area of a middle class motel which was adjacent to Balboa Park. Everything was just as he'd ordered. He had to remember to give Karla a bonus and be extra good to her during this trying time. She could be one of his vulnerabilities and there were those who knew that.

Roland took his leave of the driver with instructions for their continued contact. He would be using the car throughout his time here. He entered the modest lobby of the motel and checked in as Carl Handler. He made his way to his room on the second floor and let himself in. He had no bags other than the small case he carried. He had inquired of the desk clerk to be certain that the shops and restaurants of Old Town were within walking distance and had been informed that they could actually be seen from the window in the rear of his room. He parted the drapes now to assure himself that everything was as he'd planned.

Will arrived at the depot in downtown San Diego mid morning and was able to catch a shuttle bus which would take him through the downtown stopping at the Gaslight area, Old Town and finally Balboa Park. He opted for the relative anonymity of the bus over a taxi and boarded it with ten or twelve other passengers. By the time they left Old Town with its Moorish, Mexican style adobes and headed for Balboa Park there were only three people on the bus including himself. Thank goodness, he thought, the Brownies had spent extra time at the depot and he was not confined in this space with them and their high energy excitability.

Will studied the other two passengers carefully. Each seemed to be alone which always raises suspicion, one man and one woman. He studied their features carefully through his California shades under the premise of looking right and left while taking in the sights of the city as if he'd never seen them before. By the time he left the bus at the park he was sure he would know either of them if he saw them again, regardless of their clothing or other trappings. He'd become careful enough during this dangerous game to not take things at face value. Just because someone wore Bermuda shorts with dress shoes and trouser socks with a camera hanging around their neck didn't make them a nerd tourist. He looked through those exteriors now in a way he'd never done before. *The deadliness of this exercise in intrigue had taught him a great deal*, he thought. He hoped he didn't have more to learn.

Will left the bus at its first scheduled stop within the park and began walking along the sidewalk toward one of the museums. He made his way among the well manicured lawns and rolling hills which were literally bursting with spring color. It was still early enough in the season for the hills to retain their lush green hues from the winter rains while warm enough to encourage the beginnings of the summer profusion of colors. He was particularly impressed with the vibrant purple and fuchsia colors of the bougainvillea which adorned the old, stately buildings in the park.

He followed the signs that directed him along a pleasant walkway and found his way to the entrance to the zoo. He purchased his admission ticket, complete with the bus orientation tour and proceeded through the turnstile. There he was greeted by a huge parrot busy talking to a tour group. Directly in front of him was a large enclosure of flamingos standing around on one foot. He wondered briefly if he'd be able to keep his mind on business. He hadn't been here since he was a kid and the magic of it threatened to possess him. He recalled the deadly game then and the beauty of the animals around him disappeared as quickly as it had come. He hoped that he and Charles could return here one day.

Will had ten minutes before his tour bus would depart so he spent some time watching the animals in the vicinity of the entrance. He also kept a sharp eye on the animals coming through the turnstile.

Less than an hour later as the bus reloaded after a stop at the sea lions and harbor seals, Will did not return to his seat. He went instead up an asphalt path that led to the huge aviary and found a bench part way up from where you could sit and watch the seals cavort in their confined habitat.

He was certain that this was the place that Roland had described. He checked his watch to see how long he had to wait. He was pleased with himself to see that he had arrived within ten minutes of the appointed time.

Unknown to Will, at the same time and from across the service road, Roland watched him as he settled onto the bench to await their agreed meeting time. Roland moved his monocular carefully around through the trees and walkways. Using the monocular allowed him to fit in with the birdwatchers and it was also easier to conceal.

He hadn't wanted to handle too many bulky items and he had managed to get inside the park with his favored nine millimeter Glock at his side. He had put the silencer in his vest pocket. He hoped he didn't need to use them in a place like this. He knew that if he did it would have to be execution style. It would only be practical with the silencer in place and in some out of the way spot. This was not the kind of place you just shot at someone across the way indiscriminately. Between the risk to innocent families and calling attention to yourself within the fenced confines it just didn't make sense. Bottom line was if he needed to act, he'd have to take the time to put the silencer in place and handle the matter at close range. Under that scenario he had time to retrieve the silencer from his pocket and put it in place if and when he needed it.

He continued to scan the area around Will for the next ten minutes or so. He paid particular attention to those people who were milling about the exhibit whether with families or alone. He was not going to get careless at this point. He let Will stay there an extra thirty minutes partly to observe how he handled himself and partly to see whether anyone tried to contact him if they thought that Roland wasn't going to show. When he thought he'd left him there as long as he could he moved out of the woods and made his way up the path to the bench where Will waited.

Roland uttered the code words, "Do you know which way from here to the elephant exhibit?"

"I think it's up that service road and to your left at the top of the hill."

The two men barely looked at each other. Roland continued to scan the hillside and the path with great regularity which made Will feel all twitchy. "I didn't think you were gonna show, you're so late," Will observed.

"I've been here, just needed to be sure about the security."

"I'm certain I wasn't followed," Will continued. "I took great precautions."

"Me, too, but we can't be too careful, can we? Why don't you tell me what you know and show me what you have before we run out of time."

Will was reluctant to share the e-mail documents with Roland but he gave him a verbal rundown on what they had. He had made copies of their original printouts and he would give them to Roland but he wanted to hold them back until the man had settled down. He was really making Will nervous. He needed to know that they would get something for the 'show and tell' portion of this meeting. The quid pro quo was what was important to him.

After Will related what they had learned from the secretary's e-mail he waited for a response from Roland. There was none. Finally Will inquired, "I'm not practiced at this sort of thing, Mr. Priestly and I can't tell whether I've just told you something you didn't know, reinforced something you suspected, told you something you already knew or wasted a whole bunch of your precious time. I know that you deal with people like this as a matter of course but I don't."

Roland turned and looked carefully into Will's face. He observed everything he could about the individual in that brief moment. He said nothing, just continued to scan his environment like hunted prey.

Will went on, "Look, my only interest in this is to save the people that I love. Two of them have had very close brushes with death and that is not something that we're used to. Somehow my sister stumbled on to something dangerous and it's putting at risk her life as well as mine and others I love. I just want this whole nightmare to go away. When we got these e-mails I thought possibly that you were in danger from the same people and I'd hoped that you might team up with us to end this whole scourge once and for all. If I'm mistaken just say so."

Roland growled, "Shut up."

Will was taken aback but continued, "Look, you must think there is something to all this or you wouldn't have gone to the trouble of coming here to meet with me. That is unless you've come here to kill me. If that's the case...."

"Shut the fuck up!" Roland growled at Will now. "Get up and walk slowly up this path. You will find a wire gate there that is the entrance to the aviary. Follow the path up the hill through the aviary and when you come out the other end, turn left. About 50 feet down that road on you right there is a display of penguins. You can go in behind the glass enclosure and sit down there to watch them. I'll see you there in a little bit. Do not leave before I get there. If you think someone is trying to kill you and you absolutely have to leave, call me at this number and ask for Carl Handler. Do not, however, call until after 3 p.m."

Will took the paper with the number on it and tried to read it as it quivered in his hand. There was no wind, he must be shaking. When he looked up from the paper all he could see was Roland's back as he turned right at the bottom of the path and disappeared.

Will was dumbstruck and frightened beyond belief. He just sat there for a moment taking in what he'd just heard. God, the guy was cold, *if I think someone's going to kill me? How would I know unless I'm looking down the barrel of a gun and then it's too damn late.*

Will knew he needed to get up and move but his body seemed unwilling to listen to the commands that his brain was giving. He wondered if his legs would hold him if he did get up on them. After what seemed an eternity, but was only moments, the numbness of his mind subsided some and was replaced with a wave of nausea. He did manage to get to his feet and start moving up the path though he wondered why and what toward. As he walked he tried to measure which was more frightful, the possibility that someone might try to kill him in the next few minutes or that cold, icy, demanding voice and stare that Roland had just used on him. He shivered in the warmth of the day.

Roland made his way along the service road where he had seen the man leave the road and enter the woods. Having just spent the better part of an hour in the same basic spot, he knew there was no good reason for someone to be in there. In this pristine of a park you didn't need to use the woods to take a leak. They had clean and well serviced restrooms at every turn. Besides, he was sure he recognized him.

He entered the woods about twenty feet further down the path than where he had seen the potential stalker go. As soon as he passed the first tree and some low growing brush he reached into his vest and removed the silencer. With his other hand he extracted the Glock from his pocket. As he walked soundlessly through the natural area he attached the silencer to his weapon and held it just inside his jacket out of sight. His challenge was to continue through this undergrowth soundlessly. Not easy unless he paid close attention. He was grateful that the majority of it had been left in chaparral vegetation leaving it sparse and with very few twigs on the ground.

It was then that he caught sight of the man. He was talking animatedly with another. He knew them both. They were both men who had done work for Gazelle in the past and who would recognize Roland anywhere. He'd once considered them friends. They'd even worked together in Paris. That had been a very long time ago, back when he drank to end the pain of every day. These were two of the finest. Roland knew in that moment that he was a very high priority for his "friends" within Gazelle. *What the hell?* he asked himself.

Roland had not been in this side of the work for many years but he kept himself fit and he liked to think he hadn't lost a step over the years. Maybe a half, he let himself muse, but he was certain he could pull this off.

He found just the right tree, between the men and the road. This would cut off their natural instinct to bolt in the direction from which they'd come. He searched the area around him and found a softball sized rock which he carried in his left hand. In his right hand was the comforting weight of the Glock with the silencer in place. He knelt down behind a bush and checked that the magazine was in place and a round was chambered. He was ready to go.

He moved behind the tree and with his left hand he lobbed the rock up over the heads of the two men. As he had hoped it made a rustling and then a thudding sound as it crashed through the brush and landed hard on the floor of the woods. Both men turned in the direction of the sound immediately but only one instinctively reached for his weapon. Roland moved from behind the tree and with one quick motion he was upon them. There was less than 10 feet between them when he popped the one who'd drawn his weapon. The bullet entered at the base of the skull and exited in the vicinity of his pug nose. The second man whirled back to face him, just as the second bullet entered his brain above his eyes which were wide open with shock.

Even though thoroughly distracted, Will couldn't help but smile as the playful penguins swam and dove in the icy waters in front of him. They seemed to play and taunt one another with a mischievous affection not unlike human beings. He was lost in their world when Roland slipped onto the bench beside him. "We don't have long to talk. Meet me at the Chile Pepper restaurant in Old Town at 4 o'clock. Make sure you're not followed though I doubt you will be. Just take care to lose a tail whether you think you have one or not." Roland couldn't help but think that between him and this amateur sleuth it had been he that had been followed not Will. He would have to tighten his own security, he thought.

Before Will could respond Roland got up and left moving quickly toward the exit to the zoo.

Will found himself with nothing to do for the next hour and a half. He must have sat there with the penguins for another twenty minutes or so until he decided to begin his circuitous trip to the Chile Pepper and Roland.

The bells dangling from the front door called out as he entered the comfortable little restaurant just a few minutes before four and found Roland already there and relaxing in the back corner. Will observed that they were the only patrons in the entire establishment. He made his way between tables and joined Roland in the booth. Will's back was to the entrance since Roland, as was his custom, had carefully positioned himself where he could see the entire room including the door. Unknown to Will, Roland felt the comfort of the Glock resting against his leg on the seat.

Will didn't notice that no one came to wait on them until Roland beckoned. Will ordered a beer and Roland stuck with his usual, Perrier. Will knew from the instant that he entered the restaurant that there was something different about Roland and he could sense now that this was his meeting and he would control it, including the time and location.

Will had barely taken a sip of his recently delivered beer and Roland was still pouring his water when he began, "I'm going to put this out to you straight, Will, we've got our hands full and I would like to pursue the possibility of handling this mess together. I want to be up front with you, however, so you'd better listen to what I have to say before you decide how you want to proceed."

Roland held back very little about the current situation as he described for Will what they were up against. He chose not to reveal much about the past, however, including the long history of Gazelle.

"The reason I separated from you in the zoo was because I saw someone that I recognized from previous work with Gazelle. While you watched the penguins I followed the man and found him in conference in the woods with another whom I also recognized. It is clear to me that I was being followed. Whether they were on surveillance or a hit I can't say right now, but we won't be concerned with those particular two again. I am just as certain, though, that there will be more to come."

"I'm not sure if I follow what you're saying," Will sort of stammered the words out. "I'm trying not to be too naïve about all this but am I to assume that you killed them?" Will looked over one shoulder then the other as he barely whispered the word as if no one should hear him even utter it.

Roland looked at him somewhat apprehensively. "Look I know you're a good boy with very clean hands and a straight mid-western ethic but please know that I was once also. I don't relish this sort of thing but it has come to me out of necessity. I don't have time to sit here and make excuses or explanations. You need to decide what you're going to do. You may ask me whatever you like and I will either answer you or not, as I choose. Then maybe you can decide whether to associate with the likes of me and I with you."

Will's stomach was turning over and he seemed paralyzed in the jaw. He couldn't think of anything to say or ask. He prayed for some divine direction.

"Will, let me explain this much. I got involved with Gazelle because I believed whole heartedly in making things better for the average American. I know that sounds overly simplistic but that's how it is. I had no idea going in that I would ever end up taking so many shortcuts and doing the harm that I have. It has only been recently, when I've seen the people with whom I've been associated move this to another level that I have come to realize that I've lost sight of my original goal.

"I have a sense of where they are going and I can only say that they need to be stopped. I know that I'm probably the only person who can do that. I could use your help but I can also get along without it. You may be more trouble than your worth, I'm not sure yet. The thing is you seem to have made some inroads and I think you're as motivated to expose these people as I am. Just let me be really, really clear with you. This is a deadly game we are playing. In deadly games, people get killed. In all probability you and I will be among the dead. It is our objective to be otherwise. So please put away your shocked and appalled expression and decide what you're going to do."

Will finally found his voice, "What would you expect from me? I don't think I could kill anyone, even after what they've done to us. I, naively, would like to see them brought to justice."

"Actually that's my first choice as well but I'm not above bringing them down, however I need to. The best of all worlds would be to expose them or help them self-destruct."

They continued their conversation for nearly an hour. Will finally came to his senses and began to understand the depth and gravity of the situation. He also came to believe that he could either work with Roland Priestly or be taken out by him. He didn't think the man knew of any middle ground. You were either with him or against him.

Where had he heard that familiar phrase before? What was it about such people that they could see no gray area? It didn't have to be all one way or the other; there were people who were neutral on a subject. Sometimes compromise could be found. Things just aren't that simple. Once again Will pondered the danger of people who thought this way, these were the true extremists. Those who saw only black or white saw the world through one extreme or the other. In that moment he decided that he would rather work with Roland, at least to some extent, than to have yet another person trying to kill him and Amanda.

Will heard Roland asking him where he was staying.

"I haven't registered anywhere yet. I'll find a place around here when we finish."

"Don't do that, there are rooms upstairs, I'm going to stay here and I'll have them accommodate you as well. Gina?" He gestured to the waitress.

"She came to the booth with both a smile and concern on her face. "What is it?" she asked.

"Please prepare accommodations for the night for my friend. We do not wish for him to register locally, you understand."

"Yes, of course, he will have the room next to you, Senor," she replied.

"That done, I suggest that we retire to our rooms and continue this conversation in an hour or so. I don't know about you but I'm famished and I would really like to freshen up before dinner." Roland gracefully scooped up his gun, slipped it in the back of his waist and slid from the booth. He stopped to give Gina a peck on the cheek and turned to gesture for Will to follow him.

They left through a back door which put them in a lovely, blossom filled courtyard. Several other doors opened onto the terraced veranda and a large fountain spilled water into a catch basin below. The tinkling sound was as soft as a kitten.

They ascended a vine covered, wrought iron staircase and once inside the door they stepped into a short hallway. There were only four doors which displayed room numbers and Roland took the first gesturing for Will to use the one adjacent to it.

The door was unlocked and Will entered a graciously appointed and comfortably furnished room complete with a private bath and a turned down bed. He was grateful for the solitude and collapsed into one of the chairs in front of the window.

He wasn't sure how long he'd slept there but it was completely dark outside and he realized that he had awakened to the music of Mariachis playing in the courtyard below. He thought for a moment that he could have been in Mexico.

Will managed a shower and shave with the provisions that were provided by his hostess. He also found a freshly laundered nightshirt to sleep in which had been carefully hung in the closet. He would look forward to that later. Right now he needed some quality thinking time. He stretched out on the top of the bed covers and looking up at the ceiling he began to assess his options. .

Chapter Eighteen

Nate was busy at his new terminal in the bunker analyzing the data in front of him. Someone was trying hard and repeatedly to hack into the e-mail and they had been thwarted by the new system. They'd been getting these reports from the system for four or five days now and they'd been trying to track down the source. Today had brought success. Whoever it was had carelessly or unknowingly left a fingerprint. They had them now, the remainder was just legwork.

Just down the hall the secretary was dealing with some news of his own. His was much more shocking. He now had to find a way to tell the senator that the surveillance team that he'd put on Roland Priestly had been found dead, more precisely, assassinated. They hadn't yet had the meeting where they were to finalize the plan for taking him out. He wondered why his men had been hit. Surely Roland had no way to know that he was hot. The men had only been tailing him.

He needed to talk to the senator and wasn't sure whether he'd rather do it over the phone or in person. With all of his new equipment in place he was absolutely safe talking on his secure phones but also because of that equipment he hadn't been out of the bunker for almost a week now. There was getting to be less and less need to move about in the outside world.

He decided that today's meeting was a good reason to leave his confines and meet with the senator in person. He also needed to get some face time with the man in order to assess his position within the organization. Sometimes it was just too hard to do all of your business over the electronic equipment that had become so much a routine. There was nothing like sitting in the room with someone. You could observe every change in posture, every nuance of movement or expression; sometimes you could even smell their fear. These were things that just didn't come through even on the video conferencing they'd been using. He set out for the city on a bright, spring day in Virginia.

He hadn't been in the meeting with the senator very long when he wished he'd handled this over the phone. He could sense every tense muscle, every frayed nerve end and what he smelled was not fear but the lust for blood, his he presumed. While it was true that he had some real damage control to take care of and he needed to be there face to face to do that, it was not his favorite part of the job and he wished it could be avoided once and for all.

He had to keep proving himself, over and over. Perhaps that was because things kept getting screwed up, over and over. He didn't see it as his fault but he knew that with men like the senator, Harry Axelrod and the powers that be blame was a relative term. All they wanted was results and if they didn't get them someone was ultimately at fault. After about so many of those in your area of responsibility and you were gone. He knew that for a fact. He'd been taking care of that end of the business for long enough that he didn't need to be convinced that these guys meant business.

He watched the senator pace impatiently around his office. He knew he was losing confidence in him and his ability to handle the hard stuff. He reflected for a moment on the kinds of things that he had handled over the years and tried to assess why things were in such disarray now. Why could he not rise to the occasion? What was keeping him from growing and developing his team in stride with the rest of the organization? He was definitely the weak link and he knew that if he didn't come through this time, changes would be made. He knew that the senator dreaded that but he also knew that he had just ordered a hit on a man who was like a son to him. He wouldn't hesitate to have him taken out. He also knew that the senator trusting him with this all important assignment was literally a do or die. He had gone to bat for him, had vouched for him and it was important that he come through for him now. There was so much riding on it.

Once the meeting from hell had ended and he was making his way back to the relative safety of his bunker he reflected on what he must do. The senator had been clear about his expectations, he couldn't say that the man hadn't been forthright and direct. Everything hinged on tomorrow's meeting with the lieutenants and the plan that they would come up with for disposing of Roland, Amanda Chambers and her brother. It had to be good, it had to be foolproof. That was a good term, he thought, fool proof because he felt like all he had to work with were fools. Maybe this job was impossible.

He hoped Nate's newly inserted leadership would offset some of the keystone cops stuff that had been happening and provide a clearer path. He laid his head back on the seat, took a deep breath and silently hoped that tomorrow would be a better day.

He arrived back in the womb of the bunker just after noon and was met with news that caused his hopes to buoy. The intruder who had been trying to hack into their system for the last week had been found in southern California and had been eliminated. Maybe his team was beginning to come together. Perhaps they could get the job done. They'd found the guy on the internet, identified him in two short days and taken him out within two days of the ID. Less than a week from discovery to death. He'd certainly make the senator aware of that little success.

They were all so puffed up from their success and busy high-fiving each other that it never occurred to him or anyone on his team to try to find out why the little, techie nerd wanted their e-mail.

Back in San Diego Roland sat in his room above the Chile Pepper and pondered his direction. He had contacted Will, comfortably and safely ensconced in the room next door, and arranged to meet him downstairs for dinner at eight o'clock. He still had an hour or so and he needed to let his mind work, let it go wherever it might take him. Free thinking association, he'd always called it. It was his way of clearing his mind and making room for whatever strategizing he needed to do.

The one thing he knew was that he could right some terrible wrongs in his life if he could get Amanda and Will through this nightmare safely. He needed to do this for them but he needed more to do it for himself. If he could also expose the players, that would be a plus. He had himself to think about as well. He wasn't ready to give himself up. This didn't need to be a suicide mission.

It had first come to him back in Switzerland when he had begun to question where Gazelle was going and whether he wanted to go there with it. He had sensed then that Harry was trying to push him into assassinating innocent people. Roland had been involved in that part of the business in the earlier years, but he prided himself on the fact that he never killed anyone who wasn't a killer themselves. He had his own moral code, twisted as it might seem to others, and he was true to it always. He realized now that Harry had known that Roland wouldn't go there and it was his way, not of pushing Roland to do it, but of pushing Roland out of the organization and away from the senator. Well, Roland hadn't wavered, he remained proud of that, but Harry was also getting his way as Roland was certainly history.

He concentrated on thoughts of the senator. He couldn't help but wonder why the man he so admired and believed in had turned his back on him now. There was something that Harry had said to him that morning when he had barged into his office. That seemed so long ago now, but it had only been a few days. He got his focus back. Harry had said something about the senator selling him out. Roland began to pace as he wondered what Harry had meant by that.

He didn't realize how much time had passed until he heard Gina knocking lightly on his door and calling to him. It was well past eight and she was concerned that he had not come down to join his dinner companion. Gina had always taken good care of him. They had met over twenty years ago when he was not long out of school and still looking for his life's calling. He had spent some time in California working as an aide in the state legislature and since one of the representatives that he worked for had his constituency in San Diego,

Roland had spent a great deal of time in the area and Gina had taken him under her motherly wing.

She'd been a bar maid in a sailor's hangout near the port at that time. He'd always known that she had more than a passing interest in him. She'd lived in the same complex that he stayed in when he was down from Sacramento and their friendship had blossomed over late night drinks and talks sitting beside the pool. He called to her through the door that he'd be right down.

He arrived downstairs to find Will seated in the same booth they'd occupied earlier casually enjoying a beer and Gina's company. Gina jumped up as she saw him approaching and gave him her side of the booth. Roland thanked Gina for reminding him of the time and made his apologies to Will as he sat down to continue their business.

Roland had come to some clarity and he put it to Will now. "I've been giving this matter a great deal of thought, as you can imagine." He paused and took a deep breath as if trying to capture the illusive truth of the moment. "There is something I'd like to say to you that may influence your direction. I realized some time ago that I was beginning to question Gazelle's direction and methods and had not decided what I was going to do about it when all of this blew up. What I'm trying to say, Will, is that I feel a great deal of responsibility toward you and your sister. I mean around the mess you find yourselves in now. I'd like to help. It would be my feeble attempt to make amends, I guess. I'd expect nothing back from you other than your cooperation in what I'm trying to do to unravel this mess and expose some very bad players."

Will felt the tension flow out of his mind, down his trunk and drip out the end of his limbs like tree sap on a warm spring day. His feeling of relief was surpassed only by his anxiety at what this resolution would look like and where it might take them. He hoped the hell that he had seen the last of the danger, the last of being the point man on a team headed for certain destruction. It would be good to be able to trust that someone like Roland was going to call the shots. Perhaps even put this nightmare behind them once and for all. Oh, God, he wanted to believe, please let this be the answer he had longed for but could not find. His mind leapt to Charles.

Roland misunderstood Will's silence and continued, "I don't want you to feel that I don't think that you can look after yourself and your sister. Will, this is something I really need, really want to do. It would go along way toward my own redemption. As I said I'm doing this for myself as well as for you. What do you say?"

Will responded, "Roland, I'm delighted, it says a lot about you. As you know, your reputation precedes you and I have to admit that until this moment I've been about half scared of you. I trust what you've said to me tonight, partly because of the sincerity with which you've presented yourself, partly from my own assessment and partly from the sell job that Gina did on me before you arrived. I guess a side of me wants all this to be so, wants to trust you, that makes it more convenient, doesn't it?

"To be perfectly honest, Roland, I'm about at my wits end and have run out of places to turn. I'm hard pressed to come up with a next step. Having said that I must add that I'm frightened for Amanda and for myself to play in the league you move in. It scares me to think where you may take us. Anyway, I do welcome your assistance, no, your leadership and Amanda and I will do whatever it takes. I don't know how to thank you, Roland, really."

"Just put your life back together and go on. I'm sincere, Will, I know it sounds really trite but nothing gives me greater satisfaction than to see people safely going about their lives because most of them, sooner or later, find their benevolent side and spread their good fortune. It's a beautiful thing and I hope you can think of me as one really bad example. I tried too hard; it's like holding a fragile bird in your hand and I squeezed too hard, Will, nearly killed it. I hope I can fix it now, just hope it's not too late."

Will observed the look of utter despair that moved across Roland's face. He was almost despondent. He wondered if anyone really knew this complex man. He also wondered what the next few days were going to rain down on his life.

With the passing of that brief moment of remorse, Roland was back in the present, "Let's eat," he suggested.

Just a short distance to the north Amanda was devastated to learn of the death of Bradley Duncan. The story first came to her in the coffee shop that she frequented. She had been sitting there reading the Desert Sun when one of Brad's friends from the university approached her.

"Horrible news about Brad, isn't it?" His head hung down and he looked genuinely forlorn. "I know you hung out with him, kinda, I just wanted to say sorry, ya know," he stammered all over himself until she'd made him realize that she had no idea what he was talking about.

"Oh, I'm sorry, I assumed you knew. He was killed in a car accident."

"Again, sorry, Hey, I've gotta run." Just that fast the young man was gone and Amanda was left sitting there with her mouth open and her stomach somewhere close to the laces of her running shoes. She couldn't help but think that this had happened because of her. Her mind was beginning to go all kinds of places. Like a runaway train, one thought coupled onto the one before it and tore off down the track toward untold leaps in logic. She was determined to learn more. She left the shop in a daze but steadfast in learning the truth.

She found herself sitting alone in her living room wondering which way to turn. In using Brad had she caused his death? She thought about the woman who'd been shot by mistake in her coat. Was this another casualty of a war she didn't understand? Maybe Brad's death was just an accident. They certainly happen often enough. Maybe it was an execution. Maybe they were getting close to her again. She was beginning to panic. She needed to talk to Will but he had told her he wouldn't be available until tomorrow. He was supposed to call her then. She had to hang on, had to stay rational. She went into the bathroom and threw up.

The senator had chosen to make the trip to the bunker on this momentous occasion. This would be the first meeting of the new security team to which the safety of Operation Cloud Nine would be entrusted. It was important to him that they get off on the right foot, they had to understand what was expected of them and, more importantly, they needed to be indoctrinated into a new way of thinking. His arrival was also anticipated with mixed reactions within the security team's portion of the bunker. All the stops had been pulled out, hours of preparatory meetings were held and everything was reorganized and rearranged with the advent of the new world order in mind.

It had become increasingly clear in the last few weeks that control within the organization rested solely with the senator. His name had become synonymous with power and it was well known and accepted that the showdown between him and Harry Axelrod, though no one knew the details, had ended with the senator managing the issues and Harry responsible for the money. They had carved out their respective responsibilities between themselves and made it clear to all the others where the decision making would reside. With this done, Senator Hampton had become a very important and very powerful figure throughout the bunker though everyone seemed to know that the real power, the silent head of it all, lay elsewhere. The senator was a pawn in his own right, a powerful one to be sure, but a pawn all the same.

Over the course of the last couple of years the administration had been distracted by the war on terrorism, then distracted from that by the war with Iraq, the announcement by the North Koreans and now Iran that they were engaged in the development of nuclear weapons, the continued strife between the Israelis and the Palestinians, the domestic economy, including corporate corruption and on and on it went.

As a result of these distractions the occupants of the bunker were able to operate without control or oversight and the focus of the work had moved almost entirely from legitimate government tasks to the innovative business of changing the world. Nearly everyone working there now understood the reality of it. They all shared time in the classes each week which were designed to lead them toward greater understanding of the movement. They heard horror stories from the past and the present and were given to believe that the only hope for the future lie in the path described to them. We, as a planet, were moving rapidly in the direction of needing a strong world government. It was a pretty easy sell to those who read the morning paper.

The United Nations would never be it they were told. That organization was to the world as the current administration in

Washington was to the United States, ineffective without some outside help or shortcuts. They had really proved that with the issue of weapons of mass destruction in Iraq. It was actually laughable to the occupants of the bunker as they sat in one of their indoctrination sessions listening to the description of the inept decision making process and its impact on the entire world.

The U.N. Security Council and several world leaders had screwed around with the wording of the resolutions so long that anything that may have been vulnerable to inspections was long gone by the time they finished debating and rewording everything that came out of their meetings. It was the typical paralysis by analysis, and rhetoric, that crippled nearly every government, save for the dictators who did whatever they wished. Of course along with that form of rule came the grave deprivation of civil rights.

It was the age old struggle of the rights of the individual versus the good of the group. It had been going on since tribal times. It was a tough balancing act and had been the basis for political parties and discourse for untold generations. The state of the world today and the size of the world population had made this the time to deal with it on a macro level. Yes, they were coming to understand that a better way was needed if this planet and its population were to survive. Thank God for Senator Hampton and Operation Cloud Nine, two names synonymous with hope.

His eventual arrival and welcome to the bunker looked a great deal like that of a visiting dignitary to the White House. Though he lacked a horse drawn carriage and crown jewels his entrance could have rivaled that of Queen Elizabeth. Nearly all of the occupants of the bunker were in the hallways and aisles as he made his way to the conference room where he was scheduled to meet with the security team. He was taken aback by the reception and wondered for one brief moment if they were going a little overboard with the indoctrination program. He decided that people just naturally needed someone to look to for leadership and he had never shirked from that responsibility, his role was as the front man after all. He moved into the room with members of the security team already in attendance. The door closed behind him.

He emerged from the room nearly two hours later content with the plan for eradication of the problems. He viewed these assassinations as little more than the removal of obstacles from the path of progress to world order. In four days, that part would be over. It was important that this be cleaned up before they moved further toward implementation.

Things were on schedule and everything needed to be done on time. There wasn't much room for error in the cleanup of these little problems. If that went off without a hitch, so too would the new world regime. If there were problems with the assassinations that would negatively impact their movement. It would definitely cause a serious delay and could even preclude the enforcement of the plan altogether. That could not be allowed to happen. This is why he had attended this meeting of the security force and had inserted himself into the planning process. Something he definitely did not plan on doing in the future.

Gina hovered as Roland and Will consumed a wonderful dinner of enchiladas, frijoles and rice appropriately washed down with several Coronas. There was nothing like it, Roland thought. Will ate like he hadn't put a thing in his stomach in days and he wondered once if he had. If so, he couldn't remember it and he certainly hadn't tasted it. He'd been distracted for so long and now he was feeling the first hint of relief at having Roland on their team.

Will asked about next steps, "Have you had a chance to come up with a plan?"

"Not completely but I'm determined to have it firmly in place by tomorrow morning. It usually helps me to sleep on it."

"Can we meet for a late breakfast? I'm dying, poor choice of words, to know what's next."

"Sure, let's get together down here around ten." Roland responded.

After praising Gina for the delicious dinner and fine accommodations, they retired to their respective rooms and each set about doing some serious thinking.

Roland could not get the image of the maps he'd seen in Harry's office out his mind. He sat in his room near the window, quiet now because the revelers of the evening remained in the restaurants and bars and had not yet arrived in the courtyard. The sensual aroma of jasmine rode into his room on the soft evening air. He'd often found the environment in this area distracting. Visually appealing and grand, the vivid blue of the ocean contrasted on the nearly white beaches, the entire city framed by the outcropping of mountains with their own hint of purple. The aroma of exotic plants and blooms excited the nose so that their vibrant colors need not be witnessed for their enjoyment to reign; the sounds of a city alive with the dialects and accents that only the proximity to Mexico could bring and the way the evening and early morning air played across your skin like being embraced by fine silk. He worked to keep himself focused on his mission.

He was not sure how long he sat there but his thoughts were interrupted by the onset of the horns which literally trumpeted the arrival of the mariachi band and the throngs which they attracted. He felt bone tired and with some remorse closed the window and moved to the bed for some welcome sleep. He knew he was safe with Gina.

Will wasn't sure what had awakened him from the dream but he found relief in being away from it. The sun streamed through his window and blazed across his bed. He jumped to the table to retrieve his watch and find the time. It was nearly eight. He had really gotten some serious sleep, something else he had been missing for awhile. He glanced out the window and saw the sunlight glistening in the drops of dew that hung on the flowers adorning the side of the building. His head ached and his mouth tasted like the dregs from the bottom of a wine barrel. He moved slowly into the bathroom slightly optimistic about the day.

As he exited the shower and began his grooming routine, Will was certain that he smelled bacon cooking. He hoped it was coming from Gina's kitchen and that some of it was intended for him. First he needed to run his errand. After dressing he went down the outside stairway and made his way across the courtyard, past the fountain and out onto the street. He only had to go down two blocks to find the public telephone that he had seen on his way to the restaurant. He dialed Amanda's number.

She picked up on the first ring.

"Hi, Sandy, it's Rupert," he began. That name was one that they had used when they played together as children and it had remained a shared joke throughout their lives. They had decided to use it when they needed a code for the telephone. It brought a kind of smile to Will's face even now.

"Thank God, it's you. I've been frantic waiting to hear from you."

"Hold on, what's the matter? Are you okay?"

"Yes, no, I mean…Oh, it's terrible, my friend's been killed. They said it was a car accident."

"Whoa, what friend? What happened?"

"Brad, you know, I told you about him. I'm really upset if you know what I mean. I don't know what to do, where to turn."

She wasn't making a whole lot of sense and Will was suddenly afraid for her. His thoughts went immediately to Roland. "Sit tight. I'll call you as close to noon as I can, okay?"

"Yea, I'm okay, really, hearing your voice helps. It was just such a horrible night, I'll be fine until your call."

"Bye, Hon," was all he could get out. It was already 9:30 and, thank God, he was on his way to meet with Roland. Will hurried the couple of blocks back to the Chile Pepper and heard the now familiar tinkle of the bells on the door as he opened it and entered the restaurant. As expected Gina was there busying herself with the morning trade. She looked up and gave Will a warm and reassuring smile. He crossed the room to what he thought of as their booth and sat down to wait for Roland. Gina made her way graciously through the crowded room with the pot in her hand. "How about some coffee, Honey?" she offered.

Will nodded affirmatively and sat with his eyes fixed on the rear door waiting for Roland's entrance.

"He's gone out, left early this morning," she reported.

"He's supposed to meet me at ten; did he say where he was going?"

"Didn't say a word to me, Honey, just know he went," she responded over her shoulder as she made her way back to the kitchen.

Will was uncertain at that moment whether he'd been duped or whether, like Will, Roland had just gone to run some errands. He had that worried feeling deep in his gut that he would never see Roland again. Maybe this was all a set-up. Worse he had more and apparently bigger issues to deal with around Amanda and her safety in her present location. That matter couldn't wait. He was well into assessing his options when the rear door opened and Roland moved inside and slid into the booth opposite Will. He heard his sigh and was sure that his heart rate slowed in that moment. "I thought you were standing me up."

"It's not even ten yet. You've got to learn not to get so excited. The next couple of days are going to require a still heart and a steady hand. Think you can handle it?" he asked.

"I'll get a hold of it!" Will wondered whether to tell Roland about Amanda's danger now or wait until he heard what he had to say. He decided on the latter, just in case.

Without divulging any specifics of his plan, Roland related to Will what he saw as the challenges facing them. "What it boils down to is this; we've got to lay a trap that results in exposure and/or evidence that can be used to stop this insanity. They, on the other hand, only have to get us in the crosshairs as they say. Without a doubt, our task is much greater. Add to that the fact that they have greater resources and you know the odds are not in our favor. Lest you get too disheartened, however, we do have surprise on our side."

Will tried to make that last bit of news help him feel more optimistic. He was sure that Roland was right. No one was going to know that the three of them were working together. If they could come up with the right plan that could definitely work in their favor. That could be the tipping point.

Will decided to think positively and sat up straighter leaning in to talk closely with Roland. "Have you come up with a plan? Next step?" he asked again.

"Not totally, but I have the bones of it. Let's run through.

They ordered a hearty breakfast of bacon, eggs ranchero and even some chorizo and tortillas to try for all of the unhealthy food groups. As they ate, they talked. They drank coffee and talked some more. Will felt like they were beginning to develop a rapport and he was sure that Roland felt it too. He liked the way Roland came at a problem, the way his mind worked and he felt certain that if this mess had a solution, they could find a way through it together. It was nearly noon before Will brought up the tenuous situation that Amanda was in.

They both had the same idea and said at almost the same time, "Let's bring her here."

Will placed the call to Amanda through Roland's secure cell phone. She was pleased to be getting out of her current lair and agreed to be at the Chile Pepper that evening. She assured him that she would arrive before dark.

Chapter Nineteen

Senator Hampton rode back to his office in his big, black limousine watching the Virginia countryside slide by outside the darkened windows. He wasn't working on this leg of the journey. Instead, he was running over in his mind the events of the day in the bunker. He wondered again if he should reconsider putting his new office in such a location but he kept coming back to the same observation. New York and London were still the undisputed power locations on this planet. Even though Washington wielded its share of influence it was mostly because New York and the U.S. economy drove this country to the top of the heap. Without that foundation Washington would not maintain the same degree of importance in the world. No, he was sure that locating within the two cities he'd chosen made the greatest sense for what he had to accomplish. Besides, this should never be seen as a regime change just within the United States. This had to be seen as something larger, something new and of a much greater magnitude. He simply could not stay in Washington and achieve the world wide respect that was required. He knew that his superior agreed.

He thought about the security meeting he'd just left. He was unable to remain detached from the impending death of Roland Priestly. He really did love him like a son. They had always thought alike, reasoned the same way, had always had similar values and their visions for change were as one. At some point in the journey they had parted dramatically. The pain of reality poked at him like the stiff finger of a demanding school marm. He opened the compartment and took out a glass and a decanter of his favorite scotch. He poured just two fingers and then decided that this was at least a three finger trip. He had painfully come to realize that Roland just didn't have the guts to accompany him to this next level.

He sank back into the plush seat and contemplated the decisions that had been made. He liked the hierarchal approach of working their way down the list. It was ironic, he thought, that some of the strongest argument had been around whether to start at the top of the list and work down to the least important or the other way around. It made sense to concentrate their efforts on one target at a time. Their resources were new and virtually untried and it would not be prudent to spread them too thin.

He continued to sip his drink and the warmth that the alcohol created mingled with feelings of satisfaction both with himself and with the organization's progress. Together they produced a kind of smile inside him at the prospects that lay ahead. In less than a week he would sit atop the first and hopefully, only world government. Their reign would be long and successful because there would be no opposing power. No threat to the world order. Only if they allowed it would power flow to other entities. They would truly be in charge; they would be the ones to control tomorrow. It was only right that it be them. Not everyone in this position would use it for good. They would shape the future of an entire planet. "Heady thoughts," he remarked out loud to no one.

He continued the remainder of his ride in thoughtful silence.

Knowing that Amanda was on her way Will returned to Roland and the challenge that lay ahead. They had worked through several issues and with each exchange Will grew more comfortable and confident with Roland's mental abilities and emotional cool. The task ahead of them was difficult, their lives hung tenuously in the balance but somehow Will still managed to have an overall sense of optimism.

It had been such a help that Roland knew the characters. The personalities were numerous and complex but he knew all about how they handled themselves. Will had found solace in Roland's reasoning that the Achilles Heel of the organization would be Harry Axelrod. Apparently the man was motivated only by greed and besides that he was a bit of a loose cannon. Roland had said that Harry hated him and his thinking got clouded because Roland got under his skin. They agreed to target him as the weak link. Will was as confident as he could be under the circumstances. He was ready to put the plan into effect but they still had to wait for Amanda.

They had the entire afternoon to wait but as Roland pointed out they didn't have time to sit around counting spots on the wall. They needed this time to obtain a couple of weapons for Will and Amanda and to get some other supplies that he thought would come in handy in the execution of their plan. Roland said that he would also like to take both of his new team members to the shooting range and make sure that they could handle themselves but he knew the impracticality of that. They'd just have to go over the use of the weapons verbally and handle them unloaded, once they got a hold of them. After that they would trust that the lesson would take and if they had to use them that adrenaline would kick in and assist them in their cause.

They set out for the south part of the city to try to make a quick connection on some heat, as Will heard Roland refer to it in his inquiries. Roland knew that in this neighborhood he'd find the bars and other establishments that catered to the military trade. Also, the farther south they went and the closer to Mexico and the border they got, the more likely it would be that they could score some quality hardware at distressed prices. The price was not the main consideration for him. All he was looking for was quick and untraceable.

They found both in the person of Tommy True. After several thwarted attempts to find a connection they'd gotten lucky in a ratty little bar called the Blue Tattoo. Will didn't even want to think where they might have come up with such a name. He was just glad that they'd gotten out of there alive. He knew that the characters that inhabited the place in the early afternoon were merely the opening act for the main attractions that would permeate the premises once sundown and the cloak of night hid them from the prying and critical eyes of the functioning side of society. Will shivered slightly and his skin crawled as he surveyed their surroundings.

It had taken several of Roland's hundreds placed on the bar one at a time to get a name and location from the smarmy, unshaven bartender. They'd both taken in a deep breath of air as they exited onto the half deserted street and left behind the putrid air hanging inside the establishment, though Will was certain that it had penetrated the fibers of his clothing.

Just when he thought they could find no lower form of life they managed to locate Tommy. The good news was that he did business out of the back of a broken down van requiring them to stay out on the street. The bad news was that the street was almost as filthy as the inside of the Blue Tattoo. The garbage, trash and various unidentified wastes lay around them in the gutter and clogged any potential cleansing. The gray, warehouse buildings with broken windows and crumbling stucco reaching upward on either side of the street gave the feeling of standing in a canyon of fetid rubbish. He looked down at his feet and realized that he was literally wading in filth. The odor was rank and Will wondered what could be rotting in there to give it such a foul smell. His second thought was that he didn't want to know.

He was relieved when the transaction was completed and they drove his rental car back toward the clean and tidy Chile Pepper. He couldn't wait to take another shower and he was planning to ask Gina if he could pay her to do some laundry. He had to get the feel and the smell of today off of him. As if he'd read Will's mind Roland said, "I'm sure we can get Gina to do a couple of loads of laundry for us." Will smiled and drove around to the rear of the restaurant where they parked the car in the public lot opposite the now serene courtyard.

Back in his room before the late afternoon sun had moved from sight behind the buildings, Will immediately stripped out of his clothes and left them in the hall for Gina as they'd arranged. He got in the shower and thought he just might spend the rest of his life there with the hot water, steamy air and the hygienically fresh smell of soap lingering with the feel of clean skin and hair. He wanted to wash off the filth of the day's excursion, wanted to wash away his cares as well. While he stayed in there he seemed to be able to hold all the troubles at bay.

Will had agreed to meet Roland to go over more details. The more each of them thought about their plan the more things they came up with to iron out potential problems and to increase their probability of success. Will had a few thoughts that had come to him as he busied himself in his room after his shower. They also wanted to keep an eye out for Amanda who could be arriving anytime now. They knew Gina would be there to take care of her but both of them were now anxious about her safe escape. They didn't have long to wait.

The bells on the door to the Chile Pepper tinkled once more and Roland was stunned to see the waif-like creature who made her way into the restaurant and stopped to absorb the environment. Will saw the look on Roland's face and whirled in his seat just in time to see the look of recognition flash into Amanda's eyes. He was out of the booth and bounded across the floor in one endless motion to wrap her in his arms. "Am I glad to see you," he confessed.

Roland rose politely from his seat and extended his hand, "Good to see you again, Amanda." He wished he could have added that she was looking well, but that would have been an obvious lie. She looked drawn, fatigued and even somewhat unkempt. Her eyes portrayed the wariness of a cornered animal who was outweighed by its predator and who knew that the end was imminent.

There was little resemblance, he thought, to the capable and together young, professional woman he had last seen in Washington just weeks ago. For a moment he was dismayed at what he had done. At what he had been a part of. He wondered if he could ever work off the shame or if there was an act left to be done that could redeem him. If there was, perhaps it was the one he was attempting now.

Will guided Amanda into the booth ahead of him and then sat down beside her. All of the pleasantries were extended and everyone took some time to catch their breaths and come into the moment. The small talk lasted only a few moments. Amanda began to challenge Roland and it was quickly apparent that she placed the fault for what had happened at his feet. She chose this moment to let go of most of the rage that she had stored up over the previous weeks. Roland politely and contritely accepted the responsibility and beseeched her to trust him to make amends. With Will's help, Roland finally prevailed and they began to progress through their plans.

The evening passed quickly in the comfort of the Chile Pepper. Amanda was apprised of the plans in progress and added some information and thoughts of her own. They ate a delicious dinner prepared especially by Gina and shared a bottle of quality, California wine.

Amanda was the first to give in to her exhaustion and inquired about her accommodations for the night. Gina took her upstairs and gave her the room directly across from Will's. Her small bag carried the bare essentials and she was pleased to see that Gina's rooms had most of the items she lacked. She treated herself to a long soak in a bubble bath and took her weary body off to bed a little before nine. She sank into the soft bedding and let the feathers of the comforter float down around her. Before she actually felt them make contact with her she was asleep.

Sunrise over southern California is like no other place. On those days when the marine layer dissipates early, cities such as San Diego are awakened to the reflection and warm glow of the day's light in the glass slabs of high rise buildings lined up along busy streets. Amanda, Will and Roland awoke to such a morning. Each had taken notice of the beauty around them in their own way. By coincidence rather than prior arrangement they arrived for breakfast within minutes of each other. As was her way, Gina greeted each of them as though they were the most special guest she'd ever hosted. If you didn't look past the moment it was the start of a wonderful day. The condemned ate a hearty breakfast.

Playing it safe they decided to leave Will's car in a parking lot downtown. He called the rental company and told them that it wouldn't start and he had to catch his flight. Roland called for the car he'd hired as Carl Handler and after Will and Amanda parked the rental car the three of them made their way eastward to the airstrip where Roland had arrived. His hired plane with the discreet crew met them there. In less than an hour from the time they'd left Gina with warm goodbyes all around they were airborne and heading back to Washington with similar unplanned stops and side trips to the ones that Roland had engineered on his trip west.

"Roland," Amanda addressed him, "This is my first time on a private plane. I have to say, I can see how you could get used to it."

"Sometimes these things that come to us of necessity are the perks that we learn to covet."

"I bet you don't mind flying at all," Will added.

"Usually, I don't. I often work while in the air and I really forget sometimes to take notice of all of the amenities around me."

"Well," Will quipped, "Travel can be broadening and I have to say this trip is certainly doing that for Amanda and me."

This time, Roland thought, it will even be broadening for me. We are heading directly into the mouth of the lion and into the unfamiliar.

It was late afternoon in Washington when the tires of the Learjet carrying the unlikely alliance of three screeched against the asphalt of the runway. Ensconced in his office downtown Harry Axelrod was preoccupied as he sat across the desk from his secretary who was trying to give him a rundown on the messages she'd taken in his absence. She had lost patience with his inattentiveness and was speaking to him now in that squeaky whine that irritated him but also brought him back to the business at hand. At least to the business she was trying to conduct.

His mind was thousands of miles away, in Bangkok, and trying hard to prepare for the meetings there. They were so crucial to the plans and now just days away. It was imperative that he achieve his goals and have all of the funding from the consortium in place so that implementation could move forward. He wouldn't have much time to resolve any problems and he was concerned about running into a recalcitrant participant. His secretary was shrieking at him again, he needed to hear her out so he could get rid of her and concentrate.

She started the rundown again and his ears finally honed in on the name, Roland Priestly. He had called and wanted to see Harry, here in his office, this evening. *What*, he wondered, as he unconsciously rubbed his hand across his chin, *was this about*? He listened to the remainder of the names who'd left messages and dismissed his secretary. He dialed his secure phone.

The senator picked up. The conversation was brief and pointed. No, he did not know why Roland would want to meet with him. Given the events surrounding the surveillance team which had been on Roland, he advised Harry not to meet with him and if he could not totally avoid him to not, in any way, allow Roland to provoke him into some unwise behavior.

Harry hung up the phone peeved that the senator thought that he couldn't handle himself with the likes of Mr. Roland Priestly. He'd scolded him almost as if he couldn't be trusted. Hell, he could buy and sell the man a hundred times over and not notice the drop in his bank balance. He didn't and wouldn't fear that prickly little twit and the senator was going to have to learn to give him more respect besides. He felt twelve years old again, trying to stand out, trying to be noticed, and trying to be chosen. "Damn them all," he uttered as he made his way over to the liquor cabinet in his credenza. He poured himself a generous portion and returned to his desk and the matter of the investors in the world of tomorrow.

He stayed at his desk for a couple of hours alternating between all of the plusses for the investors and all of the minuses, in between he punctuated his thoughts with another visit to the liquor cabinet. He needed to assure himself that he could address any concerns no matter how trivial they might seem. Being prepared was his strongest tool and the reassurance he gained from the liquor went a long way toward bolstering his confidence. He had to make sure that he could maintain control of the meeting, not let some tangent or red herring take the sentiment of the group to the negative side. He wasn't exactly nervous but on the other hand he was feeling some apprehension about trying to manage a group of this importance. He knew the only way to achieve his objective was to be totally and completely prepared.

He'd spoken at length with nearly every member of the consortium and felt relatively certain that he'd heard most of the concerns. He just couldn't afford to have something come up that he wasn't equipped to handle. Something he might not have a complete answer for or wasn't prepared to put a spin on. These were sophisticated business people, many of whom had not inherited their wealth. This meant they knew how to make and how to protect a buck. He would have to be at his best.

If they watched the bottom line the way he knew they did; they would see the wisdom of the affiliation however. You couldn't sit in a room with that much money and not feel the need to go with the crowd. Control would be everything.

It was well after 7 and Harry's annoying secretary had long ago left for the day when Roland exploded through the door to the outer office and violated the inner sanctum that was Harry's private office. Harry was so astounded that he nearly fell over backward in his ergonomic, leather, desk chair as he fought to get his feet off the desk and onto the floor. His attempts to scramble upward proved futile and he fell back hard causing the chair to roll uncontrollably backward until it met the bookcase behind, confusion reigned across his face. Roland had to stifle a laugh. The glass on the desk with just a touch of amber liquid in the bottom told Roland all he needed to know about Harry's condition and his response to the intrusion. He'd been right, he observed, to come at night and not in the morning.

Harry's words were almost slurred, "What the hell you want here?'

"I'll just take a moment of your time," Roland responded politely. "I just need to follow up with you from our meeting the other morning. You remember, of course, when you couldn't wait to tell me that I'd been sold out?"

"What's your point, Mr. Prick?"

"Just wanted you to know that I've come into some other interesting news since our meeting and since you were so kind as to share what you knew with me, I feel obliged to do the same."

Harry looked at him through glassy eyes that seemed to be fighting to focus. "I still don't know why you're here," Harry continued.

"As I said, just to return the favor. Since our meeting I've nosed around a little and thought that you needed to know that your tenure with Operation Cloud Nine is about to be brought to a close."

"Fuckin' liar," Harry spat.

"Believe what you will, it's off my conscience since I shared what I learned with you. Watch your back, Harry, not everyone you count as a friend really is." Roland turned and left the office as quickly as he had entered. The first step of his plan was completed.

Harry was left sitting with his chair against the bookcase pondering what Roland knew that he did not. More importantly what was he to do about it? Harry never once considered the fact that Roland may have been baiting him.

Back in the staging area that they had set up at the small hotel in Crystal City Will and Amanda were speculating on what time Roland would return. Will was anxious to make a trip over to the rehab hospital to see Charles and Amanda, though she wanted to see Charles knew she needed to give Will some time with him alone. Consequently, she was contemplating a trip back to her old neighborhood to see what had become of her apartment. Will had been trying to talk her out of it for the last forty-five minutes.

"It's just really important that we not go around any of the places that someone would be looking for us, that's all I'm saying."

"I just think you're being over protective. I appreciate your motives, Will but I'm not going to be controlled like that," she responded.

"That's not it, Mandy, we've got to stay focused on our mission like Roland said. There'll be time to worry about your old life once we're certain we're going to have one. Going there puts the whole project in jeopardy. It's like saying you want to go to one of your favorite restaurants or if I went back to the lake right now. They're gonna follow us for sure."

"What about going to Charles, then?"

Will stood silently and allowed her words to sink in. After a few moments he spoke again, "Know what, Mandy, you're absolutely right. That is the same thing. They'll pick me up for sure. Oh, hell, I really need to see him." They hugged for several minutes each feeling that familiar support that they'd always shared. Each knowing that they would always be there for each other. This was taking such an emotional toll on both of them.

Roland arrived back at their headquarters just a little after 8 and found his two cohorts pacing restlessly around the room. Carelessly ripped open bags of junk food and snacks lounged on the coffee table and soft drink cans were assembled like colorful candles holding vigil over the mounds of crumbs. They'd obviously found a convenience store. He was just grateful that neither of them smoked. He set about tidying the place up as he was unable to concentrate with so much clutter distracting him. Neither Will nor Amanda even noticed,

"How'd it go?" Will asked.

"Just as planned, but it remains to be seen if he takes the bait."

"How'll we know?" Amanda asked.

"That'll take a little time." He made a wide sweeping gesture toward the table and chairs arranged in the far side of the room, "In the meantime, let's talk."

They pulled up to the table and before they talked about next steps, Roland schooled them on the etiquette of respecting a shared space. Both Will and Amanda looked down into their laps like chastised school children, neither knowing how to respond. Finally Will responded, "Sorry, Roland, we were preoccupied about being back in Washington and weren't thinking beyond our noses."

Roland gave a grunt of acknowledgement and began the strategy meeting as if nothing had been mentioned. He knew they were really okay and that it was his hang up but, as usual, he felt he had a right to set boundaries and have them respected whenever he was forced to spend time with others. It just wasn't where he was most comfortable; he really preferred his solitary time.

Roland began to explain the possible reactions that Harry would have to the little bombshell he'd just dropped on him. He couldn't really predict Harry's behavior but he felt strongly that he would do one of several things. He might actually bring their little project to a halt, the others, at best, would throw the group into disarray and would give Roland's team some of the time they needed.

Roland had given the matter a great deal of thought and they had concocted a plan before leaving the coast. Now it was time to act. Each of them had a specific assignment. They finalized those assignments now as they sat around the chipped Formica table with the fake wood finish. They discussed their actions, possible counter actions and their ultimate strategy. If certain events were observed, they had an idea of where that was taking them and what they needed to do in response. Operation Cloud Control had begun.

They had slept little in the nooks and corners of the hotel room. Amanda won the bed and Will and Roland had draped about in various positions on the sofa, chairs and floor. None of them looked rested but all of them looked ready.

They gathered up the weapons, tools and accessories that they each needed for their respective assignments and they talked casually about what they might encounter as they went about their work. Roland and Will watched in amazement as Amanda adroitly inserted the magazine into her weapon, chambered a round and hefted it up and down several times to acquaint herself with the feel of it. She looked up to see them both staring at her, "What?" she inquired.

Will responded for them both. "You handle that like a pro!"

"Oh, that, I used to go target shooting with Dad, remember? He taught me all about guns."

Roland decided to skip the lesson on weaponry. As often happened everyone just naturally assumed that Will would know what to do with one.

Both Will and Amanda admitted to having nervous butterflies zipping around in their insides but they both also admitted to a kind of calm which had come over them since they'd begun to execute their plan. There was an air of shared but cautious optimism permeating the room. Even Roland thought that with a little luck, they just might be able to pull this off.

They left their room together leaving everything as they'd agreed, including the fully closed blinds at all windows. The first one to return was to open the blinds as a signal to the others that they were occupying the room. Roland was the last one to leave the room and he carefully placed a small, inconspicuous scrap of paper high up between the door and the jam as he pulled it closed behind him. He had cautioned them that whoever returned to the room first should look for it before entering. "If it isn't there, don't go in," he warned. "Just keep on walking and proceed to the secondary meeting location, being sure that you're not followed." In an abundance of caution they had sanitized the room and were prepared to never see it again if necessary.

The three of them parted at the bottom of the stairs, fully focused and each proceeding to their respective location and the assignment which awaited them.

Will had always been at home in this area of the district populated with affluent offices. Several of his previous clients had their headquarters or strategic branches located here among the influential of Washington. Will's firm had even maintained a small presence in the building down the block in order to have the address and a name in this power neighborhood. Name recognition and reputation were everything in that business.

He moved easily among the commuters as he wound his way through the crowd coming up out of the metro station. He tossed a couple of coins in the filthy cup of a presumably homeless person who sat begging near the exit. He always wondered at their real story but usually reached the same conclusion. Even if they were not as desperate as they'd like you to think, if they could stoop to begging, they needed those coins more than he did.

He crossed the street against the light imbedded in the crush of people. As they reached the opposite side the crowd broke into thirds, each taking a different direction on the street. He stayed with the group that continued up 17th. He had walked just three blocks when, as expected, he spotted the plumbing van parked at the curb which flaunted the sign, "Walt's Plumbing Service." He had to love the sense of humor, under the name in smaller letters, "Let Walt Fix That Halt!" *There was a reason these guys were into electronic surveillance and not in the advertising business,* he thought.

Will rapped twice on the back door of the van and gave the code word, "Franklin." He heard rustling inside the vehicle followed by the release of the lock and the door swung open nearly knocking him down. He found himself looking into the face of an old codger, not at all what he'd expected in electronics work.

"Hi, I'm Lucas, you Will?"

"Yeah," Will responded, "And you're not what I was expecting."

"Now, that's the beauty of it, ain't it? Makes me more effective in this line of work. You a friend of Roland's or just doin' business?" he inquired as he took Will's arm and literally pulled him inside.

"Just business, I guess you'd say."

"Well we got us some business here alright." Lucas gestured to a small bench built into the rear of the van. "Sit down, we'll fill you in. Oh, this here's my partner, Doc, Will," he flung his arms around indicating the formalities were over so Will just nodded toward Doc as he sat where instructed.

Will's eyes couldn't take in all of the equipment and gadgets that were installed in the rear of this commercial sized vehicle. Red lights, green lights and some flashing amber confused his eyes as he looked over the shoulder of Doc who sat on a tiny stool, hunched over the equipment, turning dials with one hand and holding his headphones tight against his ear with the other. The opposite side of the van had wall to wall monitors. Will struggled to get oriented to what he was seeing.

Lucas seemed to read his expression and began his explanations, "This picture here is comin' from a feed we've tied into in building security. From them we can scan the lobby, the hallway, elevator and parking garage. Over here is a little gem we put in by the host's secretary. That one over there is of the man's desk. We can pick up about anything he does except pee. We left that alone. By the way, if you want to know what's on his desk we can zoom in on anything on the top. Got no x-ray ability though so if it's down in a stack of papers you're out a' luck.

Will had to smile to himself. Not only was he thoroughly impressed with the work, he couldn't help but like the little guy who was to act as his eyes and ears on Harry Axelrod. "What happens if he leaves the building?" Will asked.

"Got most a' that covered. His car's interior can be seen right there on Number 7, if he gets too far away for visual, we've got him equipped with a nice little beeper that'll tell us everywhere he goes and when, if he walks it's a little tougher visually, it jumps around a lot, but we can pick up his audio with Tammy. She's out on the street, set up with a zoom microphone that can catch his words for a good 25 yards, maybe more, that's enough to be across the street from him. She's also ready to catch any numbers dialed from a public phone if she can set up in the right position. That may be a little iffy," he explained. "I think we got Mr. Host pretty well sewed up for now," he bragged.

"I guess all we do now is wait then," Will suggested.

"Bout' it." Lucas answered and turned toward his monitoring equipment and the tasks at hand leaving Will to entertain himself.

Amanda entered the lobby of the familiar government office building that she had been coming to every day for the last six years. She had called ahead to be sure that Nate Tidwell would be available and to request clearance to enter the building. Since she was on a leave of absence her credentials would not allow her free access to the premises as she'd always had. Brandon, the regular day guard was there and greeted her as usual. If he was surprised by her change in appearance he said nothing about it. She made small talk with him while she waited for someone to come down from her department and escort her to Nate's office. She couldn't be roaming around the building on her own without employee status. She was struck by how calm she felt. She wasn't sure if it was the familiarity of the environment or the calm that had come over her regarding their plans but nerves were not part of her feelings now.

The last hint of nervousness had come when she'd left the train at Union Station and stowed her belongings, including the gun, in a locker there. For obvious reasons she could not bring it with her to a government office. Somehow and rightfully so, it still made her nervous to carry a gun around in a city. She was glad to be able to put it aside.

She looked up to see Wanda, Nate's secretary, coming toward her with a big smile on her face. They hugged and Wanda led her up to her own department, talking about family and coworkers on the way and commenting on Amanda's new hair style. Wanda left her sitting in Nate's empty office, "He'll be right here," she advised.

Amanda felt her anxiety rise slightly as she heard Nate's voice as he came down the row of offices which ended with his own. She thought she was going to panic and then reminded herself that her only task, Roland kept reminding her, was to observe responses. Her script was pretty well programmed; she'd rehearsed it so many times. All she had to do was observe Nate's non-verbal responses. She could do that, she told herself.

"Amanda, so good to see you," he entered the room with an unusually forceful presence.

"You, too, Nate, and thanks for seeing me."

"Always have time for you," he teased. "You look well."

She assumed that was his indirect way of saying, 'What in the hell have you done to your hair?'

"You said something about some questions, what are you doing with your time off? I thought you were taking a well deserved vacation."

"Not that kind of question. Nothing to do with work, really. I'm taking a writing course with some of my time and this is really about an assignment. I have some questions that we're supposed to put to a person whose judgment we respect, admire, you know," she stammered as if embarrassed. As expected, Nate leaned back in his chair, raised his arms up and laced his fingers together behind his head. His ego was sufficiently puffed up she observed. She acknowledged to herself that watching his responses would not be so difficult after all. He was pretty transparent.

Amanda moved through the questions that had been carefully scripted by Roland. He had done a good job of spacing the loaded ones among innocuous subject matter so that Amanda herself almost couldn't tell the difference. She had been schooled, however, on which ones to watch most carefully. This was like a lie detector without the electronics. Roland knew what he was doing and had even included just the right amount of complimentary statements to keep Nate so full of himself that apparently no red flags were raised. Amanda never saw so much as a hesitation and she had worked with Nate long enough to know him fairly well.

By the time she was back at Union Station retrieving her belongings she had a pretty good grasp of Nate's take on the state of today's governmental issues, particularly around energy. She was anxious to talk to the boys.

Roland was sitting on a bench along the Smithsonian side of the mall allowing the morning sun to warm him when he saw him approaching. He never failed to amuse Roland. He knew that he was anal retentive, even somewhat compulsive but this friend of his from CIA was a case study.

He was dressed impeccably in the traditionally British way. His coat reached his fingertips and was so dark as to be indistinguishable between black and navy blue. It contrasted with the handsomely cut, gray slacks perfectly. His muted stripe tie was held solidly in place by the collar pin and there was a slight touch of red at the coat's breast pocket. His fine features belied his African skin and his head was shaved bare. He held a cell phone to his ear and he spoke quietly. His posture was straight and formal but his movements had the stealth of a cat.

As Roland watched Bobby approach the bench where he sat he was reminded of their earlier time together. It seemed so long ago. They had first met in college, each representing their respective schools on their track teams. They had met at a pre-season meet and had experienced an instant comfort with one another. Roland had been a pretty fair runner back then and Bobby literally dominated the field events. As a result they'd never had to go up against each other. They had laughed many times about what the result would have been had that ever come to pass. They'd loved to debate that possibility over beers. In reality Roland knew that he could never match Bobby's talent. The name of Bobby Webster would stay in the record books for a very long time whereas no entries had ever been made for Roland Priestly. He'd often thought that if Bobby hadn't chosen government service he surely would have made a great cat burglar. Roland could observe that same natural grace as he watched him draw near.

"We meet again, my friend," he greeted Roland. The smile was broad and occupied his entire face. He had also always made the ladies swoon which had awed Roland as well.

"Indeed we do."

They walked the length of the mall to the Lincoln Memorial and back entrenched in their conversation as they went. Much had been exchanged but little had been decided by the time they retuned to their starting point. Bobby had some work to do and they agreed to meet again. "Tonight, Rock Creek Park and for God's sake wear some grubby jogging clothes. I can't believe you're very effective at what you do the way you stand out. Six o'clock at the Adams Memorial and look like a jogger."

His friend just smiled broadly and let out a soft laugh as he nodded in agreement.

Chapter Twenty

Back in the comfort of that colonial home in Chevy Chase the senator was enjoying a rare, quiet morning at home. He had decided to see his son before going to the office and he wanted to wait until his morning therapy session was over. He had called to be sure that he would not be interrupting anything critical in his schedule. He thought it would fit best to be there by ten. He carried a second cup of coffee into his den and lowered his aging frame into his favorite, leather chair. He was prepared to enjoy some quality time with the day's edition of the Washington Post. He had barely scanned the front page headlines when his mind wandered off to the heavy burden that his soul strained to carry.

He felt such remorse around the loss of Roland. He tried to examine his real reasons for giving the order. He said that it was to protect the implementation of Operation Cloud Nine but it nagged at him that his motives were otherwise. He loved Roland and it had felt right to share with him the existence and circumstances of his son, Charles. By doing so, though, he had let another person know that he had put a hit on the most important person in his son's life. What if Charles found out that he was responsible for Will's death? Charles would never understand why it had to be. His son would never comprehend the concept of collateral damage that he had learned to live with. Hell, he wondered sometimes if he really did.

Had that been his real reason for ordering Roland's demise? He hated to think so but something nagged at him. He couldn't remember the last time he had slept through the night but he was certain that it was long before Gazelle had morphed into Cloud Nine. His nightmares and fitful sleeping had gotten worse since he'd given the order, especially since the strategy meeting in the bunker with the security division. That's when the cold sweats had begun. And those horrible nightmares, would they ever go away?

He tried again to concentrate on the paper he held. He could not shake the visual image which haunted him. The nightmare that had been awakening him. The picture of him standing over Amanda's, Will's and Roland's lifeless bodies, his hands dripping in blood and only the back of Charles moving away from him down a dark tunnel, ignoring him as he called out. He sat bolt upright in the bed every time with his pulse racing and his heart thumping like it was going to come out through his chest.

He revisited his motives. He hoped he was better than to have done it solely to protect his relationship with his son. In a sense he was trading one son for the other. He knew his motives were for the greater good. For the new world order and all that would flow from it. That had to be his reason. But was it? His doubts continued to haunt him. Was there a pattern? He had left his wife and son under circumstances where he believed he had a strong calling. Where he was needed to help the nation and to achieve that he had needed to change in a way that didn't include them.

Along the way there had been the backroom deals in the Senate but that's how the business of the country got done. When that wasn't efficient enough there had been Gazelle, again for the overall good. It wasn't that he enjoyed making these tough decisions. Trade offs were always hard and there were always winners and losers. *Those who believed in win/win deals weren't in politics,* he thought.

Now, all these years later he was still taking actions which he was compelled to take. Was he repeatedly being tapped as the savior or was he just incapable of taking responsibility for his actions? No, he assured himself, this is best for the world. I know it is. I didn't make this up, they came to me. *I just need to shake off this reverie,* he told himself.

He finally gave up on the paper and the den and went upstairs to dress for his day at the office looking forward with pleasure to his upcoming visit with his son.

Roland was the first to arrive back at the grungy little room that they'd left just a few hours earlier. The blinds were still as they'd left them and the scrap of paper clung discreetly to the door jamb exactly as he'd placed it earlier. He put his key in the lock and entered the dim room which, he observed grumpily, smelled of stale cigarette smoke and musty carpet. He opened several windows inviting some of the fresh, spring air to enter the space, sat down at the table and began to read through the notes that he carried with him in his small utility bag. He had to be prepared when he met Bobby this evening.

He also took out the cell phone and dialed the contact number for Will and the surveillance team. Will picked up immediately.

"Any movement?" he asked.

"Still inside but we have some interesting contacts."

"We're still on for 11 o'clock."

"I'll be there," Will answered and they hung up.

Roland was relieved to learn that the surveillance was still in place and apparently able to monitor Harry's office. It was a relief to have Will sit with the pros. He could sort out what they learned and make on the spot decisions Of course Roland would still get the voluminous logs of information but he wouldn't have to review every word recorded with Will able to filter what he heard. He hoped that Will's reports would be concise yet complete enough that if something alarmed him he could go directly to that particular communication without getting bogged down in the trivia. Time was important to them and he knew it. Everyday that they stayed alive was a near miracle in his mind.

Roland's next call was to Amanda. She felt the vibration of the phone in her jacket pocket as she picked her way through the crowd on the transfer platform of the metro.

"Mission report," he requested.

"All solid, on my way to headquarters with positive reports."

"We're still on for 11 o'clock."

"Affirmative, I'll go directly there," she replied and hung up.

Roland half wandered and half paced around the confines of the room as he continued to roll the facts around in his mind for what seemed like the millionth time. There had been something about the team that he took out in San Diego that bothered him. He still hadn't been able to put his finger on it. There could only be one reason that those two guys were there. They were not surveillance men and if they had been one would have been sufficient. There were two and they were both high level exterminators.

He wanted to think that it was Harry Axelrod's doing. That he had gone off half cocked as he'd been known to do so many times with Gazelle, but those particular men, he knew with certainty, came from the secretary. He remained uneasy about their assignment. Something about it didn't compute. He knew it would have done no good to try to learn anything from them. They were pros and that is precisely why they were assigned to the kind of cases they were. They would never talk, not even to him. He needed to concentrate but there were so many things in his mind competing for his thoughts, screaming for attention. He couldn't satisfy them all. He found that he was most uncomfortable in the unfamiliar role of the hunted.

He continued to try to analyze the details one step at a time. His mind was rebelling at the demands and was becoming numb to the agony. As soon as he sat down he fell asleep.

He awoke with a jolt and reached immediately for his weapon. His old habits were returning with his lapse into self-preservation mode. He hadn't reacted that way for years. He struggled to ascertain what had awakened him and then he heard the voices. It was outside, on the walkway near his door. He sat quietly and listened to the muffled sounds, two men he calculated. He took his weapon and moved over to the door careful not to allow a shadow to fall across the window nor to permit his silhouette being observed from the outside. He listened intently to the voices and determined that it was simply new hotel guests making their way to their rooms. His heart thumped in his chest and he lowered his weapon and returned to the sofa. He realized that he was sweating even though it was not particularly warm in the confines of the room.

He checked his watch and found that it was time to leave for the meeting with Will and Amanda. He gathered his belongings, returned them to his utility bag and secured it around his middle. He slipped the weapon into his waistband in the middle of his back and his jacket went on over the top easily concealing both. Less than thirty minutes later he joined his two associates on a partially shaded, bench in front of the Air and Space Museum. There were so many people, students and families, milling noisily around the entrance that he was certain no zoom microphone or filtering system could blot out the cacophony of the various voices that refused to stay in the background.

They began their progress reports in the safety of that environment.

Will gave a summary of what he'd overheard in Harry's office. Besides some whining that he had done to one of his associates or superiors, the thing of most interest was a call to someone in Bangkok by the name of Paul. Paul seemed to be working with Harry to set up a large and apparently very important meeting that was to take place in conjunction with the world summit meeting on energy. Will had the transcript of that call with him, but the salient point was that this meeting was outside the summit itself and apparently held some importance for Operation Cloud Nine. Will handed the transcript to Roland, "What is really amazing is that their equipment can take audio input and convert it to text," he said somewhat in awe.

Roland ignored his observation on the state of the art technology and asked absently, "What was the whining call you mentioned?"

"Rather disgusting really, he called someone and went on in this shrieky, little voice about how you had assaulted him again and when were you going to be reined in? Also, that he thought the matter was settled. Stuff like that."

"Do you know who he called?"

"Not right now because there was some kind of block on the number but Lucas is checking it out and should have it for us shortly. Also, I have to say, I think there was something familiar about the voice but I can't be sure. It was a man, sounded annoyed at him for carrying on, but he spoke very quietly so it was hard to hear him well."

"Sounds like your morning's been productive, Will. How'd yours go?" Roland asked turning his attention to Amanda.

"I'm totally pumped," she responded. "Nate's so full of himself that he just went on and on with little prompting. The most important thing is this bit about the energy summit. He's nervous and apprehensive and can't wait until it's behind them. I've never seen him like that before. With all of the summits he's done in the six years I've worked for him, never once has his face looked like that. I'm telling you something's up and now I wonder how it connects to what Will just said about this other meeting. What do you think, Roland, have we got something?"

Roland let a brief smile creep across his face. Her verve could be contagious. He'd admired that about her as he'd watched her work and it was all the more compelling now. He felt a stir inside him that was more than casual interest. He fought to keep his mind on the issue. "Yes, he responded, "I think our morning has been pretty fruitful. I met with my friend that I told you about and he is going to get some information for me. I'll meet him again tonight. I think we can be hopeful at this point. Who wants to eat?" he asked with a playful twinkle in his eye.

Will and Amanda looked at each other with raised eyebrows. This was a Roland Priestly that neither of them had seen before. They responded in the affirmative and the three of them headed off to the cafeteria in the basement of the Museum of American History just across the mall.

After a lunch laced with more conversation, analysis and hypothecating Will decided to walk the distance back to the surveillance van. It was a pleasant day and he needed to stretch his legs. The air was pleasantly fresh but not really cool. The sun gave a glow to the monuments along the mall in stark distinction to the depressing gray of the more functional government buildings he passed. This was a city of contrasts in more than just ideology.

He hoped Lucas would have more information on the identity of the man that Axelrod had called. He was trying his best to figure out why the voice seemed familiar. It was not just the voice itself but something in the speech pattern perhaps, in the cadence of his words. Maybe, he told himself, it was just a regional or colloquial speech pattern that he'd heard before and not really related to the identity of the speaker. Anyway, he was anxious to move along and he was sure there would be some transcripts to review when he got back.

He decided to take a few minutes out and call Charles. He found a public telephone and dropped in his coins before dialing the now familiar number.

Just minutes later, Will resumed his journey back to join Lucas and Doc. He felt renewed after hearing Charles' voice. He was sounding better and better. Even though their conversations had to be brief, it seemed to energize him every time they spoke. Today Charles had told him that the senator had come to visit him this morning, he still would not call the man his father. He always seemed to be a little down emotionally after being with him but it had been good to hear the enthusiasm in his voice when he told Will that he had a surprise for him. Will knew that Charles was getting anxious for him to visit. It seemed like an eternity since they'd seen each other, since they'd been able to look in each other's faces and utter words of love. Maybe in a few more days, Will was optimistic.

He decided that when time permitted he would call Charles' father and get an update on his progress and a first hand assessment of how he looked. Will was sure that would make him feel better, feel closer to him. The senator had given him his personal phone number and had invited him to call.

Roland and Amanda left the cafeteria at the same time as Will but they headed in the direction of the Hart Senate Office Building. They were headed into the mouth of the lion.

The senator sat frozen in his chair unable to move, unable to respond. The speaker phone was delivering Marge's perplexed voice again, "Senator, did you hear me? Are you still there? I said Mr. Priestly is here to see you with a Ms. Chambers. Shall I send them in?"

He finally was able to respond, "Hold them, Marge. Tell them it will be just a few minutes. Have them sit down and then get in here."

He had to think through the consequences of his response, decide what should be his next move. Roland knew there was a hit out on him. He'd made that clear from his response in San Diego. He'd sent an unequivocal message. If he saw him now he'd have to own up to his part in Roland's demise and he wasn't ready to do that. He'd just have to be evasive.

What of the Chambers girl? Why had Roland brought her? Same reason, he thought. Roland knew that he would be able to read the guilt in his eyes. He knew him too well.

If I see them he will know that I am implicated in his peril. He already knows I've ordered the take out of the girl and her brother. He sank back against the plush chair and let out a sigh which seemed to take all of the vigor from his body. This was it, Roland had him cornered. If he saw him, it was all out in the open. If he didn't see him, the message was just as strong, *I'm guilty and I do not want to look into your face and see the mask of imminent death.*

Not seeing him now had one other consequence. Roland knew where to find him if he wanted to, his home, his car or his other office. His only option was to accelerate the time table. They were so close, he couldn't afford to let things get out of control now. It wasn't a question of whether to have them taken out, it was only a decision of when. The cost was too large, this project had been underway for far too long. There was too much at stake and his superior would never understand if it got derailed now over something personal like this.

Marge came through the door and crossed the office to stand directly in front of his desk, both hands on her hips and a look of pure exasperation on her face. "What in the world is going on with you?"

He was in no mood for her prying. "Go back out and tell Mr. Priestly that I cannot see him and advise him that I have summoned security."

"Well, I never," she sputtered but from the look on his face she knew he meant what he was saying and she did exactly as instructed.

Moments later Roland and Amanda were outside on the street with

Amanda badgering Roland for an answer. "What was that about? I thought we were going to talk to him."

"We got our information, Amanda. He told us everything we need to know. He didn't want to see me because he's given the order to have all three of us killed. I was not completely honest with you before. He is one of the highest operatives in Gazelle and, I believe, also one of the powers behind Operation Cloud Nine. He's just confirmed my suspicions. Come on, we need to hurry. Let's grab a cab."

The second try proved successful and as they crawled into the rear of the taxi Roland gave the driver the address of their hovel of a hotel. They both sat back to endure the ride in silence. They were anxious to talk about their strategy but knew it had to wait until they were back to their headquarters. A couple of minutes into the ride, Roland pulled out his cell phone and summoned Will to meet them there. Roland was experiencing a certain clarity knowing that Senator Hampton had definitely crossed him off the list of those with a future. Even though he knew it wasn't personal, he was still questioning what he had done to bring him to that point.

It was just mid-afternoon when the threesome sat around the table while Roland played spill-your-guts. He described to Will and Amanda his long standing relationship with the senator and how he had been more than his mentor, almost a father figure for Roland. The behavior of the senator this afternoon had made it abundantly clear to Roland that they had very little time. Whatever the time table had been on their termination, he advised them, it had just gotten shortened.

He openly questioned the wisdom of what he had done but all of them agreed that under the circumstances, he had to know the truth. Roland had shared with them more than he ever had with anyone but he'd decided that if these were their final days, they needed to know everything about him and he about them. This was not the time to play the cards close to your chest and you never knew when some small detail might be helpful. They were definitely in this together and their interests were as one. They had to watch each other's backs.

After listening intently to Roland's story Will felt the greatest empathy for the man. He was glad that he had gotten to know him even if it was under such bizarre circumstances. There was a lot of substance to him and Will felt that Roland had done what he had with Gazelle in an effort to make things better. It was an example of someone doing bad things for distorted but honorable reasons. Sometimes people just believed in the wrong things. The hard part was knowing what was real, what was good and what was bad. We all have our own view, our own vision of reality and we all have our blind spots.

Amanda's heart had gone out to Roland the minute she saw the look in his eyes in the outer office of the senator. She had seen a vulnerability that she'd not observed before. It was only there for a second but it had sucked her in completely. She wanted to put her arms around him and comfort him. She could sense how he was hurting though the façade was in place and he was definitely back in charge.

Will was focusing more intently on the exigencies of their plan. "Roland," he asked, "Is there any way we can get to this guy? Any way to get him to call this off, or to keep him from moving up the time? You know him pretty well, where's he vulnerable?"

"That's a good question, Will, and last week I would have had a very clear answer for you. This week I'm thinking I don't know this man at all. He and Axelrod seemed to have gotten into this bigger and more aggressive organization that is determined to control world energy, I'd guess at any cost. You're probably on the right track though, everyone's vulnerable."

Amanda chimed in, "What about exposing him to other members of the senate or to the press? Can we bring him down that way?"

"We don't have time for that even if we had enough evidence, which we don't," Will replied. "Do you think stirring up Axelrod against him is going to do any good, Roland?"

"I don't know, time is the key to that strategy and Axelrod doesn't seem to be going anywhere. Why don't you call Lucas and see if anything's changed." As an afterthought, Roland added, "And while you have him on the phone, see if he has the resources to put a team on Hampton's house out in Chevy Chase. I know we can't mess with his office but we might pick something up out there."

Will stopped in the middle of dialing the cell phone and looked across at Roland with an expression which caused Roland to look over his shoulder to see if he was in imminent danger. "What is it, Will, what's the matter?"

Amanda urged, "Will, are you all right? What's happened?"

Will finally found his voice, "Did you say Hampton, Senator Chastain Hampton?"

Harry rode through the damp streets of the District comfortably settled in the back of the big limousine with the darkened windows. He had instructed his driver to take him around the monuments and across the bridges. The uniformed man gave him an affirmative nod and a, "Yes, Sir," while trying to cover his questioning look. The truth was he just wanted to take some time to appreciate and enjoy the trappings that went into making this place what it was. *The seat of power,* he reflected, *at least for now.* It would be sad to think of all of this stripped of its influence and brokering ability but time marches on. The important thing was that although he wouldn't be driving the cause, he would be riding shotgun. Just as he directed his driver to take him where he wanted to go today, so would he direct the world once the new order was in place. He didn't need to be the out front man. He still would call the shots because he would control the money that controlled the energy. It went without saying that whoever controlled the energy had the power, and that was in both senses of the word.

The sun was making its way down toward the tops of the buildings and the shadows were long. People bustled along the sidewalks and the streets choked with the stream of cars and trucks going about the tasks of a busy and powerful city. There was a certain energy in this environment. It was heightened even more as serious men and women labored under the stress of world altering work. Everyone looked like they had important things on their mind, probably they did.

He reflected on the changes that were to come. He put his head back and turned to watch the sights slide by the window. The tint in the glass gave the city a muted appearance. The unimaginative, gray buildings were almost sinister in tone and tenor. He was so satisfied with himself that his work was about to culminate. The agreement would be executed in Bangkok. He had prepared to the point that nothing could stand in the way of the accord. He had spoken with every one of the participants at least three times and he had held some conference calls where pros and cons were argued at length. Each time the debates had been meaningful and had concluded with his colleagues agreeing with the terms. He was about to finish a project that had consumed a great deal of his time and energy for nearly two years.

He had a moment of melancholy as he wondered what would occupy his every waking moment in the same way. He still needed stimulating work in his life and it had not occurred to him that he would feel a sense of loss at the conclusion of the project. Sitting atop the power position had been so appealing but it suddenly sounded a little dull. He was astounded at his reaction. A wave of remorse swept slowly over him causing a chill to settle in the confines of the lavish car.

He asked himself how he had gotten here. He'd heard of people who worked their entire lives with one goal in mind and when they reached it they got depressed, apparently from the struggle having ended. Was it possible that people had to have that to be happy? He'd always thought that if he could reach the pinnacle of power, the ultimate in control, that he'd be happy. He wondered now if he would.

Well, he wasn't exactly there yet so perhaps he was getting ahead of himself. There was still the formality of the summit to go through and then he'd see. He could only hope that the senator had his part as clearly defined, his plan as carefully laid and his homework so thoroughly done. They could not afford to have that side of the movement blow up. He assured himself that even after the coup there would still be a great deal more work to do. One didn't just casually run a whole planet after all. It would still take a great deal of management.

He let his thoughts drift to Roland. That arrogant prick was nothing but trouble, God, how he got under his skin. He'd decided to let the old man take care of it. He had the bunker brigade to put on it and it was high time they earned their keep out there. He was disgusted that they were taking so long though, the sooner they were rid of him the better. It would be important to watch how this was handled. If the secretary and his sissy entourage weren't up to the task he'd have to insist that

that beehive be cleaned out and they start over with a security crew who could measure up. Once they were up and running there would be more than enough enemies, plenty of challengers to require a highly competent security squad and system. It would be like playing, "King of The Hill." He shook off the painful childhood memory.

It remained to be seen if the secretary was their man. He had yet to be tested with his new organization and his shitload of new equipment.

If this Roland thing wasn't done right and done now he would take control of it himself. He knew now that he'd been wise to have him followed. He didn't know why Roland was meeting with this Webster fellow but it couldn't be good news. Harry had learned that the man was CIA and that didn't bode well. It had been wise to have his men check out his place and see if he was working with Roland.

There would always be problems and he had been foolish to think that he wouldn't have enough to do when the funding was in place and the operation under way. He had to look over everyone's shoulder it seemed. It had probably been unwise to have Nate send those two hit men to tail Roland but there was no real harm done. He probably shouldn't be going around the secretary like that. The old adage, "If you want it done right, do it yourself," was really true. There were only so many tasks that it was appropriate to delegate. A great deal of it would stay right on his plate, just like always.

The senator, he knew, had to be managed and maybe he'd eventually take all the others out and sit in the power spot alone. He lifted the handset out of the arm of the seat and dialed. While he was waiting for the connection he picked up the intercom and instructed his driver to take him home. There was so much still to do before he left for Thailand.

The phone on his desk had been ringing incessantly all morning as it was now. Margaret Blanchard's assistant finally picked it up and answered in an annoyed tone. He was surprised to hear Harry Axelrod on the other end. He never risked calling him at work.

"One of your boys has been meeting with a very dangerous player," he began. "I want you to check him out. See what he's doing there in the office. I've covered his house but I have reason to think something more is going on. His name's Webster, Bobby Webster. Call me at the regular number when you've had a chance to check it out."

The young man was pale with fear. He knew the player that Harry was; he'd been on his payroll for two years now. He'd fed him all sorts of information on Ms. Blanchard and had even copied a file for him once or twice. There was just no way that he could tell him that he'd already given Bobby Webster access to some of Ms. Blanchard's personal files. He'd have to lie and just hope that Harry never learned the truth. If he did, he was sure he'd be dead.

As Harry made his way home, a dark car left the Hart Senate Office Building and wound its way to a simple, but heavily guarded, three-story, glass building on the edge of Georgetown. It slowed just enough for the guard in the kiosk to recognize the driver and for the signal to be given. They were waved through under the raised parking control arm and proceeded down the ramp into the underground parking. The car stopped in the reserved area adjacent to the garage elevator and two figures emerged from the back doors. They stepped directly into the elevator closing the doors so promptly that it was nearly impossible to identify either of them even though their faces frequently appeared in the news media.

Amanda just sat and listened as Will and Roland excitedly exchanged notes about the Senator Chastain Hampton that each of them knew. The story which emerged was one of a tortured man with a deceptive and self-serving character. Roland was amazed to learn that the man he'd so admired had left his young son and the boy's mother to fend for themselves as he climbed the ladder of influence.

Will, on the other hand, was learning that Charles' father was a despicable man who had repeatedly taken the law into his own hands in order to accomplish his ends. Sometimes to better society and sometimes not but always for what he thought was right. "Who did he think he was?" Will asked. "How could one man think that he knew what was best for everyone without the benefit of open debate or a free exchange of ideas?"

More importantly, Will was sickened to learn that Charles' own father was responsible for his injuries, the near death of his own son, as well as Will and probably Amanda. He asked himself what kind of monster this man was. He couldn't possibly have a conscience. Yet he had sat with them for long hours at the hospital and talked to them both reassuringly about the future. *My God,* Will thought, *We asked him to help bring Amanda home safely and it was he who was trying to have her killed. This is insane.*

This time it was Amanda's turn to play the authoritative role. She let the two of them continue on until they were over the greatest part of their shock and then she brought them back to focus. "I know you've both had quite a jolt of reality thrown at you but we've got to stay on track. What we've just learned makes it all the more important that we get moving. We have a man who is out of control, has been for a long time and it sounds like he now has delusions of taking over all of the energy resources of the world and playing God with them. Besides all that he's out to kill us. I think you'd both better wake up. You can lick your wounded pride later, for now, get over it."

Will and Roland both turned from Amanda at the same moment and looked at each other. All three of them fell into uncontrollable laughter.

Moments later they'd regained their composure and the work resumed in earnest. They had learned so much through the course of this day. They needed to get a monitor on the senator sooner rather than later. They knew now who their enemy was and they needed to know what he was up to. They could think of no better way to find what they needed than electronic surveillance. They had exhausted their alternatives, even considering using Charles as bait.

They talked about Roland getting into the senator's house or office but the risk of detection was too great. If he was caught, there would be every reason in the world for the government to lock him away for the rest of his life and they would never have what they needed to expose him.

After hearing from Lucas they were all certain that he could get what they needed. His equipment was very sophisticated, he and Doc were two of the best outside the FBI and CIA, and his plan seemed flawless.

By four o'clock Walt's Plumbing Service was parked close to the corner near the senator's home. In order to keep from raising suspicions, Lucas had gone to several of the homes in the neighborhood and let them know that a number of the houses in that vicinity were having trouble with one of the sewer mains. He inquired if they were having any similar difficulty and when they replied that they weren't, he informed them that he would be working on the problem and he gave them a number to call in case any symptoms arose. In any event they would be on the street for the next few days. Satisfied that they were safely hidden in plain sight, he and Doc began their work.

Not two hours into their vigil Lucas was sure they'd struck gold. He called Roland immediately with his report.

Roland hung up his cell phone and turned to Will and Amanda, "We may have something," he said. "Grab your equipment bags and weapons, we've gotta hurry. I'll fill you in on the way."

They did exactly as told and ran out the door together with their handy bags stowed around their waists and weighted down with their weaponry. They crawled into the small, inconspicuous car that Roland had rented and they set out for their unspecified rendezvous. Roland drove through Arlington and as they headed for the Key Bridge he told them what he'd learned on the phone. "Lucas was able to get some bits and pieces of a badly broken up transmission just after getting set up. He doesn't have his equipment fine tuned to the senator's stuff yet so it wasn't as clear as he'd like nor as good as he'll get.

"He said that the conversation was with someone with very sophisticated encryption equipment. He only got what he did because the senator's is not as high tech. Lucas was just in the process of dialing down what equipment is in the house when he picked this up." Roland made a left turn in front of an oncoming car that caused the driver to blow his horn and wave his finger out the window at them. He took the time to return the salute and mutter some expletives to accompany it. Will just sat frozen with his eyes riveted on the road ahead.

Making his way down the side street he continued with the information he'd learned, "Anyway, it seems that our pigeon is off to meet with someone pretty high up. Probably a real player in this scheme. He was picking up part of a three way conference call and what Lucas wasn't sure of but what he thinks is that at least one person is very high in the U.S. government. He picked that up from the type of encryption being used. He says he can't be sure yet but he thinks the other one might be FBI or CIA. But get this," he paused appropriately and then turned to look at Will seated next to him in the front, "One of them is a woman."

Neither Will nor Amanda found much clarity from the explanation they'd just been given. Amanda asked, "So I don't get it, where are we going?"

"Well, it gets a little complicated. The senator was talking on a phone in his Senate Office which is routed through a server he has in his house. That's how Lucas picked it up. Anyway, this woman was to pick up the senator and they were going to the office from there."

"So?" Amanda repeated, "Where are we going."

"Well, that's just it, I'm not sure, but I know the senator keeps a private office in a small building over in Georgetown. I'm hoping that's where they were headed. It's a long shot but the only one we have."

"What are we gonna do, just burst in on them?" she asked in a smartass tone.

"We've got to know who he's meeting with. If my guess about where they're meeting is correct we may be able to catch a glimpse of this mystery person," he responded. Roland locked his eyes onto the roadway ahead and began to slow as he approached the simple, heavily guarded, three-story, glass office building on the edge of Georgetown.

Roland was familiar enough with the building to know a little about the security and about the layout. He cruised past the building at a reasonable speed and noted that indeed, the lights were on in the second floor corner office. That, he knew, was the senator's private area. At least they knew where he was meeting, now if they could only determine with whom. "The fact that the other player is a woman and is either high up in the government or is CIA or FBI is going to pare down the list of possibles to something pretty workable," he explained. "Lucky for us there just aren't that many women with those credentials."

Roland went around the corner and pulled over to the curb in a red zone. He instructed Will to take the wheel and drive around the area, avoiding the front of the office, until Roland called on the cell phone. Amanda pulled out her cell, turned it on and laid it on the seat between her and Will as she took up her position in the front seat and Will slid over to drive. He pulled away from the curb as Amanda turned and cautioned Roland to be careful.

He gave her a broad smile and a playful salute as he made his way toward the rear of the building. All Amanda could see as they made their way into the next block was Roland stepping into the shrubbery which surrounded the building and enclosed the portion of the garage which had been left open for ventilation. She hoped he knew what he was doing. She found that she was beginning to worry about him more than she really wanted to.

Will was silent giving all of his concentration to his driving. This gave Amanda time to let her mind wander. She thought about Alex, back in Bulgaria, and wondered how he was doing. She knew that he'd been traumatized from the death of that woman and wondered how he was coping with it. She found herself back in the present and worried about why they hadn't heard from Roland yet.

She glanced at the time display on the dashboard of the car and realized that Roland had only been out of the car four minutes. She went back to thinking about him as a man. She was surprised at what she had learned about him in the last couple of days. She'd thought that he was attractive but had assumed that was because he had an aura of danger around him. She found him to be quite different from what she had imagined. He really was very gentle and kind. Besides that, she observed, he was just plain sexy.

She looked at the display again and saw that only another three minutes had passed. She needed to do something to pass the time or she'd be crazy before this was over. She was startled out of her reverie by the ringing of her cell phone.

She picked it up, pressed the answer button and said, "Yes?"

"I'm secure in the garage and I want you to contact Lucas and see if he can find out who drives this car." He gave her the make, model and license number of the dark vehicle whose driver had turned it around and now waited directly in front of the garage elevator.

"Check," she responded. "Will you call back or don't you need it down there?"

"Just jot down whatever he can get you," he whispered. "I'm going to wait here for our players to appear and see what I can learn. Now that I've seen the car my suspicions are growing. I'll call you when I need a ride." He hung up abruptly and switched off his phone.

Roland had wedged himself into the only undetected place where he thought he could catch a glimpse of the occupants of the elevator when they moved to the car. It had required that he loosen the light bulb in one of the units when the driver had his back turned. Gratefully, he was busy visiting with the guard and the two of them needed to walk as they talked. This enabled Roland the few seconds he needed to turn the fluorescent tube to disable it without them noticing the subtle change in the darkness. From there he bided his time until he could make his way over toward the safety railing and pull himself up into the airway which housed the huge fan system for automobile exhaust removal. He was sure the system was set to come on only when the exhaust level in the garage reached a certain level. The only thing he had to fear once he was inside was the driver deciding that he needed to start the car and leave it idling while he waited for his boss. He doubted that one car would be enough to activate the system but given where he was and the parts of his anatomy that were at risk, he didn't want to find out.

Roland was sure that he was in for a wait so he decided to use his time to assess where they were with the situation. This business about the senator had been an emotional blow to Roland personally and he had not had the time to consider what this might mean for their cause. He needed to step back from the emotion and weigh the gravity of it. His first thought was that this man was more driven and more calculating than Roland had ever imagined. This made him all the more dangerous and meant that all options had to be considered in bringing him down. At this point it was eat or be eaten. There was absolutely no doubt left in his mind that all three of them would be killed if they didn't stop this organization first. The senator seemed to be the kingpin in the plot.

Roland lay doubled up in the ventilation tube for over an hour going over every aspect of this war. By the time his attention was diverted to the car in front of the elevator he thought he had drawn on every last bit of his expertise and had the beginnings of a good plan.

He watched as the driver started the car and got out from under the steering wheel to open and stand alert at the rear door closest to the elevator. From his post in the guts of the building he could hear the hum of the elevator as it made its way to pick up and transport its passengers down into the garage. He moved slightly to assure himself of the best possible view and in doing so he got his foot caught on some type of cable. His effort to extricate his limb created a scraping sound which reverberated through the garage. The driver heard it even over the sound of the car's engine and turned abruptly in Roland's direction. His hand was inside his jacket and it rested on the weapon in his shoulder holster. He was saying something to the guard who was now positioned halfway between the elevator and the car door. Roland was sweating and only taking half breaths as the driver began to walk over toward his hiding place. The guard called out, "Those damn stray cats crawl around in here all the time, guess they keep the rats outta here anyway."

The driver, looking only half convinced, turned right under Roland and returned to his post next to the open rear door of the car just as the bell chimed the arrival of the elevator. Roland watched intently as the doors separated down the middle and slipped slowly off to the sides revealing Senator Chastain Hampton and Margaret Blanchard, Deputy Director CIA, Covert Operations. Roland had to stifle his urge to let out a low whistle. He watched as both of them got into the car and the driver closed the door after them. As the car pulled out of the garage he felt a huge sense of relief and was certain that his latest brainstorm would be successful. Now all he had to do was free himself from this living tomb and call Amanda and Will to pick him up. He was actually excited about the prospects that lay ahead for the three of them.

Roland had to wait only another fifteen minutes before the guard took a walk around the perimeter of the garage. Once he was on the opposite side, Roland turned his body so that his feet would come out of the tube first and hung precariously for a moment before dropping to the floor of the garage. Once on the ground he used the railing to boost himself back out through the slightly overgrown shrubbery and then he made his way down the street looking like every other Washingtonian out strolling in the Georgetown neighborhood. He took out his cell phone, switched it on and dialed.

"Yes?" she answered.

"Pick me up, same place," he instructed.

Bobby Webster not only looked like a jogger he was actually doing so. He found the feeling of sweat running down his back and chest totally reassuring and it always reminded him of how good he felt when his clothes fit to perfection and his body was trim and firm. He loved to give the ladies a thrill. It had been that way ever since he first found the track team back in high school. He never tired of checking himself out in any mirror, window or other reflecting surface when he got himself all duded up. He had decided that if Roland wanted him to look like a jogger for their meeting he might as well make the best of it. Besides it was giving him an opportunity to turn over in his mind the information he'd found. He found it troubling and needed to be sure that he was drawing the right conclusions. He didn't want to be fooled on this one.

He slowed to a walk to begin his cool down as he passed through the gates to the cemetery in Rock Creek. The walk to their meeting place would be just about right to keep him from getting too stiff after his run.

He couldn't tell if his friend had arrived ahead of him due to the wall like structure that surrounded the seats at the Adams Memorial. He approached the enclosure with care. He was the first to arrive. He checked his watch to see if he was early and noted that their meeting time had passed. Roland was so anal he was usually early or made an entrance at the exact time. He wondered if something had happened to his friend.

It hadn't taken long to discover at headquarters that the game that

Roland was playing in had pretty high stakes. He'd had to pull in some favors and make some moves to get the information. Most of the files that contained the data that Roland needed had been taken from the regular file pool and moved into a secure location under the control of the assistant to the Deputy Director. He had found this curious in itself but the mystery deepened when he finally gained access to them.

He had been fortunate to be able to copy the documents that he did and was relieved when he got them squirreled away safely and under his control. Roland would surely need them and Bobby had an unsettling feeling that in no time someone would be made aware of his interest. He wondered why he had persevered. Roland was a good friend but it went beyond that. It disturbed him every time he saw that someone was not following protocol. He believed deeply in his agency and in the work that they were doing but he knew that their unique position also made it easy to take matters into their own hands. Shortcuts were expedient but, in his mind, dangerous. Rules needed to be followed, everything had to be above board and transparency of transactions was paramount to the future and credibility of the agency. He guessed he'd pulled this string because he feared that shortcuts were being taken that weren't healthy for anyone.

It was not like him, however, to not think through to culmination the results of his actions. He'd had to decide in a moment whether to go forward with obtaining the data or just tell Roland that his hunt had been a bust. He was used to making such determinations. He did it every day in the field. He wondered why this seemed like a precipitous decision that he'd not properly deliberated. He knew he might have put people in jeopardy in that instant, including himself.

He glanced at his watch again wondering where Roland could be. He took a seat on the bench opposite the hauntingly vague features of the statue that was the centerpiece of the memorial and decided he'd give him another ten minutes. He had a sudden and brief sense of an odor, a familiar scent riding on the early evening air but it was out of place, a chemical, he thought. Just as his defense system was about to kick in he felt the cloth sliding over his head and everything went dark.

Chapter Twenty-one

Roland was disgusted with himself that he was nearly twenty minutes late for his meeting with Bobby Webster He knew that Bobby had some information for him but he didn't know that he'd have to spend that extra time in the ventilation tube so Bobby had no way to know that he was going to be late. He tried to raise him on his cell phone but guessed that he hadn't taken it with him on his run. He thought that strange, but then Bobby was kind of a strange guy.

Roland was convinced that Bobby had given up on him and gone home when he didn't find him at the memorial. He had no reason to doubt that he'd been there and he knew that Roland was always punctual. Given this he decided to try his cell phone again. He'd probably be back home by now.

Still unable to raise him, he gave up and went back to meet with Will and Amanda. He hadn't had time to brief them fully after his observations in the garage of the senator's private office.

The senator found himself feeling lonely as he sat at the large, hand rubbed oak desk in his office at the Senate Building. Evening was descending on the city as it changed from its sunny attire of the day to the more drab and dreary cloak of descending darkness. His meeting with Blanchard had not gone well and as was happening more frequently lately, when he was down he thought more and more about the past.

He had another one of those visions of what his life might have been if he'd not been tapped on the shoulder and asked to enter politics. It was that first calling that had changed everything. That was when he'd come to realize that it was he who was supposed to lead the people. That's what had made it so difficult to operate within the parameter of politics. He knew how things were supposed to be but so often he couldn't reach his goals without those shortcuts, without Gazelle. Now it was time to move to the next level and he needed the same type of assistance. His clarity of vision had not diminished. *I never asked for this and it has cost me so much. My life has continuously been shaped by the needs of others,* he thought.

He wondered if it was too late for him to have the things that mattered most to him. He tried to list what those would be. He tried to focus on things like world peace or food for the starving but his thoughts kept returning to family, to love. He wondered if he had changed so much,. Perhaps this was all a function of age. He certainly had been thinking more and more about his own mortality lately. He'd thought that was because he'd ordered more deaths in the last six months than at any other time in his life.

Maybe it wasn't that, maybe it was just that when a man got to be his age his priorities changed. It suddenly meant so much to him to have Charles. Having him in his life was incredibly satisfying but there was more than that. There was something about knowing that his bloodline would continue, even if his name would not. It just made a man feel more of a man to know that he had done his part to ensure the continuance of the human race. Perhaps it was just that fundamental.

Of course he wished that Charles could love him but he was sure that that was too much to hope for. He'd be satisfied to have some kind of ongoing relationship with him. They could be friends. Well, that sounded pretty trite, like something you'd tell a stepchild as you were trying to win their trust. Of course he wanted more from Charles than friendship. He wanted to be his father.

He began to emerge from his reverie and back to the business at hand. He had to get Margaret Blanchard back to thinking like a member of the team and he wasn't sure how he was going to do that. She had

303

been as stiff as a new pair of jeans during their meeting. He wondered if someone had gotten to her, changed her allegiance. It had only been a few days since he met with her last and even her demeanor today had been different. *That was one of the handiest things about working with women,* he thought, *you could tell any little change in them by their body language.* He stopped to ask himself if that was a sexist attitude, decided it wasn't and went on with his thoughts.

Margaret Blanchard was an important player in the next phase of the program. They needed her to provide the impetus for the coup. They couldn't gain control of the energy resources if they had all of these little pseudo-democratic empires and dictatorships trying to hang on to what they believed was theirs by birthright. The best example of this was probably the Middle East where every little country had their own oil reserves and they tried like hell to keep it all under control with the likes of OPEC. The problem with that was that there were still energy producers who were not a part of that organization and who often worked at odds with them. It could and would be so much simpler and ever so much more effective when it wasn't all chopped up among political entities. One leader, one thought, one way and eventually, one world.

It was Blanchard's team who would take down these dynasties, each in their own way but each swift and effective. It had taken months and months of endless study and fact gathering to find the right way to attack each of them. Now was not the time to let that facet get out of control. He wondered if the answer was that Margaret needed to be replaced. He had to be assured that the operatives were in place and ready to go.

He pulled out the files and began to review again the plan for each of the more critical locations. The names of the operatives and dates and details of the takedown plan were all clearly spelled out. Of course unlike most such plans of the CIA, the piece which was missing in all of these was the subsequent insertion of a figure of power. That would not be necessary under the new world order. He was startled out of his work by the ringing of his secure phone. He picked it up, "Yes?"

"We've got a problem," the female caller said.

Bobby Webster could feel his head throbbing before he was fully awake. He tried to focus, tried to remember where he was. He thought he must have been drinking, had a hangover, but that was certainly unlike him. He didn't think that he did that as a matter of routine. Then he became more aware of his surroundings. If he had been drinking it was bad. He must have passed out before he made it home. He was aware of the dark. It was cold and he was lying on the damp earth with a twig or sharp rock digging into his hip.

Slowly it started to come back to him. He was supposed to be meeting Roland, at the Adams Memorial. Then the resounding memory of the chemical smell intruded into his memory and the headache made more sense. Someone had snatched him out there in the cemetery, before he could meet Roland.

He sat up slowly trying not to let the headache make him nauseous. He had to move slowly. He groped around for his fanny pack, his cell phone and weapon would be there. He didn't find it on the first sweep. He struggled to get up on his hands and knees and he anxiously patted the ground around him, still no luck. He'd have to get to his feet and find his way home. He stopped to run his hands over his head hoping to get things put back into place before he tried the dizzying heights of standing on his own two feet. He didn't know what they had used on him but his body hurt like hell. He doubted all that was from the run. He wasn't that far out of shape.

Once on his feet he began to crawl up out of the ditch area where he'd been left. It was steep sided enough that he had to use branches and small shrubs to pull himself up. He assumed now that they had thrown him down in the gully while he was unconscious and that accounted for the aches and pains he was experiencing.

He didn't know what time it was or for that matter, what day. They'd stripped his watch off of him presumably trying to keep him from being identified too quickly if found by a passerby. Well, they needn't have worried, where they left him a passerby was highly unlikely. He wondered if they'd intended to kill him or only put him out of commission for a period of time. Neither scenario meant much to him at this moment. He needed to consider all of the options once his head cleared. At the top of the climb he stopped to catch his breath and to orient himself. He was sure that he was somewhere in the woods within Rock Creek Park but he had no idea where. He decided to just start walking and hope that he would cross one of the many hiking and jogging trails.

It seemed to take forever but in reality it was probably less than thirty minutes until he was on a well worn path through the woods. After that it seemed to be no time at all before he was out into the residential neighborhood that bounded the park and from there it was a short walk home. He was glad that he kept a key in the flower bed and wouldn't have to try to break into his own home in his condition.

He had three things to do once he was inside, make sure the documents were still there, call Roland and get a shower.

Bobby was only half prepared for what greeted him when he opened the door to his home. He'd been certain that they would come looking through his house but he hadn't expected them to ransack the place and bust up his belongings. His professional side told him this looked more like an act of passion. Somebody cared enough to send a message and they expended a hell of a lot of energy breaking up things that didn't matter. It really didn't look very professional.

He set one of the lamps upright and turned it on. He was glad to find that it worked. From there he cleared a path through the living room and made his way down the hall toward the bedrooms. About half way down the hall he turned into the service room off the back porch that doubled as a laundry room. He opened a tall narrow door that housed a built in ironing board that was commonly found in houses of this era. He let the ironing board down and pulled the cover off. There, taped to the board were the documents that he needed more than ever to get to Roland.

He called Roland and arranged to meet him at his hotel room. From there he headed for the bedroom taking the documents with him. He opened his closet and took down a hat box from the rear of the top shelf. Lifting the lid he removed his backup weapon and a full clip of ammunition. He was surprised they'd missed it. They must have been in a real hurry. He inserted the magazine into the butt of the grip and made sure that a round was in the chamber. He placed the gun inside the towel he had placed by the shower. Next he rolled up the documents and put them in the leg of the trousers that he'd laid out on the bed and headed for the comfort of a long, hot shower and a load of aspirin for his aching head and body.

The senator was both surprised and relieved to hear Margaret Blanchard on the phone. She had asked to meet with him again saying that something had come up and she needed to brief him. She told him that new information had come to her since they talked earlier.

They agreed to meet back at his office in Georgetown in thirty minutes. That didn't leave him much time to get there but he felt he needed to accommodate her. He summoned his own car this time and headed quickly out of his office. In his rush he neglected to secure the documents he had been looking at.

Margaret was prompt as usual and he was glad that he had hurried. They pulled into the parking garage close enough in time that they could ride the elevator up to his office together. As he punched the code into the key pad adjacent to his office door the lights came on inside the reception area and the chime sounded indicating that the locks on the door were released. He held the door for her to enter and made his way around her to provide passage into the office itself. Once inside he gestured to the chairs in the corner of the room away from the windows and offered her a drink.

She sat facing the door they had just entered and declined the drink. She wanted to get this over with.

Amanda, Roland and Will were all seated around the little table in their obscure headquarters when Bobby knocked on the door. Roland rose and crossed the room with his weapon in his hand. He pulled back the drapery just far enough to assure himself that it was safe to open the door.

Bobby entered the room with his usual savoir faire and went immediately to clasp Amanda's hand while he introduced himself. He loved the ladies and the ladies loved him. His dress was toned down a bit but, as always, he was a picture of fashion. Roland introduced him to Will and pulled a fourth chair over to the table.

The three of them interrupted where they were in their meeting and quickly shifted gears to concentrate on the information that Bobby was bringing them. There would be time when he was finished to continue their plans.

Bobby extracted a handful of documents from the inside pocket of his coat and began his verbal explanation. He wanted to be sure that they understood what they were about to see and the context within which these particular copies were found. He began by allowing himself a recap of what he had gone through to get them and keep them. He'd been brief with Roland on the phone but he wanted to impress upon this little group just exactly what they were involved in.

Finally he laid the precious papers out on the table in front of them and began to explain the detailed descriptions that each of them contained about the takedown of the governments in certain, apparently targeted countries around the world. There was also, he pointed out, a direct correlation between the first twenty names on the master list and how much oil that particular country controlled.

He had saved the best for last. When all three of them were head long into reading and studying the intricacies of these plans he sprung it on them. "The other thing I learned is that Margaret Blanchard is acting as a double agent in this terrifying little consortium." He waited for the news to register with the three curious faces.

Roland regained his composure first, "Double agent?"

"That's right. Lucky for you she's got the goods on the whole mess. As a matter of fact she's meeting with the precious Senator Hampton as we speak, but the best news for you is that she's wearing a wire."

"Oh my God," was all that Roland could get out. Finally he stammered on, "We've got the documents and she's getting corroborating evidence?"

"That's right, Buddy Boy," Bobby answered. "Before we're through here she'll be back at CIA Headquarters in Langley with all the proof needed to put an end to the good senator and his little nest of vipers."

"This is almost too good to be true," Will added.

"That's for sure," Roland echoed. "Bobby, will you be in touch with her? How will we know if she's been successful? As I told you before, our lives are on the line. The contract's out." He stopped to contemplate the effect of this news. What he had seen in the parking garage could verify this or it could be a cover. He decided to give Margaret the benefit of the doubt for now.

Bobby just smiled that sweet, affable smile of his and patted his coat, "She'll call me on the cell as soon as she's got it," he reported. "All we have to do is wait. That shouldn't be too hard. Hey, anybody bring any cards to this party?"

The senator sat across the small table from Margaret and watched the panel of lights over the door to his private library. There was one in particular that kept blinking an alarming orange color. He knew instinctively that it was from the sensor for recording equipment. Margaret Blanchard was bugged. He let her prattle on as he tried to think about how best to handle this predicament. It could mean only one thing. He did wonder whether she'd been disloyal to the cause from the beginning or whether something had happened to make her change her allegiance. Either way it was time to deal with it.

He kept her involved in small talk as he moved across the room. "Are you sure you wouldn't like something, Margaret?" he asked. "If you don't mind I'm going to fix myself a drink."

He couldn't push the silent alarm and just have her taken away by security, then what? He'd just have to evade her attempts to lead the conversation, stay totally off the subject and then beg off on the meeting.

Returning to the chair across from her, he continued, "Margaret, unless this news you have is of the utmost importance to the security of this country, I'd really like to beg off. Suddenly I'm not feeling very well."

She looked at him with a questioning look. She was practiced in this game of subterfuge and her first inclination was not to let him off so easily. She decided to try to obtain even the slightest incriminating conversation by making him acknowledge the project. If he wouldn't give her that much she'd know that he was not really ill but instead that he was on to her. "This isn't about the security of the country, Senator, it's about Operation Cloud Nine, the new world order, of course."

Time seemed to stand still for both of them in that moment. For her it was the wait to see if he would speak openly of their plans or if he knew of her treachery to the cause. For him it was the defining moment of acknowledging her sabotage or putting himself on the hook with irrefutable evidence of his clandestine work. The atmosphere filled with tension like a slowly inflating balloon being filled to the point of bursting. The air hung heavy with the anticipation of the moment. Who would blink?

All at once the senator slopped the liquid from the glass as he nearly threw the drink down on the table, covered his mouth with his hastily extracted handkerchief and literally ran for the bathroom which adjoined his office. A "Sorry, Margaret," was expelled through the cloth and with that primitive exit the line was drawn in the sand between them.

She reached inside her jacket and switched off the activation button of the voice operated recorder. Nothing would be gained from this meeting and probably not from any other. All of her months of work had just gone up in smoke. With her cover blown she was, for all intents and purposes, useless to the cause. She sat there awaiting the senator's return so she could at least leave with some sense of decorum.

When he returned to the office several minutes later, still making his apologies, he was both delighted and amused to see that the warning light for the recording sensor had stopped flashing. She had gotten the point and turned off her little evidence gatherer. *They would live to engage another day*, he thought. The gravity of what had just happened was only beginning to settle over him.

He apologized one last time as he showed her to the door still clutching the handkerchief over his mouth. "I just don't know if it was something I ate or if I'm coming down with something," he lamented. "I'll call to reschedule."

He closed the door behind her and waited until he heard the doors of the elevator open and close before he left the outer reception area and went back into the confines and safety of his office. He locked the door behind him and sank into the huge chair behind his desk. He realized that he was sweating.

Margaret Blanchard rode the elevator down into the parking where her driver, Donny, had positioned her car directly in front of the doors. She stepped quickly from the enclosure and slipped into the rear seat settling safely behind the darkened windows. She put her head back on the seat and felt her heart racing as her pulse, she was sure, reached well over 120 beats per minute. What, she wondered, had just happened? She knew it had been a close call and had it not been for her position in the agency and her high profile she'd be toast. She wondered how he had known and then realized it really didn't matter.

She picked up her secure phone and dialed the cell phone of Bobby Webster.

Roland, Will, Amanda and Bobby had moved from the table to the more comfortable seating in the pathetic little room. They had been talking about the diabolical plan they had uncovered and each had something to add from a different perspective. Together they had spun a tale of enormous proportion which pretty well spelled out the purpose and long reaching effects of what they'd happened on to.

Bobby had just been explaining that it wasn't until after he'd met with Roland and he'd returned to Langley Headquarters that he found that all of the files that contained the key words that Roland had asked him to research were pulled out of circulation and were under the personal control of Margaret. He had pulled in some favors owed to him by her assistant to sneak a look at what they had that pertained to Gazelle and that had told him enough to cause him to go directly to the woman, herself.

It was she who had briefed him on the magnitude of Operation Cloud Nine and the new world order. It was then that Senator Hampton's name had been tied to the whole action. She had explained to him, her long standing relationship with the senator going back to their days in southern Michigan and her early involvement in state politics there. He had been a mentor. This really touched a chord in Roland and he was saddened by the chasm that had opened between the two of them.

Bottom line and the phrase that resounded in the ears of the three listeners was her sharing with Bobby that the senator had approached her and solicited her assistance in planning and implementing coups in several countries which were rich in oil. It was at that time that she became a mole in the organization known as Operation Cloud Nine. Bobby's intriguing story was suddenly interrupted by the long awaited ringing of his cell phone.

"This is Bobby," he answered.

"Bobby, it's Margaret. I've been made. I don't know how much time I have but I can't imagine my life's worth a plug nickel right now."

"Jesus," he responded letting a look of alarm engage the features of his face. "What the hell happened?"

"I don't really know right now and that's not the issue, moving forward is. I think we need to meet so I can fully brief you. If something happens to me this thing's got to be stopped and you know almost as much as I do. Where are you now?"

"With the targets who put me onto this. Do you want to come here? Or I can meet you at headquarters, wherever you say."

Margaret thought for a moment and then responded, "I think we'd better keep this within the agency for now."

Bobby gave her a meeting place and they hung up.

He turned to the other three occupants of the room and delivered the bad news. The faces all sagged at once like children who'd just gotten the news that Santa wouldn't arrive this year.

Bobby gathered his jacket and other items he'd strewn about the room and made his way to the door. He turned with his hand on the knob and told the three of them that he would be in touch right after he talked with Margaret. He cautioned them to try to get some sleep because he had this ominous feeling that after meeting with her their days and nights would become one until this business was finished. At that he turned and left leaving the remaining occupants of the room in various stages of shock.

Bobby made his way to the front of the miserable little hotel where, after ten minutes or so, he was finally able to hail a cab. He had the man drive him to the metro where he rode inbound on the blue line. At this time of night the train wouldn't stop at the Arlington Cemetery stop so he'd ride it to Rosslyn and walk the short distance back to the Iwo Jima Memorial where, he hoped, Margaret would be waiting in her car. As he left the station the wind had picked up and he automatically hunched his shoulders and turned the collar of his jacket up against the onslaught of cold air that was trying to reach down inside his garments as he began the walk.

Moments later he saw her standing outside the car. She was intermittently leaning against the rear door and pacing around the back. Her hands were jammed down into the pockets of her light raincoat and her eyes seemed to be darting about indiscriminately, looking everywhere while seeing nothing. It was apparent, even if he hadn't been trained to make such observations, that she was a bundle of nervous energy. He braced himself for the encounter.

As soon as she saw him approaching her hand shot up in the air in a half wave. She immediately turned, got in the backseat of the car and shut the door. He made his way to the other side and slid in beside her. "You're late." She admonished.

"I didn't know we'd set a time," he responded.

"She looked him in the eye and he knew that what she needed as much as a colleague was a friend. He reached over and put his arm on her sleeve. "We're gonna make this thing happen, Margaret," he assured her.

She gave a half smile, "I hope we can pull it off, Bobby, I really hope we can."

The car pulled away from the memorial slowly and began its trip around the city. Donny had been given his instructions and he was quite used to his boss conducting secret meetings in the rear seat of the automobile. He drove slowly and cautiously. He knew that it didn't matter where he went as his passengers would have no idea where they were. He glanced in his rear view mirror regularly staying alert to his surroundings and aware that they might be followed. He would just drive around keeping everyone safe and wait for further instructions.

In the rear of the vehicle with the privacy screen securely raised Margaret began to lay out for Bobby everything she knew about the operation. She told him of the involvement of the secretary and also of Harry Axelrod. She had been trying to determine whether there were other major players but she was most focused on the senator initially. At this time she was not certain whether there was someone directing the senator. She had only suspicions in that regard.

For his part, Bobby took in and assimilated information about as fast as anyone in the agency. He rarely made notes as they could and often did fall into the wrong hands. As the briefing progressed he got a sense of the gravity and was at the same time formulating a preliminary plan. As she talked, he adjusted his proposed actions accordingly. This was what Bobby Webster did best. He was determined to pull this off. There were too many lives at stake. An entire way of life was hanging in the balance. While he valued all human life, he was particularly loyal and wanted to watch the backs of both Margaret and Roland. Before this assignment concluded he would reach further down inside himself than he could now imagine.

Harry was still pacing around his office well into the evening. He was nervous about the upcoming meeting in Bangkok and he was getting tense over his staff's inability to locate Roland. He knew he was still out there, if he'd been taken out Harry would know that. He was also concerned that the CIA man, Webster was moving around as well. They'd lost the tail on both of them and while Harry knew that it was only temporary he didn't like the idea that they were probably together and continuing to probe into his business. He was sick of killing people right and left, not because it bothered him morally, but because he knew that it would eventually arouse way too much interest.

He hadn't wanted to waste the agency man, just send him a message and while they were at it give his house and office a toss for sensitive materials. Now he was concerned that he and Roland were too far along on their trail to be safe. He didn't want to put the searchlight of suspicion on the organization but neither did he want them terminating the cause.

He continued to pace and ponder. Sometimes he found himself just inches from taking over the whole program. It would be easier to waste the senator, secretary and the sneak who never showed himself and just run the whole show from behind the magic curtain. Sometimes it was like being in the Land of Oz.

When this had begun, each of them brought something to the table and their unique strengths were assets. Now it seemed to him that they were rapidly becoming liabilities. He couldn't rely on them for even the simplest assignments. They seemed determined to screw things up. He preferred to rely only on himself.

He decided to keep a hand in the middle of their backs until after the coups had taken place and the organization had control of the energy before seriously considering eliminating them. The head man in particular, the sneak, as he called him, was beginning to give him pause. He didn't like the way the man stayed in the background and made all of his moves by manipulating the senator.

For now it would fall to him to cleanup behind them again. He'd have to step up his forces and take care of all of the enemies of the cause. Perhaps he could find a way to get them all at once. That would be handy, he thought. Especially in this day of fear and panic about terrorists he was sure he could arrange a hit that would look like a terrorist cell had struck. Hell, they could even call the media afterward and take credit for it. He decided to call in his specialist. He hadn't used the man's unique skills since the labor strikes in Venezuela. It was time to renew such an old acquaintance.

Given the ease of operation from there, he decided that it would be best to send the man directly to the secretary out in the bunker and let them put the plan together. They could present it to him and he would just tell the senator to get over it when he whined at him about going behind his back. He was getting too hard to deal with and he'd been so sullen lately that Harry had wondered if he was going soft. No, he'd have to do this himself and there was absolutely no doubt that it needed to be done sooner rather than later. Time was of the essence. He liked the idea of giving the secretary's team some on the job tutoring by a real pro. It may come in handy later.

Roland, Amanda, Will and Bobby sat in the coffee shop and weighed their options. After Bobby's meeting with Margaret they had learned even more about the purpose and the plan of Operation Cloud Nine and thanks to what they'd gotten from Lucas they knew that Margaret Blanchard filled the role from the conference call of the woman and also the representative from the CIA. They now knew that the main players were Senator Hampton, Harry Axelrod and Secretary Denton and then of course there was Deputy Director Blanchard in her dual role.

Roland had been both relieved and dismayed at what they had learned. It made sense to him now; he knew why he had suddenly become expendable. He had become an obstacle that this new world order needed to remove from their path. It was becoming clearer but no less painful.

Roland pointed out the obvious to the others, they had a limited amount of time to find a way to stop this scheme. They reasoned that their choices were to eliminate all of them, to expose and discredit them completely or to somehow thwart their efforts. They decided that the murder of 3 or 4 well known people was probably not a choice at all. Pulling that off undetected and avoiding prosecution did not present favorable odds.

In considering the second option they determined that the hole in that plan was the corroborating evidence. They had the documents which proved that someone was planning to foster coups in several oil rich countries and take over the allotment of energy resources to the world but without Margaret's tapes there was nothing to tie those plans or those documents to any of the guilty parties. They had the e-mail that Amanda and Bradley Duncan had obtained to incriminate the secretary but that didn't bring down the bigger players. The last alternative was beginning to look like their only choice. Also, with the time crunch they had to work fast and sabotaging the implementation of this maniacal plan was probably the quickest way to stop it. All they needed was a fast, fool proof way to do that.

Bobby and Roland were kicking ideas back and forth between them while Will sat and doodled on a piece of paper. Amanda was drumming her fingers on the table and humming. Each of them had their own preferred way of working. The tension at the table and the mental effort being expended were almost palpable.

Amanda brought them back together by announcing, "I've got some thoughts that might get us started in the right direction."

Everyone stopped what they were doing and looked at her with various expressions ranging from amazement to doubt. There was a part of each of these men who still saw her as weak and vulnerable. Someone they had to take care of or rescue. She was not the one that they looked to for solutions but each was polite enough to listen.

"It seems to me that we have a threshold question to answer. Do we attack each of these individuals separately or do we go after Operation Cloud Nine as one big enemy?"

The men looked at each other and each seemed to be deferring to the others to address her question.

"Look, damn it, I'm sick of you guys treating me like I don't have a brain or a life at stake here. What I'm thinking is this. Instead of trying to keep Operation Cloud Nine from going into effect through force, infiltration or some other crazy method you might think up and don't have time for, doesn't it make more sense to get one of these players to stop it themselves? We might get them to go after each other even. I mean, I don't think there's any love lost between the senator and Harry Axelrod from what Roland's described. How about using that for instance?"

The furtive looks that were flitting around the table bordered on sheepish. Will broke the silence, "She might have something there, you guys. I was on a different but somewhat similar thought myself. I keep thinking that the Senator Hampton I've met and the one Roland describes is down inside this man somewhere. I had thought that we might bring pressure to bear on him by threatening to expose him to Charles. It's kind of far out but I just keep wondering."

Again, Roland and Bobby looked at each other half amazed. All at once Bobby broke out his big, jovial smile, "Why have I been racking my brain? You guys are onto it. We need a serious plan here."

Roland scooted his chair up closer to the table and leaned forward in anticipation, "Will, I think you're onto something, Amanda too. I agree with you both, what I know of the senator he has a very vulnerable spot for his long lost son. Will get your paper out, let's make some rough notes. My suggestion is that we take each of the targets and see if we can find a weakness that we can exploit. Something that will bend them," he added

Will acted as the recording secretary as the group began to brainstorm in earnest about the objects of their plan. Undoubtedly Harry was the easiest. Everyone who knew anything about him decided that greed was his weakness. He would do almost anything for money. They were also all in agreement that the senator was soft where his son was concerned. Roland added the observation that he'd made of late that the man seemed to feel compelled to do what he must for the good of mankind. It was like he was driven.

The wild card in this system would be the secretary. Little was known about him outside the bunker and his department and he kept a low profile by design.

When it came time to divide up assignments it was almost as though they'd been preordained. It was obvious that Amanda should take the secretary since she worked for him and knew more than the others about the system. Also, she was the only one with even a prayer of getting inside the bunker.

Roland and Will were the natural choices to take the senator. They both had a relationship with him and, due to his importance, he merited having them both work on him.

By default, Bobby was left to deal with Harry. Not that it was a perfect fit but Bobby probably had the right kinds of skills to deal with someone like "Dirty Harry," as Bobby had taken to calling him.

Since they didn't have much time to brainstorm; all the minds needed to have input to get the best and safest action plan for each target.

The overriding plan was to get the individual to sabotage the project out of fear or coercion. Failing that, they wanted to plant information or do whatever they could to bring dissension to the ranks. If they could not get the plot axed they needed to stir up the hornet's nest that might bring them down from the inside.

With their respective plans ready, they headed out to the four winds.

Chapter Twenty-two

The ordeal with Margaret had left the senator totally drained. It seemed sometimes that the harder he tried to help people the more obstacles they placed in his path. He wondered why people couldn't just trust him or understand that he was moving things in the direction that was ultimately to everyone's benefit. He knew that a bright woman such as Margaret would come around. She'd just gotten off track. Of course she knew that this was best. The question for him was whether to wait for her to come to her senses or to deal with her now. He didn't think she would sabotage the operation, she was smarter than that plus she'd been loyal to him since she was just a young girl. He was certain she could be trusted but what in the world had made her act like that? It certainly seemed as though she were trying to set him up. His mind couldn't accept such absurdity, not Margaret.

Suddenly he felt very tired. There were days like this one where he was sure that he was carrying the entire weight of the world on his shoulders. It was never easy being a leader but some days and some decisions were just a lot harder than others. There was some saying, he thought, about the head that wore the crown not getting any rest. No, he was mixing his metaphors. He was just so tired, exhausted, he decided to stretch out on the sofa in his office and rest for ten minutes or so. That should help. He turned off the overhead light and left the small work light burning. Just a few minutes of rest and quiet and he'd be able to get back at his work.

He was startled awake by an unfamiliar sound. It sounded like scratching. Almost like a rodent in the wall, but no, not that. It was cautious and intermittent. He raised his head and turned it slightly, inclined it in the direction of the noise and listened more carefully. There it was again. *My God,* he thought. *Someone's trying to get into the outer office.*

Roland's earlier time in the ventilation tube of the senator's office building had given him some familiarity with the routine followed by the guards on the building. The fact that the senator was meeting Margaret here and not in his Senate office led Roland to believe that he had segregated his work around Operation Cloud Nine to this location. It would either be here or his home. Since Lucas was already in place at the residence, Roland had decided to start with the office and then visit Chevy Chase only if he still had the need to do so. He desperately hoped that he would find what he needed right in here.

He was having problems picking the lock and since it didn't appear to be all that sophisticated, he assumed he was grossly out of practice. He removed the tools, stood up to stretch his neck, took a deep breath and started again. Once he had the two probes inserted, he began again to move the pick counter clockwise while feeling for that now less than familiar click that would occur when the pin holding the bolt released. Finally, there it was, he was in. He allowed himself to exhale and gained a little self satisfied expression on his face.

He had been in this office enough times to know that he didn't need to go through the same agony to gain access to the inner office. Once inside the reception area he could go through the small, access door from the guest restroom and emerge in the senator's private bathroom thereby gaining access to his office. This route was only locked when the senator was in the shower. He liked to leave it free in case he needed to leave in a hurry, unnoticed. A healthy touch of paranoia.

Roland walked through the bathroom as planned and emerged into the spacious and grandly appointed office. He knew where the file cabinet was and decided that he would begin his search there. He'd pulled open the top drawer and placed the flashlight in his teeth to free up both hands to pull and review files quickly when a thought raced through his mind. He'd better check the desk just in case something was left out, perhaps in haste. He turned from the file cabinet and began to make his way across the room. Some of the brightness from outside, mostly street and security lights, allowed slants of illumination to pierce the darkness and highlight the desk and chair in front of the windows. Roland was attempting to go around the end of the desk where he might also access the drawers when he thought he saw something move.

He stopped abruptly. It must have been a shadow from the outside, he thought, but as he stared straight ahead he knew that the chair moved. The pounding of his heart inside his chest left him deaf. His mouth was too dry to speak and his rubber legs prevented any movement of retreat. He just stood there frozen in his steps. The form was anonymous but the voice was memorable, "Good evening, Roland, I wasn't expecting you."

Roland had one of those moments where every alternative for action that comes to mind seems worse than the one before it. At least time seemed to stand still giving him an opportunity to assess his options. He knew he was fried and decided that it was best to own his guilt and just play it out.

"Good evening to you, I thought it best not to announce my arrival. I was afraid you wouldn't see me under the circumstances."

"Yes, you were right to make that assumption. Tell me, what is it you're looking for in my files. Perhaps I can save you some time."

"Well actually, anything that would incriminate you and save the lives of my friends, and my own as well."

The senator leaned over and illuminated the room with the flick of a switch. "I'm truly sorry about all of that, Roland, I wish you knew just how sorry, but sometimes people have to be sacrificed for other causes. I know you understand about that."

Roland looked at the man and thought that he hardly recognized him. As he observed him he had to wonder when the last time was that he'd slept through the night or truly rested. Even in this dim light he saw a bundle of burned out energy and listlessness that he didn't remember being part of his demeanor at any other time since he'd known him. Roland wondered if he was on some sort of drug. He ultimately determined that he may be more vulnerable than he'd thought and he decided to push this advantage.

"Both Margaret and Charles are worried about you." Roland was certain that he saw him wince. "So am I for that matter. Actually one of the things that brought me here tonight was your earlier meeting with Margaret. She said you were ill. Are you feeling better?" He thought he saw a slight softening in the eyes.

"Well that doesn't really matter right now. Other things, such important things require my attention. I'll rest later."

His look was distant but his eyes kind of darted about like they were looking for something he'd misplaced. Roland was almost overtaken with sympathy, but then he remembered his purpose. He could taste the bile of anger heaving in his throat and he knew the shell of a man across from him was not the man he'd known and loved. He had to think of him as the monster he was.

"Did I remember to tell you that I heard from Harry Axelrod?" he inquired.

"That fool will be the death of me yet and, if I don't watch him the undoing of this project. I just hope to God I can hold it together."

"Well that's just what Harry wanted to talk to me about. I probably shouldn't be repeating this to you but I feel like I owe you, we go way back and I feel some sense of loyalty, even now. Anyway, I guess Harry is working with the secretary and their thinking it's time to take you out of the picture. Something about you being distracted, going soft, I don't know. He didn't make a lot of sense to me. I wasn't really listening, just let him go on, but I felt an obligation to inform you nonetheless."

Roland was sure that he'd struck a chord. The old man pulled himself up straight in his chair and set his jaw in determination. He muttered something under his breath that Roland couldn't hear. He was sure that he was making progress in driving a wedge between the less than happy couple. He may not leave here with any hard and fast evidence against the senator, he may not leave here at all, but if he did he hoped he'd started the inner feud between the players that would throw a wrench in the works, at least temporarily.

He decided to press on. "I probably shouldn't bring this up either, but I thought it was pretty unfair. Harry was threatening to go to your son and expose you if you didn't start listening to him and giving him a freer rein in the day to day operation." That did it, he knew. The senator bent forward placing his elbows on the desk and took his head into his hands. He looked like he had the headache from hell. It saddened Roland to devastate him so badly but, he reminded himself, he was not the one that started this little dogfight. Right now he just hoped to be around to finish it.

He opted for this moment of self indulgence by the senator to try to make his escape. He turned and bolted toward the bathroom, sliding through the door the way he'd come in and was across the reception area in several large steps. Once he gained access to the hall he ran down the back stairs pausing at the stairway exit door on the ground level just long enough to listen for footsteps or voices. Hearing neither, he punched out through the door and made his escape through those now recognizable shrubs without looking back. He couldn't tell if anyone had seen him. He just ran the whole time expecting to hear or feel gunfire.

He didn't stop to breathe or look over his shoulder until he reached the corner where Will was waiting in the car with the engine idling. He nearly squealed the tires when he pulled away from the curb he was so anxious. He told Roland that he looked like a cat burglar running down the street in his dark clothes and his small bag tied around his waist. Will was concentrating hard on his driving not wanting to call any attention to them as he pumped Roland for the details of his visit to the senator's office.

Roland was quick to place a call to Bobby on his cell phone. He picked up before it had stopped ringing, "Yo!" he answered.

"Glad I caught you, where are you?" Roland asked.

"Just making the turn into the high rent district of our greedy friend. How can I help you?" Bobby teased.

"I've just left my target's office and the only success I had was starting up those engines of discontent with your man. He's acting strangely, I must say. I think if you can further that cause it would be most helpful."

"Gotcha! I'm your 'can do' man." Bobby hung up the phone just in time to swing his car into the short term parking area of the high rise office building which housed Harry Axelrod's suite of offices.

While Bobby and Roland were having their brief conversation on the phone Amanda engaged in a brief but productive call with the secretary. She had gotten through to him fairly easily since technically she was still one of his employees, even if she was on leave. He seemed surprised to hear from her but he was cordial enough. The real purpose of the call had been to set up his secretary, Donna. She had gone through her and asked to speak with the secretary so that she would know that they'd had a conversation. She made some small talk with him around being about ready to come back from leave and asked about his summer vacation plans. She was sure she had probably left him scratching his head and wondering what that was all about.

Immediately after hanging up from her conversation with him she called Donna. "Hi, Donna, it's Amanda again. As you know, I just hung up from the secretary and we made an appointment for tomorrow but I went to calendar it and can't remember whether we settled on 9 or 10. What did he tell you?"

"He hasn't given me any appointment yet," she responded. "But looking at his calendar he's already got a 10 o'clock so it must have been 9."

"I thought so but then I got myself confused after I hung up."

As Amanda had hoped she would, Donna added, "I'll just go ahead and put you down. He'll probably forget to calendar it himself. He gets so much on his mind that I'm sometimes the last to know."

"I know what you mean. He amazes me how many balls he can keep in the air. I suspect a big part of that is your support. By the way, Donna, he said he'd clear me at the gate. He'll probably forget that too without your help. Will you call for me?"

"Of course, Amanda, and I look forward to seeing you."

"Me too, maybe we can grab a cup of coffee or something," she suggested. "Get caught up." They hung up on the best of terms and Amanda's fingers were crossed that she could slide through the security gate in the morning.

Amanda was shaking as she hung up the phone. She wasn't all that sure that she knew how to find the bunker. The few times she'd been there before she'd always taken the shuttle. She considered all of her options and determined that the best course of action would be to leave tonight and stay in a motel out in the vicinity of the Sommerset Inn. That way she could allow herself more time in the morning to find it. She wouldn't have to drive for hours to get there and then drive around looking for the right golf course.

She was scurrying around putting some things into a bag when Will called in. She explained to him what had transpired and what her plans were. "Since you've got the car Roland rented, I'm headed for National Airport by Metro to rent a car for the drive out to the bunker." She promised to call when she got checked into a motel and let him know that she had arrived safely.

Amanda took her small bag that had the emergency supplies in it that Roland had provided them as well as her overnight things which she'd stuffed into a backpack and headed downstairs to try to find a cab. She waited what seemed like an inordinate amount of time before she was able to hail one down. This seedy little hotel had very few amenities and a doorman or bellman was not among them. Guests were on their own to find transportation and you almost had to step in front of their car to get them to stop, she observed.

After a harrowing ride to the metro station, she left the taxi, tipping conservatively and made her way down to the ticketing machines. Things were pretty quiet at this time of the evening. Most of the commuters were home by now. She checked the display board to make sure of the fare and purchased a ticket for the exact amount. She went through the gates and down along the track to await the train. She had barely gotten off the escalator when the lights began to flash that a train was entering the station.

Amanda rode the blue line with just two other passengers in her car.

She was the only one from her car to exit at the airport and she walked the short distance across to the terminal and the rental car counters. She chose the company that gave her frequent flyer miles with the use of her credit card and waited patiently for the pimple faced youth to make his way through the tedious paperwork. His sell job on the insurance options needed work as she managed to refuse all coverage and feel no fear for having done so. She selected a small, non-descript, white car and went outside for the journey to the lot where she would pick it up. In no time she was on her way out into the Virginia night.

She was cruising along in a carefree manner when she remembered to check the fuel gauge. Even though the tank was supposed to be full when you picked up a rental sometimes, she'd found, that wasn't the case. It registered full so she let herself relax a little more. She decided some music would make a nice companion on the drive. She fiddled with the dials on the radio until she found an "Oldie" station that came in loud and clear. She had her handwritten driving directions that she'd extrapolated from various sources next to her on the seat.

She thought things were pretty much under control for the duration of the drive.

She cruised along that way, trouble free looking for her numbered exit from the interstate. It was at least an hour before she saw the warning that it was going to be just two miles ahead. She moved over into the far right lane and prepared to take the exit. It came up quickly and was a little hard to see in the dark but she found her way to the end of the ramp where a stop sign greeted her. She needed to make a left hand turn across traffic so she was being cautious about picking her time to go. It seemed to her that this secondary road had a lot of truck traffic on it.

She finally made the turn and was surprised at the response she got from the little car as she shoved down hard on the accelerator pedal. "This thing feels like a tin can with a rocket in it," she observed. She also noticed that it had a tendency to fishtail if the wheel was pulled too quickly. She decided that this would not be her candidate for car of the year.

Once she was out on the two lane road she noticed that the windshield had some sort of foreign substance on it that made the oncoming headlights look like a rainbow. She wondered once about pulling off the road and trying to get it off but she had nothing with her to clean it with. Besides she knew it wasn't wise to pull over on this kind of a road if it wasn't absolutely necessary. She thought she could manage with it as it was and perhaps the traffic would thin out as she got further from the highway.

She settled in for the duration. She had a long way to go before she had to worry about finding her next turn. She started to sing along with the tunes on the radio.

Bobby found a well placed parking space adjacent to the stairwell and backed his Beemer into it ignoring the signs insisting that cars be parked headfirst only. He was pleased to observe that the lights in the lot were on alternate sides and that there was no light directly over his space. He got out of the car and left it unlocked just in case he was in a hurry when he returned. He looked around to observe the exits available and to assess the pros and cons of using each of them. Satisfied that he was prepared for his inevitable departure he headed for the front entrance where the bank of express elevators to the top floors was located. His first hurdle would be the guard in the lobby.

It was still early enough in the evening that the doors into the grand and spacious lobby were unlocked. Bobby entered and went directly and aggressively to the guard at the desk. "Where do I sign in?" He inquired. "I'm late for a meeting with Mr. Axelrod."

The guard was slightly taken aback with Bobby's command of the space and moment and he turned toward the log book hardly realizing it. "Mr. Axelrod didn't put anything in here about an appointment and he hasn't called down. I can't let…"

Bobby interrupted, "Bet I'm not the first one he forgot to call about. I just got a call from him on my cell. He's hoppin' mad and demanded I get my ass in here." Bobby smiled real big, "Hey, be my guest and give him a call. It'd please me to have him take it out on someone else. Spread the wealth," he laughed.

The guard sized him up once more and decided he didn't want to get his butt chewed by Axelrod. He'd had that fine experience a few times before. "Go ahead on up," he directed, "But you gotta sign the book here."

Bobby took the pen and signed, "Julius Ceasar," in an illegible hand. He smiled to himself. Not only had he gained access to the building but he knew that Harry was still in his office. The guard would have said if he wasn't.

He proceeded directly to the express elevators and pressed the call button. As he waited for the door to open he glanced back at the guard and gave him the finger across the throat gesture, letting him know that he was just some flunky on his way to get his throat slit by a mad boss. The guard smiled and gave a half nod of recognition as Bobby stepped into the waiting elevator and the doors closed. He punched the button, not for Harry's floor but for the one just below it. As was his habit when he prepared for tense or dangerous work, he felt in the back of his waistband for his weapon and was reassured by the safe and secure feeling it gave back.

Bobby's quick research had shown that the offices directly below Harry were occupied by a large accounting firm. He had feared that it would be one of the many law offices in the building and that it would be filled with young associates trying to earn their way onto the partner track by living in their offices and billing for everything except brushing their teeth. Instead he'd lucked out with the accountants and with the tax season just concluded things were slower in the evenings now. He stepped off the elevator into a small lobby which encompassed the elevators. There were doors on both sides of the space. One lead to the main reception for the firm and the other went directly into the office area.

He chose the latter. It was not a very sophisticated security lock and it took just moments to gain entry. When he stepped inside he found himself in a service area which contained copy machines, faxes and shelves of supplies. He was relieved to see that the security lights were the only ones on. They provided plenty enough light to move around. He'd only have to worry if one of the offices he passed had lights on and an occupant. He began to move slowly down the hallway toward the sign that glowed, "Exit." That identified the stairwell he sought.

He was lucky, only one office seemed to be occupied and the door was only slightly ajar. He moved past it unseen and unheard thanks to the plush carpet in the hallway. He pulled out his flashlight and flipped it all around the stairwell door looking for a sensor which might automatically trigger an alarm. Finding none he pushed slowly on the crash bar until the click of the release was heard. He paused in that position, not moving, waiting to see if the occupant of the office down the hall had heard it. After a safe time he determined that all was well and he slipped through the door. Before closing the door he removed the duct tape from his fanny pack and tore off several lengths. He placed them over the catch of the door so that once it was closed the lock could not engage. He pressed hard on the tape to make sure it was set and that he had enough on it to keep from being locked in the stairwell. Again he anticipated that he might be in a hurry when he returned.

He carefully brought the heavy fire door back to its closed position and listened for a moment to make sure that the lock had not engaged. "Damn you're good," he complimented himself. He began to make his way quietly up the stairs, cautiously placing each step, to the floor above and Harry Axelrod, himself.

Upon reaching the top floor the first thing he did was check the door to make certain that it was the same standard issue as the rest of the building. He needed to be sure that the security had not been beefed up for the heady heights of the penthouse. Everything was standard and he set about the lock picking process. He prided himself on his ability in this area and took on the task with great confidence. As if he could will the cooperation of the lock, he gained entry on the first try and in a matter of seconds. He took out the tape again and taped the lock as before. Not to allow for an exit this time but to keep the click of the lock engaging from being heard in the suite.

He again found himself in a service area. This time the copy machine and supplies had been replaced by a tidy little kitchen. The only downside to this entry was the lack of carpet on the floor. He needed to be extra cautious in the placement of his steps. He drew his weapon and held it out in front of him as he moved stealthily across the room and peeked his head warily around the edge of the doorway. He saw no movement so he lingered there for a few moments taking in the lay of the land.

He was sure that he could identify which was Harry's office. Roland had sketched out what he knew of the arrangement and it looked pretty true to what he'd described. Also, the whole arrangement of things pointed to where the head honcho could be found. There was a flow which led your eye to the office that mattered. It was the center of everything and the massive double doors stood open allowing light from the inside to flood the reception area like sunlight between the clouds on a spring day.

He had also learned from Roland that there was a second door that led into the office from the far side of the suite. He wasn't sure if it was an adjoining office or a private bathroom. Bobby knew he needed it whatever it was and he needed now to find access to it without being detected. He waited in the kitchen a few more minutes trying to assess whether anyone other than Harry was working the nightshift.

Finally, satisfied that he and Harry were the only two present he slowly made his way over to the open door to Harry's office. With his gun at his side and watching to make sure that he was not creating a shadow he peered through the crack between the door and the jamb where he could observe Harry at his desk with his eyes cast downward intent on the papers in front of him. Bobby slipped stealthily past the open portion of the door on tip toes stopping on the other side to again peek through between the matching door and the jamb. Harry had not moved. He was almost there.

Bobby crept cautiously onward until he found a door on the same side of the hall as Harry's. He turned the knob slowly and the door moved open freely. Bobby ducked inside the room and secured the door behind him. He paused to take a breath feeling a moment of relief, even if brief, before pushing on.

He was forced to work with his flashlight once again and in the corner of the room he found what he was looking for, the executive style bathroom that was an integral part of Harry's connected offices. The room Bobby was in was a conference or meeting room attached to the main office and the bathroom was accessible from both. He needed to utilize this entrance in order to come up on Harry from the rear.

He pulled out the knit cap and ski mask that had been stuffed inside his jacket and pulled them both on over his head. He crept silently through the bathroom and emerged into Harry's office. He was just behind his line of sight and off to his right. With one graceful move he was instantly behind him and while putting the gun to his temple he spun the chair around and away from the desk precluding Harry from hitting any alarm buttons. Harry barely got out, "What the," before Bobby had him in a choke hold. Harry stopped struggling realizing quickly that every time he moved it was harder to get air. Bobby quickly bound him with the coil of nylon rope he pulled from his pack and proceeded to gag him with his own linen handkerchief, unceremoniously ripped from his breast pocket, and a few more lengths of that duct tape.

Once he had him secured he spoke to him in a contrived voice. "All you need to know, Harry Baby, is that I was sent by your friends, Margaret and the senator. Seems they've got a little business to conduct and they need to make sure that you can't interfere. It'll only be for a little while and then you'll be found. No lasting effects, I'm sure." As he spoke he rolled him into the bathroom in his plush, leather chair with ball bearing rollers that made it ride like a Rolls Royce. Bobby further secured him into the chair with a combination of nylon rope and duct tape. Once he was finished, he walked out through the reception area, removed his hat and mask and waited patiently for the elevator to respond to his call.

He rode the express car down to the lobby where the guard was struggling to stay awake. "One hell of an ass chewing," he lamented as he walked over to the log book to sign out. The guard looked at him sympathetically and responded, "I feel your pain." They both laughed out loud.

Before Harry would be found by his secretary the next morning his anger at the senator and Margaret would have reached a murderous pitch. It was bad enough to be sabotaged in your own office by your own business associates but he had been forced to urinate in his Armani suit and Calvin Klein briefs. He would never forgive them.

Amanda was beginning to have trouble staying awake. She was just outside the small town of Bradenton which meant her turnoff was approaching. She picked up her directions and tried to read them in the dim light from the display on the dashboard. She wanted to double check the route number even though she had it memorized. She decided that she would keep an eye out for a restaurant or convenience store where she could grab a cup of coffee to go.

Just on the outskirts of Bradenton she spotted a gas station with a convenience store in it and a sign up in the air promising coffee and snacks. She had slowed her speed to stay in compliance with the local law and now she flipped on her turn indicator and pulled into the drive to take advantage of their invitation for junk food and caffeine. It felt good to step out into the night air. She hadn't realized that she'd gotten a little stiff from sitting tensely behind the wheel of the car for that long. She rubbed at her neck and did a couple of stretches before heading into the store to find the restroom and some goodies.

Back on the road and all the happier for her brief stop, Amanda saw the sign for the secondary road that she sought. She made her left hand turn right behind a big, gravel hauling type truck and settled in for her trip to Hightower where she was sure she would be able to obtain accommodations for the night. She estimated that she had less than an hour to go. The radio stations weren't quite as plentiful out here so she fiddled with the dial again to find one that would keep her company on her final leg of the journey.

She found a suitable station that she thought would keep her awake without jangling her nerves too badly and tried to find just the right setting. She looked up from the radio and into two huge headlights rushing directly at her. She responded by hitting the brakes at the same time that she steered the car toward the ditch on the right hand side of the road. Her mind could hardly comprehend what her eyes were seeing but her instantaneous assessment was that a large truck had been passing a slower vehicle and had ended up facing her down in her own lane. She also assumed that in addition to her own, the onrushing vehicles would be making some diversionary moves that would keep them all from becoming a mound of scrap metal and human parts.

As she bounced from the road surface to the shoulder it was as if the steering wheel had been rudely ripped from her hands. She was literally bouncing around the inside of the car even though she wore the safety belt. She couldn't seem to keep her hands securely on the wheel. Every time she got a grasp of it and started to turn she flew up in the air again and her hands were wrenched from their hold. She had a remote sense that the braking was having some effect as the whole panorama that was rushing by her windows seemed to be slowing even if too gradually. She realized that she'd been deafened by the horrific blast of an air horn as this wretched scenario played out. She wondered for a split second how anyone in this predicament had time to put their hands on the horn.

The car was definitely slowing and the bouncing was diminishing as she realized that her hands were remaining on the wheel now. She was however, headed through a wire fence if she didn't turn immediately. She pulled hard to turn the car to the left and was rewarded with a feeling of careening back toward the roadway.

Through her side window now she had only a sense of the wheel of the huge truck. It was enough to make her believe that it was passing beyond her and if she could regain the road she might wrestle back some control. Pulling on the steering wheel so hard had sent her little car into a fishtail maneuver that first rocked her to the right, away from the onrushing truck and then immediately back to the left where all she could see was the huge rear end and the loading step about to come through her windshield. She literally jerked the wheel back the other way and the fishtail reversed its direction once more.

She had a confused sense of horns, squealing brakes and someone screaming. As her car finally slowed and straightened out its course she realized that the screaming had been hers. She pulled totally off the side of the road and brought the car to a complete stop. All she could do was sit there, unable to move and wait for the wracking sobs and uncontrollable shaking to subside. She did manage to look into her rearview mirror and see the lights of the other two vehicles diminishing in size as they rambled off into the night.

On the one hand it seemed like she sat there for hours, on the other she thought she'd just come to a stop when she hesitantly headed out again. Back up on the road and with her headlights piercing the dark night she vowed that she would not take her eyes off the road for an instant. She didn't even want to blink. The trembling continued unabated.

She didn't think she'd ever felt such relief in her life as she did when she saw the sign for the city limits of Hightower. She chose the first motel that she came to on her right. It looked like it was up to her standards and it was flashing a vacancy sign. She went into the office and was registered for one night by a motherly looking woman who Amanda wanted very much to pour her heart out to. Instead she took the key and headed to her room for a much needed rest. She thought to herself that tomorrow would be a cake walk compared to tonight's horrors.

Amanda awoke just before dawn. She had slept in fits throughout the night but all things considered she felt pretty good. She headed off for the shower and once the water hit her she realized what she'd been through. Her first clue was the stinging when the water hit her hands. She looked down and saw two blisters on her left hand. She'd had no idea that she had worked so hard with that steering wheel. She made a complete assessment of her body then and realized that her left hip was showing some color from being knocked against the door and all of its handles and other protrusions. She wouldn't be surprised if the top of her head was bruised from the repeated encounter with the roof of the car as well. She ran her hand through her hair and probed for sore spots.

Once she had taken inventory of her body parts and had herself dressed for the day she was careful to pack up her "kit" that Roland had given them. She knew for sure that she would need several of the items in there and most would probably come in handy. Only the day would tell her that. She reflected on her challenge for a moment and realized that she was experiencing some strange combination of fear and excitement. This must be what cops and firemen go through every day, she thought.

Packed up and ready to go she spread her map open on the little table in her room and reviewed again the last part of the journey that would take her to the Sommerset Inn, Resort and Spa. She knew she wouldn't be looking at the map while driving. Once she had the remainder of the drive in her mind she folded up the map, picked up her other items and headed out to the car for her meeting with destiny. She was shocked when she saw the dirt, various grasses and clumps of sod that clung to the once white car. She dreaded getting back in it.

On her drive to the bunker she stopped to fill the car with gas and used the hose at the island to clean some of the earthy deposits from the car's paint job. She didn't want to stand out in any way when she reached the security check at the bunker.

Amanda was pleased that the sun was shining brightly as she pulled up to the security gate. This enabled her to wear her dark glasses and she'd also pulled on a golf visor to complete the look. Her hair was pulled back in a pert little pony tail giving her a younger look than her regular do. Now she just needed to turn on the charm. She was out of the car and bounded up to the security kiosk so fast it almost dazed the men on duty there. She looked at the badge of the one closest to her and read his name as quickly as she could. "Hey, you're Bart aren't you?" she inquired. "I remember you."

He looked surprised and responded, "Should I know you?"

"Oh you probably wouldn't remember me. No reason to, it's just, well, you've always been really nice to me when I come out here. Nothing but a gentleman mind you, but I don't forget a good looking guy with manners." She smiled brightly and watched as he gave a sideways glance toward his companions and co-workers. They'd surely want to tease him about this one.

"Anyway, I'm back for some more of this drudgery we call work. The secretary should have left my name for clearance, Amanda Chambers." She purposely stood very close to Bart as he checked the book. She knew her breath was reaching the back of his neck as she saw some hair move slightly and she leaned forward just enough to allow her breast to come into contact with his arm.

Bart was having trouble remembering how to read. "Yes, here it is, Ms. Chambers. We'll just have to do a search of your vehicle here while Al over there scans your thumb print. It's standard operating procedure and then we'll get you off to work."

Amanda decided to push it while they were still in front of the others, "Aren't you gonna frisk me Bart?"

He turned about twelve shades of red as the snickers from his colleagues echoed in his ears. "Uh, that's probably not necessary this time," he responded. "We only have to do that randomly." He new his buddies would be teasing him for months for not taking the opportunity to cop a feel. He hated it when they acted like that.

Bart and a co-worker accompanied Amanda back out to the car where she unlocked and opened the trunk for them. Additionally, another guard brought a dog from around the back and directed him to sniff around the outside of the car. Amanda took this opportunity to return to the security kiosk and give her thumb print to the computer. She didn't know much about the training of these dogs but she hoped that electronics or garlic weren't part of what he could ferret out. Her little waist pack was sitting conveniently in the small of her back under her golf sweater.

Once the security men had run their routine Amanda gave Bart a really warm and lingering smile that couldn't be missed by the men who remained in the guard shack. She took her parking pass, placed it on the dashboard of the car and waved as she pulled away and made her way up the winding road, through the golf course and up to the bogus resort building. She pulled into the parking lot on the north side of the building and took a moment to sigh and take a deep breath. She'd done it. She was in.

Amanda knew enough about what the security badges looked like to replicate one that would look okay from a distance. It only had to hang around her neck unless someone questioned her. Those who knew her would just assume she'd come back to work, the ones who didn't, she hoped would just not pay any attention to her as long as she looked like she knew what she was doing and that she belonged where they found her.

She pushed open the heavy fire door and entered the bowels of the building. She headed straight for the supply room on Level C which she planned to use as her launching pad. It would fit her purposes perfectly. It was large yet had enough shelves and tables in it to provide small, cozy areas that were relatively secure and mostly went unnoticed by others who found a reason to use the room, rare as that was. She had used it a couple of times when she'd been working out here legitimately. She found an area back in the rear corner of the space. It had a small utility table with folding chairs around it that was almost entirely cut off from the rest of the room by tall shelving units weighted down by manila files filled with all sorts of government twaddle that had been reduced to paper and carefully and alphabetically saved in perpetuity.

She rearranged a few things so that she could sit at the table with some work in front of her if anyone wandered into that area. Additionally, she wanted to be arranged so that she could see out through the myriad of files and have a clear view of the door and larger open area if necessary. The last amenity that made this the ideal location was the small, janitor's closet that was accessible through a door that was just off the end of the table. In there was a seldom used mop sink and more storage shelves which held all manner of cleaning tools and chemicals. More importantly, a second door from the closet opened into the utility hall from which you could access all of the levels of the bunkers and the rear stairs.

After rearranging her work area she went into the closet and found an old smelly jar that contained some chemical residue, she removed the plastic explosive encased in garlic that Roland had given her, placed it in the jar screwing the lid back on and stored it on a higher shelf toward the back. She went back into her little launching area and removed her waist pack before sitting down at the table. She placed the items on the table and proceeded to sort out the ones that she would carry with her and the ones she'd leave behind here at her temporary, bunker headquarters.

The last thing she did before striking out for her destination was call Will's cell phone to be sure that hers would work from down in the bunker. There was a booster through which all cell phones bounced to get up out of here but she had never understood exactly how that worked and didn't know if only certain phones would be operational. She was pleased to hear Will answer immediately.

"My God, Mandy, I've been worried sick. I thought you were gonna call me last night and let me know you were okay."

"Sorry, Will, I didn't mean to worry you but it was an extraordinary trip that I will tell you about some day. For now, I'm in and I'm set up. I'll be on my way down to start reconnaissance in less than five minutes. Everything steady there?"

"Ya, we're good, making progress anyway. Call me in a couple of hours and let's see where we are."

Amanda thought it was a good sign that Will had not stayed angry with her about not calling. She thought to herself, *He could have called me,* then remembered that she'd not had her phone turned on all night. Well, he seemed to get over it quickly which she took to mean he was working too hard to focus on her forgetfulness. She hoped that meant they were making headway with the senator.

She had to think forward not back. She was ready to make her move out into the bunker and take her big step into clandestine operations. She hoped she could remember everything that Bobby and Roland had tried to teach them as they'd sat around in that motel room and waited. Right now it was Lucas' instructions that were ringing in her ears.

Harry was pacing around his plush quarters this morning while congratulating himself on the fine set up he'd achieved. He had chosen to use the secretary and his newly formed teams from the bunker to give them a chance to work with a real pro. He knew they'd learn something working with him and under his tutelage that they'd never get with the secretary. It was time that security group got tough. He had met with the leader and liked his way. He had assured Harry that he had his team prepared. All that was left was for Harry to get the targets to a place where the pseudo terrorists could strike. He was sorry for the distractions of the morning. He had several important phone conferences set up with some of the more jittery investors and he couldn't take time out right now to finalize the preparations for the hit. He looked forward to getting this morning behind him and taking the afternoon to relish the pleasure of the final arrangements.

In the meantime he had to take care of the money men and deal with the treachery of the senator and Margaret who'd not only double crossed him but also humiliated him. God, he would make them pay.

He readied himself for the office and called down to have his car brought around. He was pumped and ready to take on the day.

He left his penthouse condominium and rode the private elevator down to the main lobby of his building. During the winter he had met his car in the basement not wanting to subject himself to the dismal weather even though the car would pick him up under the roof and not subject him to the elements. He preferred to stay in the garage where he didn't even have to look at what nature was tossing on them. He could go from the garage of his condo to the garage of his office working as he went and never have to deal with the real environment.

Today, however, it was spring, the sun was shining and he instructed the driver to pick him up under the portico on the ground level. He wanted to appreciate the fine weather, he thought. Bobby watched as he strode through the lobby with his briefcase in one hand and his cell phone held to his ear with the other. He was talking to his office and ordering people into a frenzy before he was even in the car. The doorman pulled back the large, glass door well before he reached it so that it was standing fully open by the time he went through it in full stride. His car waited at the curb just a few steps away and the driver was at the rear door fully anticipating and accommodating his every move. For several seconds, the sun shone on Harry Axelrod's face and shoulder as though Mother Nature herself were trying to remind him of the sweetness of life. Harry entered the car totally unaware and untouched by his surroundings.

He was ensconced in his office and fully engaged on the phone conference when he turned his chair and noticed the sun reflecting on the Washington Monument in the distance. He remembered that he'd meant to enjoy the spring weather this morning.

The thought left as quickly as it had come and he began to focus on getting even with the senator while the participants of the conference proceeded to allay each other's fears and concerns without his input. All he was doing was monitoring the call he noticed.

He began to wonder if it didn't make sense to include both Margaret and the senator in the unfortunate terrorist attack which was about to take place. He needed to think of just the right place for this. It had to not seem odd to have all of these people in the same place at the same time. To keep suspicion down about who was taken out, the collateral damage had to be high. If Roland, Amanda, Will, and Bobby and Margaret Blanchard, both CIA were among ten who died that would look suspicious, if they were among a thousand, say, no one would raise a brow. He had to come up with just the right place and a way to get them all there.

Further, he needed to really consider the wisdom of taking Margaret out before the new world order was in place. There was still the matter of the coups and he'd found a great deal of support for her leadership among the consortium of investors. He didn't want to do something stupid, something that would jeopardize the entire project just because his pride was hurt. He had to really think this through.

His attention was drawn back to the conversation on the phone. Everyone was back on board and they were ready to sign off. Harry was again relieved that this side of things seemed to be sticking together so well. He wasn't sure if it was because of him or in spite of and he wasn't going to waste brain energy on that with everything else that was on his plate. He signed off from his colleagues, punched the button that disconnected his end of the line and pulled out one of his favorite pads of paper to doodle and scribble on as he made surreptitious notes for his eyes only. The first such note was, "Union Station," followed by several large question marks.

After a lot of doodling and a lot of thinking he had a plan, his choice was made, Union Station would be perfect for their needs. There were hundreds and, at certain times, thousands of people about. Between the commuters, shoppers, travelers and those who were eating or drinking in the various bars and restaurants it had all of the flexibility required.

He began working on the set up. After a couple of hours, everything was planned. It was brilliant, he thought. He'd be able to lure Margaret there by meeting her for drinks. Roland he'd snag by sending him a key and a message that there was valuable information about the clandestine activities of the senator locked in a storage locker there. He knew he'd go for that. He was getting desperate. Will and Amanda had required a little extra thought. He finally decided to simply send them both messages on their cell phones that Roland needed to meet them there and that he'd explain when he saw them. The same was true for Bobby. Though Harry didn't much care if he was taken out or not, it would be a little cleaner if he was.

With all the pigeons coming home to roost he'd gone to work on getting his terrorists in motion. He thought his plan was brilliant because it took so little set up or organization. After he'd concluded his call with the leader he felt certain that it would come off without a hitch. Sometimes he even surprised himself with what he could come up with. Now it was all up to those boys from the bunker in concert with his man. He'd see what they could do under real leadership.

He leaned back in his leather chair with that self satisfied look of his, put his feet up on his polished walnut desk, lit a cigar and reveled in the moment. He was sorry in some ways that the senator wasn't going with them but he already had that matter under control.

Margaret had been dreading the meeting with the senator. Although she had a perfectly good explanation for her actions he had not been himself lately and she wasn't sure that he was focused enough to comprehend the meaning behind her behavior. She hadn't usually been kept waiting in his reception area as she was today and that irked her.

Finally, the young woman who'd been fixing her broken nail with a file, fabric and some kind of odoriferous glue spoke to her, "He'll see you now." She gestured toward the office door.

Margaret strode into his office like the armies of the Third Reich into Poland. "I'm not amused by your behavior," she began. "I recognize a power play when I see one. Don't keep me waiting like that again or I will leave. The only reason I'm still here now is because I owe you an explanation and I thoroughly intend to give it."

He looked up at her from behind his desk and she suddenly realized how old and pitiful he looked. What had happened to him in such a short time?

He responded to her entry with some mumbling which was incoherent. He gestured toward the guest chairs and she sat down opposite him.

"Let me begin by explaining why I came in here the other night wearing a wire. You've got to be wondering what that was all about."

"That would be nice if there really is an explanation. I'll gladly give you the courtesy of hearing you out."

He was suddenly cognizant and very present, she thought, compared to where he was just a moment ago. "I've had all of the files on Gazelle and Operation Cloud Nine under my clearance code for months now so that I would know exactly who was looking or trying to look at them at any time. Twenty-four/seven as we say. Anyway I learned a couple of days ago that Bobby Webster, one of mine in covert operations was making inquiry, remarkably, under both names. Since, as you know, there has been no link from one to the other such an inquiry raised my suspicions. To make a long story short, I had to convince Bobby that I was a double agent, working undercover for the agency to sabotage the operation. As a part of that, I got backed into a corner and had to wear the wire to keep from being exposed on that end. There was no way I was going to let you incriminate yourself on the tape. I know you already know that. I had my hand on the power switch ready to claim malfunction if I heard you go anywhere near the issues." She studied him across the desk and tried to read his expression but none was on his face.

"Plausible," was all that he responded.

She waited a respectable amount of time for him to say something more. He didn't. He just looked out into space as if he was seeing something there to capture his attention that no one else saw.

"If we've got that behind us I'd like to move on. What in the hell is wrong with Harry? Have you done something to set him off? I got the meanest message from him telling me that I owed it to him to meet him for drinks after what you and I did to him. Want to tell me what he's talking about?" she inquired.

"No idea," was all that she heard before more incoherent rambling or muttering. She was really worried now about his state of mind as well as his physical health. What could be happening? He wasn't old enough for senility or Alzheimer's she told herself. Has he had a stroke or something? She was genuinely worried about a man whom she'd admired and respected for most of her adult life. If things hadn't been as they were with Roland she'd have called him. He had always sort of looked after that side of him. Now she couldn't think where to turn.

With the meeting with the senator apparently going nowhere fast, Margaret checked her watch and decided that she'd have to table it for now. She was going to be late to her meeting with Harry even if she left now and hit no traffic.

She made some concluding comments to the senator and stood to leave, "I'm late for that drink with Harry," she said, "Are you sure you don't know something that I should before he pounces on me?"

There was no response. She turned and left abruptly and as she rode the elevator down to the garage she found that she was preoccupied with the sense that he was not well, "Perhaps he'll come around when he's had time to absorb what I just told him. Maybe it was just too much to take in right now," she thought.

She stepped out into the parking garage where Donny had her car waiting in front of the elevator doors and as he slid into the driver's seat after securing her in the back. She told him, "Union Station, Donny, and we've got to hurry, I'm late as usual."

Chapter Twenty-three

There were an even dozen of them. Two unmarked, windowless vans pulled up near the Roosevelt entrance to Union Station and turned on their emergency flashers. They would only be able to sit in the "no parking" zone for a few moments so it was imperative that each of them had their pack on and were ready to exit the vehicles at once.

The side door slid open on both vans at almost the same moment and one by one the twelve terrorists stepped out onto the sidewalk and headed into the grand hall of the old, refurbished train station. Once inside each went to an assigned exit and began their tasks.

Once their packs were removed they opened them and removed a wireless, two-way radio which was clipped onto the small loop on the left shoulder with the battery pack slipped into the rear pocket of the coveralls. A hearing piece was placed in the left ear.

Next the body belt was unpacked and carefully placed around the waist and trunk. It was secured with Velcro closures which ran from the navel to the neck. A small coil of steel reinforced, nylon tubing was attached to the canisters that the pack held tightly to the body. The tubing ran over to the left wrist where it was secured leaving enough slack for a punch operated valve on the end of it to reach into the left hand. From there protruded a wide spraying nozzle not unlike the one used to fertilize grass. It could deliver the contents of the canisters over 8,000 square feet in less than 3 minutes. The contents of the canisters had sufficient elemental weight to keep it in the lower portions of the enclosure and do its work within the allotted time.

The last items out of the pack were several lengths of steel hardened chain and three heavy duty padlocks.

They turned the valve on the compressed air tank which remained inside the pack to start the flow of pure, life saving air. Finally, each of them took the air regulator which was attached to a full frontal mask and placed it over their faces securing it with a strap that went around the back of the head. They slung the packs up onto their backs.

As they took up their assigned stations around the exits people around them began to take notice and panic was beginning to set in. At the moment they concluded dressing, the leader mounted the huge, marble steps with his bullhorn and advised everyone that they could not leave the building. All exits were blocked by members of his team caring canisters of lethal gas which would be released unless everyone did exactly as they were told.

The biggest mistake made that day was the compliance by the stunned crowd with the demands of the terrorists. If they had run at that moment the outcome may have been different. While nearly a thousand good people with ordinary lives and from all walks of life stood in that large hall and tried to absorb what was happening and what they should do, the terrorists were chaining the exits leaving no escape.

The terrorists assigned to the gates leading to the tracks were allowing people in but no one out. Whether by design or simply by chance the first of five daily commuter trains arrived from New York City and an extra three hundred commuters entered the impromptu gas chamber just as the signal was given to the fellow terrorists to activate the valves on their canisters.

At approximately the same moment, Harry Axelrod picked us his phone and dialed the editor's desk at the Washington Post. He related a description of the massacre to the man who answered and informed him that more such incidents would follow. It was the intent of this terrorist cell, The Architects of Mid-east Peace (AMP), he told him, to keep making Americans suffer the same plight as their ancestors until the United States government stood up and unequivocally brought peace to the Middle East.

Harry didn't even flinch at the horrible action he'd prompted nor at his exploitation of people who'd already suffered great losses and who deserved so much more than the continued abuse and hatred he fostered. His immorality knew no bounds. He truly was a man with no conscience and a man to be feared.

Margaret's car sat outside Union Station with her bewildered driver inside, uncertain of what to do. The scream of sirens split the air all around him gradually diminishing to irritating whines and finally just whimpering into an eerie silence as one emergency vehicle after another came to rest around him. Nearly every rescue group in the district was represented in less time than it took for him to register that something was amiss and get back out of the car. He headed over toward the door that Margaret had entered just minutes ago. She'd been gone such a short time that he hadn't had time to move the car from the loading zone to a proper parking place. The police, fire department and almost every other emergency crew that could be summoned was on the scene. People milled about talking excitedly but no one seemed to be saying anything that made sense. Some were running, terrified, away from the terminal building, some were weeping. He couldn't bring order to the chaos, couldn't figure out what was going on.

He approached a fireman who was standing still only because he was struggling into his heavy gear next to the truck that had wailed its way up and onto the curb.

"What's happened?" he inquired.

The man looked at him sideways while not missing a beat in his suiting process. "Can't really say for sure, our call was that some dangerous gas was escaping or something. Better get yourself out of here," he cautioned as he turned away and began pulling equipment from the rear of the truck.

Donny continued around this way getting bits and pieces of information from various sources until a picture began to form in his mind. He knew his boss was inside, he'd seen her enter before he got back in the car. He always waited until she was safely in whatever building they were visiting. He thought it a courtesy that she deserved. He kind of liked feeling responsible for her safety even though that was not in his official job description.

He opted to wait at his post until he could learn her fate. It occurred to him to call into headquarters to let them know where they were and what was happening. On that call he learned the truth of what had taken place in this grand, historic building that even now cast its ominous shadow across him and brought a chill to the back of his neck. He was speechless.

Donny's observation had been correct. One of the terrorists had politely held the door open for her just before he placed the chain through the crash bars and secured it with a padlock. Once inside it had taken a moment for Margaret's eyes to adjust to the light and to gain perspective on what was happening. She saw fright on the face of the people directly adjacent to her and then she began to take in the words she was hearing.

Her last realization was that the sounds emanating from the bullhorn weren't the only thing raining down over the crowd. There was a fog of sorts settling over the entire scene and she noticed that the huge, cavernous room had lost the echo of busy voices that had greeted her just moments ago. People were beginning to settle onto the floor and she had the sense that order was coming to the crowd. The quiet grew like a great malignancy spreading throughout the hall.

She found herself sitting when she hadn't known that was her intent. She propped her head on her hand and tried to listen to the program that was coming over the PA system now but she was too tired to focus. Just like happened to her when she invested in theatre tickets, she thought. "If only I can stay awake until intermission."

Although both the swat and terrorist teams had been deployed the twelve terrorists had safely made their escape as planned out through the metro tunnel and leaving all of their paraphernalia of death behind. By design everything that was abandoned had been purchased or otherwise obtained outside the U.S. making the charade more plausible.

Once in the crowd they managed to blend in with everyone else who was getting word of the horrific event that had transpired as trains were stopped in the tunnels and stations, and cars and busses on the streets were delayed and rerouted. Televisions and radios were tuned to the all news stations, everyone was craving information. In no time, all of Washington, D.C. was either in shock, in panic or in mourning. "The horrors of terrorism," everyone thought.

Chapter Twenty-four

Amanda readied her pack with the equipment that she knew she'd need and a few items that she thought might come in handy. She slipped the waist pack around her middle and pulled her blouse down over it fluffing it out so that no telltale bulges were evident. Her greatest tool was her strong resolve as she set out for the lower levels of the bunker.

She went out through the janitor's closet and paused briefly after opening the hallway door just a crack. Hearing no one but unable to see in both directions she slowly moved the door wider and finally, gauging it was safe she stepped fully into the hall closing the door behind her. As she started down the hall she heard voices coming from around the corner. She stepped back into a small recess which housed a drinking fountain and made herself as flat as she could. The voices, now accompanied by footsteps, went straight along the intersecting corridor oblivious to her presence and leaving her safely behind. She continued her trek down the hallway and entered the little used service stairs.

The bunker had been designed and built during World War II and it had been built of the strongest, steel reinforced concrete walls. This thickness alone made it impossible to hear anything from one room to another. Offices were assigned to particular personnel with that in mind. The secretary's was one of the soundest.

During the post war years many changes had been made and the level of paranoia in the government at that time was obvious if one just looked at those modifications. There were now a number of rooms which had two way mirrors and others had small, undisclosed passages between them. It had been in the years of the McCarthy witch hunts, when the government was trying to ferret out its communists that many men and women engaged in government service had been sent here believing that they were doing one job when in fact they were being observed and tested as to their loyalty. It was an ugly blot on the history of the United States and one that was not often spoken about.

The first employees sent to the bunker under the current administration's creation of the shadow government had made a find of many of these adaptations. Amanda and several others had been sent out here first when there were no desks or other furniture in the offices. It had been their responsibility to assist with equipping and arranging the offices. They had worked hand in hand with the electricians and telecommunications people who were wiring the entire premises for phones and computers.

Not having the hollow walls of most office buildings had proved to be a challenge until the passages had been found. Using these obscure hallways had enabled them to keep the lines out of the work environment where people would trip on them. Having had the run of the place for at least 8 hours a day while this was going on, they had begun to make a game of the passageways and finding ways to sneak up on each other. She hoped this would come in handy now.

She remembered that the secretary's office was one of the most secure. They had been careful at the time to select a room with no passageways bordering it. He sat back in a corner of the lowest level completely protected from above by the security monitoring room and with only two interior walls, both of which were part of the huge footings which acted as anchors and support for the bunker and the resort above it. Although there had been a mirror in that room they had considered it a fake as it was on an exterior wall and no passageway led to it. What they hadn't known was that behind that wall was an observation room and an entirely separate entrance that was unknown to all but a few.

She knew she wouldn't get anything from his office without a bug actually being placed inside it. For the moment that was not an option.

She concentrated for now on several of the offices close to his. He had chosen to have particular members of his staff close to his office for the convenience of meetings and conferences. She knew that one such person was Nate Tidwell but there were others as well.

Amanda was standing in a passageway listening for any activity around her. She had taken out the small flashlight and was sweeping the light around inside the tiny corridor. She observed the myriad of cables and lines that wound together like strands of spaghetti and continued on for as far as she could see with the aid of the light. She'd have to be very careful not to become entangled in them as she walked. The computer people had been very busy in here getting everyone networked and hooked in to the internet.

She continued forward with the aid of the flashlight and stayed aware of every step she made. Periodically there was a huge support column which would impede her progress and require her to turn sideways to slide past. She tried not to let her thoughts go toward spiders or other varmints who might have taken up residence in here. She had to keep her mind on her work and stay focused. *Panic is not an option,* she cautioned herself.

By her calculations she had gone almost far enough to reach the first of the offices that they had targeted. She stopped and turned the waist pack around to the front where she could access its contents more easily. She located and took out the first amplified microphone that she had gotten from Lucas. The difficult part of this was going to be getting a good enough contact on the wall. The concrete was a rough texture by nature and there had been no attempt to smooth them out or put another surface such as plaster or wall board over them. They had given her a jelly like substance which they could only hope would help make the required contact with the wall. If the contact was good enough it should be sufficient to pick up through the relatively porous substance of concrete.

She smeared the jelly on the cup-like pickup and felt around for what seemed like the least rough area on the wall. She pressed it firmly against the concrete and held it there for the recommended ten seconds. The small wire lead had already been attached and she was careful to make sure that it hung down freely from the pickup. This would act as an antenna hopefully relaying whatever it picked up back out to Lucas and Doc once they were in place.

She continued down the passage attaching her microphones at the prescribed locations or as close to it as she could. She had totally lost track of how long she had been making her way through this maze. She was pretty sure that she knew which way she'd come in and cursed for a moment that she hadn't left a string or something to follow back. It would be easy to get disoriented in here. Anyway, she thought, it was time to talk to Will again; he'd said a couple of hours. Hopefully, when she got him they would know whether or not they could pick up any conversation from the offices. She turned and started back down the passageway in the direction of her entry.

It seemed to her that she'd been going back longer than it had taken her to get there in the first place. On top of that she'd had to keep stopping and hooking up the mikes on her way in. "Don't tell me I'm lost," she murmured to herself. She kept moving along in the direction she thought she should and soon realized that her entry point was not even on the horizon. To make matters worse the flashlight seemed to be dimming. She decided that she had failed to make one of the turns on the way back so she turned and retraced her steps as quickly as she could without getting caught in the cables.

When she got to the first intersecting passageway she shone the light down it and determined that it was not one she'd been in. She continued on. Not until the third intersection did she believe that she'd found her way out. She turned to the right and had gone just a few yards down it, sliding past two huge pillars when she saw one of her microphones hanging vigilantly on the wall with its tiny wire dangling downward. She heard a sigh of relief slip from her lungs and she continued along cautiously toward her secret access door.

The senator dined alone in his office. He often did so even though there were so many luncheon meetings and various colleagues who wanted to meet with him over lunch to discuss this or that. Marge had been adamant that he stay in the office and do so today. She was always kind enough to send out for his food and prepare a tray for him. He could tell that she was worried about his state of mind. *Rightfully so,* he thought.

While he chewed on those flavorless salad greens he ruminated about Harry. He was convinced now that he had to do something about him. He was completely out of control. He was a vital link to the monetary side of the project but he was fast becoming a liability. He had called Harry immediately upon hearing of the unfortunate demise of Margaret Blanchard and had hung up appalled at what he'd heard. Without actually saying it, he was certain that Harry was taking credit, if you could call it that, for the horrible events that had taken place at Union Station. At first he'd been unable to absorb it. Now he realized it had Harry's fingerprints all over it, especially Margaret. She'd just told him that she was on her way to meet Harry for a drink, at his insistence.

The senator spent the rest of his brief lunchtime considering options for dealing with Harry Axelrod. He was astute enough to know that if Harry had been the one to order the death of Margaret he would do the same to him. The only thing that would keep him alive was if Harry believed that he needed him. He congratulated himself for the hard work he had put in on his relationships with the money brokers and how he had managed to make himself indispensable to his superior. It seemed that Harry had gotten the message.

His first concern was the initiation of the coups. They were on the eve of implementation and the effect that Margaret's death would have on them could be devastating if it wasn't handled carefully. His superior had always insisted that the operation not be dependent on certain individuals but expedience had overcome that logic and they had proceeded with the smallest team possible. He now had to deal with the consequences of that decision.

He was beginning to think that the entire project was doomed. Perhaps he should recommend that they consider pulling the plug and reforming. He realized that he was so angry at Harry that it may be clouding his thinking. It was then that he knew that they had to deal with Harry before the operation could move on. If not canceling, they at least had to postpone the implementation. "Damn you, Harry," he murmured.

The senator decided to call in his most trusted minions for an afternoon meeting. In just a couple of hours they could go over every aspect of the project and decide how to postpone or forestall all of the key tasks that were necessary to buy some time. He knew that he had no more than a few days to do what needed to be done and begin the project moving forward again. If he couldn't implement in that time it would all have to be scratched. He would wait until he'd made that determination to inform his superior, however.

He had been ordered to put Harry as the first item on his 'to do' list. Although the senator was not comfortable with direct orders and was seldom issued them, he was completely on board with this one. The truth was that Harry had pretty much completed everything that he'd been asked to do. The funding of the coups and the alignment of the money men would all be in place well before the time of the Bangkok meeting. He had convinced Harry to obtain all of the signatures on a letter of intent leaving the signing of the actual accord as a simple formality. This made Harry completely expendable to the project. He rolled over in his mind the advisability of taking him out before or after the summit. After some serious consideration his plan was made ready. He made the call then that would put that plan into action.

He prided himself again on the fact that he had been very thorough in establishing himself as the front man of this new world order. He knew that eventually there would be attempts to replace him but for now he had the complete support required to put everything in place and set the direction for the foreseeable future. He was right where he needed to be, the power was finally in his hands. It had been a long and difficult struggle to get here but he was convinced that in just days he would be able to bring a better way of life to a struggling world. It would be such a relief to not have to wait and wrangle every time a change was needed. If he thought it, it could happen. The idea of it made him feel relaxed and quite at peace. *Just days,* he thought.

He was having a tough time trying to stay awake. He'd been having difficulty getting enough rest recently but it was totally unprecedented for him to be this sleepy at mid-day. This was the peak of his work time. He'd had only a light lunch, no reason to be so tired. He succumbed to the overwhelming urge for a nap and went to stretch out on his sofa for a few minutes. He closed his eyes and gave one more thought to how close they were to their ultimate success. His eyes would never re-open.

A few moments later his secretary, Marge, entered his office and removed the drinking glass from his lunch tray. On her way to lunch she dropped it in a trash can several blocks down the street as instructed. Continuing on she stopped at the designated pay phone and placed a call to Harry Axelrod confirming that his directions had been followed.

She'd been assured that there would be no investigation. It would all come out as a hard working man under too much stress. In the unlikely event that someone did check further it would simply be a case of an overdose of his heart medicine. He hadn't been himself lately; perhaps he got confused on his dosage.

While Roland and Will were busy meeting with Lucas and Doc, Bobby was back at Headquarters in Langley, Virginia gathering some more information about the bunker in rural Virginia. While he was there he picked up a message from a buddy of his with the bureau. The FBI had intercepted some communications during a stakeout that may have some international consequences. This guy was always doing this to him. He would leave some vague message suggesting international involvement to cover his own ass and would lob it to Bobby making him have to put all of the footwork into figuring out whether it was anything for the agency or not. He never had enough facts but he always got it off his desk. The only thing Bobby liked about this guy was he loved to jog as much as Bobby did and they had some good runs together followed by a few beers. He assumed this was just another one of those lobs of his until he saw the names.

Bobby went immediately back to his desk and placed the call. He hung up a few minutes later a whole lot wiser. A team of operatives, the secretary's own little militia it seemed, whose objective was Roland and company had gathered at a known safe house on the south side of DC. The numerous references to an explosives expert who was due to arrive tomorrow from Jakarta had tipped the scales far enough into the international area to merit alerting the agency. Best of all there had been references, now on tape, to link the secretary, the hit team and the bunker. While it wasn't anything that would stand up in a court of law it was finally something that could be used as persuasive evidence in a court of public opinion at least. Maybe they were finally going to get somewhere. He was sure that this had to be related to Union Station as well.

Bobby stuffed the notes in his jacket pocket and went back to what he had come to headquarters to do. He had already ordered the vehicles. They were almost ready; he'd gone down to the shop to check on them. Everything had to be right. Sometimes those guys in the shop got squirrelly and cut corners. He didn't want any shoddy workmanship on this operation.

Now he was off to the documents department with passport photos in hand to get the ID's they'd need. After that he'd swing by and get the uniforms fixed up and he was out of there. He figured he'd be on his way by noon. The rendezvous would be at two and everything would proceed from there.

Two hours later he was on the phone with Roland. He didn't take the time to tell him what he'd learned from the FBI guy; there'd be time for that later. They had to be precise in their plans and he didn't want to delay the meeting or the plan.

Bobby left his conversation with Roland and packed up his materials. He had one large laundry bag that contained numerous, smaller plastic bags. Each plastic bag had a small label on it identifying for whom it was intended.

Additionally, he had numerous forms of identification in his pocket for each of the participants. He took his large parcel and headed for the motor pool. As he entered the underground garage area where he was to meet his drivers he was amazed to see the transformation that had taken place in such a short time. All of the vehicles stood there ready to go with the drivers loitering around them. Bobby gave them a wave and reminded them again of the meeting point. It would not have served them to take the same route.

Bobby opened the door of the large tanker truck and threw his bundle inside. As he did he noticed a sharp reflection from the paint on the door which identified the oil company by name. "Geez, you guys," he called across to the technicians. "The damn paint's still wet."

One of the men turned and came over to where he stood. "I'll take care of it," he responded. He pulled a large, infra red, heat lamp over to the door and focused it on the wet area. From a roll around tool chest he pulled out a prissy, little hair dryer from the local five and dime and began to blow hot air on it as well. A few seconds later he said, "There you go, all set."

"Yeah," responded Bobby fretfully, "Not your ass out there."

One by one the vehicles pulled out of the garage and up to the guard's booth at the exit. Each driver presented his credentials and like bees leaving the hive each set out on their respective routes to the Virginia countryside. Reflecting on the wet paint Bobby couldn't help but wonder as he bumped along in the truck what else hadn't been taken care of as carefully as it should have been.

Chapter Twenty-five

Amanda was back in her handy little headquarters in the rear of the storage room. She had been disappointed to learn that the pickup from the microphones she'd placed had not been sufficient to give Lucas what he needed. She had been further thwarted in her efforts to gather information when she had tapped into the computer network cable as Lucas had shown her. Again, the result had been useless. This time they had discovered that the communications moving on the network were encrypted and they were unable to make any headway with it from outside.

That was when they'd decided that they needed to get Lucas inside the bunker. He would tap into the memory bank where the messages were held while they were in their encrypted form. When one computer sent the message, regardless of the recipient, it went into the bank to be encoded. There it sat until the receiving computer requested it. At that point it was put back into decipherable language by the software program and appeared on the reader's screen in the same language that it had left the sender. That was where they needed to attack the messages. Lucas was confident that he had the equipment and software to do it but he needed a direct tap into the cable to keep from being detected. While he was at it he would place bugs in several key offices.

Everyone thought it would be impossible to get him inside given the security at the bunker but again Amanda had come up with the idea that Bobby had begun to implement. Judging from her watch the fist step in the execution of that plan was just minutes away.

Bobby was the first to arrive at the small, neglected campsite that was just one of many public areas that the county couldn't find the funds to look after. He parked his truck adjacent to the cinder block building that functioned as a bathroom and shower facility and went around toward the rear. There the access door presented itself to him and he took just moments to jimmy the catch and disable the lock. He returned to the truck and removed the large canvas bag that contained the other's uniforms.

He was just turning to approach the building again when he saw the police cruiser pull up behind his truck. He had barely finished complimenting his man on his promptness when they were joined by the third vehicle.

Bobby checked his watch and calculated that they had less than five minutes to wait. One of the drivers lit up a cigarette and the two were just beginning a discussion of the Oriole's season when the non-descript, rental car bounced off the road and into the campground. That was the fourth vehicle in the row. Not wanting to call attention to the gathering Roland, Will, and Lucas got out of the newly arrived car and walked quickly over to Bobby. He gave each man their respective plastic bag from the larger one he had removed from his truck and gestured them toward the shower building he had opened.

Roland paused long enough to give the keys to the car to one of the other men and then hastily made his way into the building.

The drivers crawled into the rental car and wished Bobby well as they departed leaving their delivered vehicles in his care.

Will and Lucas were ready and out of the building first with Roland just seconds behind. Will, dressed as a county patrolman with his ID in place and a holstered weapon on his side took his place behind the wheel of the police cruiser. He and Bobby gave a quick check of each other and Bobby turned and swung himself back up into the tanker.

Roland and Lucas lingered in the campground for awhile monitoring the radio in their vehicle with the insignia of the county and large letters identifying it as belonging to the Haz Mat Unit. Across the rear appeared the message, "In Case of Hazardous Material Spill, Dial 1-800-CLEANUP."

Bobby led the parade that was to make its way to the Sommerset Inn Resort and Spa. It was less than a ten minute drive and he was feeling the importance of this assignment throughout his digestive track. It was more than butterflies, it always was. It felt as if someone had taken his alimentary canal and tied it in a square knot. He knew that he could neither eat nor drink until the execution of this assignment was complete. This was the part of his job that he hated and the part that he loved. He moved his head rapidly back and forth to clear his thoughts and lock himself into the personality that he had to become.

He could see his turn coming up less than a hundred yards down the road. He put his foot in on the clutch and slipped the big tanker down into third gear as he neared the turn. His left leg allowed the clutch pedal to release a little faster than normal causing the big engine to let out a low, growling beller that could be heard at least a quarter of a mile away. He hoped the guards in their little kiosk had allowed it to register in their consciousness. One more down shift and he cranked the wheel to take the truck around the corner and onto the road of the target. He stepped down hard on the accelerator and shifted back up into progressively higher gears as he picked up the speed he would need for execution. He reached down and brought the five-point, webbed harness up between his legs and as he slipped one arm through it at a time he steered the huge tanker toward its destination.

With the harness buckle inserted in the receptacle he heard and felt the click which told him he was secured to the seat. He pulled on the tab to tighten the harness as tightly as he could and he felt it respond by pinning him to the back of the seat. He had just enough reach to manage the wheel. His last act before implementation was to pick up the helmet off the seat beside him and quickly pull it on over his head. The quick clasp allowed him to secure it with one hand and he felt for the release before bringing his hand back to the task of steering. He saw the spot in the fence that had been carefully scoped out and taking a deep breath he jerked the wheel hard to the right and sent the tanker truck down into the ditch and directly at one of the panels of vertical, steel rods with the perfectly shaped, little spears on the top.

Bobby wasn't sure that he had kept his eyes open for the entire ride but he heard the engine of the truck groan and then whine as the wheels engaged the soft earth and then became airborn with nothing to pull against. Truck and driver soared through the air for a brief moment which registered on Bobby's conscious mind as something approaching five minutes or more. The percussive wallop that erupted when the truck met the earth and the fence at approximately the same moment seemed to duplicate a sonic boom in both volume and vibration.

As the truck came to rest Bobby hit the release clasp on the helmet and literally tore it from his head forcing it behind the seat of the cab. His second movement was to detach the five-point harness from the standard seat belt and stuff it under the seat. His third and final critical move was to give a vigorous pull on the lever that was barely visible under the dashboard. Having done so, he opened the truck door and leaned out to assure himself that the liquid had begun to flow from the tank onto the ground. He reached back inside the truck, and as he had been shown, he jerked the lever soundly to the right. As promised, it remained in his hand. He threw it as far down the ditch as he could.

Right on cue he became aware of the high pitched wailing of the siren on Will's cruiser followed by that mournful wind down as it came to rest behind the truck. Will hopped out and checked with Bobby to make sure he was okay before slipping into his role as county officer. Just seconds later they could see the parade of jeeps approaching as they took the straightest route across the golf course. Their timing had been perfect so far.

At least eight men alit from the jeeps with weapons drawn and aimed. "What the hell's goin' on?" The man with the most adornment to his uniform asked.

Will stepped forward with all of the arrogance of a real county mounty, "Seems there's been a little mishap here, don't it?"

"You're on government property! This is a security breach. I demand you get off the premises at once," the lead guard stammered. This apparently was their first attempt at actually protecting the grounds. Heretofore they had busied themselves with searching, inspecting and patrolling around the perimeter. Things like this only happened in their Saturday drills.

"Not gonna be that simple, I'm afraid," Will retorted. "Got a couple a problems here. This here tanker is leaking fuel like a racehorse taking a piss and besides the driver's gotta be checked out for alcohol and drugs." Will was playing his part so well that Bobby had a moment of concern that he was in some sort of trouble.

The security guard continued to act as if this whole unfortunate event was about him personally and considered it a personal affront that someone had crashed through their fence.

Will calmly continued on, "I've radioed in for the Haz Mat Unit to get over here. That's a federal law now whenever fuel or some unknown substance is released at an accident scene. Seems like you fellas oughta know that, it's your law. Anyway, I'll take the driver here with me. Says he isn't hurt but we gotta give him that blood test. Those Haz Mat boys should be screaming in here any minute." Will had just finished his sentence and taken a hold of Bobby and led him over to his cruiser when the siren could be heard splitting the afternoon air. Roland and Lucas were arriving.

Will stuck Bobby in the back seat and returned to the truck to add to the confusion for the benefit of the security guards who were now pretty much reduced to standing around looking at each other with various expressions of confusion reigning on their faces. This was not the most elite branch of federal security units.

Roland pulled his Hazard Materials Unit truck up behind the tanker and Lucas jumped out to join him as they began pulling out cables and hoses and hooking up all kinds of gauges and meters. They were calling out statistics to each other and walking around and looking under the leaking vehicle like the Lilliputians sizing up Gulliver on the beach. Will had to stifle a chuckle.

Not far into the charade Roland made it clear to the guards that he and Lucas had to be taken inside the grounds and into the bunker. The guard protested strongly and was utterly appalled at the thought.

Roland gave his best impersonation of a chemist who specialized in petroleum and made it clear that since they were with the county and this facility was in their jurisdiction they knew what went on out here and even had blueprints for cases of emergency like this one. The guard remained adamant but was losing fervor.

Roland continued to push, "Look, you can have it one of two ways. Either I'm standing in front of the man who is in charge of this facility with this measuring equipment in my hand within ten minutes or this place will be evacuated. If you think your security is breached now wait until the evacuation equipment including about eight National Guard helicopters on loan to the Haz Mat Unit descend on this place. Security will just be a word that you find in the dictionary somewhere between 'safe' and 'sorry.'"

Moments later Lucas and Roland were being escorted into the bunker with some official looking gauges and meters in their hands and were heading straight for the secretary's office on Level C. In addition, Lucas carried a bright, shiny metallic case with the Haz Mat insignia emblazoned on the side but with his computer hacking tools and software hidden inside. Simultaneously, Will and Bobby were pulling away from the accident scene and moving out along the road as Doc pulled up in a wrecker to begin the removal of the offending vehicle. "I can't believe the agency has gotten so environmentally conscious," Will observed to Bobby as he glanced at him in the rearview mirror.

"Federal law is federal law," he replied, "We had to come up with that sweet little mixture to smell like gasoline while not polluting the soil. Otherwise we'd be staring at a very stiff fine." Bobby was wearing that patented broad grin that made him and everyone around him feel good.

Will looked up out of the open window of the car to watch a rapidly moving, private helicopter move overhead and make its way off into the direction of the Sommerset Inn. He had no idea that the occupant would also be entering the bunker.

Harry was making preparations for his departure for Bangkok. Everything was in place at the office. As usual the only things that were not specifically assigned to someone were those things which were unexpected. His elaborate technical and communications equipment kept him totally in the loop in this age of electronic tethers.

Out on the tarmac at Dulles his Gulfstream was being made ready. His capable crew was finalizing the pre-flight checks, filing the flight plan for Bangkok's Don Muang Airport and overseeing the loading of provisions aboard for the comfort of their boss on the longer trip into Asia.

Everyone, pilot, co-pilot and cabin attendant was busy with their own aspect of the preparations. No one took specific notice of the man who struggled ineptly with the task of fueling the aircraft from the gas truck which sat adjacent to its right wing tip. Though highly skilled he was not in the business of servicing private aircraft. While the access panel for the fuel connector was open he deftly placed the explosive device inside the compartment. He activated the timer on the detonator and closed up the access panel. As the door closed he noticed that the timer now showed 3 hours and 48 minutes.

Harry was as excited about the flight as he was about the meeting. He loved that aircraft and every moment he spent in it. Sometimes he found himself looking for reasons to go to one place or another just so he could revel in its opulence. Of course Tina and her massages were a part of that comfort. He let his mind linger on that pleasure for a moment as he continued to gather up the documents he needed.

He was really pleased that he had taken the senator's advice to prepare and circulate the Pre-Accord Agreement. It had allowed him to have every single delegate to the summit sign their name agreeing to all of the provisions that had been hammered out and confirming their intent that the ceremony where they would sign the actual accord in Bangkok was but a formality. In essence his work was done. It made the idea of his time in Bangkok much more appealing. It was almost a junket at this point.

He continued around his office putting files and documents in the appropriate cases and found himself resisting the urge to whistle. Life was good and to his way of thinking was only going to get better.

By the time his car arrived at the airport and he was on board the aircraft there had been a sudden and severe change in the weather. The pilot advised Harry that the tower had passed along the FAA's recommendation that they consider a variation from the flight plan they'd filed. He informed Harry that it would add a couple of hours to the first leg of the trip. The alternative would be to delay their departure for about five hours. Harry considered the alternatives and eventually chose to leave as scheduled and make the change to the route. It was a choice that Harry would never second guess and a flight plan that would never be completed.

After parking the gas truck back in the vicinity of the hanger the driver removed his uniform coveralls and left the airport immediately. As he drove he placed a confirming call to Senator Hampton's secure phone. He had to leave a coded message.

The private Bell Ranger helicopter flew past the site of the tanker truck accident and continued on in the general direction of southern Virginia giving no indication that it would be landing soon. Once beyond the ridge of the gently rolling hills it dove behind the larger peak and lowered itself gradually onto the familiar pad that it called home. It was immediately joined by its companion conveyance that was housed at the same location, a charcoal gray Chevrolet Suburban with blackened, bullet proofed windows and reinforced plating in the body. As with other such security vehicles, the engine had been beefed up to overcome the inertia that the added weight inflicted and to make its moves more responsive.

A tall, stout man in a dark suit stepped from the passenger side of the vehicle and held the door open to give their passenger access to the safety and security of the rear seat. The bulge under his coat would be noticeable to only the most observant and coupled with the wire from the earpiece that he wore he'd quickly be identified as Secret Service. The man rejoined his counterpart who waited behind the wheel and before the blades of the chopper had come to rest the car was away from the site and on its way to deliver its rider to his usual destination.

They followed a narrow, poorly paved road along the curving base of the hill. Less than 500 yards from the landing pad they came to stop in front of large, electrical gates with a card key access panel suspended on an arm to provide easy use from within the car. The driver took the card key from the restraining strap on the sun visor over the wheel and inserted it in the slot. A moment later the gates began to swing lazily inward inviting access to the road as it continued around the hill.

Just around a sharp curve to the right the Suburban came to rest with its nose nearly pressed against a set of steel doors that appeared to give admittance to the hill itself. A second card key was used and the doors swung inward permitting the vehicle and its occupants to enter the bowels of the underground. Everyone was familiar with this routine which had been repeated at least twice a week for the last ten months or so.

The man in the front seat jumped out as the vehicle came to a stop. He opened the rear door again and gave his hand to the man inside offering him assistance as he departed from the vehicle and entered a small replica of the large steel doors through which they had come. The Suburban moved on to its assigned waiting space just as the visitor was swallowed up by the bunker

Once inside the man made his way down the short hall and making a right turn he inserted his key into the sophisticated lock and gained access to his private room. He threw his case up on the small work table and took a seat in his chair which faced the large glass window with a vertical row of monitors running up each side. The window was actually the back side of the mirror which looked directly into the secretary's office. He picked up the headphones which dangled from the arm of the chair where he'd stowed them last and placed them over his ears. He fiddled with the dials in the arm of the chair to control the volume and select the location he wished to monitor. He checked in on all of the pertinent locations like any red blooded, American male channel surfing with the TV remote.

As he monitored the working lives of the bees in his hive he reflected on the larger situation. He loved this spot and the calm that it brought to him. He began to run the traps of his mental 'status reports' and 'to do' lists.

He started with the big picture as he liked to think of it. Operation Cloud Nine and the new world order were very close to reality but now, he admitted, it would not be. He reflected on the current state of the project. The leadership had been strong but was not what would be required to bring it all together. He needed more time to garner support for the real vision. For this to be sustained the key participants, the leaders in the various locations throughout the world had to believe strongly in it as a way of life.

It had been no problem to get the energy producers together; they were always floundering for leadership and understanding of how to maximize the reward that their countries and they personally could receive from such a commanding resource. His problem was in making them see the vision. They were too short sighted. He could only assume that came from the volatility in their political structures. None of them knew how long they would remain in control. How long they would hold the power and the influence in their own country. They'd need to address that.

In addition, there was the loss of his current team. Margaret's intervention on behalf of each of these leaders would have brought them the renewed strength that was required to maintain control in their respective political structures. It could still happen without her but at a minimum it would take additional time to restructure. Even after the coup there was no guarantee how long each could remain in control without her ongoing support of them.

Harry's dirty little terrorist attack had set them back dramatically and caused him to order the senator to have him taken out. At least the Accord could go forward, Harry had done a good job with the financiers, he had to give him that, but he was one loose canon whose shenanigans could no longer be ignored. He had definitely outlived his usefulness. He had needed to bring all of that under control, one way or another. Harry's time had come, mostly by his own doing.

The secretary was definitely a weak link in the organization. He still didn't seem to be able to oversee the kind of security force that would be necessary in a new world order. While he didn't want to create a police state for the people of the world to live under, history had proven that to have order you had to have laws and the enforcement of them. The secretary would never be the man to lead such a force.

The greatest problem, however, had been the senator himself. He'd simply gone soft and the lofty position that he was to occupy could not tolerate that weakness. It just couldn't be. Unfortunately, as a part of that softness he'd left Roland out there working relentlessly to try to bring this project down. He had some thoughts about that as well.

A feeling of sadness washed over him. Perhaps it was time to admit that he had failed. There was more going wrong than right at this moment but he'd been having these other thoughts lately and he was beginning to believe that this was not really failure, per se. What he needed was a revised version. After all NASA had experienced a lot of fizzles at Cape Canaveral before they successfully reached the moon and most financially successful men admitted to having failed attempts before making it big. There was no dishonor in learning from one prototype and improving it for the next attempt. He was feeling more and more certain that this project should be scrapped in favor of his new one.

That would also solve the problem of Roland. It was an outright horse race at this point whether the secretary's men would find and kill Roland before he thwarted the project and exposed the entire plan. Although he was sure that he was above detection he would much rather bring it all to a close himself. That way the work that had been accomplished would not be in vain and he would have a structure from which to build.

He liked the concept and thought that it had tremendous merit. He had given this new, improved version plenty of thought. He had identified exactly twelve of the countries who sat on the greatest energy resources and who already had fairly stable political environments within which they could work. Some were dictators and some were monarchs but each had been leading his country for a significant length of time and each showed the promise of longevity. He had the good sense to have begun cultivating relationships with them anyway so what he planned might not be so onerous. Because there were twelve of them he had dubbed them the Disciples of Destiny and the more he contemplated the entire situation the more certain he was that it truly was his providence to bring them together and lead them to this more pure vision.

Roland knew that they could not allow the overly conscientious guard to take them to the secretary. Once inside the bunker he and Lucas watched for their opening. It would have been easy to take the two men out on the elevator but you never knew what would confront you when the doors opened. They couldn't wait much longer. As they stepped from the elevator the older guard stood to the side to let the two guests go ahead. That put them with one in front and one behind them. Roland looked at Lucas and gave him an imperceptible nod at the same time he stopped and squatted down to tie his shoe lace.

He set his Haz Mat items down next to him while he manipulated the laces and when he came up the short, weighted stick was in his hand. He swung it hard making contact with the closest guard's head just behind and above the ear. He went down like someone had removed his backbone. At the same time Lucas struck and disabled the younger man and they began to drag their respective prey around the corner and out of the main hallway.

Lucas stood over the two unconscious men as Roland checked a couple of doors. On his fourth try he gained access to a small room filled with electrical panels and the like. He went back and helped Lucas drag the men inside with one hand while he held Lucas' case in his other and precariously balanced the other instruments in the crook of his arm. Once they had them thoroughly bound and gagged they closed the door and while inside the room they placed their call to Amanda.

In no time Roland and Lucas had met up with Amanda in the hallway as she'd described it and she had led them back to her little staging area in the rear of the work room. Lucas began at once to tap into the cable that Amanda had identified as the one which networked the computers on the LAN for the bunker. While Lucas worked, Roland called Will to be sure that everything had gone well on the outside and to assure him that they were inside and beginning their operation.

It was on that call that Roland learned of the death of the senator. Roland had never watched someone literally lose their mind before and he had been saddened to see it happen to his mentor. Witnessing that and now with his untimely death it allowed him to excuse a great deal of the unpleasantness that had come between them over the last month or so.

Roland had managed to convince himself and the others after looking at the evidence that it was the secretary who controlled these hits. Even if the senator had been involved in the plan for a new world order it was the secretary who was giving the actual orders that put them in peril.

In their last conversations before departing on their separate assignments, all of them had been in agreement that there ultimate mission was with the secretary. Now, with the senator dead, they'd reasoned that was the only course open to them. They had to get control of him and force him to abort the kill order that was out on Roland, Amanda and Will. It was the only way that they could even think of being safe and perhaps returning to a normal life. The evidence that Bobby had gotten from the FBI had been the clincher that put them all in agreement about who was controlling the order to have them killed.

In their last meeting with the senator Roland and Will had found an ill and prematurely aged man. Roland had let go of a lot of the baggage that he had around the treachery that he had suffered at his hands. Will on the other hand had not been so kind. He had been all over the senator. He had called him everything but decent and he had verbally pounded on him for what he had done to his own son. He had shamed the man so badly that it had just seemed to drive him further into his confused state of mind and the ramblings and disjointed responses had only gotten worse. Roland had finally gotten Will to back off but his parting shot had been that if it weren't for the fact that it would break Charles' heart he would expose him for what he was. Roland had taken a hold of Will's shoulder to lead him out of the house and he had felt Will trembling with rage.

Roland collected his thoughts now as he readied his bag of equipment for the confrontation. He had convinced Amanda to remain and provide cover for Lucas and his work. In case Roland was apprehended or in some way unsuccessful they would still need to continue their efforts to gain evidence to derail the implementation of Operation Cloud Nine and ultimately save their own lives.

Amanda described to Roland how to reach the secretary's office from where they were located and watched as he packed a few key pieces of equipment in his jacket. He was still dressed as a member of the Haz Mat Unit and she couldn't help but notice that he cut a fine figure even in that makeshift uniform. She asked herself how she could think of such things at times like this and wondered if there was something wrong with her. She had to admit that she was strongly attracted to him as well as interested. She was embarrassed when their eyes met briefly and she was sure that he had somehow read her thoughts.

When Roland wasn't asking Lucas how much longer, Amanda would quiz him about whether or not he would be successful in getting the evidence they so desperately needed. Lucas politely dismissed them both.

Time dragged on as Lucas worked untiringly on the encryption. Roland found himself distracted from what waited for him down the hall once Lucas was finished. He was watching Amanda and just enjoying the feeling that he got when he was around her. He knew he was attracted to her and refused to let his mind play out the consequences of that attraction.

They tried to make small talk hoping that the time would pass more quickly and also trying to diffuse the tension that they could both feel between them. When they were in each other's presence there was always this intensity, unspoken and deeply felt. It hung in the air between them now making words awkward and looks almost painful. At the same time it was the most easy and contented sensation in the world.

The mood was interrupted by Lucas' grunt, "Here it is."

Roland thought those were some of the sweetest words he'd ever heard. "Do you have it all?" he asked.

"This is it, Baby, the whole enchilada. I'm burning your little disk of evidence right now. You better pack up and head out. The ball's in your court now."

Roland and Amanda both rose from the table at the same time and while Roland was completely focused on his preparations Amanda seemed to be bouncing off the walls with excitement as she turned one direction then the other wondering what she should be doing. She finally gained enough composure to realize that it might be helpful to Roland to know exactly what they'd found. Over Lucas' shoulder she started reading the contents of the disk out loud to Roland as he continued gathering together the items he'd need. As they had thought, the secretary was the man they needed.

Her heart felt light and she was so hopeful that she was beyond anything that might even resemble calm. She wasn't sure how much of it was Lucas' good news and how much was her previous and unspoken communication with Roland.

Once he had everything in order Roland took the precious disk from Amanda and tucked it carefully into his shirt pocket along with the documents Bobby had gotten from the FBI man. "While I'm gone make about four or five more of these, will you, Lucas? They're our ticket to tomorrow."

Roland took Lucas' hand and shook it in gratitude. He turned toward Amanda and gave her a quick peck on the cheek. She was so startled that she couldn't react. He gave her a crooked little smile, saluted them both and said, "Wish me luck," as he turned and went out through the janitor's closet that Amanda had shown him.

Roland didn't want to make the receptionist outside the secretary's office suspicious so he stopped and introduced himself and said that he had to put some monitors in the inner office. He kept his head down slightly and stood off to the side as she announced to her boss that he would be coming in and the purpose of the intrusion. She turned and nodded to Roland, "Go right on in," she said as she held the door for him. Once inside she closed the door behind him and returned to her desk.

Roland felt confident that she would have no reason to be suspicious but he positioned himself where he could see the door just to be safe. The secretary had hardly acknowledged his presence as he took a semi-dismissive attitude about him entering his office. Once in front of the desk and positioned where he could see the door, he addressed the man directly, "Well, Mr. Secretary, we meet again."

The secretary looked up with a start at the words and then nearly rocked over backwards in his swivel chair when he recognized the man standing over him aiming a silenced gun directly into his face.

On the other side of the mirror the unknown observer could only murmur, "Holy Shit!"

Roland made sure that the secretary moved slowly away from his desk so he could be sure that no alarms were activated. Once he had his full and undivided attention he laid it all out for him. At the same time that Roland was standing guard over him there were others strategically placed at his home and at his son's school. "This isn't just between us, Mr. Secretary; you have caused a number of people that I care very deeply for to live in terror that their lives will be snuffed out at any moment. Now you and some of the people that you love can either live with the same feeling or we can make it reality if you try to do one thing other than what I am about to tell you. Are we clear so far?"

The secretary could only nod in the affirmative, "What do you want me to do?"

"Who's your Number Two on this hit?" Roland inquired.

"Tidwell, Nate Tidwell," he answered.

"Buzz him in here."

The secretary did as ordered. In two minutes or less there was a muffled knock on the door and when it opened the consummate bureaucrat stepped through it. He got only, "What," out when the door was pushed shut from behind and he saw the gun.

"Come in and sit," Roland ordered as he gestured toward a chair.

The man in the observation room sat with his hand on the alarm but something had stopped him from activating it. He watched in amazement as Roland held the secretary at gunpoint and now had Tidwell in there as well. It was like watching a movie. He was realizing that perhaps one or even two of his problems might be resolved for him if he just watched and let this unfold. He sat back and listened with his hand poised above the alarm.

Roland took a pad of paper from the top of the secretary's desk and ripped off the top sheet. He handed it to Tidwell and gave the remainder of the pad to the secretary. He turned the secretary in his chair so the two men could not have eye contact and instructed, "Write the name of the contact for the hit and your method for contacting him. I advise you to be as thorough as necessary for if we do not reach them on the first try you will both be dead."

Both men picked up writing instruments and began to scratch away on the paper. Moments later each looked up at Roland like young students finishing their exams.

Roland took the papers and began to read aloud. The versions of contact were similar enough to convince him that he had what he needed. He instructed the secretary to make the contact and abort the hit. It was to be complete and unequivocal and the entire squad was to be off the street and released from the contract by 6 p.m. The contact man was to confirm when it was done.

The secretary was nervous as he tried his best to use his new communication equipment again. Under the circumstances he was having difficulty remembering his name let alone the obtuse directions he'd been given when he last tried to simply dial out. He usually had someone walking him through it. His first attempt didn't go through and he immediately began to plead with Roland. He explained his ineptness with electronics and was successful on his second try. Once the instructions were given Roland settled back to wait.

To further his intimidation he placed two phone calls to Amanda reporting that he was in place and on schedule. Then he inquired of her whether her targets were still under surveillance and within reach. The secretary looked at him with eyes which half pleaded and half hated. Roland had no idea at that moment whether they would all come out of this alive.

Time doesn't really exist some have said. It is merely a method that man has devised to measure change. Roland could have easily been convinced of the truth of that theory in the next hour and ten minutes. The secretary's receptionist called in twice and Roland had to monitor the conversation between her and the secretary to be sure that he wasn't arousing any suspicions outside that room.

Finally the all important call came. The hit had been called off and the team was released. "Any further instructions?" the caller asked.

"Take yourself a vacation," the secretary responded, "It doesn't look like there's much work on the horizon."

Now that the immediate danger had been removed it was time to take care of the future. Roland could either eliminate these men or he could play the intimidation card. Time again seemed to stand still for Roland as it did for the observer on the other side of the mirror. He watched now to see where Roland would go next. In many ways what Roland decided would determine his own fate and course of action as well.

He watched Roland intently. He could almost read what was going on in his mind. Although he was not aware of his recent epiphany and his attraction to Amanda he knew that Roland had a strong conscience and he wondered if he would kill the two men in front of him. The old Roland would not have hesitated.

If Roland killed them now it would set his course for heading out directly to develop the Disciples of Destiny. With Margaret and the senator already out of the picture and Harry well on his way, if Roland eliminated the secretary he would be free of any awkward encumbrances around Operation Cloud Nine. There would be no one to tell the tale and he would definitely be free to ride on.

On the other hand, if Roland wasn't up to killing the men he was left with three choices. He could call the guards and have him arrested. That wasn't a pleasant thought as he'd certainly have a lot to say which might place his own veracity in question even if he wasn't directly implicated. It might destroy a level of trust that he could not afford to lose. His reputation was everything in this business.

His second option was to kill them all himself. He found that rather sticky but a definite possibility.

Lastly, he could leave quietly and let them all think that matters were exactly as they thought. Only he would know the truth. He thought this was the preferable alternative. Everything quietly tucked away with no scandal brought into the bunker and only a slight delay before his better plan could be developed.

He'd watch this unfold and try to determine if he was in any way at risk. He doubted that anyone knew of his involvement but even if they suspected that there was someone else in charge he wouldn't dare let them live. The next few moments would determine the destiny of many.

Roland continued to feel the agony. He felt the sweat as it beaded up on his brow and trickled down his chest. He thought that a drum was pounding in his ears but realized that it was his own heart.

He knew he wanted a new life, one that would take him out of this environment. He was tired of the intimidating, the coercing, the killing. He wanted to come home from work at five and be met by his wife and children. He felt the rage as it worked its way from a burning in his gut to a fire in his lungs and finally threatened to make his head explode with fury. As long as these thugs lived there would be no life for him, no dream of a home and family. It was men like these who took that from others. Who killed fathers and brothers and sons. It was these very men who were robbing him of his chance at such a life.

He had never seen himself as cold blooded, had always prided himself that he'd only killed those who had killed others. Now even that didn't seem like enough.

He realized that he had changed over the last few days. He had even gone so far as to fantasize that he might have a life with Amanda. He admired her down to the core, found her wonderfully attractive and delightful to be with and he had this need to care for her and keep her safe always. He really believed that he might be able to fall in love again. He really liked who he was when he was with her.

It was this thought that held him now as he agonized over his decision. The hope of a different life and the contempt he felt as he looked down at these pitiful men.

He took out his cell phone and called Amanda again, "It's over," he told her. "Both of you get out. I'll meet you as planned or call within an hour."

"Give me the code word so I know you're not being coerced," she demanded.

Roland responded, "Tallyho."

Amanda and Lucas gathered up their remaining equipment and left the bunker in the car that Amanda had arrived in. They met Will and Bobby at a small cafe less than ten miles down the road. There were relieved hugs shared upon the reunion. Even the men could muster up enough relief to merit more than a handshake. Only Roland was missing, everyone was still a little tense about him getting out safely. Amanda reported that he had sounded very confident and she was sure he'd be along.

Roland turned the secretary back toward his desk and standing over him pulled the disk from his shirt pocket. "Put this in your computer and pull up the directory," he instructed.

The secretary did so and he began to read what was on the screen out loud. At the conclusion he turned toward Roland, "I'm going to assume that there is more than one copy of this."

"You're quick," Roland responded. "I'm sure you know how the rest of this goes but just so we have no misunderstanding let me say it. If one hair on the head of Amanda, Will or me is disrupted for as long as you or your partners in crime live, those copies will be anywhere and everywhere that will bring you and your nest of vipers to justice. I would also remain very worried about the members of your families, none of your loved ones will ever be safe."

The secretary was nodding as Roland spoke. He knew their security had been penetrated and knew that Roland held the power now. "You have my word that none of you will be targeted by me. Please leave my family out of this," he pleaded.

"Can't do that I'm afraid, you're the one that opened this up to hard ball. Suffer the consequences," Roland spat the words at him.

He took no joy from seeing the look in the secretary's eyes. He knew that he was causing him to live with a fear that would haunt him day and night for as long as he lived.

What Roland didn't know was at the same time he had made his momentous decision to allow the secretary and Nate Tidwell to live, he had also set the course for the man who lurked in the shadow of the bunker and much of the world beyond.

He put the gun in the back of his waist band and turned and walked out of the office. He thanked the receptionist for her assistance and advised her that the secretary did not wish to be disturbed until he called her.

He walked calmly down the hallway and pressed the call button for the elevator. As he waited the few moments for the doors to open he realized that a weight had been lifted from him back in that office. He stepped onto the elevator, nodded at the only other occupant and rode up to where the clean air could be found. A shower had moved through the area and he could smell the sparkling, unsullied freshness of it before he stepped outside. Once he left the bunker behind he climbed into the Haz Mat Unit truck and headed for the little cafe down the road.

The feeling of what he was leaving behind was as profound as his decision back there had been. He had no idea what lay ahead for him. He knew he had to atone for some of the things he'd done, he vowed to find a way. He hoped that some of what he was seeking was waiting down the road at a grungy little cafe.

He placed a last call and identified himself again as double zero, ten, twenty-two. He was assured that everything was in place at his new home and his arrival was anticipated. The funds, the identification papers and even his clothes would all be waiting. He let himself wonder if Mr. Reynaldo Perez would be arriving in Mallorca with a wife.

Back in the bunker, the man lurking in the shadows behind the mirror tried to weigh carefully how this would affect him. It was clear from what was on the disk that he had neither been implicated personally nor even known of in the abstract. Roland's evidence had placed all of the responsibility on the secretary. *How fortuitous,* he thought. He wouldn't have to play out any of the alternatives he'd anticipated. It would serve him well to leave things as they were and continue his life of public service.

Well, Mr. Priestly, he said to himself, *you've just made one hell of a decision for both of us.* He allowed a slightly satisfied smile to break over his face as he contemplated his next move.

Moments later he removed the handset from the arm of his chair and pressed the call button to summons his Secret Service men. With just one ring the call was answered. "I'm ready to leave the bunker and return to my office in the District," he announced.

"You're car is waiting. The helicopter should lift off in 6 minutes, Mr. Vice-president."

Printed in the United States
35810LVS00005B/40-102